THIEFTAKER

TOR BOOKS BY D. B. JACKSON

Thieftaker
Thieves' Quarry (2013)

THIEFTAKER

D. B. Jackson

A Tom Doherty Associates Book

NEW YORK

This is a work of fiction. All of the characters, organizations, and events portrayed
in this novel are either products of the author's imagination
or are used fictitiously.

THIEFTAKER

Edited by James Frenkel

Map production courtesy of the Norman B. Leventhal Map Center
at the Boston Public Library

Design by Heather Saunders

A Tor Book
Published by Tom Doherty Associates, LLC
175 Fifth Avenue
New York, NY 10010

www.tor-forge.com

Tor® is a registered trademark of Tom Doherty Associates, LLC.

Library of Congress Cataloging-in-Publication Data

Jackson, D. B.
    Thieftaker / D.B. Jackson. — 1st ed.
        p. cm.
    "A Tom Doherty Associates book."
    ISBN 978-0-7653-2761-1 (hardcover)
    ISBN 978-1-4299-4732-9 (e-book)
    1. Magic—Fiction.   2. Boston (Mass.)—History—Revolution, 1775–1783—
Fiction.   I. Title.
    PS3610.A347T48 2012
    813'.6—dc23

                                                                2012011659

First Edition: July 2012

Printed in the United States of America

0 9 8 7 6 5 4 3 2 1

For NJB,
Again, and always

A PLAN of
THE TOWN of BOSTON

References to the Town.

A. Christ Church
B. Old North Meeting
C. Anabaptiste Meeting
D. Faneuil Hall
E. Town Hall
F. Old Meeting
G. Prison & Courthouse
H. Kings Chapel
I. Work House
K. Granary Public
L. Province House (General ____)
M. Old South Meeting (the Riding House)
N. Trinity Church
O. New South Meeting
P. Prison Meeting
Q. West Meeting

Scale of Yards.

THE

Dry at Low water except in the Mid. Channel

all this Part is dry at Low Water

Boston, Province of Massachusetts Bay,
August 26, 1765

than Kaille eased his knife from the leather sheath on his belt as he approached Griffin's Wharf, the words of a warding spell on his lips. He had sweated through his linen shirt, and nearly through his waistcoat, as well. His leg ached and he was breathing hard, gasping greedily at the warm, heavy air hanging over Boston on this August eve. But he had chased Daniel Folter this far—from the Town Dock to Purchase Street, over cobblestone and dirt, past storefronts and homes and pastures empty save for crows and grazing cows—and he wasn't about to let the pup escape him now.

The western horizon still glowed with the last golden light of day, but the sky over Boston Harbor and the South End shoreline had darkened to a deep indigo. Hulking wooden warehouses, shrouded in a faint mist, cast deep, elongated shadows across the wharves. Clouds of midges danced around Ethan's head, scattering when he waved a hand at them, only to swarm again as soon as he turned his attention back to his quarry.

Ethan stepped onto the wharf and peered into murky corners, expecting Folter to fly at him at any moment. The boy had shown himself to be a fool; now he was desperate as well, a dangerous combination. Ethan preferred to handle this without casting, but he already knew what spell he would speak if he had to.

"You're mine now, Daniel!" he called. "Best you come out and face what's coming to you!"

No answer. He crept forward, wary, his gaze sweeping back and forth between the warehouses that loomed on either side of the pier. He heard small waves lapping at the timbers, and the echoing cries of a lone gull. But Ethan was listening for the man's breathing, for the scrape of a shoe or the whisper of a blade clearing leather.

After a few more steps, Ethan halted, afraid to stray too far out onto the pier lest the pup sneak past him. If he lost Folter to the tangled streets of the South End, he would have to begin his search anew.

"You shouldn't have stolen Missus Corbett's necklaces, Daniel!" Ethan pitched his voice to carry, but his words were swallowed by the hazy twilight air and the sounds of the harbor. "Her husband is angry. He's paying his hard-earned money to get her jewels back, and to have some justice meted out on her behalf."

He waited, listening, watching.

"Your only way out is through me, lad. And I'm not going anywhere."

Still no response. Doubt started to gnaw at Ethan's mind. Had Folter found some other way off the wharf? Or was he simply smarter and more patient than Ethan had allowed?

Neither, as it turned out.

Ethan heard a footfall to his left and wheeled quickly, his knife held ready. Folter stepped from the darkness, the faint glow of twilight shining in his eyes and glinting off the dagger he carried.

"Corbett can rot fer all I care!" he said. Brave words, but his voice trembled, almost as badly as his blade hand.

Ethan shook his head and approached him slowly. "You know better, lad. Mister Corbett is a man of means. He decides who rots and who doesn't."

Folter was bigger than he remembered. He stood a full head taller than Ethan, with long limbs and a thin, bony face. His hair, damp and lank, hung to his stooped shoulders. His breeches were torn at the knees, his waistcoat stained; the sleeves of his shirt barely reached his narrow wrists. His knife had a long, curved blade, and though he passed it from one hand to the other, wiping his sweaty palms on his breeches, the movements were deft. Ethan guessed that he would be a formidable foe in a knife fight if it came to that.

"Tha's not true," Folter said. "Not all of it, anyway."

Ethan stopped, leaving some distance between them. Folter's gaze met his for a moment before darting away, first to one side, then to the other. He was looking for a way out or past—or through, if need be. Ethan sensed that Folter had already taken his measure and convinced himself that he could prevail in a fight if he had to. He was wrong, but he had no way of knowing that. Ethan didn't exactly cut an imposing figure. He was of medium height and build, and looked like a competent fighter, but not one to be truly feared. His hair was starting to go gray at the temples, and his face was lined and scarred. Folter would see in him someone too old and too small to be a true threat. Others had made the same mistake.

"I done a bit o' work fer Pryce—Miss Pryce—back a year or two. If she could see her way clear t' let this slide . . ."

"I don't work for Pryce," Ethan said.

Folter stared at him. "Then why are ya—?"

"I work on my own."

The pup actually laughed. "Yar own? Ya think Sephira Pryce will stand by an' let another thieftaker work anywhere in Boston?"

Ethan shrugged. "She has for the last few years."

Folter's smile faded. "Who are ya?" he asked.

Ethan twirled his knife casually between his fingers. "I was hired by Ezra Corbett to retrieve the jewels you're carrying. My name is Ethan Kaille."

The pup's eyes widened at the mention of Ethan's name. "Kaille," he repeated. He tightened his grip on the hilt of his blade. "I've heard o' ya."

"Good," Ethan said. "Then you know that you'd best be giving me what I'm after."

"Ya'll take them an' then give me t' th' lobst'rbacks. I'll be fourteen years at hard labor."

"It doesn't have to come to that."

The young man shook his head, panic in his eyes. "I don' believe ya." He shifted his weight just slightly toward his right, his knees bending, his shoulders tensing. Subtle changes, but taken together they were all the warning Ethan needed.

By the time Folter lunged at him, leading with his blade, Ethan had already started to spin away. He had every intention of countering over Folter's off hand, but at the last moment he saw that the boy— more cur now than pup—somehow had drawn a second knife. Only another spin saved Ethan from being skewered.

But in evading Folter's attacks, Ethan had opened a path of escape. Folter looked at the thieftaker once, perhaps weighing another assault. Instead, he ran up the wharf back toward Purchase Street.

With the harbor at his back and the air heavy with moisture, Ethan had enough water at hand to cast an elemental spell. He spoke it quickly under his breath—"*Imago ex aqua evocata*"; illusion, conjured from water—and at the same time made a small flicking gesture with his hands, directing the charm so that the image formed directly in front of Folter.

Instantly the air around him felt charged, as it did when a storm came upon a ship at sea; as it did any time he conjured. Ethan felt the hairs on his neck and arms stand on end.

The old ghost appeared at Ethan's side, glowing a rich reddish brown like the moon when it hangs low in the night. His eyes gleamed like brands, and they held a hint of annoyance, as if Ethan had torn him away from something too important to be interrupted for a mere illusion spell. Not that the ghost could refuse him. He was Ethan's guide, a spectral guardian of the power-laden realm between the living world and the domain of the dead. Folter wouldn't be able to see the specter; no one who wasn't a conjurer could. But he would see the conjuring that Ethan's ghost made possible.

For this illusion, Ethan summoned the first image that came to mind: a great white horse with a flowing mane, like the one he had seen earlier that day leading a chaise through the streets near the Common. Ethan cast the spell quickly, with little preparation; at midday, the creature might have looked insubstantial, but in the gloaming it appeared solid and huge and wild. It bore down on Folter as if intent on trampling him, and the pup did exactly what Ethan had hoped. He halted, dove to one side, and wrapped his hands over his head to shield himself. He gave no sign of noticing that though the beast looked real enough, its hooves made no sound on the wharf.

Ethan sprinted forward just as Folter scrambled to his feet.

The young man looked around frantically, his knives still in hand, though seemingly forgotten for the moment. "Where'd it—?"

Ethan didn't allow him to finish the thought. He crashed into him, sending him sprawling. Ethan fell, too, rolled, and was on his feet again. One of the knives had flown from Folter's hand; Ethan kicked the other one away. He aimed a second kick at Folter's jaw, but the pup was too fast for him. He grabbed Ethan's foot and twisted viciously, flipping Ethan to the ground.

Folter threw himself onto Ethan, and for a few harrowing moments the two of them grappled for control of Ethan's blade. Folter was younger, quicker, stronger. He tried to pry Ethan's fingers off the knife, and though Ethan fought him, he could feel his grip on the weapon slipping.

He wrapped his other hand around Folter's throat and squeezed as hard as he could. Immediately the younger man stopped trying to tear the knife away and instead grabbed at Ethan's other hand. Ethan, his blade hand now free, drove the heel of it up into Folter's nose. He heard bone break, felt hot blood splatter on his cheek. An instant later, Folter rolled off of him, both hands clutching his face, blood running over his fingers.

"Damn ya!" the pup said, his voice thick.

Ethan got to his feet and kicked Folter in the side. The pup gasped and doubled up.

"Where are the jewels?" Ethan demanded.

Folter groaned.

Kneeling beside him, Ethan laid the edge of his blade along Folter's throat. The young man stiffened.

"Don't try it, lad," Ethan said. "I don't want to kill you, but I will." Folter didn't move; Ethan began to search his pockets with his free hand. In no time at all, he had found three bejeweled golden necklaces. "Was this it, or were there more?" he asked.

When Folter didn't answer, Ethan pressed harder with his knife, drawing a small trickle of blood from the pup's throat.

"Tha's all," Folter said sullenly.

Ethan didn't release him.

The young man looked up at Ethan, fear in his eyes. "I swear!"

After holding him for another moment, Ethan removed the knife and stood once more.

"Are ya going t' kill me now?" Folter asked. He sat up, eyeing Ethan, his body tensing, coiled.

"I can tell you that Mister Corbett wouldn't object," Ethan said. "The Admiralty Court would probably thank me for performing a service. And I promise you that if I meant to, you couldn't stop me."

"But ya're going t' let me go," Folter said with disbelief. "Ya really don' work fer Pryce, do ya?"

"No, I really don't. I'm giving you this one chance, Daniel. I'll let you go, but you have to leave Boston and never return. Corbett instructed me to give you over to Sheriff Greenleaf; he would be happy to see you transported to the Carolinas, or the Indies." Ethan felt a twinge in his foot at his mention of the islands, the remembered pain of an old wound. "But Diver Jervis is a friend of mine, and he wouldn't want to see you come to that end. I'm risking a great deal by letting you go. If I see you again, I'll turn you in. Failing that, I'll have no choice but to kill you."

"I's born here," Folter said. "I ain' never been anywhere else."

"Then this is your chance to see the world," Ethan told him. "But one way or another, you're leaving the city."

Folter opened his mouth to argue.

"I'll give you one day, Daniel," Ethan said. "If you're still in Boston after midnight tomorrow, I'll know it, and I'll find you. Then you'll have the sheriff to deal with."

The young man nodded glumly.

"Go," Ethan said.

Folter started away, then stopped, turning again. "My knives—"

"Leave them. And when you get to wherever you're going, try not to make a mess of your life."

The pup frowned and glanced about as if he had barely heard. "Say, where did tha' horse go?" he asked. "Th' one tha' nearly ran me down."

"I didn't see it."

Folter eyed him curiously. "Ya had t' have seen it."

"Good-bye, Daniel."

The young man stared at him for a long time. "Ya're a speller, aren' ya?" he finally said. "Tha's why I'd heard o' ya. Ethan Kaille. Sure, tha's it. Th' speller wha' does thieftakin' here in th' city. I remember now. Tha's where tha' horse came from. It was bloody witch'ry. An' tha's how ya can compete with Sephira Pryce."

Ethan retrieved Folter's knives and put them in his pocket. He made no answer.

"I could tell someone," Folter said. "I could tell Pryce or one o' her men." A smile crept over his thin face. "I could get ya hung fer a witch."

"You could," Ethan said, meeting his gaze. "But if I really am a speller, what's to keep me from killing you in your sleep if I think you're a threat to me? What's to keep me from tracking you down whenever I want to, and giving you smallpox or plague?"

Even in the failing light, Ethan could see the pup's face go white. In truth, the fact that Ethan was a conjurer—a speller, as Folter put it—wasn't as much of a secret as he would have liked. He suspected that Sephira Pryce already knew, and it was possible that some on the Admiralty Court still remembered the names *Ruby Blade* and Ethan Kaille. But he didn't want word of his talents spreading farther than necessary, and he surely didn't want Folter thinking that he had any advantage over him.

"I'm not sayin' I'd tell," Folter told him. "I was jus' . . . I wouldn' tell anyone."

"Go, Daniel. Right now. Get out of Boston, and you won't need to worry about me ever again. Remain here, and I'll make Sephira Pryce seem like a kindly aunt. Understand?"

The pup nodded, and began to back away from him, his eyes wide, his face still ashen save for the bright blood that trickled from his nose. After a few steps, he turned and ran.

*E*zra Corbett and his wife lived only a few streets
west of the South End waterfront, in a house on Long Lane along
the edge of d'Acosta's Pasture, a broad ley within the confines of
the city. Ethan made his way up from the water's edge, crossing Purchase
Street once more, and then Cow Lane. The sky had darkened almost to
black. A gibbous moon hung in the east, its glow dulled and made
faintly yellow by the summer haze that had settled over Boston.

As Ethan approached the Corbett house, he caught the scent of
smoke riding the warm breeze, and he thought he heard the excited
babble of many voices in the distance. He wondered if another mob
was abroad in the city, drinking Madeira wine and making mischief.
Only two weeks before, such a rabble had made its way to Kilby Street,
just a short distance from Henry Dall's cooperage, where Ethan leased
a room, and had destroyed a building belonging to Andrew Oliver, the
king's newly designated distributor of stamps here in the province.
The crowd had been loud, vulgar, and violent. Ethan sat out front for
several hours guarding Henry's cooperage, while the rioters disman-
tled Oliver's building, ransacked his home, which was also nearby, and
finally built a bonfire at Fort Hill. In the end, they didn't approach
Cooper's Alley, but Ethan didn't relish the idea of spending another
sleepless night listening to the drunken cries of agitators.

The Corbett house was no more grand than its neighbors, but neither was it any less so. It was built of stone and oak, its few windows

thrown open to coax inside whatever breeze drifted along the lane. Ethan rapped on the door with the brass knocker and stood with his hands behind his back. His shoulder hurt where he had run into Folter, and he was sure that he would be sore come morning. Twenty years ago he could fight in the streets without worrying about such things. Not anymore.

A pretty young servant opened the door and led Ethan into a small sitting room before going in search of her master. He surveyed the room: wooden floors, simple furnishings, an empty hearth in the center of the south wall. The subtle aroma of roasted fowl and fresh bread blended with the bitter scent of spermaceti candles. There were finer houses in town—mostly on Beacon Street and in the North End—but it was obvious the Corbett family didn't want for much.

Ethan strolled around the room, looking at the paintings of Corbett's wife and his two daughters. After several moments, a door opened at the far end of the chamber. Mr. Corbett stepped in and closed the door quietly behind him. Facing Ethan and eyeing his clothes, he faltered, a frown on his homely face. Belatedly it occurred to Ethan that he must look a mess. His breeches were filthy from his struggles with Folter on the wharf, and there probably were bloodstains on his waistcoat and shirt.

"Mister Kaille," the merchant said grimly. "I didn't expect to see you again so soon. Is there a problem?"

He was a short, round man whose clothes didn't fit him quite right. They were too long in the sleeves and legs and too tight around the middle. He was bald except for tufts of steel gray hair that poked out from behind his ears, and he wore spectacles on the end of his nose.

"There's no problem, sir," Ethan said, producing the necklaces and laying them on a small table beside the hearth. "I've come to return your wife's jewels."

Corbett's entire bearing changed. His eyes widened, and as he crossed to the table he actually broke into a smile. "You've found them already! Well done, Mister Kaille!"

"Thank you, sir."

"And the thief?" Corbett asked, examining each necklace by the light of an oil lamp.

"Daniel Folter."

The merchant looked at him. "Daniel? You're sure?"

"Yes, sir. You know him?"

Corbett hesitated. "He did some work for me a year or so ago. He even expressed interest in courting my older daughter, though I didn't encourage him in that regard." He shook his head. "Still, I'm surprised. I never figured the man for a thief."

"No, sir."

Corbett studied the necklaces a moment longer before facing Ethan again. "Well, these look to be none the worse for their adventure. I take it Daniel has been dealt with?"

"He won't trouble you again, sir," Ethan said, holding the man's gaze.

"Very well. I owe you another ten shillings, don't I?"

Ethan bit down on his tongue to keep from laughing. He had dealt with merchants before. "Actually, I believe you owe me fifteen."

Corbett raised an eyebrow. "Fifteen is it?" he asked.

"Yes, sir."

"Hmmm, I suppose that's right." The merchant dug into a small pocket on his vest and pulled out a coin purse. He poured its contents onto his desk and began to count out Ethan's payment. "An acquaintance of mine said I shouldn't hire you," he said as he piled the coins.

Ethan tensed. "Is that so?"

"Yes," the merchant said, not meeting Ethan's gaze, lamplight reflecting off his glasses so that the lenses looked opaque. "He said I would have been better off hiring someone . . . safer."

Ethan didn't know whether to laugh or yank out his own hair. There was only one other thieftaker in Boston; Corbett's friend thought Sephira Pryce would be a safer choice than Ethan.

Corbett went on. "I think he was concerned about your past."

"Of course," Ethan said.

"I bring this up because I wanted you to know that people still speak of it, those who remember anyway."

He knew this already, of course. Nearly twenty years had passed since the *Ruby Blade* mutiny, but few who were old enough to have heard of the incident when it happened would have forgotten. Mutinies were scandalous enough; add to that whispers of witchcraft and the result was enough to cause quite a stir.

"Thank you, sir," Ethan said stiffly.

The merchant finished counting out the money and returned the coin purse to his pocket. "I intend to tell my friend that he was wrong about you," he said.

I don't give a damn, Ethan wanted to say. Instead, he thanked him once more.

"Here you are," Corbett said, handing Ethan the stack of coins. "Well earned, Mister Kaille. I hope that I won't require your services again, but should I have further need of a thieftaker, I'll be certain to call on you."

"Thank you, sir. For your sake, and that of your family, I hope that won't be necessary."

Corbett smiled and led him back to the front door. "My wife will be most pleased," he said, pulling the door open.

"I hope so, sir."

The smell of smoke had grown stronger. Corbett wrinkled his nose and frowned. "More trouble," he said sourly. "I don't hold with lawlessness, Mister Kaille. And I don't choose to associate with those who do. Do you take my meaning?"

Ethan was about to answer, but in that moment he felt the pulse of a spell, the air around him thrumming like a bowstring. Ethan's first impulse was to ward himself, and his hand flew to the hilt of his blade.

"Mister Kaille?"

An instant later, Ethan realized that the spell had not been intended for him, that it hadn't even been cast in this part of the city. Which meant that it must have been a powerful conjuring. He stared into the night, trying to locate the conjurer, wondering who could have cast such a spell.

"Mister Kaille! I asked you a question!"

"Yes, sir," Ethan said, far more interested in the spell he had felt than in whatever Corbett had said. "I beg your pardon. What did you ask?"

"I said that I don't hold with those who would flout the law in pursuit of political aims, and I asked if you took my meaning."

"I do, sir." He wanted to go. Right now. He wanted to find the conjurer who had cast that spell. But Corbett had paid him, and might well hire him again. Kannice would tell him that he should give the man his undivided attention.

The merchant gazed out into the night. "Do you support them?" he asked. "These agitators?"

In recent days, Ethan had heard arguments on both sides of this issue. There was nowhere a man could go in the city without overhearing discussions of Grenville's Stamp Act. Like much of Boston, all the people he knew were beginning to align themselves according to whether they supported or opposed Parliament's latest attempt to raise revenue. Corbett had made his position clear, and Ethan thought it best to give the safest response he could, even if it didn't exactly answer the man's question.

"I'm a subject of the British Crown, sir," he said. "I recognize the authority of Parliament in all matters pertaining to the colonies."

Corbett nodded. "That's most wise of you. This sort of villainy and licentiousness will be the ruin of Britain."

"Yes, sir," Ethan said. "Good night."

"And to you, Mister Kaille."

Ethan stepped out of the house, followed the path back to Long Lane, and turned northward. As he walked, he wondered if Corbett and his acquaintances knew only of the mutiny and Ethan's time in forced labor, or if they knew as well the role that conjurings played in all that happened aboard the *Ruby Blade*. Just how many people in Boston knew that he was a conjurer? Three or four months might pass without anyone speaking to him of his spellmaking abilities. And then he could have days like this one, when it seemed that everyone knew.

He had his share of enemies in the city, and none of them would hesitate to use his secret against him if they thought themselves safe from his retribution. But fear of conjuring ran deep, even among the wealthy, even among the likes of Sephira Pryce.

Corbett's coins jingled in Ethan's pocket, bringing a smile. Combined with the seven and a half shillings Corbett had paid upon hiring him last week, it was money enough to last him a while. He wouldn't need to work again for at least a month, perhaps longer. Maybe this would be a good time for him to stay out of sight; let talk of his . . . talents die out. Particularly if there was another conjurer in the city casting spells as potent as the one he had just sensed. And in the meantime, he could spend a few days with Kannice.

He was headed to the Dowsing Rod now. She would want to know that he had found Folter and managed to avoid getting himself killed in the process.

Ethan strode through the heart of the South End, passing by the brick edifice of the Third Church, its steeple looming dark and tall against the moonlit sky. The smell of smoke grew stronger as he walked, and he could hear shouts coming from different parts of the city—the area just north of Cornhill as well as the North End. He wondered if there were two mobs loose in the streets, or if there might be even more. As he neared the First Church and the Town House, he saw the glow of the fire he had been smelling.

He slowed. Ezra Corbett wasn't the only client who might look askance at Ethan's involvement in any mischief, and Ethan had no interest in attracting the notice of officials of the Crown. He had already endured enough British justice to last a lifetime.

A sound behind him made him spin; his knife was in his hand almost before he realized that he had reached for it. Two shadows emerged from behind a dark house and trotted up to him. Shelly and Pitch: a pair of dogs who lived in the streets, and spent most of their time scrounging for food at Henry's door. Ethan lowered his blade, laughing at himself. But his heart continued to hammer as he sheathed his weapon and squatted down to greet the dogs. They licked his hand, tails wagging.

Shelly had first shown up at the cooperage several years before, not long after Ethan took a room there. She was a large dog with a short coat, mottled gray and white. She had a splash of tan on her snout, and pale gray-blue eyes. Henry had named her Shells because he said her coloring reminded him of the shells that washed up on the harbor shore. But before long he and Ethan were both calling her Shelly.

Pitch, who showed up a few months later, was a bit smaller, and entirely black, save for his deep brown eyes. His coat was long and silky. Ethan often wondered if he had once belonged to a wealthy family; dogs as pretty as Pitch generally didn't live in the streets.

"No food," he told them, as they continued to lick his hand and sniff his clothes. "Sorry."

He scratched them both behind their ears. Judging from their response, this made up for the fact that he had nothing to feed them.

Standing again, he backtracked to School Street, and followed Treamount northward, the two dogs flanking him. He hoped to keep his distance from those abroad in the streets. He soon realized, though, that rather than avoiding the mob, he was walking directly toward it. The closer he got to Queen Street, the louder the noise grew. He could hear raucous laughter and shouted curses, the shattering of glass and the splintering of wood. As he crossed the lane and gazed eastward, he saw men tossing broken furniture and bundles of parchment from the window of a stately home directly across the street from the courthouse and prison. The irony of it nearly made him laugh out loud.

One man stood in the middle of the lane, holding a bottle of wine in one hand and what looked to be a table leg in the other. He spotted Ethan and shouted, "Hey, you!" The man sounded so merry, one might have thought that he was celebrating the coming of a new year rather than the sacking of someone's home. "Care t' join us?" the man asked. "Th're's plen'y t' go 'roun'!"

Ethan waved a hand and shook his head without breaking stride.

"Wha'samatter?" the man called after him, his voice hardening. "Don' like wha' we're doin'? King's man, eh? Well, damn ya t' hell!"

Ethan walked on, allowing the man to shout at his back. But he spoke a spell under his breath. *Veni ad me.* Come to me.

The air around him hummed, and the ghost of the old man appeared at his shoulder again and fell in stride beside him. The drunkard continued to shout after him, but he didn't follow. Shelly and Pitch broke off, whining slightly as they headed back to the South End. This wasn't the first time Ethan had seen the dogs flee at the first appearance of the ghost. He regretted scaring them off, but he felt better knowing that he could summon his power instantly if he had to. Too much was happening this evening. The spell he had felt, these rioters; he had grown cautious over the years, and if ever there was a night that called for care, this seemed to be it.

Ethan felt the ghost watching him, but he kept his eyes trained on the street ahead. He wished he knew more about this glowing figure who materialized at his side whenever he conjured. The man was tall and lean, with a trim beard and mustache, and close-cropped hair that looked like it would have been white had it not been for the shade's reddish glow. He was always dressed the same way: in a coat of mail and an ornate tabard bearing the leopards of the ancient kings, like those worn by medieval knights. Ethan guessed that he had lived hundreds of years ago, and he assumed that the old man was one of his mother's forebears. All Ethan knew for certain was that every time he spoke the words of a spell, the ghost materialized to blend his power with whatever source Ethan had chosen to complete his conjuring.

The ghost couldn't speak; at least, he had never said anything to Ethan, although his bright eyes and bushy eyebrows could be quite expressive. Over the years, Ethan had taken to calling him Uncle Reginald—Reg, for short—after one of his mother's older brothers who had a prickly personality.

At last, as he continued to walk up Treamount, Ethan glanced at the wraith, who was still eyeing him with that familiar vexed expression.

"Something on your mind?" Ethan asked.

By way of answer, the ghost pointedly glanced back toward Queen Street and then nodded toward the knife on Ethan's belt.

"Yes, I could have spoken a spell when I needed you. But the castings are faster when you're already here." He grinned. "Besides, you're such pleasant company."

The specter glowered at him.

They reached Hanover Street, and Ethan heard more commotion coming from down the lane. Two weeks ago the agitators had concentrated their ire on Oliver; tonight, they were casting a wider net. Best to get off the streets.

When at last he reached the Dowsing Rod, Ethan turned to Uncle Reg again. *"Dimittas,"* he said within his mind, not bothering to speak the words aloud. I release you.

The ghost touched a glowing hand to his own brow and then began to fade from view. Ethan gazed back toward the center of the city, where smoke continued to billow into the night. Shouts echoed through the streets, punctuated occasionally by strident cheers. If anything, there was more commotion now than there had been earlier. He could guess who was behind these riots, and he knew that only trouble could come of them.

T he Dowsing Rod was owned and run by Kannice Lester, who had become the sole owner of the tavern several years
ago, after her husband Rafe died. Kannice served decent ales at
a reasonable price, but she was known throughout Boston for her
stews, which most people, Ethan included, thought were the best in
the city.

From without, the Dowser looked clean and reputable. Kannice
wouldn't have had it any other way. She made it clear to all her guests—
even Ethan—that she wouldn't tolerate gambling or whoring or any
other sort of mischief within the walls of her inn.

"Leave it in the streets," she always told them. "Or you won't be
welcome here again."

Ethan had yet to meet anyone brave or foolish enough to defy her.

Stepping into the tavern, Ethan expected to be greeted by the usual
din of laughter and shouted conversations. But the Dowser was half
empty, unusual even for a Monday night, and those who stood at the bar
or sat at tables arrayed around the hearth spoke in hushed voices. The
air within was heavy with the smell of candles and pipe smoke, and the
mouthwatering aroma of one of Kannice's famous fish stews. Though
the crowd was small, Ethan saw several familiar faces, including Devren
Jervis—Diver—an old friend who occasionally helped Ethan with his
work.

Of all the people Ethan knew who frequented the Dowser, Diver came closest to getting himself banned from the tavern. He did so with some frequency, and, as Kannice had pointed out on more than one occasion, if it wasn't for Ethan's friendship with the man, Diver would have been tossed out into the street long ago. He sat alone at a table near the back of the tavern. Catching Ethan's eye, he raised his tankard and gave it a little wave.

Ethan had to laugh. The evening mist and a few stubborn midges still clung to his waistcoat, and already Diver was asking him to buy his next ale. Ethan walked to the bar, where a few men stood drinking ale and eating oysters.

"Evenin', Ethan," said Kelf Fingarin, the hulking barman. "Wha' kin I getchya?" Actually, he said it so quickly that it came out as a single word: WhakinIgetchya? Ethan understood only because he had been in this tavern a thousand times. Newcomers weren't so lucky, and in addition to being the size of a Dutch merchant ship, Kelf also had a quick temper. He was certain that his words were as clear as an autumn morning in New England.

"What's Diver drinking?" Ethan asked.

"Th' cheap stuff, as usual."

Ethan wrinkled his nose. "You have any of the pale left?"

"From Kent, you mean?"

Ethan nodded.

"I might have a bit."

Ethan tossed two shillings onto the bar. "I'll have two. And keep them coming."

Kelf grinned and grabbed two tankards. "Someone jest got paid."

"Where's Kannice?" Ethan asked.

Kelf was already filling the first tankard. He jerked his head toward the entrance to the kitchen. " 'N back, gettin' more stew. I'll tell 'er ya're here." He placed the first ale on the bar, began to fill the second.

"There's another mob out in the streets," Ethan said.

"Don' need t' tell me," Kelf said. "Look 'round. Half them who're supposed t' be here are with th' rabble, an' th' rest are too scared t' leave their homes."

"You know why?"

The barman shrugged and put the second ale on the bar next to the first. "Stamp nonsense again."

Ethan took the ales. "My thanks, Kelf."

He wove his way past tables and chairs, nodding and smiling to the few people who met his glance and offered a greeting. When he reached Diver's table, he placed one ale in front of his friend and sat.

"I'm grateful, Ethan," Diver said. "I'll get the next one."

"We're paid through a few rounds," Ethan said. "You can pay next time."

Diver raised his ale. "Well, then!"

Ethan tapped his friend's tankard with his own and they both drank, Diver draining most of his.

Diver wiped his mouth on his sleeve and peered down into his drink. "The good stuff, eh?"

"I got paid," Ethan said. "Enjoy it."

Diver sipped from his mug again. But he said nothing more and soon began to drum his fingers nervously on the table.

"You all right?" Ethan asked.

"Fine!" Diver said. "Just . . . I'm fine."

A cheer went up from the bar; looking past Ethan, Diver smiled. Ethan turned in time to see Kelf and an attractive, auburn-haired woman emerge from the kitchen carrying a large tureen of what had to be more fish stew. Kannice Lester was willowy and stood at least a full head shorter than the barman, but her arms were corded from years of lifting pots of stew, of keeping her tavern clean, of making sure there was wood for the hearth and for the stove in her beloved kitchen. At a word to Kelf, she and the barman hoisted the tureen onto the bar in one fluid motion. She began to ladle the soup into empty bowls as patrons converged on her from all around the room. After a few moments she spotted Ethan, and a smile lit her face. She whispered something to Kelf, who immediately returned to the kitchen. Kannice continued to serve out the stew.

"So who paid you?" Diver asked Ethan, leaning close.

Ethan tore his gaze from Kannice. "Corbett," he said. "His wife's got her jewels back and I've got my coin."

Diver's eyebrows went up. "Already?"

"Don't look so impressed. It was Daniel."

"Daniel? He swore to me that he'd given up thieving."

"Well, he's as much a liar as he is an idiot." Ethan narrowed his eyes. "Did you have business with him?"

"Of course not," Diver said, suddenly interested in the tankard in front of him. "I know Daniel's trouble. I stay away from him." He glanced up at Ethan, though only for an instant. "Is he . . . did you . . . ?"

"I didn't give him up to Greenleaf," Ethan said, lowering his voice to a whisper. "And I didn't kill him, either, though Sephira wouldn't have been so forgiving. I told him to leave Boston, so if he owes you money, I'd suggest you collect in the next day."

"I told you, I have no dealings with him." Diver said the words forcefully enough, but he wouldn't look Ethan in the eye.

Diver was nearly ten years younger than Ethan, and had long looked up to him as he might an older brother. They had known each other for more than twenty years, since Ethan first arrived in Boston and Diver was just a boy working the wharves. The younger man was clever, but he had been orphaned as a small boy and raised by an uncle who never liked him. Early on he had turned his wits to activities that might well have landed a less fortunate man in prison or on a boat to a British penal colony. He put to sea as a hand on merchant ships for a time, and about five years ago, around the time Ethan was released from his servitude in the West Indies, Diver came back to Boston to work the wharves once more. In the years since, he had also helped Ethan track down the occasional thief. He actually seemed to have a knack for such work, though Ethan often wondered if this might not be because of Diver's own shady dealings and his connections with Boston's less virtuous citizens.

Ethan had every intention of pressing his friend further on his association with Daniel, but before he could ask more questions he felt a smooth arm snake gently around his neck, and soft curls brush against his cheek.

"I didn't expect to see you tonight," Kannice whispered in his ear. Her breath smelled lightly of whiskey, her hair of lavender. Over the past few years he had grown fond of the combination. She kissed his temple, and when he turned to her, kissed his lips softly.

"This job worked out better than I hoped it would," he said, brushing a strand of hair off her brow. "Hope you didn't have other plans."

She shrugged, blue eyes wandering the tavern. "I figured I'd have to make do with one of these others," she said airily. "But since you're here . . ."

He smiled, as did she. Then she looked over at Diver and straightened.

"Derrey," she said, a trace of ice in her voice.

"Stew smells good tonight, Kannice," Diver said with brittle cheer.

She inclined her head toward Ethan, though her eyes never left Diver's face. "You going to make him pay for your meal, too?"

Kannice was younger than both of them and, so, far closer in age to Diver than Ethan. Her husband, whom Ethan had never met, was nearly twenty years older than she, and when he died, back in 1761, leaving her to run the tavern, she was barely more than a girl. But she always spoke to Diver this way, as if he were a wayward child, and she his older sister. Or his mother.

"I was glad to buy him the ale," Ethan said, keeping his voice low. "I just got paid."

She pursed her lips, but held her tongue. Diver had enough sense to shut his mouth as well. A moment later, Kelf showed up with a bowl of steaming stew, which he placed in front of Ethan.

"Thereyago."

"Better bring another for Derrey here," Kannice said.

Kelf eyed each of them in turn and tromped back to the kitchen to fetch another bowl.

Kannice turned her back on Diver and looked down at Ethan. "I'll deal with you later," she said, a coy smile on her lips. She started back to the bar, shouting, "Tom Langer, I swear if you spill another ale in my tavern I'll banish you for a year and a day!"

Several men behind Ethan laughed uproariously.

"She's a hard woman, Ethan," Diver said, watching her walk away.

"Only with you. And I'm not sure it's undeserved."

Diver frowned and drank the rest of his ale. Kelf brought a second bowl of stew, placed it in front of Diver without saying a word, and returned to the bar.

"I want to know what you had going on with Daniel," Ethan said as Diver started to eat.

"I told you," Diver said, his mouth full. "Nothing at all."

"That's the first time you've looked me in the eye since we started talking about him."

Diver's cheeks reddened. He was a handsome man, his face still youthful, his black curls as yet untouched by gray. Kannice's hostility notwithstanding, women were drawn to him. He was tall, lean, and dark-eyed, and he had a winning smile and was quick with a jest. But if Ethan had a daughter, he would have done everything in his power to keep Diver away from her.

Ethan continued to stare at his friend, saying nothing, until at last Diver put down his spoon and glanced around, as if to make certain that no one could hear.

"Was Corbett your only job?" Diver asked in a low voice.

"What?"

Diver leaned closer and lowered his voice even more. "Are you working on anything else right now?"

Ethan let out a small laugh and shook his head. "What have you gotten yourself into, Diver?"

"Answer the question."

"No, I'm not working on anything else. In fact, I'm thinking I should lie low for a time. It seems everyone I meet right now knows too much about me, if you catch my meaning."

Diver's eyes widened. "Really? You think Pryce is spreading rumors about you?"

"They're not rumors if they're true. And no, I don't think she would bother with something like this. If Sephira gets tired of having me around, she'll just have me killed and be done with it." He took a spoonful of Kannice's stew, which was savory, just a bit spicy, and as delicious as usual. He never took his eyes off of Diver, though, and now he added, "But we were talking about you."

"I'm getting to it." Diver took a breath and scanned the room again. "It's not as bad as you think."

"I don't think anything, yet," Ethan said, which was not entirely true.

"Well, then it's not as bad as it's going to sound. There's a group of merchants who have put in together to buy a shipment from a French merchant."

"A shipment of what?" Ethan asked, though he already knew.

"What do you think? He's French. Wine from France—fifty casks— and a few hundred gallons of rum from the French West Indies. Course the merchants can't sell any of it the usual way. They can't have the casks showing up in their warehouses, and they need people to sell them outside the usual places, where the lobsterbacks can't see."

Of course. Since Parliament passed the first of the Grenville Acts the year before, it had been illegal for anyone in the colonies to import or sell any wine from France or any rum from the French West Indies. The problem was, as much as the British here in the Americas hated the French, they still had a mighty thirst for French wines and spirits. Since the 1730s, American distillers had purchased smuggled molasses from the French West Indies. Now Grenville and his friends in Parliament had lowered the molasses tariff and banned the import of French rum, in the hopes of ending that illegal trade. All they had done, however, was create a new and lucrative illegal market in spirits from the islands.

If the customs men caught Boston merchants selling French goods, they would confiscate what they found and fine the merchants. But if they found someone like Diver selling them, they would leave the merchants alone and deal harshly with him.

"So they want you to sell them," Ethan said.

"I get paid two pence for every gallon of wine or rum; and that adds up. I could make more in five days selling this stuff than I make at the wharf in an entire season."

You could also get yourself thrown in the stocks. Or worse. Ethan kept that thought to himself; Diver was a fool, but he understood the risks.

"Daniel was supposed to sell them, too, wasn't he?" Ethan asked.

Diver faltered. "Aye."

"When does the shipment get here?"

"Tonight. It might be here already. I'm waiting for one of my mates from the wharf. He's supposed to tell me when it arrives."

Ethan shook his head and ran a hand over his face. Daniel wouldn't be leaving the city after all. He couldn't refuse that kind of money. Ethan had to hope that Folter would manage to avoid Corbett until he sold his share of the contraband.

"You think I'm mad," Diver said.

"I have for years. Why should it start bothering you now?" He grinned, as did Diver. "No, I was thinking about Daniel. I told him to leave the city. But he won't go if he's waiting for this shipment."

"He might, if you scared him enough."

"Would you," Ethan asked, "if you knew the casks were coming?"

"Probably," Diver said, dropping his voice once more. "But I've seen what your spells can do." He took another spoonful of stew.

They ate in silence for a time. Diver eyed the tavern's entrance, while Ethan pondered what might happen if Ezra Corbett learned that Daniel was still roaming the streets. Ethan depended on men like Corbett— merchants and craftsmen of means—for his livelihood. If word spread through the city that he had let Daniel go, they would think twice about calling on him when they needed a thieftaker. Sephira Pryce, Ethan was sure, would be all too happy to take their business.

"There we are," Diver said suddenly.

Ethan looked up to see that his friend was already standing, his eyes fixed on the doorway. A burly man stood in the tavern entrance, motioning to Diver.

"I'll see you later, Ethan," Diver said.

"Watch yourself," Ethan told him. "There are plenty of men in this city who would be willing to sell the wine and rum themselves, and who would think nothing of taking them from you and leaving you a bloody mess."

Diver nodded and crossed to the doorway. He and the man spoke briefly, the burly man shaking his head repeatedly as Diver's expression grew grimmer by the moment. At last, Diver turned and walked slowly back to the table.

"What happened?" Ethan asked, as his friend lowered himself back into his chair. "Ship delayed? There's been more talk of privateers in the waters off Boston and Europe."

"No," Diver said, sounding morose. "The ship's put in, but the shipment wasn't on board. There's no telling when it'll be getting here." He stared at his empty bowl. "Damn!" he muttered after several moments.

"You need another ale," Ethan said. "And so do I. Tell Kelf that you're buying off the shillings I gave him before."

Diver got up again, eager as a puppy. "You're a good man."

Ethan finished his stew, and when Diver brought back the ales, he turned his chair so that he could see the rest of the room. Kannice spent most of her time behind the bar, helping Kelf with the ales and whiskeys. But occasionally she came out into the common area to joke with her patrons or settle down a group that was getting too boisterous.

She might have been small of stature, but there was steel in her voice and ice in those blue eyes when she had need. Ethan had yet to meet a man who wasn't cowed by her. At one point she glanced his way and saw that he was watching her. She smiled, her color rising, and then went back to what she had been doing.

"Why don't you marry her?"

Ethan glanced at Diver and sipped his ale. "That's none of your concern."

"If you're still thinking that you and Marielle—"

"I said it was none of your concern, Diver."

He didn't raise his voice; he didn't have to. Diver knew him well enough to understand that he had sailed into dangerous waters.

Marielle Harper—Elli, Ethan called her—had once been his betrothed. Among the better families of the North End it had been said that she was too fine for him. She was the daughter of a wealthy shipbuilder; he, the wayward son of a captain in the British navy. But she loved him, and he adored her. Still, in all their time together, he never revealed to her that he was a conjurer, and when he was accused of taking part in the *Ruby Blade* mutiny, of using "witchcraft" to subdue the ship's captain, she wrote a letter to him that to this day he could recite from memory. In it she said that he had betrayed her trust, and she vowed never to see him again. By the time he returned, bitter and maimed, from the plantation in Barbados where he had labored and bled and, on more than one occasion, nearly died, Elli had married another and borne the man's children.

She had since been widowed, but she still insisted that she wanted nothing to do with Ethan or his spellmaking. Ethan knew better than to expect that she would ever change her mind, even as he also knew that a part of him would always long for her.

Kannice knew about Elli. Having ruined one romance with secrets and lies, Ethan vowed never to do so again. He sensed that Kannice harbored hopes that eventually he would forget about his first love and agree to spend the rest of his life with her. She rarely spoke of it, though, and that was fine with Ethan; the last thing he wanted was to hurt her.

For long minutes Ethan and his friend sat in uneasy silence, until at last Diver drained his tankard and set it down smartly on the table. "Well, then," he said, getting to his feet. "Looks like I'll be working the wharf again tomorrow, so I'd best get some sleep." He flashed a smile, though it appeared forced. "Good night, Ethan. My thanks for the ale."

"Take care of yourself, Diver."

"I always do," Diver said, and left the tavern.

Ethan remained where he was and drank his ale slowly. No one approached him. Most of those who knew him either feared him for his ability to conjure or saw him as an unrepentant mutineer. He had few friends, though those he had he trusted.

Eventually, as the crowd in the tavern began to thin and the noise died down, Kannice approached his table again.

"Derrey was in a hurry to leave," she said, pulling Diver's chair around and placing it beside Ethan's.

"Not really. He has to work the wharves come morning."

"Who was that came to talk to him?" she asked, her eyes fixed on her hands as she toyed with one of the silver rings on her fingers.

She doesn't miss a thing.

"One of his mates from the wharf, I think."

A faint smile touched her lips as she glanced up at him through her eyelashes. "Why do you protect him?"

"Why do you harry him?"

"If ever there was a man who needed harrying . . ." She trailed off, letting the words hang.

He knew better than to argue. "I'll tell him to keep it outside next time," he said, an admission in the words.

"Thank you."

They sat in silence for a few moments. Eventually Ethan took her hand. She met his gaze, smiled.

"You say it went well with Corbett?" she asked.

"It did. I found all that his wife had lost. He was pleased."

"And the thief?"

Ethan exhaled and made a sour face. "Daniel Folter."

Kannice rolled her eyes. "Another fool."

"Aye," Ethan said, conceding the point as far as Diver was concerned.

"You let him go?"

"Of course." He started to tell her that doing so might well prove to have been a mistake, but thought better of it. That would have carried the conversation back around to Diver, and Ethan didn't want that.

"Why is it that you're so forgiving of fools?" she asked him.

"Maybe I see enough of my younger self in them to think they're not beyond hope."

She shook her head, the corners of her mouth quirking upward again. Then she stood, moved to stand behind his chair, and began to knead the muscles in his neck, her small fingers deft and strong. He closed his eyes and tipped his head forward.

"Just because there's hope for them doesn't mean it's your job to save them all," she whispered.

"Now you tell me."

She kissed the top of his head.

"That feels good," he said, as she continued to rub his neck.

"It's supposed to."

He smiled, but just as he did she moved her hands down and began to rub his shoulders. Ethan winced, sucking air through his teeth.

"What's the matter?"

"I had to fight Daniel to get back those necklaces. My right shoulder's sore."

She kissed the side of his neck. "That's a shame. And your leg?"

"It hurts, too."

The air around them was redolent of her perfume. "Poor baby. You're probably too tired and sore to do anything but sleep."

He laughed. "I'm not sure I'd go that far," he murmured.

Kannice giggled. "I'm glad to hear it," she said. She took his hand. "Let's go then."

"Don't you have to clean up?"

She waved a hand vaguely toward the bar. "Kelf will get most of it. I let him leave early a few nights ago. He owes me."

Ethan grinned. "I've always liked Kelf."

She stopped. "Well, if that's what you prefer . . ." She held his gaze for several moments, struggling to keep her expression neutral. Finally, she began to giggle again. "Come on," she said, tugging on his hand.

Before they reached the back stairs leading up to her chamber, the door to the Dowsing Rod swung open and several men rushed in.

"Did ya hear?" one of them asked of no one in particular. "They're sacking Hutchinson's house!"

Ethan and Kannice had stopped, and now Kannice took a step toward the men.

"Who are?" she demanded.

"Mackintosh an' his boys," the man said.

And another added, "They got Story an' Hallowell, too!"

"Idiots!" Kannice said. She glanced at Ethan. "They can't think any good will come of it."

He shrugged. She knew well enough what he thought of the agitators. After the attack on Oliver's house, they had argued about it for two days. But he was thinking once more about that conjuring he had felt. Had there been spells at work in addition to whatever else stirred the mobs to attack?

Regardless of the answer, Kannice was right: Attacking the homes of William Story and Benjamin Hallowell was one matter. Story, of the Admiralty Court, and Hallowell, the comptroller of the Customs House, were two of the most hated men in all of Boston. But Thomas Hutchinson was lieutenant governor and chief justice of the province. To be sure, he had enemies among those opposed to the Grenville Acts, but he was also one of the most respected leaders in the colony. If these men were right—if Hutchinson's home had been attacked—it would anger not only the Crown, but many of those the leaders of these demonstrations hoped to draw to their cause.

"Has anyone been hurt?" Kannice asked, sounding disgusted.

"Not tha' we know," the first man said. "Hutchinson an' his family have got away, an' so did th' other two. Bu' their homes are wrecked."

One of the men behind him suppressed a chuckle and looked side-long at another. This man laughed, too.

"All right, you lot," Kannice said. "You've had your say. Now get out."

"Bu' we're thirsty," the first man said, sounding aggrieved.

"Well, you'll have to find your drink elsewhere."

They looked like they might argue, but at that moment Kelf stepped out from behind the bar, and planted himself in the middle of the great room, his massive arms crossed over his chest. The men grumbled among themselves, but shuffled out of the tavern.

When they had gone, Kelf faced Ethan and Kannice. "Ya think it's true?"

"Hallowell's place is on Hanover Street, isn't it?" Ethan asked.

"Yes," Kannice said. "And I think William Story lives near the Court House."

"I heard them," Ethan said. "There were mobs at both houses."

Kelf looked from one of them to the other. "But Hutchinson—he lives in th' North End, don' he? Did ya hear anything from there?"

"It was hard to tell," Ethan told him. "But if the rest of it's true . . ."

"Then this is, too," Kannice finished for him. "And there'll be hell to pay."

Chapter
FOUR

*S*oon after the men left, Kannice and Ethan went upstairs and immediately fell into each other's arms, forgetting about Parliament and street mobs for a time. After they made love, though, Ethan made the mistake of asking if Kannice was ready to admit that the Stamp Act agitators were ruffians and fools.

"The ones who attacked Hutchinson's house?" she said. "Clearly. But that doesn't mean all of them are."

He should have left it at that. But he didn't, and they were up half the night arguing about the rioters and what they had done. Kannice, who believed that Parliament had overstepped its authority by enacting the Stamp Act in the first place, blamed the mob for going too far and ransacking the Hutchinson house. But she refused to say categorically that the riots led by Ebenezer Mackintosh and his men were wrong.

Ethan could hardly contain himself. "So what you're saying is that they were justified in attacking Andrew Oliver's property, but not Thomas Hutchinson's."

"Oliver has been made distributor of stamps!" she said, as if that was answer enough.

"That is what you're saying then!"

Kannice raised her chin defiantly. "Yes!"

"So, you think it acceptable to destroy the property of those who disagree with you! And you'd be fine if people who support the Stamp Act tore the Dowser to the ground!"

"That's not what I said!" she shot back. "And you know it! Oliver will be enforcing the Act. What was done to him was unfortunate, but justified. Tonight was different."

"There's no justification for destroying a man's home," Ethan said in a low voice. "I don't care who he is, or what he's done. If that's the freedom these men speak of, then I want no part of it." He rolled over and pulled the blanket up to his chin.

Ethan could tell that Kannice was watching him, thinking of more to say. But at last she blew out the lone candle burning in the room and lay down beside him. She touched his arm lightly and Ethan reached back to give her hand a quick squeeze. Soon after, he fell asleep.

When Ethan woke, Kannice was already up. The room was cold, though the bed was still warm where she had lain. She had pulled on a long, plain dress and was plaiting her hair.

Seeing that he was awake she said, "Good morning. Are you hungry?"

Ethan nodded and tried to rub the sleep from his eyes.

"Bacon? Bread? Eggs?"

"Aye," he said.

Kannice laughed. "Fine. Don't take too long getting yourself out of bed. Unlike some people, I have to work today."

"Yes, ma'am."

She came to the bed, kissed him, and slipped out of the room.

Ethan lay there for a few minutes more before finally sitting up and reaching for his breeches, which were slung across a chair next to the bed. He had barely gotten them on when the door opened again and Kannice came in, wearing a mild frown.

"Is everything all right?" Ethan asked.

"I'm not really sure," she said. "There's a man downstairs—no one I've ever seen before. He says he's looking for you."

"Lots of people saw me here last night. And it's no secret that you and I spend a great deal of time together."

"I know," she said, still troubled.

"What did he look like?" Ethan asked. "What's he wearing?"

"He looks harmless enough. Older than I am." She paused. "Probably older than you are, too. Fine clothes. A silk shirt, linen waistcoat and matching coat and breeches. But he looks too rough to be a merchant or a shop owner."

"A servant?"

"Maybe."

He reached for his shirt. "All right. I'll be down shortly."

She nodded and left the room once more. Ethan finished dressing, making certain to strap on his blade. Then he left the room and descended the stairs to the tavern.

The man stood beside the doorway, his hands in front of him clasping the brim of a black tricorn hat. As Kannice had said, his clothes—the white silk shirt and pale blue ditto suit with its matching coat, waistcoat, and breeches—were of fine quality and fit him well. His hair was silver, but his face was unlined—Ethan wouldn't have wanted to hazard a guess as to his age. His eyes were pale, and his nose looked like it had been broken at least once. Even before he spoke, Ethan guessed that he was a Scotsman by birth.

"Yah're Kaille?" the man asked, as Ethan approached. "Th' thief-taker?" His brogue was heavy—definitely Scottish.

"I'm Ethan Kaille. Who are you?"

"I represen' a man who wishes t' hire ya." He indicated the closest table with an open hand.

Ethan hesitated, then took a seat. The stranger seated himself across from him.

"Who is it you represent?"

"Have ya heard of Abner Berson?"

Who hasn't? Ethan wanted to ask. Berson had made a fortune importing and selling hardware and firearms from England. He owned a wharf and warehouses in the North End off Ship Street, and was one of the richest men in Massachusetts. "Everyone's heard of Mister Berson."

"I suppose. Ya wouldna heard that his daughter was killed last night, in th' middle of all that unpleasantness."

"I'm sorry to hear it," Ethan said, his eyes flicking in Kannice's direction. She was wiping the bar with a cloth, but he could tell she was listening. "I hope you'll convey my condolences to Mister Berson and his wife."

The man accepted his words with a nod.

"They had two daughters, didn't they?"

"Aye. This was th' older one. Jennifer."

Ethan knew why the man had come, and though he sympathized with the merchant and his family, he needed to make it clear that he couldn't help them.

"You understand, sir, that I'm a thieftaker. I recover stolen items for a fee and I deal with those who are guilty of thievery. But I don't track down murderers."

A wry smile touched the stranger's face. "O' course ya don't, Mister Kaille. There's no profit in it."

Ethan bristled. "That's not—"

"I mean no offense. Ya have a trade. Ya have t' make a livin'. I understand. As i' happens, Mister Berson has need o' yar talents as a thieftaker. His daughter had on a brooch when she was killed. It was taken. Th' family wants it back." He pulled a small pouch from the pocket of his coat and placed it on the table. Ethan heard the muffled clink of coins. "Tha's ten pounds. More will come t' ya when ya find that brooch."

Ethan's eyes strayed to the pouch. "And if I happen to find Jennifer's killer while I'm recovering the brooch . . ."

"Obviously, Mister Berson would be most pleased."

Ten pounds. And more when he found the brooch. Ethan had to admit that he was tempted. But only the night before he had decided to keep out of sight for a while, to live off the money he had gotten from Ezra Corbett. More to the point, in all the time he had been working as a thieftaker he had tried to avoid taking jobs involving murders. They were far more dangerous, and he could never justify sparing the life of a thief who also killed, which meant that he himself might have to take a life. He had vowed long ago never to do that again.

"I'm afraid I can't help you," he said, meeting the stranger's gaze once more.

"If it's a matter o' more money . . ."

Ethan shook his head. "It's not. I don't work murders." He stood. "Please thank Mister Berson for his offer."

"He asked for ya specifically," the man said quickly. "And he doesna like bein' refused. Ya might wan' t' consider if Abner Berson is someone ya want as an enemy."

It wasn't the threat that stopped him. He had heard far worse in his years as a thieftaker in this city. But the other part . . . *He asked for you specifically.*

"Why would he want me?" Ethan asked.

The man shrugged; the expression on his face didn't change at all. "It's no' my place t' ask. But he did."

Now that he thought about it, Ethan realized that this should have been his first question. He usually worked for men of middling means— merchants like Corbett, craftsmen like Henry, for whom he had recovered a valuable set of tools before taking the room above his cooperage. Men as wealthy as Berson didn't come to him. They went to Sephira Pryce. Pryce was better known; she was as wealthy and influential as they were. If word got around Boston that Berson had come to Ethan instead of going to the Empress of the South End, as many called Pryce, both Ethan and the merchant could expect visits from her and her toughs—never an appealing prospect.

Kannice would have told Ethan that this was all the more reason to send the silver-haired stranger away, to follow through on his plan to avoid the streets for a time. But that had never been his way.

"Have you approached Sephira Pryce about this?" he asked.

For the first time, Berson's man seemed unnerved. His face paled, and the corner of his mouth twitched. "No," he said. "Mister Berson sent me here."

"Has he had dealings with Miss Pryce in the past?"

"It's no' my place t' say," the man said. He seemed unsettled by the question. "Mister Berson sent me here."

"You already said that."

"An' will ya accept his offer?" He shifted in his chair, then straightened, regaining some measure of his composure. "Most men o' yar . . . station would leap at th' chance t' work for Mister Berson."

"Most men of my station wouldn't be offered the opportunity."

"Ya make my point for me, Mister Kaille."

"Right, but what I'm wondering . . ." He stopped in midsentence, staring at the man.

"Yes?"

Of course. It came to him in a rush, along with his memory of the conjuring he had felt the night before. He should have understood immediately. If he was going to risk angering Pryce, he couldn't afford to be this slow-witted.

"All right," Ethan said. "I'll do it."

The stranger looked genuinely surprised. "Ya will?"

"Aye. I'll need a description of the brooch and some information about Mister Berson's daughter—where she was killed, and exactly when; where she had been, and where she was going. If possible I'd like to see her corpse."

He had expected that this would trouble the man, but the stranger merely nodded, as if he had expected Ethan to request as much. What did it say about the streets of Boston that a merchant's man should be more disturbed by the mention of Sephira Pryce than by the dead body of his employer's daughter?

"She's a' King's Chapel," the man said, "downstairs in th' crypt."

"The crypt? She's already been buried?"

"No. Tha's where her body was taken. She's t' be buried on th' grounds there."

Naturally. The King's Chapel Burying Ground was the oldest cemetery in Boston, and the only one a man like Abner Berson would have deemed appropriate for the interment of his child.

"Mister Caner, the rector there, knows yah're comin'," the man went on. "Once yah've seen her, yah're t' come t' th' Bersons' home."

"All right," Ethan said, although he was already having second thoughts. He had his reasons for taking the job, but he had also had his reasons for refusing at first. Perhaps the stranger read the doubt in Ethan's eyes, because he stood, put on his hat, and strode to the tavern entrance, as if determined to leave the Dowser before Ethan could change his mind. He paused by the door and looked back at Ethan.

"Until later, Mister Kaille," he said, and left.

For several moments Ethan sat staring at the door, wrestling with the urge to run after the stranger and give him back Berson's money. At last, knowing that by now he had waited too long, he reached for the pouch, which still sat on the table. He held it in his palm, enjoying the weight of it, the soft jangling of the coins. Then he stood and slipped it into his pocket.

Turning toward the bar, he froze. Kannice was watching him, her brow furrowed, her lips pressed in a thin line.

He walked over to her. "You have something to say to me?"

"I thought you weren't taking any jobs for a while."

"This one's different," he said. "I couldn't say no."

She didn't respond.

"That man works for Abner Berson. His daughter's been killed."

"I heard," she said, her voice flat. Ethan had been sure she would have much to say about him working on a killing, but if she did, she kept it to herself.

"They want me because there were spells involved. He didn't say it, but I'm sure. I think I might even have felt the conjuring that killed her. That's why Berson didn't go to Sephira Pryce."

"And do you have to work every job that calls for a conjurer?"

"Would you rather I left it to Sephira or the sheriff? They know nothing about spells. Or rather, they know just enough to cast suspicion on every speller in Boston, myself included. It has to be me, Kannice. I'm the only one who knows enough about conjuring to find the truth."

Kannice went back to wiping the bar, rubbing at the wood with such fury that Ethan half expected her to take off the finish.

"She died last night," Ethan said. "Berson's man made it sound like she was killed by the same mob that destroyed Hutchinson's house."

She frowned, but she didn't look at him. "You don't believe that any more than I do," she said quietly. "The men who wrecked those houses might be fools, but they're not murderers."

"Not all of them. But one of them might be."

Kannice cast a hard look his way, but continued to clean the bar.

"I have to go," he told her at last.

She nodded, a strand of hair falling over her forehead. He started to reach out to brush it away, then stopped himself.

"Will you be back here tonight?" she asked, pushing the strand away herself.

"I don't know. Probably not."

Her frown deepened.

"Anyway," he went on. "It'll probably be a late night."

She straightened, her eyes meeting his. She draped the polishing cloth over her shoulder and tipped her head to the side. "If you change your mind . . ."

"Aye," he said. Both of them knew he wouldn't. He stood there another moment, neither of them speaking. Finally, Kannice went behind the bar, and retreated into the kitchen.

Ethan left the tavern.

The warmth of the previous night had given way to a cooler morning. The sky was a clear, bright blue, and a freshening wind blew in off the harbor, carrying the smell of fish and brine, and sweeping away the heavy pall of smoke that had been inescapable the night before. The streets were crowded with carriages and men and women on foot making their way with grim purpose to shops or to the markets at Faneuil Hall.

When Ethan first came to Boston, twenty-one years before, he thought he had never seen a finer place. The city was small by English standards, but it was clean and alive. Its streets bustled with activity. It was everything Bristol, his home in England, was not.

Two decades later, hard times and war had taken their toll. Every day, Boston felt more like the sad, gray cities of England. It had grown torpid, weak. Where once it had been the leading city of British North America, it was now the indolent older sister to New York and Philadelphia, surpassed by its younger, more vibrant siblings.

King's Chapel sat at the corner of Treamount and School Streets, only a few blocks from the Dowsing Rod. It was one of the older churches in Boston, though it had been rebuilt only ten years before, its wooden exterior enclosed within a new granite façade. The wisdom of that choice had been borne out in the years since, as Boston was ravaged by fires, including one that began on Cornhill and swept down to the wharves, damaging literally hundreds of shops and homes. Some had suggested that the rebuilt church should now be called Stone Chapel, but it remained King's Chapel to most in the city.

The still incomplete structure had a ponderous look, much at odds with the more graceful lines of the older churches in the North and South Ends. But the chapel was the first in the colonies to affiliate itself with the Church of England. Its congregation included some of the wealthiest and most influential families living in the central part of the city, particularly those with close ties to the Crown.

Ethan didn't worship at any of Boston's churches. In his years as a soldier and then as a prisoner, he had seen too much brutality and suffering, and had done things for which he could not forgive himself. He had lost a third of his life, part of his foot, and the one woman he had ever truly loved. At this point, whatever faith Ethan might once have had in the existence of a just and merciful God was gone.

This was another point of contention with Kannice, who every Sunday went to the Old Meeting House in the South End, and who assured him that God had taken his toes to save his life and had eased his ague before it killed him. But even if Ethan believed her when she said that God was watching over him, he knew better than to think that His servants would be so kind. Ethan was a conjurer, not a witch, and few of those who had been hanged or burned as witches in New England's dark history could actually cast true spells. But that hadn't stopped men like Cotton Mather from railing at magicking in their sermons, and it didn't stop the present crop of ministers and vicars from doing the same.

And of all the churches in Boston, there was none that he avoided so assiduously as he did King's Chapel. That was how Bett, the older of his two sisters, and a member of the chapel's congregation, wanted it. Usually, he was more than happy to honor her wishes. Today he had no choice but to ignore them.

He entered the churchyard through the gate on Treamount, ascended a low set of steps to a pair of heavy oak doors, and entered the chapel. The building was far more attractive within than it was from the street. Pairs of columns with ornate carvings at their tops supported a high ceiling with shallow vaulting. Two stories of windows allowed sunlight to flood the main sanctuary. Boxed pews lined the central aisle, which led to a rounded chancel beyond the altar at the far end of the church. The walls and ceilings had been painted ivory, the columns darker shades of tan and brown, and the pulpit and gallery fronts pale pink; the pews were natural wood. Given the chapel's somber exterior, the cheeriness of the sanctuary surprised Ethan.

A robed man, tall and narrow-shouldered, stood at the pulpit, poring over the Bible. He looked up as soon as he heard Ethan enter.

"Yes?" he called, his voice echoing through the sanctuary. "What do you want?"

"Mister Caner?" Ethan asked, walking forward.

The man frowned and descended the curving stairway to the stone floor. He had a thin, bony face and a somewhat sallow complexion. His nose was overlarge, his eyes were small and hard, his lips thin and pale. His robe was black and he wore a stiff white cravat at his neck.

"No, I'm not Mister Caner," the man said, waiting for Ethan at the base of the steps. "I'm the curate, Mister Troutbeck. And you are?"

"My name is Ethan Kaille. I was sent by Abner Berson. I'm to see his daughter's body."

The minister's frown softened. "Yes, of course. Mister Caner mentioned that you might be coming. This way."

Ethan followed Troutbeck through an archway into the vestry behind and to the left of the pulpit, and then down a broad set of marble stairs.

The air grew colder and damper as they went down. At the bottom of the stairs, they turned onto a broad corridor lined on each side by stone walls. The basement was poorly lit; a few candles burned in iron sconces set in the corners, but there was no other source of light, and after the brightness of the sanctuary Ethan's eyes were slow to adjust. He could tell, though, that the walls of the corridor were marked regularly with stone plaques, all carved with names and dates. The crypts.

In the middle of the corridor stood a stone table. A delicate figure lay upon it, her dark hair spilling over the edge of the slab. She was covered to her neck with a white cloth. A censer had been placed in a corner by the stairway, and fragrant smoke rose from it, barely masking the sickly smell of decay and the pungent scent of the spermaceti candles.

Ethan started toward the corpse, walking slowly, his boots clicking loudly on the stone floor. His vision was still uncertain, and so when a figure in the far corner moved, rising from a small wooden chair, Ethan nearly jumped out of his skin.

"That is Mister Pell," Troutbeck told Ethan, amusement in his voice as it reverberated loudly off the stone. "He is sitting vigil with the body. I trust that if you need anything he can help you."

The curate turned to go.

"Who brought her here?" Ethan asked, his pulse still racing from the fright the second minister had given him.

Troutbeck stopped and faced him once more. "Pardon?"

"Who brought the body to King's Chapel?"

"I don't know. I wasn't here last night."

"Two men of the night watch," said the minister in the corner. "They said they had been called by a man who found her lying in a deserted lane, and that Berson requested they bring her here."

"You see?" Troutbeck said. "Mister Pell should be able to answer any questions you have." He nodded curtly to Ethan and then to the minister before returning to the stairway. This time, Ethan made no effort to stop him.

Once the sound of Troutbeck's footsteps had faded, Ethan approached the stone table. Mr. Pell did the same.

Pell was young and slight; despite his black robes and cravat, he looked more like an altar boy than a minister.

"Did the men of the watch tell you where she was found?" Ethan asked, as he stared down at Jennifer Berson's face. She had been an attractive girl, with a wide, sensuous mouth, large, widely spaced eyes, and a straight, fine nose.

"They said she was found on Cross Street. But that's all."

"And what time was this?" Ethan asked absently, his gaze still on the girl.

"Forgive me," the minister said. "Who are you, and what are you doing here?"

Ethan looked up at that. "Mister Caner didn't tell you?"

Pell regarded him placidly. Even in the dim light Ethan could see that his eyes were pale. He had straight dark hair. A powdered wig sat on the stone floor beside the chair on which he had been sitting, but

Ethan couldn't help thinking that with a face as youthful as his, Pell would have looked odd wearing it.

"Mister Caner might have mentioned something about expecting a visitor," the young minister said, taking some care in the choice of his words. "But I wish to hear an answer from you."

Ethan resumed his examination of the girl, bending closer to get a better view of her face. Let the man play his games. Ethan had work to do. "My name is Ethan Kaille," he said as he searched her head and neck for wounds. "Abner Berson has asked that I look into the death of his daughter and the theft of an item she was carrying when she died."

"And you're a thieftaker?"

"Aye."

"Do thieftakers often investigate murders?"

"Are you interested in hiring me?" Ethan asked. "Or are you making conversation?"

The minister shrugged, looking sheepish. "I was merely curious," he said quietly.

"I'm not sure this is the time for indulging your curiosity. Please answer my question: When did they bring her?"

"It was close to midnight, I believe."

"Had she been dead for long?"

The minister glanced at the girl before quickly averting his eyes again. He stood a few paces from the table, and his hands trembled. "You mistake me for a physician, Mister Kaille. I couldn't tell you."

"Then you have no idea how she died?" Ethan asked.

Pell licked his lips. "None at all."

"Forgive me, Mister Pell," Ethan said. "But this can't be the first time you've seen a corpse."

"Of course not," the young man said, his voice unsteady.

"And yet, you seem shaken by the sight of her."

The man hesitated, his eyes now fixed on the girl. "She's about my age. And the men who brought her said that she had been murdered. I've seen the dead before, but never anyone who was . . . killed in that way."

"I understand," Ethan said. "I'm going to uncover her. I want to see if I can learn something of how she died. All right?"

Pell nodded.

Ethan pulled back the sheet to reveal the girl's body. She was dressed in a pale silk gown—a soft shade of yellow, although it was hard to tell in the dim light. Her petticoats were darker—perhaps green—and she wore a stomacher of white silk. Ethan bent closer, examining the exposed skin of her shoulders and chest, searching for any marks that might explain her death.

"Bring me that sconce," Ethan said, gesturing vaguely at an iron tree in the far corner of the chamber.

Pell retrieved it and brought it to Ethan, setting it beside him so that the glow of the candles illuminated the girl.

Even in the better light, Ethan saw no stab wounds, no dried blood, no obvious bruises. He searched her limbs, checked her clothing for rents or cuts in the fabric. At last he rolled her onto her side to examine her back. Nothing.

He wasn't surprised; this was why Berson had wanted him and not Sephira Pryce or some other thieftaker. This was why he had been thinking about that pulse of power ever since seeing Berson's servant in the Dowsing Rod. Even so, he was troubled.

"There are no marks on her," Ethan said, straightening and meeting the young minister's gaze.

"What does that mean?" Pell asked.

"Well, it means she wasn't killed in any of the usual ways. She wasn't stabbed or shot. Her throat wasn't slit. Her neck wasn't broken."

"Could she have been strangled?"

Ethan looked down at the girl again and shook his head. "That would leave bruising on her neck, whether done with a rope or bare hands."

"What about poison?"

He considered this for several moments, staring at the girl's face. Her expression in death was peaceful; she could well have been sleeping rather than dead. It was hardly the face of someone who had died by poisoning.

"I suppose it's possible," Ethan said.

"But you don't believe it."

"No."

"Perhaps she wasn't murdered after all."

"Perhaps," Ethan said absently, still regarding the body. "Mister Pell, I wonder if you wouldn't mind getting me a cup of water?"

"What?"

"Some water. Or better yet, wine. Like you, I'm . . . I'm troubled by the sight of this poor girl. I need something to drink."

"You're lying to me," Pell said, sounding young and just a bit frightened.

"I assure you—"

"You're lying," he said again. "And I want to know why."

Ethan smiled faintly. "No, you don't."

"What do you mean I don't?" Pell said, frowning deeply. "Of course I do."

"Do you know my sister, Mister Pell?" Ethan asked. "She's a member of the congregation."

"Your sister?"

"You would know her as Bett Brower, the wife of Geoffrey Brower."

"You're Missus Brower's brother?" The minister leaned forward, scrutinizing Ethan's face. "Yes, I suppose I do see some resemblance. What about her?"

"Has she mentioned me to you?"

"No, why would she?"

It was a fair question, though perhaps not as Pell meant it. Bett was too protective of her status in Boston society to risk calling attention to her rogue of a brother, who also happened to be a conjurer. Thinking about it, Ethan realized that he should have been surprised that she had spoken of him even to dear Geoffrey.

"No reason in particular," Ethan said at last. "I merely mention her to make you understand that you have no reason to distrust me. If you can simply get me some wine, I would be grateful. I'll stay with poor Miss Berson—she won't be alone for even a second."

Pell said nothing, but he continued to eye Ethan, a thoughtful expression on his face.

"That's not what you were going to say," the man said at last. "Is it?"

"I don't know what you mean."

Pell stared at him. "You do know what killed her, don't you? You just don't want to tell me."

"I don't know anything," Ethan said, trying to keep his voice even.

"Not for certain, you mean. But you have some idea. It's there in your eyes; I can hear it in your voice. What is it you're not telling me?"

Ethan didn't answer, but he watched as the minister worked it out for himself.

After a moment, Pell turned back to the corpse. "She wasn't stabbed or strangled," he muttered. "She wasn't shot or poisoned or killed in any of the other, more conventional ways. But she *was* murdered." He glanced at Ethan again, his brow furrowed in concentration. And then it hit him. Ethan saw it happen. He blinked, his eyes widening. Even in the faint candlelight, Ethan saw the color drain from Mr. Pell's cheeks.

"Oh," the minister said. And then again, "Oh."

"You understand?" Ethan asked gently.

"I believe I do," Pell whispered.

"Then you understand why I need you to go."

He squared his shoulders. "What if . . . ?" The young man paused and took a slow breath. "What if I won't let you do this? What if I call for Mister Troutbeck right now?"

"And tell him what?" Ethan asked.

"That . . . that you're . . . that you're a witch."

"You could do that," Ethan said. "You could make your accusations. I've done nothing that you could point to as evidence to support your claim. But still, he might believe you. He might have me arrested and burned or hanged. Is that what you wish to see them do to me?"

Pell looked away. "Of course not."

"A young woman is dead. I believe she died at the hands of a conjurer. I understand that the mere mention of the so-called dark arts is enough to make some who wear those robes fall into a panic, but her family has hired me to learn the truth. And I believe that even Mister Troutbeck would want to see her killer punished."

The minister glanced at the woman's corpse. "What is it you want to do to her?"

"I want to find out what kind of spell killed her, and, if possible, who cast it."

"You can learn those things?"

"Yes, I can."

"But only by using witchery yourself. Isn't that so?"

"Aye," Ethan said.

"What kind?"

"What?"

"What kind of witchcraft would you be using?"

Ethan frowned. "Why would you care about—?"

"What kind of witchcraft?" the minister asked again, his eyes meeting Ethan's. "Your sister isn't the only person who came to this chapel with . . . with strange powers in her blood. I know something of conjuring, and before I risk being banished from the ministry by letting you cast on these sanctified grounds, I would like to know what you intend to do." When Ethan still hesitated, he said, "This calls for more than an elemental spell, doesn't it?"

"That's right," Ethan told him, surprised to hear that the minister really did know something of conjuring. "It would have to be a living spell."

"So you'll need to spill your own blood."

"Unless you'd like to stay and let me bleed you."

The minister paled again, but managed a smile. "No, I think not. But a living spell could draw the attention of other conjurers."

"Any spell will," Ethan said. "There's nothing to be done about that."

They stood eyeing each other for several moments, until at last the young minister dropped his gaze to the body. "Very well, Mister Kaille. I'll trust you not to do any more conjuring than necessary, and you can trust me to say nothing about this to Mister Troutbeck or Mister Caner."

"Thank you, Mister Pell. I'll do this as quickly as I can."

"I'll be in the sanctuary. Please call for me before leaving the crypt." Pell glanced at Jennifer Berson once more. "She shouldn't be alone."

His gaze lingered briefly on the corpse. Then he left the corridor, his footsteps echoing in the stairwell. When Ethan couldn't hear him anymore, he removed his waistcoat and pushed up his sleeve, shivering in the cool, still air. He paused over the girl for a mere instant, studying her face once more. Her expression was so serene; she couldn't have known what was about to happen to her. She hadn't feared her murderer. This might well have been done by someone she knew, perhaps even someone she trusted.

He pulled out his blade and dragged its edge across his forearm, making a cut long and deep enough to draw what might have been a spoonful of blood. Laying his knife on the table beside Jennifer, he dabbed his forefinger in the welling blood and traced a single dark line across the girl's brow, and a second one from the bridge of her nose, over her lips and chin, down the length of her throat, to her breastbone.

"*Revela potestatem,*" he murmured in Latin, "*ex cruore evocatam.*" Reveal power, conjured from blood.

The words rang in the dark chamber, as if they had been spoken by several voices at once. The stone beneath his feet hummed with power, and the air around Ethan felt even more charged than it had the previous night, when he conjured the horse. This was a stronger spell; he also wondered if perhaps these grounds held some power that he didn't fully understand.

The ghost appeared beside him, his glowing eyes fixed on the dead girl, a hungry look on his russet features.

Ethan felt the blood on his arm turn to vapor, as sweat on the brow dries in a cooling wind. He watched the blood he had placed on her face, throat, and chest vanish, as if wiped away by some unseen hand. The candles beside him guttered and the hairs on the back of his neck stood on end.

And then the body of Jennifer Berson began to glow. The light emanated from just to the left of her breastbone and spread slowly, radiating out over her entire body, spreading up over her face and head, out to the very tips of her fingers, and down to the soles of her feet. At first Ethan thought the light had no color, that it simply reflected the hue of the candle fire. But when he moved the sconce away and looked at the girl's body once more, he saw that the glow was actually pale silver, the color of starlight.

Usually the spell Ethan had cast would have concentrated the glow at the point where the murderer's conjuring had struck her, but the light surrounding Jennifer's body was as even as moonglow on a snow-covered field. And that shade of silver . . . Every conjurer's power had a different hue; the variations were subtle but distinctive. Ethan's was rust-colored, like the brick façade of the Boston Town House in the late-afternoon sun. His other sister, Susannah, was also a conjurer. Her spells left a residue of greenish blue, the color of the ocean on a clear day. But never had he seen power like this before. It was as if all the color had been sucked out of the conjuring, and this silver was all that remained.

Old Reg's ghost flashed a mocking grin. Then he vanished again.

Ethan had no doubt that Jennifer had been killed by a conjuring, but he couldn't imagine what kind of spell had been used against her. It was possible that the way the glow had spread over her body offered some clue. An attack aimed at her heart might have produced such an effect by following the flow of her blood, though in Ethan's experience such an assault, when revealed by the spell he had cast, should have left a gleaming spot over her chest.

There was another spell he could try, one that could tell him what the murderer had used to fuel his spell. Every conjuring had to draw upon its source, be it one of the elements—fire, water, earth, or air— for the simplest spells, or something drawn from a creature or plant for living spells. The revealing spell Ethan had just tried demanded his own blood. Other living spells could be cast using herbs or tree sap or wood.

Just as every conjurer left his or her color on the residue of a spell, so the source left an imprint as well, if one knew the casting required to reveal it. Ethan did. And perhaps knowing how the spell had been cast would help him learn a bit more about the murderer. He had told Pell that he would speak only the one spell. But this would likely be his only chance to examine the girl's corpse, and it struck Ethan as foolish not to do everything in his power to learn the identity of her killer.

The wounds he made to conjure began to heal themselves almost as soon as he spoke his spells, which meant that he needed to cut himself again for this second casting. He retrieved his knife from the table, bared his arm, and laid the blade against his skin.

Before he could draw blood, however, he heard a light footfall behind him.

"Don't you dare!" a voice warned, echoing off the ceiling and stone walls. "Not in this place!"

*E*than turned slowly, holding up the knife and extending his arm to show that he hadn't cut himself again.

"Hello, Bett."

His sister frowned at him and then shifted her gaze to Jennifer's body. "What have you done to her? Why does she look like that?"

"I tried to learn something of the conjurer who killed her."

"She was killed by witchery?" Bett said. She walked past him, her satin dress and petticoats rustling. "You're sure?"

"Look at her," Ethan said.

"You did that."

"I merely made the power reveal itself. Her killer did that."

Bett stared at the dead girl for a long time, chewing her lip; he remembered that from when she was young. She and Ethan had never gotten along, even as children. He and Susannah, on the other hand, had been inseparable, which probably had made matters worse for their middle sister. Bett had always been so serious, so righteous, far more like their father than their mother. She even looked like Ellis. She had his straight brown hair, his dark blue eyes, his square, handsome face. Susannah was Sarah's daughter in every respect. Not only did she resemble their mother; she also had Sarah's sharp wit and hearty laugh. Ethan had always felt a kinship to both of them. But except for the scars he now bore, he looked just like Bett and just like their father. Throughout his life he had thought this ironic, though he couldn't help thinking that those who knew him best—Kannice, Diver, Henry—wouldn't have seen the irony. They thought him grave, even ill-tempered at times, and they were right. The years had left him far more like Bett and his father than he had been in his youth.

"It's an odd color," Bett finally said, her voice low.

"I was thinking the same thing before you came in." He regarded her slyly. "Maybe you have a knack for conjuring."

One might have thought from the smoldering look in her eyes that he had accused her of thievery, or worse. "That's not funny."

Susannah would have laughed. So would Mother. But he kept these thoughts to himself. When they were young, their mother had taught all of them to conjure. But while Ethan and Susannah had quickly shown an aptitude for spellmaking, Bett had not. It was one more reason why Ethan and Susannah had been so close to each other and to their mother. As a boy he had thought Bett difficult; only later did it occur to him that she had probably felt left out, lonely.

"I don't know what that color means," he said. "I suppose it could be the color of the spell that killed her, though I've never seen conjuring power that looked like this. It's more likely that her killer is strong enough to mask his or her castings." He glanced at her. "That's why I was going to try the second conjuring. It might tell me something more about the spell itself."

"You shouldn't be using witchery in here. Not for any purpose."

He gestured toward the body. "Not even to find out who killed this girl?"

"If God wants us to learn the identity of her killer, He will reveal it to us in His own way."

"I was just noticing that my conjuring feels stronger in here than it does anywhere else in Boston. Maybe this *is* His way."

The look she gave him would have kindled damp wood. "You are speaking of witchcraft in a house of God!"

"Witchcraft?" Ethan repeated, his voice rising. "You know better, Bett! I expect that kind of nonsense from people who know nothing of conjuring, but not from you!"

"Why not from me? Just because I'm your sister, that doesn't mean—"

"Yes, you're my sister! If you're going to call me a witch you have to accept that you're one, too!" His words echoed loudly through the corridor, and belatedly he thought of the two ministers upstairs in the sanctuary.

"I'll thank you to keep your voice down," she said with cold intensity. "You may have forsaken the Lord and His word, but I have not. Neither has Geoffrey, nor our children. This is our church, and I won't have you desecrating it."

Ethan inhaled and exhaled slowly, trying to keep his temper in check. "I haven't desecrated anything. This murder is the true desecration. I merely want to find the person responsible. Is that so terrible?"

Bett stared at the girl again. "You've gotten Mister Pell in some trouble, you know."

"Pell had nothing to do with this."

"*Mister Pell* was asked to keep vigil over this girl," she said. "Instead, he left her with you. He should have known better."

"I sent him away, Bett. I asked him for a cup of wine. That's why he left me."

She pursed her lips, and Ethan held his breath, hoping that Pell had been smart enough to tell a similar tale. Apparently the minister was better at all of this than Ethan had thought, for at last Bett said, with some reluctance, "He told Mister Troutbeck the same thing."

"Then perhaps you should believe him," Ethan told her, masking his relief.

"Still, he shouldn't have left her side."

"Perhaps," Ethan said wearily. "I hope you'll be kind enough to speak with Tr—with Mister Troutbeck on his behalf. Feel free to blame me. That should come naturally."

Her expression soured, but when she spoke again, her tone had softened. "You might also wish to consider the danger to yourself. I felt your spell, Ethan, and so did anyone else who . . . comes from a family like ours. Even if you don't respect this church you should be fearful enough for your own life to keep your blade in its sheath and your blood in your veins."

"Unless you believe that Mister Caner and Mister Troutbeck are conjurers, I really don't think I have much to fear on that account. Anyone saying that he felt my spell would be declaring himself a conjurer as well."

Bett frowned. Clearly this hadn't occurred to her. She had spent too many years pretending that she didn't have spellmaking abilities.

"Well, then," she said, drawing herself up. "If you don't care about yourself, and you won't respect this church, then I have no choice. I'll reveal you as a witch myself. I'll tell Mister Troutbeck exactly what you were attempting to do."

"Even if it means that you also will be revealed as . . . as a witch?"

"I'll tell him that our mother was a witch, and that she lured you to her ways. Mister Troutbeck knows that I'm a pious woman. And Geoffrey will vouch for me. He's as well respected as any man in Boston."

Ethan had always thought that Bett's husband was a prig and an ass. But he was also a fairly well-placed British customs official, and that probably counted for something among those in Bett's congregation.

"Fine, Bett." He sheathed his knife and began to roll down his sleeve. "It's been a pleasure seeing you as always."

She looked disappointed, as if she hadn't expected him to give up so easily. "You're sure that a conjuring killed her?"

He threw his hands wide. "I don't know how many different ways to say it! Yes, she was murdered with a spell! I don't know what kind or who cast it, but a conjurer killed her."

"And you've been hired to find her killer? I didn't know you did that." She said it without any trace of malice, which surprised him.

"Actually, I don't," he said, lowering his voice. "I recover stolen property, and that's what I'm doing here. Something was taken from her, presumably after she was killed. Berson hired me to find it, no doubt hoping that I'll also find the person who killed her."

She said nothing.

Ethan finished rolling down his sleeve and reached for his waistcoat. "Good-bye, Bett," he said, starting toward the stairway.

"Wait."

He stopped, sighed. His sister still faced the stone table, her back to him.

"Was your spell really stronger here?"

Ethan nodded, then realizing that she wasn't looking at him, said, "I don't know. It felt stronger. Would that really be so surprising?"

She glanced back at him, her expression dark. "Of course it would."

"Why? If I could paint like Copley or work silver like Revere, you would tell me that my talent was a gift from God. Why is this any different?"

Ethan wasn't sure he had ever seen her more offended. "Don't you dare claim your . . . your black art as a gift from the Lord!" she said, her voice trembling. "When you're alone, or with your witch friends, you can justify your conjuring any way you like! But in this chapel, in my presence, you will say no such thing!"

Ethan started to respond, but stopped himself. He and his sister had battled on similar terrain too many times before, and too many of their wounds remained raw. "Very well," he said, turning once more to go. "I'll leave it to you to explain to Abner Berson why I couldn't find his daughter's killer. It's really not a conversation I wish to have."

"That's unfair," she said, actually sounding hurt. "You know how I feel about this, Ethan. I haven't said anything today that I haven't told you a thousand times before. What did you expect?"

"I expect nothing, Bett. But however much you hate me—"

"I don't hate you. I've never hated you. I pray for your redemption every night."

It would have been rude to laugh. "Thank you for that. What I meant to say is that whatever you might think of me and what I do, you must know that I never seek to do harm with my conjurings. Surely you understand that I never use my spellmaking to kill."

"I know."

"But whoever murdered Jennifer Berson did just that. Wouldn't you like to see that person punished?"

He watched her, hoping in spite of all he knew of her that she would listen to reason this once. But she showed no sign of relenting and at last Ethan crossed to the archway leading back to the stairs.

"All right," she said, her voice echoing so loudly that it startled him. Then she said more softly, "Speak your spell. You've already desecrated our church. You might as well learn something of value."

Ethan didn't say a word or hesitate, lest he give her an excuse to change her mind. He put down his waistcoat once more and walked back to where she was standing. He eyed her briefly, expecting her to leave. When she didn't, he pulled out his knife, pushed up his sleeve, and cut himself for a second time. Ethan felt self-conscious with Bett there watching him, no doubt disapproving of everything he did. But he tried to ignore her as he dabbed blood on the girl again in the same pattern.

"*Revela originem potestatis,*" he said, "*ex cruore evocatam.*" Reveal source of power, conjured from blood.

Again, the air in the chamber came alive. The ghost appeared beside Ethan, and Bett let out a small gasp. Reg leered at her. Ethan saw Bett shudder and fold her arms over her chest, even as he felt the blood on his arm evaporate and watched it vanish from the dead girl's face, neck, and chest. The glow surrounding the corpse flickered briefly, like a flame in a sudden breeze, but otherwise the light didn't change at all.

They stood utterly still for several moments. At last Ethan frowned and cast a quick look at his sister. He half expected her to gloat at the apparent failure of his spell, but she merely continued to stare at the still form on the slab and rubbed her arms to keep warm.

"Well, that was damned peculiar," Ethan said eventually.

She shot him a disapproving look. But instead of chiding him for his oath she said, "You expected more to happen."

"Aye." Ethan thought about trying the spell a second time, but he didn't think Bett would stand for it. He also didn't expect that it would make any difference. The killer had gone to great lengths to mask the nature of his—or her—conjuring, something Ethan hadn't thought possible.

This conjurer possessed skills that Ethan couldn't fathom, much less match. Where had he—she?—come from, and what had brought such a cursed presence to Boston?

Bett had been watching him, and now she said, "There's blood on your shirt."

Ethan glanced down at the stain. "It's from last night. And it's not mine."

"You should put on some clean clothes. You look like a ruffian."

He laughed. "Do I?"

"I'm serious, Ethan," she said, sounding so earnest, the way he remembered from when they were children. She had always been far more concerned than he with social niceties.

"I'll change before I see Mister Berson. You have my word."

Bett nodded, then turned back to the body. "What will you do?" she asked. "About the girl, I mean. Now that the spell didn't do what you thought it would."

Ethan shrugged. "I'll find another way to track her killer. That's what I was hired to do."

Her laugh was dry and humorless, just the way he remembered. "You actually sounded like Father when you said that."

"He wouldn't be pleased."

Bett dismissed the comment with a wave of her hand and turned to leave. "That's not true and you know it. Good-bye, Ethan."

"Thank you, Bett."

She stopped at that and regarded him with obvious surprise. "For what?"

"For not interfering with the spell, even if it didn't work."

Her brow creased, as if she realized for the first time that she had done exactly that. "I did it for the girl," she said. She glanced toward the body. "Will that glow go away, or do you need to cast again?"

He could have claimed that he needed to do one more conjuring. That way he could try the second spell again. But he couldn't bring himself to lie to her in this place.

"It'll fade on its own. She should look normal by nightfall."

"Good," Bett said, and left him there.

He put away his knife and pulled his sleeve back down. Then he picked up his waistcoat and shrugged it on. He paused at the doorway to look at Jennifer once more. "Grant her rest, Lord," he whispered.

Ethan climbed the stairs back to the sanctuary. Troutbeck was nowhere to be seen, but Pell stood by the altar. Ethan raised a hand in farewell and continued to the door.

The young minister merely watched him leave.

Ethan thought about making his way directly to the Berson home, as Abner Berson's man had instructed. But Bett's remark about the blood on his shirt had reminded him that he ought first to change. He walked down School Street and then on to Water. With each step the stink of the harbor grew stronger.

Dall's cooperage, which had been built by Henry's grandfather, stood on the east side of a lane named, appropriately enough, Cooper's Alley. It was a modest building, but sturdy, with a small sign out front that read simply "Dall's Barrels and Crates" and a second sign, on the oak door, that read "Open Entr." Blue-gray smoke rose from a small, crooked chimney on the roof.

Shelly and Pitch lay together outside the door. At Ethan's approach they raised their heads, their tails thumping the cobblestones in unison.

Ethan stepped over them, pushed the door open, and entered the shop. It was warm within. A fire burned brightly in the stone hearth. Henry sat on a stool by his workbench, his leather apron covering a worn gray shirt, the sleeves of which he had pushed up. The cooper was a small man with a lined, grizzled face, a bald head, and thick, muscular arms. Whenever he worked he furrowed his brow in concentration and opened his mouth in a sort of grimace, revealing a large gap where his two front teeth should have been. That was how he looked now, as he struggled to set the final hoop in place on a large rum barrel. There were fewer distillers in Boston now than there had been as recently as five or ten years ago, but Henry still did a steady business supplying barrels to those that remained.

He was working the hoop into place with a large mallet that he had covered with cloth so that it wouldn't damage the wood or scrape the hoop. Seeing Ethan enter, he raised a hand in greeting, but continued to work. Ethan remained by the door, watching, saying nothing, until Henry gave the hoop one last whack, threw his mallet onto his workbench, and pushed himself off the stool.

"Damn hoop'th th' wrong thizthe," he said, with his usual lisp.

"Is it from Corlin?" Ethan asked.

Henry nodded, frowning with disgust.

"Well, he'll make you another. He's been smithing for you for ages."

"I know. But I wanted this one done by today. I have other things t' do."

"Well, this should brighten your day." Ethan pulled from his pocket the pouch given to him by Berson's man and handed two pounds to the cooper.

"That should pay for my room through the rest of the year."

Henry stared at the coins as if he had never seen so much money in one spot. "I should say it does. Where'd ya get all this?"

Ethan shook his head. "Not important," he said. It wasn't that Henry didn't approve of thieftaking; in fact, he enjoyed the stories Ethan told about his past jobs. But he grew alarmed whenever he knew too much about what Ethan was working on at any given time. Ethan wasn't sure how much of his concern was for his shop and the room above it, and how much was for Ethan himself, but he couldn't deny that the old man fretted after him, as if he were Ethan's father. Truth be told, the diminutive cooper worried about him far more than Ethan's father ever had.

"Well, thank you, Ethan. Ya're welcome in that room for as long as you want it."

Ethan patted the man's shoulder. "You're just saying that because you've been paid."

Henry grinned at him, wide-mouthed and gap-toothed. "Aye," he said. "In advants, no less."

The thieftaker laughed as he walked back to the door and pulled it open. "I'll see you later, Henry."

The old man was still grinning. But he sounded deadly serious when he said, "Be careful, Ethan. That much money—ya're bound to attract someone's eye."

Ethan glanced back at him. "Aye, thank you, Henry."

Once outside again, Ethan saw that both dogs were still awake. Pitch was on his feet, his tail raised, his ears pricked. Ethan looked around, but saw nothing. As he started away, he heard the dog growl.

Wary now, he walked around to the back end of Henry's building, and climbed the wooden stairs to his door. Just as he reached for the door handle, he heard footsteps on the stairs below him. Glancing down, he saw a large man making his way up the stairway. He was dark-haired, young, and when he looked up at Ethan, catching his eye, he leered menacingly. No wonder Pitch had been on edge.

Ethan quickly ducked into the room and locked the door behind him. He had just started to consider what kind of spell he might use on the man when he felt a powerful hand grab his shoulder and spin him around. Ethan found himself face-to-face—or rather, face-to-chest— with another large man, this one yellow-haired with a long, horsey face. Two other pairs of hands grabbed his arms, pulling them wide.

"Get his knife," a woman's voice commanded calmly from behind Yellow-hair.

The man in front of him yanked Ethan's blade from the sheath on his belt. The other two released his arms, but before Ethan could move, Yellow-hair dug a hammerlike fist into his gut, doubling him over and stealing his breath. One of the other men knocked him to the floor with a hard chopping clout high on his cheek.

Before he could clear his vision or remember how to inhale, a pair of hands hoisted him to his feet. Someone pounded him in the gut a second time, and then they set to work on his face. A blow to the jaw, another to the eye, a third to the cheekbone. Ethan felt his knees buckle, felt blood trickling from his mouth and from a burning cut just below his right eye. He was tempted to conjure, but wasn't sure he could incapacitate more than one man at a time. And before he could think of a spell, a fist to the stomach made him heave, though he managed somehow to keep from throwing up. They straightened him, and Ethan braced himself for another blow.

"Enough."

One word, but it stopped his attackers cold. It came from Ethan's bed, as had the demand for his blade. He didn't have to see Sephira Pryce to recognize her voice, but he would have preferred to look her in the eye.

The hands holding him up released him, and Ethan's legs gave way. He fully expected to fall to the floor, but someone had placed a chair behind him. He flopped into it.

He heard the door rattle behind him.

"Someone let him in," the voice said, sounding both bored and amused. "Gordon's going to be disappointed that he missed all the fun, Ethan. You shouldn't have locked the door."

Ethan forced his eyes open, and then concentrated on the face swimming before him.

As it came into focus, he was reminded once again of how dangerous it could be having any dealings with Sephira Pryce. Everything about the woman lent itself to seduction. Her voice was low for a woman's, and slightly gravelly, so that with every word she sounded like she was purring. Reclining on his bed, her shining black curls cascading over her shoulders, she looked like some lithe, preternaturally intelligent creature from the wilds of North America. Her oval face tapered to a sharp chin, but her other features were soft, womanly. Her cheekbones were high, but her cheeks retained enough roundness to give her a pleasant look—some might even have called it friendly. Her eyes were large and bright blue, the kind of eyes that should have belonged to a child. They could convey innocence, even kindness. God knew they could be alluring, at times brazenly so. But more often than not, they were hard, shrewd, and watchful, as they were now. They were always moving, scanning faces, appraising her surroundings, preparing for a fight even as she purred and charmed her way through another negotiation.

Her nose was lovely, finely upturned and as perfect as it was the day she was born. No one who spent his or her life working Boston's rougher lanes could avoid scars, and Sephira had plenty: small ones on her cheeks, her brow, her temples, and one long one along her otherwise smooth jaw.

But those whose work found them in the streets of Boston usually had broken their noses at least once. Not Sephira. Actually, this was something she and Ethan shared. At least for the moment. Who knew what this encounter would bring?

She always smelled subtly of lilac and she wore more jewelry than the king's consort: glittering gemmed earrings, rings of gold and silver on her hands, and bracelets to match. The only concession she made to her profession was in her dress. She wore breeches, a blouse, and a waistcoat, like anyone who worked in the lanes, although her blouse was cut lower than a man's, and her waistcoat was just a shade tighter. The effect could be distracting for even the most disciplined man. Already this day Ethan had been beaten and kicked, and he couldn't be certain that Sephira didn't intend to have him killed in the next moment or two. Yet he couldn't keep his glance from straying to the gentle swell of her bodice as she reclined before him on the bed.

Noting this, she smiled and sat up. "You've missed me," she said, as if they were old friends.

"No," Ethan told her. "I can't say I have."

She replied with a small pout, stood, and began to pace the room. There was a taut grace to her movements—again Ethan saw something animal in the way she stalked across his floor.

She stood as tall as Ethan, and while she looked at first glance to be as slender as she was fair, the appearance was deceiving. He had seen her fight; once, he had felt the bite of her blade. She was as strong and quick and cunning as any man Ethan had ever battled. But her sex remained her greatest weapon. Her hair, her body, her eyes—she was bewitching. Ethan couldn't help but watch her as she walked, and, he noticed, neither could the men who worked for her.

And yet, for all her sensual beauty, she seethed with pent-up violence. Sometimes it simmered below the surface. Sometimes it manifested itself in those who traveled with her, like the toughs who had beaten Ethan and still loomed over him, threatening to renew their assault at any moment. On occasion Sephira herself lashed out. Ethan had seen her beat a man senseless in a tavern brawl simply because the poor fool had failed to recognize her and had ordered an ale without waiting for Sephira to be served.

Despite her talents with a blade and a firearm, despite her reputation for ruthless cruelty and the lethal storm that always raged around her—or perhaps because of all these things—Sephira was renowned and respected throughout the city. Rather than hiding in shadows, with other thieves and ruffians, she walked the streets as if she were royalty. She spoke with the confidence of someone who knew beyond doubt that she was the mistress of her own fate and the fates of everyone she met. She was several years younger than Ethan, but she dispensed wisdom—or what she took for wisdom—like a sage. Ethan thought of Sephira as little more than a glorified brigand, lovely to be sure, but wicked in every way. But he took great care in concealing his true feelings. Because everyone else in Boston, including Sephira herself, considered her nearly the equal of no less a man than Thomas Hutchinson, or even the governor of Massachusetts, Francis Bernard.

It wasn't just that she was the most important thieftaker in Boston, in all of the American colonies. She was also responsible for much of the thieving and violence that made thieftaking necessary. At least half the gems and jewelry and other riches she returned for reward were first stolen by men in her employ. She took with one hand, gave back with the other, and was paid handsomely for doing so.

Those like Ethan, who lived their lives in the streets, saw the woman for what she really was: a charming, clever villain. But to the unsuspecting, particularly the wealthy, she was the person who kept Boston's streets safe. And by dint of having forged this reputation, she had built an empire for herself. For if she profited from her efforts to keep order in the city and see to it that stolen property was restored to its rightful owner . . . well, who could begrudge the woman a bit of coin?

She watched Ethan now as she circled him, a half smile on her exquisite face, an appraising look in her cold, pale eyes, as if she was weighing whether or not to have her men beat Ethan a bit more.

"You've been hired by Berson," she said at length.

Ethan would gain nothing by denying it. Little happened in Boston without Sephira knowing of it; chances were she had known Berson was going to hire Ethan before the merchant's man ever reached the Dowsing Rod. But Ethan saw no reason to confirm her suspicions. He stared back at her as the pain in his gut and his cheek gradually faded.

After several moments, Sephira flicked her gaze up to one of the men standing behind Ethan. One quick glance, that was all it took. Immediately the man behind him—Yellow-hair—grabbed Ethan by the hair, pulled his head back, and laid the edge of a blade against Ethan's throat, much as Ethan had done to Daniel the night before.

"I believe Miss Pryce asked ye a question," Yellow-hair said, giving Ethan's hair an extra yank.

"Actually, she didn't," Ethan said, his voice strained. "She made a statement."

The man looming over him frowned, then looked to Pryce, apparently unsure of what to make of this.

"Let him go," she said.

The man released Ethan's hair, but then smacked him across the top of the head. Ethan winced.

"This is why I choose to let you live, Ethan," Sephira said, her laugh deep and throaty. Even mocking him, she sounded enticing. "You amuse me. And I'll admit that you have some courage, as well, though the line between bravery and folly can be a fine one."

"I didn't realize that my life was subject to your whim," Ethan said.

In an instant, her expression changed to a sneer. "Then you're a greater fool than I thought. The life of every man, woman, and child in this city is subject to my whim."

Ethan wanted to challenge her on this. Surely Sephira didn't mean to imply that even officers of the Crown were within her reach. But he held his tongue. If she did wield such power, over even the king's men, Ethan wasn't certain he wanted to know about it.

"I'll ask it as a question this time," Sephira went on a moment later. "Have you been hired by Abner Berson in the matter of his daughter's murder?"

"Yes, I have," Ethan said. "Actually, that reminds me: Can you account for your whereabouts last night?"

Pryce rolled her eyes and nodded to one of the men behind Ethan.

A fist to the temple sent Ethan sprawling to the floor again and knocked over the chair. One of the men kicked him in the stomach; another kicked him in the small of the back. A wave of nausea crashed over him and once more he could barely manage to draw breath.

"Get him up," Sephira said.

One of the toughs righted his chair, and the others lifted him off the floor and dumped him back into it, none too gently. Ethan hung his head, gasping for air, his elbows resting on his knees. He could feel Pryce watching him.

"Don't make me do that again," she said.

"You know he hired me, Sephira," Ethan managed to say. "You've known it all along. What's all this about?"

"What do you think it's about?"

"I think you don't like it when wealthy men come to me. You don't mind me working for the likes of Ezra Corbett, because he's hardly worth your time, but when someone like Berson hires me you feel like I'm taking money out of your purse."

Sephira smiled, and the entire room seemed to get colder. "You see? You can be clever when you want to be."

"You don't want this job, Sephira. Believe me you don't."

"Because she was killed with witchery?"

Ethan stared back at her.

"Yes," she said, "I knew that, too."

"Do you know who killed her?"

She shook her head, reclining on the bed once more, like some woman from a prisoner's dream. "I'm not sure I'd tell you if I did, but as it happens, I've no idea."

Something occurred to him in that moment, but he kept it to himself. He would have time to satisfy his curiosity later in the day, provided he survived this charming interview.

"I've been happy to let you have the jobs involving witchcraft," she told him, "because until now it hasn't cost me much to do so. But that changed when Berson hired you."

"Do you know much about conjuring, Sephira?"

"I know enough to have taken your knife from you as soon as you entered the room. You need blood, or something of the sort, to attack me with anything more than an elemental spell. And I know enough not to be afraid of elemental conjurings. Those are illusion spells. They can't really hurt me." Her smile this time was fleeting, though no less icy. "How am I doing so far?"

"Fairly well," Ethan said. "But you can't conjure, can you?"

By now, no answer would have surprised him. Still, Ethan knew a moment of profound relief when Sephira shook her head and said, "No, I can't."

"Then you know as well as I do, that you can't hope to find the person who murdered Jennifer Berson without getting yourself killed. That's the reason her father came to me."

"Yes, it probably is."

"So then what are we doing here, Sephira?"

"We're making sure that you understand just that. Witchcraft is the only reason Berson hired you instead of me. And witchcraft is the only reason I'm allowing you to keep the job. The Ezra Corbetts of the world are yours. The Abner Bersons belong to me."

Ethan eyed the woman another moment, then shook his head and let out a small laugh.

She sat up abruptly, her expression deadly serious. "You think I'm joking?"

"I know you're not. I just find it hard to believe you've gone to all this trouble because you're worried I'm taking jobs that you think should be yours."

"Well, believe it, Ethan. I've tolerated you working in Boston because there are certain jobs I would rather not take on. The last thing I need is to fail a few important clients and ruin my reputation, all because some idiot conjurer has taken to thieving. In some small way I need you, so I let you work at the fringes of my trade. But make no mistake: You work in this city—you live and breathe in this city—because I allow it."

Sephira glanced past him again, which gave Ethan at least some warning that another blow was coming. Not that it helped much. One of Pryce's men grabbed his chair from behind and pulled it out from under him, so that Ethan fell face-first to the floor. Two others lifted him and pinned his arms to his sides, and Yellow-hair resumed the beating. This time Sephira let them have their fun for what felt like an eternity before finally calling them off. Yellow-hair drove one last punch into Ethan's side before the other two released him, leaving him to crumple to the floor.

Every inch of Ethan's body hurt, and he could feel blood flowing freely from his nose, his split lip, and more cuts on his face than he could count. He didn't try to move, not even when he felt one of the men rifling through his pockets.

"Here it is," the man said.

Ethan heard the ring of coins, and knew that they had found Berson's money pouch.

"Found these, too."

More coins. Those would have been the shillings Corbett had given to him.

"Take it all," Sephira said, standing over him. "You'll make more, won't you, Ethan?"

"Sure," Ethan said, the word coming out as a whisper. "What's a few pounds between friends?"

"Well said. You know, Ethan," she went on, though Ethan just wished the woman would shut up and go away. "You need me as much as I need you. More really, though you don't know it."

"Would you care to tell me why?"

"Not really."

"You know, I don't need my knife to cast," Ethan said. "There's blood on my face. I could speak a spell that would kill all four of you."

"Actually," Sephira said, "I was just thinking the same thing."

Ethan heard something clatter on the floor next to his head. Opening his eyes, he saw his blade lying beside him.

"But we both know that you're not going to do that," she went on. "It hasn't been that long since you were a prisoner in Barbados, or wherever it was. And I imagine those memories fade rather slowly."

"Many people know I'm a conjurer."

"I'm sure. But it's one thing for people to know that, or to hear rumors of a few small spells cast in the capture of a thief. It's quite another for you to use your witchery to kill a person, especially someone like me. They'd have you in shackles faster than you could say 'God save the king.' Or maybe they'd just hang you. Don't you agree?"

Ethan gave no answer.

Sephira laughed again. "Nothing to say? Very well, then. Goodbye, Ethan. I hope you find the girl's killer. It would be unfortunate if you mucked it up."

He heard them leave, listened as they descended the creaking stairway. But even after they were gone, he simply lay there, his eyes closed, waiting for the pain to subside.

Chapter
SIX

*E*than? Ethan, y'all right?"

The voice reached him from far away, as from a distant passing ship on still waters.

"Ethan?"

But as soon as he felt someone touch his shoulder, his hand shot up of its own volition and grabbed the speaker's wrist. He heard a small gasp and, opening his eyes, saw poor Henry kneeling beside him, staring wide-eyed at Ethan's hand. Ethan let go of him and let his arm fall back to his side.

"Sorry, Henry," he muttered.

"Godth, Ethan!" the cooper lisped. "What happened to ya?"

Ethan forced himself up off the floor into a sitting position. His head spun a bit, but less than he had feared it might. Still, his body ached as it hadn't since his days laboring on the plantation; he wondered if Yellow-hair and his friends had broken a few of his ribs.

"Sephira Pryce was here," Ethan said. "She and her men were waiting for me." He glanced at Henry. "You didn't hear them earlier?"

Henry looked hurt. "O' course I didn't. Ya think I'd let ya come up, knowin' they was here?

Ethan shook his head. "No, I don't. I'm sorry, Henry."

The cooper's face colored. "I did hear some commotion and . . . well, I was afraid to come up. But then I heard them leave. That was all I heard, though. I swear it."

"I believe you. And it's probably best that you waited. There's no telling what they might have done to you."

"She was really here, eh?" the old man said, gazing wistfully at the door, as if he might still catch a glimpse of Sephira and her men. "Th' Empress herself?"

Ethan had to laugh, though it hurt to do so. "Aye. It's my own fault. I saw one of them coming up behind me on the stairs. I should have realized that he wouldn't be alone."

"Wha' does Sephira want with you?"

"New job I'm working on," Ethan told him. "You really don't want to know." He probed his face gingerly with his fingers. Everything felt swollen. "I must look a mess."

"Ya do," Henry said. "I'll get some water and help ya get cleaned up." He stood, hitting Ethan's knife with his foot as he did. "They leave that?" he asked.

Ethan shook his head. "It's mine. It's pretty much the only thing they didn't take."

Henry glanced around the room. "They took stuff?"

"Just my money. Good thing I paid you before coming up here."

Henry grimaced sympathetically, but he didn't offer to give Ethan back any of the rent money. He left the room, still looking around, perhaps, Ethan thought, hoping that he might spot something that Sephira had left behind. Ethan thought it likely that nothing he had done before had impressed the old man as much as getting thrashed by Sephira Pryce's men.

While Henry was gone he gently probed his ribs with his hands, trying to decide if any were broken. It felt like at least one of them was, but Henry entered the room again before he could cut himself and cast a healing spell. For all their years of friendship the old man didn't know that Ethan was a conjurer. Or if he did, he acted as though he assumed Ethan didn't cast anymore, for he never mentioned spell-making or "witchcraft" in front of Ethan.

Henry had brought a bucket of cold water, several pieces of clean cloth, and a bottle of what Ethan guessed was rum. He helped Ethan climb into the chair and then began to clean the wounds on his face. The old cooper was surprisingly gentle and deft, though he worked slowly. It wasn't long before the cloths were stained red with blood. Henry continually wrung them out into the bucket, and soon the water had shaded toward pink.

"Lot o' blood," the cooper said after a lengthy silence.

"I was noticing that. I think I'm glad I don't have a looking glass."

"I have one," Henry told him. "I can get it if you like. Ya don't look so bad. Probably feels worse than it looks."

"Aye, probably. My thanks, Henry."

The cooper finished cleaning him up, and then opened the rum and poured a bit onto a clean cloth.

"Is that necessary?" Ethan asked.

Henry shrugged. "They say i' keeps away infection."

"I'm going to smell like a distillery. People will think I've been drinking."

"I'd drink if I looked like you do," Henry said, cackling.

Ethan frowned, but then gestured for the cooper to use the rum.

Henry leaned forward and began applying the soaked cloth to Ethan's various cuts.

Ethan spent the next several moments inhaling sharply through his teeth again and again. "Damn!" he said after the sixth or seventh time. "Do you have to use that much?"

The cooper glanced doubtfully at the bottle. "I didn't think I was using a lot."

Ethan closed his eyes briefly and shook his head. "I'm sure you weren't. Just . . . keep doing what you were doing. I'll keep my mouth—" He winced again as Henry touched the spirit-soaked cloth to another spot on his temple. "—closed."

Henry grimaced again. "Ya want me t' stop?"

Ethan stared at him briefly before picking up the bottle, pulling out the cork, and gulping down a mouthful. It burned, but it tasted good. "Don't stop."

The cooper nodded his approval, a toothless grin on his face, and went back to work.

When at last Henry had finished, Ethan had to admit that he felt somewhat better. He stood stiffly, and began to pull off his waistcoat and shirt.

"Ya should rest," the cooper said.

"I can't. I have to pay a visit to Beacon Street."

"Beacon Street!" Henry repeated. "Who d'ya know there?"

"I have a meeting with Abner Berson."

The cooper's mouth dropped open and he shook his head. "Pryce and Berson in one day. Ya're movin' up in the world, Ethan."

Ethan didn't say anything. It probably would have amazed Henry to see the house in which Ethan had grown up. His father had taken great pride in being able to afford a home within a block of the Bristol Cathedral. Ellis Kaille would have been ashamed to see his son living in this single room on Cooper's Alley.

"My thanks again, Henry. I'm in your debt."

The old man gathered his bucket, cloths, and rum, and paused at the door. "Not at all. Have a care though. I don' want t' have t' do this again. Never liked blood o' any kind."

Ethan watched him go. Once Henry had descended the wooden stairs, Ethan sat again and checked his ribs, determining that only the one was broken. Taking a long breath to prepare himself, he pushed the broken bone back in place, gasping in agony, and fighting not to be sick. When he had set the bone as best he could, he pulled out his knife, cut his forearm, smeared some blood on his side, and said, "*Remedium ex cruore evocatum.*" Healing, conjured from blood.

Uncle Reg appeared, took one look at Ethan's face, and began to laugh silently. If Ethan could have punched the ghost in the nose, he would have. Despite the specter's mockery, the effect of Ethan's spell was immediate. It felt as though cool water were flowing over the bone and surrounding flesh. He hadn't realized how much it hurt each time he took a breath until he could inhale without pain.

Ethan wished he could do more for his wounds, but Henry had seen the bruises on his face and would notice if he healed too quickly. He would have to be satisfied with mending the broken bone. Healing spells were taxing, and after the beating he had taken, he would have liked nothing better than to take Henry's advice and rest. But one didn't keep a man like Abner Berson waiting, and Sephira's visit had served only to make Ethan more determined to begin his inquiry. He changed into clean clothes and left his room. One of his eyes had swollen shut, making it difficult to see, and his split lip would make speaking a chore.

He had lost track of the time, but the sun was still up, angling sharply across the shops and lanes of Boston. The day had grown warm, and a steady wind blew in off the harbor, carrying the scent of rain.

He walked back up Water Street and School Street, passing King's Chapel once more, and also the Granary Burying Ground, before turning onto Beacon Street. The night before, while waiting for Ezra Corbett in the merchant's sitting room, Ethan had remarked to himself how much nicer Corbett's home was than his own. Now, walking past the mansions at the base of Beacon Hill, he wondered if Corbett felt the same way when he came to call on men like Berson.

Referring to these manors as houses failed to do them justice. They might have been situated within the bounds of the city, but they resembled the country estates of Braintree, Milton, and Roxbury as much as they did even the finer houses of the North End. Beacon Street itself was clean and pleasant, offering fine views of the hill. There were no beggars asking for coin or miscreants lurking in alleys. Each house had its own stone wall and iron gate, and the grounds surrounding the homes were neat and well tended.

Abner Berson's home was no more grand than those around it, and it was modest when compared with the Hancock estate farther down the road. But still it was impressive. Constructed of white marble, it was solid and square and stood three stories high. A wide flagstone drive led from the street to the door. Before it, broad marble steps led to an ornate portico supported by proud Corinthian columns. A carriage waited by the house, a large chestnut cart horse standing before it with its head lowered, a grizzled driver seated behind the beast. He eyed Ethan with unconcealed curiosity as the thieftaker approached.

"Wha' happ'n'd t' you, mate?" the man asked. "I once hit a felleh with my cart—looked a bit like you do now."

Ethan chuckled. "It wasn't a cart," he said, and climbed the steps to the front entrance.

The servant who answered his knock was a white-haired African man, smartly dressed in black linen. He regarded Ethan dubiously, even after the thieftaker told the man his name.

"Mister Berson is expecting me," Ethan said. "If you don't believe me, you can find the man with the silver hair and Scottish accent who hired me earlier today."

This convinced the servant, who waved Ethan into the house even as he continued to cast disapproving looks his way.

"Wait here," the man said, and walked off, leaving Ethan just inside the door, in a spacious tiled entrance hall with a high ceiling. Brilliantly colored tapestries covered the walls, and a large, round fixture that held no fewer than a dozen candles hung overhead. Ethan could hardly imagine how much work it took to light and extinguish the flames every night. Rather than smelling of spermaceti, though, the house was redolent of sweet scents: bayberry and beeswax.

He could see into the next chamber, which was also huge. The floors in there were made of some dark, fine-grained wood, and the furniture was of better quality than anything he had seen in the Corbett house.

No wonder Sephira didn't want Ethan competing for her clientele.

Curtains had been drawn across every window Ethan could see, and in the sitting room a cloth was draped over what he assumed was a looking glass. Even in the wealthiest households, mourning superstitions remained the same.

The click of footsteps on tile and a brisk "Mister Kaille" made Ethan turn.

Abner Berson was striding toward him, though he slowed upon seeing Ethan's face. "God have mercy! What happened to you?"

He forced a broad smile, which hurt, and walked to where Berson had halted, extending a hand. "A disagreement with a colleague. It's nothing, sir."

Berson took his hand and shook it absently, but he continued to study Ethan's face, frowning as if pained by what he saw. "You call this nothing?"

Silently cursing Sephira, he said, "Not really, no. But I can't do anything about it now, and you and I have more pressing and difficult matters to discuss."

"Aye," Berson agreed soberly. "That we do."

He started toward the large sitting room, gesturing for Ethan to follow. They stepped through that chamber into a small study, the walls of which were lined with shelves holding more bound volumes than Ethan had ever seen in one place.

"I collect them," Berson said needlessly, watching Ethan as he scanned the shelves. There were volumes here by Rabelais and Cervantes, Butler and Newton, Hobbes and Locke.

"Most come from England," the merchant went on. "A few are from France, and some of the newer ones were produced here in Boston, by Edes and Gill. Though I must say that I don't think much of the quality of their volumes. Do you read, Mister Kaille?"

"Yes, sir, I do. There was a time when I read a lot."

"You don't anymore?"

"I have less time for leisurely pursuits now than I did in my youth." *And less coin.*

Berson nodded, staring at the volumes. He was a portly man with a thick neck and a jowly face. His eyes were heavy-lidded; his nose was round and red. A few strands of coarse black hair stuck out from beneath a powdered wig of white curls. He wore a black silk suit and a white cravat.

"William told you why I require your services?" he asked after some time, still avoiding Ethan's gaze.

The silver-haired man. "Yes, he did, sir. You, Missus Berson, and your younger daughter have my deepest sympathies."

"She was . . ." Berson stopped, then swallowed, his eyes misting. "Thank you," he said roughly. "At a time like this, a stolen brooch may seem like a trifle, an extravagance. But . . ." He shook his head, his lips quivering.

"I think I understand," Ethan said. "I'll need a description of the brooch."

"Of course. Jennifer's girl can help you with that."

"I also have some questions for you, sir. If you can spare me the time. And if I may speak with Missus Berson—"

"I think not, Mister Kaille," Berson said. "I'll tell you what I can. But my wife is troubled enough just now. And with you looking the way you do . . . I don't think it would be good for her."

"I understand, sir."

Berson sat in one of two large cushioned chairs before an empty hearth. He indicated with an open hand that Ethan should take the other.

"Thank you, sir," Ethan said, lowering himself carefully into the chair. "Please forgive me if some of my questions strike you as . . . indelicate. I need information, and where murder is concerned one can't always mince words."

"Of course, Mister Kaille. Proceed."

"Can you think of anyone who would have wanted to do your daughter harm?"

Berson shook his head. "Not a soul."

"Did she have suitors, men she might have spurned?"

"She's had but one suitor for some time now. Cyrus Derne, the eldest son of Fergus Derne, of whom you might have heard."

Ethan had heard of the elder Derne. He was nearly as successful as Berson—another man Sephira would have wanted Ethan to avoid.

"How long had Mister Derne and your daughter been acquainted?"

"They've known each other since they were children," Berson said. "And he had been courting her for the better part of a year. I expect they would have been married sometime in the fall."

"There weren't any others, even men she might have known before Mister Derne and she became close?"

"None who had reason to hurt her," the merchant said.

Ethan wasn't entirely certain that he believed this. Berson's daughter had been young, beautiful, and wealthy; such women were bound to attract at least a few rogues along with more appropriate suitors. Then again, a spurned lover was apt to be more violent in wreaking his vengeance than Jennifer's killer had been.

"Then what about your enemies, sir?"

"Mine?" Berson said in a way that told Ethan the man hadn't even considered the possibility.

"A man in your position is bound to have rivals. Is that not so?"

"Well, of course, but—"

"Do any of them dislike you enough to strike at your family in this way?"

"I—I don't know."

Ethan eyed him closely. "Then there are some who might."

"Well . . . I suppose that . . . some . . . Derrin Cormack, for instance. He and I have disliked each other for years. And Gregory Kellirand—he and I had a falling-out some years back over a shipment of wine from Spain. I've never forgiven him, nor he me. I suppose you could list Louis Deblois and his brothers, or even Godfrey Malbone."

"I thought Colonel Malbone lived in Newport," Ethan said.

"He does," Berson said, growing more impatient by the moment. "My point is that these men are merchants, as am I. We are all of us rivals, and therefore can be said to wish each other ill in some sense. But we are also successful men, and we try to leave our business and our disputes in the warehouses and the markets, where they belong. Why would any of them kill Jennifer for her brooch?"

"I don't know that one of them did," Ethan said. "I'm a thief-taker, and I've little experience with murders. I have to start somewhere. Thieves can be quite specific in choosing their victims, but they can also be random. If your daughter had wandered into the lower lanes of the South End and been robbed, I probably wouldn't be asking such questions. But she was murdered, and though my experience with killings is meager, I believe that such acts are less arbitrary. Someone might have killed her to steal the brooch. Or might have stolen it as an afterthought. Or perhaps she was killed for some other reason and the villain took the brooch to confuse matters, to conceal the true purpose behind her murder."

Berson's face had paled and his hand trembled as he rubbed it across his mouth. But he shook his head vehemently. "I believe you're thinking about this the wrong way, Mister Kaille."

Ethan didn't so much as raise an eyebrow, though he wanted to. Did Berson now fancy himself a thieftaker? "Is that so, sir?"

"Yes. No doubt you've heard of the unpleasantness last night."

"The destruction of the lieutenant governor's home."

"And the homes of Hallowell and Story," Berson said pointedly.

It took Ethan a moment. "You believe this crowd also killed your daughter?" he asked.

"I believe this *rabble* was capable of the cruelest sort of mischief. They were obviously determined to do as much injury as possible to

Boston's finer families. Is it so hard to credit that they would also harm my poor girl?" His voice broke on these last words.

Ethan began to respond, his voice gentle. "I suppose—"

"She was found last night on Cross Street," Berson went on, growing more animated by the moment. "She was only a few steps from the path these ruffians followed from the Hallowell home to Thomas Hutchinson's house. She left here only a short time before the fire was lit at the Town House, and by the time the mob had finished with Hutchinson's home, she was dead."

It occurred to Ethan that if he was right about that pulse of power and its connection to Jennifer's murder, he could have pinpointed the time of her death even more precisely. For now, though, he kept this to himself.

"Forgive me for asking, sir, but why was she abroad in the city so late in the evening?"

The merchant rubbed a hand over his face once more. "I don't know. I've been asking myself the same thing."

"And who found her?"

"A young man walking home from the wharves," Berson said. "A customs clerk, I believe. I never learned his name or those of the men of the watch for that matter."

There was a knock at the door and at Berson's reply the African servant who had greeted Ethan at the entrance stepped into the room.

"What is it, Nathaniel?"

"Forgive me, sir," he said, addressing Berson. "But Missus Berson is asking after you."

"Of course," Berson said, standing. "Tell her I'll be along shortly."

The man withdrew, leaving Ethan and Berson alone once more. Ethan stood, but remained by his chair, though he could tell Berson wanted him to go.

"I have just a few more questions, sir, and then I'll be on my way."

"Yes, all right."

"I went to King's Chapel today, as your man instructed. Have you been to see your daughter's body as well?"

"Of course I have!" Berson said, his brow knitting in anger. "What kind of question is that?"

"Did anything strike you as odd about what you saw?"

The merchant started to answer, faltered. At last he said, "I'm not sure what you're getting at, Mister Kaille. Perhaps you should just come out and say it."

"All right," Ethan said. "Why did you hire me, sir?"

The man stared back at him, his expression unreadable. Finally, he looked away and said, "You're a thieftaker, aren't you? I'm paying you handsomely. I thought you would be eager—"

"Why not Sephira Pryce? She's far better known than I am. To be honest, I'm surprised you had even heard of me."

A humorless smile flitted across Berson's face. "Come now, Mister Kaille," he said in a low voice. "There was a time when everyone in Boston knew your name. You and the *Ruby Blade* were quite the sensation some years back."

"It's not the same," Ethan said. "Sephira Pryce is the most renowned thieftaker in all of Boston. So again I ask: Why did you hire me?"

Berson eyed him a moment longer, and then sagged. "You saw her," he said. "There wasn't a mark on her, nothing to tell us what had killed her, much less who. At first we didn't even suspect foul play. But then we realized that the brooch was gone. And that mob was still in the streets."

"Did you think perhaps that she had died of natural causes, and that the brooch was stolen after?"

A spark of hope lit Berson's eyes. "Is that what you think happened?"

The man deserved the truth, but Ethan needed answers first. "I'm trying to understand how you came to hire me, sir."

"Isn't it clear? Jennifer was dead, and for no reason we could see or understand. She was a healthy girl, and there was no indication that anything had been done to her. It had to be . . . devilry." He stumbled over the word and his face went white at his own mention of it. He even took a step back from Ethan, seeming to realize that he ought to be frightened of him. But then he went on.

"That's the only explanation for what happened to her. I thought about going to Pryce. Of course I did. But she would be the first to admit that she doesn't know much about your kind. And so we . . . we asked around. I've always known there were spellers in Boston. A person just needed to know where to look. And when I heard that there was a thieftaker who was also a speller . . ." He shrugged. "Well, how could I not seek you out?"

"Who told you I was a conjurer?"

"I don't know. I have men who work for me. I've had them combing the streets for information since last night. I suppose one of them heard of your . . . talent." Berson said all this without meeting Ethan's gaze, leaving the thieftaker to wonder if he was being completely truthful.

Still, the events of the last day had made it clear to Ethan that too many people knew his secret. The last thing he wanted or needed was for every man and woman in the city to be talking about his past and the fact that he was a conjurer.

"I won't tell anyone else, if that's what you're worried about," Berson said. "You have my word."

"Too many people know already." He exhaled heavily and raised his gaze only to find the merchant already eyeing him. "It was a conjuring that killed her. I know that beyond a doubt. I used a spell at the chapel and . . . well, you don't need to know the details. But there is no doubt in my mind. I don't know who cast the spell that killed her, but he or she is powerful. There can't be more than a handful of people in all the colonies who could have murdered her that way."

"So, do you . . . do you think you can find the person who did this?" the man asked, sounding both hopeful and frightened.

"Yes, sir. I believe I can."

Berson nodded, his gaze drifting toward the door.

"I'll leave you to your family, sir," Ethan said. He started to leave. Then he halted and faced the merchant again. "Is there really a brooch, Mister Berson, or was that just something you and your man made up to get me to take the job?"

Berson shook his head again, his eyes wide. "No, the brooch is real, and it's missing."

"All right," Ethan said. "Then if you'll direct me to your daughter's servant, I'll begin my inquiry straightaway."

Berson led Ethan out of the study back into the large chamber with glazed windows. The merchant called for William, the white-haired man who had come to the Dowsing Rod that morning, and sent him in search of Jennifer's servant. He then bade Ethan farewell.

William returned a few moments later accompanied by a plain-looking young woman with reddish hair and freckles. Her eyes were red-rimmed and her face was blotchy, and even after William introduced Ethan to her she continued to stare at the floor. She looked frightened; Ethan thought it likely that his bruised face did nothing to set her mind at ease.

Ethan smiled at her, but she barely met his gaze. "This won't take long," he said gently. "I just need you to tell me about the brooch stolen from Miss Berson."

A tear slipped from the girl's eye and ran down her cheek. "It was oval," she said in a low voice. "With a gold setting. There was a large round ruby in the center, and it was surrounded by small diamonds. And then around them were more rubies. Small ones." The ghost of a smile touched her lips and was gone. "It was my mistress's favorite. Mine, too."

"Is there anything else you can tell me about it?" Ethan asked.

The girl shook her head.

"It belonged t' Jennifer's grandmother," William said. "Missus Berson's mother. Her initials are etched in th' back: CN. Caroline Neale."

"I didn't know that," the girl whispered.

"I've worked in this house a good many years," William said, eyeing Ethan. "Little escapes my notice."

Ethan heard a warning in the words. He held the man's gaze until at last the servant looked away. After thanking the girl, he allowed William to lead him to the entrance.

"Th' brooch is worth more than they're paying ya," the Scotsman said, as Ethan stepped past him out into the cool twilight air.

"That's usually the case," Ethan told him. "It's never stopped me from returning an item."

"An' why is that?"

"People won't hire me if they don't trust me."

"One brooch like this one an' you'd never need t' work again."

"Are you trying to tempt me, William, or warn me?" Ethan didn't give the man a chance to respond. "I have no interest in stealing from the Bersons, or anyone else for that matter. Believe it or not, I like my work."

"Ya can say tha' looking as ya do right now?"

Ethan laughed. "Remarkable, isn't it?"

The man surprised him with a smile. "Rather, yes."

"Good-bye, William." Ethan started down the stairway.

"Wait."

Ethan turned again. The servant stared at him another moment, tight-lipped, his brow creased. He glanced behind him into the house, before descending the steps to where Ethan had stopped.

"Ya know tha' Miss Berson was . . . was being courted?" he asked in a hushed voice.

"By Cyrus Derne," Ethan said. "Mister Berson mentioned it."

"Not all of us were as pleased with th' match as Jennifer," the man said.

William sounded more like a concerned uncle than a servant. Abner Berson probably would have thought it impertinent had he heard. But this man, whatever his station, cared about the family he served.

"Do you suspect Mister Derne of doing her harm?" Ethan asked.

William shook his head. "Nothin' so . . . heinous," he said. "But he strikes me as a careless man, someone who coulda led her int' peril." He glanced back toward the door. "If my master knew that I was telling ya this—"

Ethan raised a hand, stopping him. "He'll hear nothing of this conversation from me. Derne would have been the first person I sought out regardless. Now I'll meet the man armed with your perceptions of him. Thank you for that."

William ascended the steps. "Watch yourself, Mister Kaille," he said over his shoulder. "Judging from th' way ya look, I'd say ya have some trouble with that."

Ethan was in no condition to argue.

*L*ike the Bersons, the Derne family was well enough known that Ethan didn't have to ask William or Mr. Berson how to find their house. The Derne mansion stood at the corner of Middle Street and Bennet's in the North End, among some of the most opulent homes in that part of the city.

To get from Beacon Street to the North End, Ethan had to walk past or near all three of the houses that had been attacked the previous night, as well as the spot where Jennifer Berson's body was found. He decided to go just a short distance out of his way, so as to follow the path taken by the Stamp Act mob. He began by walking back to Cornhill Street and then making his way to the Town House, where the offices of the provincial government were housed. It was a grand brick building with a soaring steeple and striking statues: a lion on one side of the gable, and a unicorn on the other. These figures framed the building's clock and the carved façade in which it was fixed. In front of the building, a pile of ash and the charred ends of wooden beams marked the spot where the bonfire had been lit.

Following Queen Street west from the site of the fire, Ethan soon came to William Story's home, which had been ill treated the night before. Windows had been broken, shattered furniture lay in the yard and the street, and the gardens and walkways around the house were littered with torn and partially burned papers. A small crowd had gathered in the street in front of the house to gawk, and several more people wandered through Story's yard, picking through ruined furniture and personal effects as if they lived there.

William Story meant nothing to Ethan, but still Ethan was tempted to demand that these people leave the man's home alone. He had no authority, of course, and he doubted that anyone would listen to him. But not for the first time, he wondered if Boston wouldn't be better off with a stronger sheriff and a constabulary. True, such an office would render thieftakers like himself and Sephira Pryce unnecessary, but he would find other work. And he liked the idea of Sephira begging someone for a job. Not that this was likely to happen any time soon. He cast a last look at the gawkers and continued up Brattle Street to Hanover, where Benjamin Hallowell lived.

The damage done to the Hallowell home was even more extensive than that inflicted on Story's house. The wooden fence surrounding Hallowell's property had been knocked down, many of the windows had been shattered, and Hallowell's furniture had been wrecked and pieces of it strewn about. Papers, pieces of clothing, and empty bottles of wine had been scattered about the yard and into the street fronting it. The crowd gathered outside this house was far larger than that at the Story home. Benjamin Hallowell was better known and even less well liked than William Story. It stood to reason that the destruction of his property should draw more interest.

Ethan didn't linger at the Hallowell home. After crossing over Mill Creek into the North End, he came to Cross Street, where Jennifer Berson's body had been found, and followed it toward the harbor. Compared with Hanover and Middle Streets, Cross Street was quiet and peaceful. There were no crowds of curious onlookers, no men of the watch, no sign that a young girl had been killed here the night before. A few people strolled the lane; a chaise rattled past. But that was all.

Still, Ethan knew he needed to be careful. He wished to cast a spell that might reveal the nature of the conjuring that had killed the Berson girl, but he knew better than to draw blood on the open street. Instead, he casually picked a few leaves off tree branches overhanging the lane.

"*Revela potestatem*," he muttered under his breath. "*Ex foliis evocatam.*" Reveal power, conjured from leaves.

Reg materialized beside him, pale and insubstantial in the failing light. Ethan felt the spell thrum like a bowstring, but he saw nothing to indicate that his conjuring had worked. Reg stared at him, shaking his head slowly, his expression grim.

"This conjurer hid his handiwork well, didn't he?" Ethan whispered to the ghost.

Reg nodded.

"Is there another spell I should try?"

A woman eyed him as if he was mad and hurried off.

The old ghost shook his head again, even as he faded from view.

Discouraged, Ethan walked back to the main thoroughfare and made his way to the Hutchinson house on Garden Court Street, off North Square.

As he drew close to the square, Ethan slowed. The damage that had been done to the Story and Hallowell homes paled next to what had been done to Thomas Hutchinson's house. Ethan had little regard for the rioters, but he had never imagined that they could be capable of such wanton destruction.

Until the night before, this had been one of the more stately homes in the North End. It was similar in many respects to the Berson house; three stories high and perhaps fifty feet across, with a simple, classical design: a solid home befitting one of the most important men in the thirteen colonies.

But in a single night, it had been laid waste. Every window across the front of the house, twenty in all, had been completely shattered. The door had been destroyed, as if by axes, and parts of the roof had been torn away, as had the cupola. The garden fence had been torn down, and all the trees in the yard pulled over or hacked down. Personal effects belonging to the lieutenant governor and his family littered the yard and the narrow street. The crowd of gawkers here dwarfed the gathering Ethan had seen at the Hallowell home, although they remained in the street, seemingly afraid to venture into the lieutenant governor's yard. Ethan could see people moving about inside the house, but he didn't recognize Hutchinson himself.

"Got wot he deserved, if ya ask me."

Ethan turned and saw a young man standing near him. The lad wore shabby, ill-fitting clothes and a stained cap.

"Hutchinson, I mean," the young man added, unnecessarily.

"Aye," Ethan said, fighting to keep the rage from his voice. "I'm sure his wife and children did, too."

"Come again?"

"His wife and children." Ethan pointed to several dresses and petticoats lying in the yard, soiled and torn. "They deserved to have their home destroyed, and all their belongings pillaged by a crowd of strangers. They're lucky they didn't get worse, right?"

The lad frowned. "Well, I don' know 'bout that."

"Isn't it their fault that Parliament's burdened us with this Stamp Act?"

The young man pulled off his cap and scratched his head. "Well . . ."

"Think about it," Ethan said, and started away.

"Right!" the lad called after him. "Right, I'll do that."

The Derne mansion was only a block or so from North Square. It wasn't as impressive as either the Berson or Hutchinson houses, but it was of a similar design: a square, three-story building with large windows spaced evenly across the façade, and impressive columns flanking the main entrance.

The man who answered the door in response to Ethan's knock was several years younger than William, and quite a bit larger. Burly, tall, stone-faced, he more closely resembled one of Sephira Pryce's toughs than a house servant. Ethan attempted to explain that he had been hired by Abner Berson and needed to speak with Cyrus Derne, but the man simply glowered at him. When Ethan finished, the man informed him that Cyrus Derne was not at home, and promptly shut the door.

Ethan considered knocking again, but decided against it. It was growing dark. The night watch would begin rounds before long. And men like Cyrus and Fergus Derne would be making their way home from the waterfront. Ethan strolled back to the street, but he remained near the Derne house, nodding to strangers as they walked past, laughing under his breath at their reactions to his battered visage.

He had never met Cyrus Derne or his father, but he knew them as soon as they turned a far corner onto Bennet's Street. They were both well-dressed in ditto suits as was the current fashion. The younger Derne's was beige; Derne the Elder wore dark blue. Both men sported dark cloaks and black tricorn hats with elaborate black cockades, and both carried canes tipped with brass. The men were of medium height, the father thicker in the middle and heavier of face. The son was lean, the long gray hair of his wig framing a square chin and high cheek-bones. Ethan could see how a young woman might be drawn to him.

Father and son spoke in low tones as they walked, oblivious of all around them. When they were only a few paces from where Ethan stood, he cleared his throat loudly to draw their attention.

The older Derne halted immediately, a frown clouding his face. The son slowed, but put himself between Ethan and his father, firmly gripping his cane.

"Is there something I can do for you?" the younger Derne asked in a strong, cold voice.

"I hope so," Ethan said, smiling so that his lip and cheek hurt. "I'm looking for Cyrus Derne."

The younger man hesitated for only a moment, although the knuck-les on the hand holding his cane whitened even more.

"You've found him."

"Forgive me if I've alarmed you, Mister Derne. My name is Ethan Kaille. Abner Berson has hired me—"

"Of course, Mister Kaille," the younger Derne said, striding for-ward and offering a hand. "Mister Berson told me he intended to hire you. Terrible business. I'm still . . ." He shook his head. "Well, I'm at a loss for words. Jennifer was quite dear to me, as Mister Berson might have told you."

"He did. I'm terribly sorry for you loss."

"Thank you."

The elder Derne joined them and offered a hand as well, even as he examined Ethan's face.

"You look like you've had quite a day, Mister Kaille," the older man said.

"Yes, sir, I have." He was growing weary of hearing comments on his cuts and bruises, and he had yet to see Diver or Kannice. "If I may,

Mister Derne," he said to the son, "I would like to ask you a few questions. I won't keep you long."

Cyrus and his father exchanged glances.

"Of course," the young man said. "Would you mind if we walked? I've spent most of my day in our offices; I wouldn't mind a bit of air."

"That's fine, sir. Thank you. A pleasure meeting you, sir," Ethan said to the elder Derne, "despite the circumstances."

The elder Derne smiled coldly, glanced once more at his son, and then walked toward the house.

"Shall we?" Cyrus said, gesturing with an open hand for Ethan to lead the way. "I take it you've already spoken with Mister Berson."

"I've just been at his home."

"And you came straight to me." The younger Derne's smile was much as his father's had been a few moments before. "Should I make anything of that?"

"I assure you it was simply a matter of convenience. I don't spend much time in the North End. And with the Berson home so close to yours—"

"It's all right, Mister Kaille. I was attempting a joke. Apparently I failed." They came to a corner and continued down Fleet Street toward the wharves. "You have questions for me," Cyrus prompted.

"Yes, sir. When did you last see Miss Berson?"

"Yesterday," the man said. "I had some business elsewhere in the city that required my attention, but I wished to see her. I try—" He winced. "I tried to see her each day, even when we hadn't made plans as such. I stopped by late—several hours past midday. We spoke briefly in the sitting room. She wanted to go for a walk, but by then it was growing late, so we sat and . . ." He paused, looking thoughtful. "And then I left."

"Did she mention that she intended to leave the house?"

Cyrus shook his head. "No."

"So you don't know why she would venture out after dark."

He stared at the street before them, shaking his head again. "For the life of me, I do not."

"Do you often have business that takes you into the streets at night, sir?"

Cyrus smirked. "You're bold, Mister Kaille." He looked away, so that he was staring straight ahead. They turned another corner and walked past a line of warehouses. The smell of the harbor was heavy here. Flocks of gulls perched on rooftops, preening and crying out mournfully, and a lone osprey circled overhead. "Occasionally, yes. I'm a merchant, from a family of merchants. The Dernes have business in every part of Boston, as well as in Newport, Providence, Norfolk, Newbury, Hartford, even Halifax. And our business doesn't always end with the setting of the sun."

"Can you tell me where you were last night?"

"I'm not inclined to, no," Derne said in a flat voice, his expression unchanged. Still, Ethan could tell that the merchant's patience had started to run thin.

Ethan said nothing, allowing the silence to stretch on until Derne seemed to grow uncomfortable.

"If you must know," Derne said at last, "I was home. My father will confirm that if you ask him."

"Thank you, sir. I don't think I need trouble him."

"Have you asked similar questions of the brutes who were abroad last night, behaving like savages and showing themselves capable of the worst kind of violence and mischief?"

"Not yet," Ethan said. "But I will."

"Good," Derne said brusquely. "It seems to me more than coincidence that poor Jennifer should be killed the same night that rabble was rampaging through the streets."

"Yes, sir. Do you know if Miss Berson had any other suitors— anyone who might have been angered by how close the two of you had grown?"

Derne halted and faced him, forcing Ethan to stop, too. "Are you trying to offend me?" the merchant demanded, his voice low. "Do you find all of this amusing?"

"Neither, sir," Ethan said evenly. "But Mister Berson is paying me a great deal, and I believe that obligates me to explore every possibility. I've no doubt that Miss Berson was devoted to you. But would it be so surprising that a woman of beauty and intelligence and, yes, means, might attract men possessed of less honor than you?"

Derne regarded him a moment longer, and then began walking again. Ethan fell in step beside him. They walked in silence for some time, turning another corner, so that the waters of the harbor were now behind them.

At last Derne exhaled softly and shook his head. "Is it your profession that makes your mind work as it does?"

"Sir?"

"Looking for betrayal and falsehood. Thinking the worst of people. I would think that spending your life among the criminal element would color your perceptions of everyone, even someone like Jennifer."

"I think no ill of her, sir."

"Perhaps," Derne said coldly. "But your questions can hardly be deemed flattering." He looked at Ethan briefly. "You're right, of course. It is conceivable that she had other suitors of whom I knew nothing, and that one of them did her harm. It's not a possibility I've considered. I would like to tell you out of hand that there was no one, but I don't know for certain. Satisfied?"

"I take no satisfaction in offending you, sir. You have my word on that."

Derne appeared unconvinced. "Did you ask her father about any of this?"

"I did. He said he knew of no one. But I thought perhaps he sought to protect her, or that maybe she had hidden such things from him." Ethan shrugged. "There probably was no one. I apologize for upsetting you." This last he added for Derne's benefit. In fact, angering the man had served its purpose. He now knew Cyrus Derne's composure could be shaken. That knowledge might eventually prove valuable.

They again lapsed into silence. A cart rumbled past, hoofbeats echoing off the nearby buildings. Two cats slunk across the lane ahead of them. A few faint stars shone overhead.

"Have you more questions for me?" Derne asked at length, a chill still in his voice. "I've had a long, difficult day."

"I'm sure you have, sir." Ethan hesitated, considering how best to word his next question. Finally, he said, "How much do you know about the circumstances of Miss Berson's death?"

"Very little," Derne answered. "I know that she was murdered, that she was found near where these . . . these agitators had been, that her grandmother's brooch was taken. Is there more that matters?"

"Have you . . . have you gone to view her at King's Chapel?"

The merchant shook his head. "Not yet. I haven't had the chance. And to be honest I've been dreading it. Why? Is there something I ought to know before I do?"

"No, sir," Ethan said. "It's nothing like that." Again he faltered. "Do you have any idea why Mister Berson came to me with this matter?" he asked at last.

Derne frowned. "What an odd thing to ask. Why should I care why you were hired? Why should you, for that matter? I should think you would be grateful for the work."

Apparently there was at least one man left in Boston who didn't know that Ethan was a conjurer. Which probably meant that Derne truly didn't know how Jennifer had died. Berson might have been too ashamed or too frightened to tell him. "It probably shouldn't," he said, eager now to explain away his question. "I'm . . . I'm a bit out of my element. I'm a thieftaker. I usually don't involve myself in murders."

They turned one more corner and Ethan realized that Derne had steered them back within sight of his home. No doubt this was the man's way of telling Ethan that their conversation was at an end.

"I won't trouble you more, sir," Ethan said as they approached the Derne house. "Except to ask you the same thing I asked Mister Berson. Can you think of anyone who would have wanted to hurt Miss Berson, or anyone who wanted to hurt you so badly that he would take vengeance on her?"

Derne sighed, sounding genuinely weary. "Jennifer had no enemies," he said. "I can't imagine anyone wanting to hurt her. But her father, and my father and I are another matter entirely. We're merchants. We make enemies every day, and yes, some of them might go to great lengths to get back at us." He raised a hand to forestall interruption. "I'm not thinking of someone in particular. I'm just saying that the pursuit of wealth makes men do foolish things, dangerous things."

He said this last with such earnestness that Ethan was forced to wonder if he did in fact have someone specific in mind. But he had already pushed the man hard enough, and he had no desire to provoke him further, at least not yet.

"I appreciate your candor, sir," he said, as they stopped in front of the Derne house. "If you think of anything that might help me find Miss Berson's killer, I hope you'll let me know."

"Of course," Derne said, his tone businesslike. "How might I get in touch with you?"

"I live in the South End, above Dall's cooperage. And a message can be left for me at the Dowsing Rod on Sudbury Street."

"Very well." Derne put out his hand and Ethan gripped it.

"Good night, Mister Derne."

"Mister Kaille."

Ethan started away, aware that Derne was staring after him. He kept his gaze fixed on the street ahead of him, however, and after a short while the feeling of being watched faded.

He was hungry, and he considered making his way to the Dowser for some of Kannice's stew. But Kannice hadn't been happy with him when he left the tavern that morning—was this really still the same day?—and he had given her good reason. If he had kept his word to himself, and had refused to take any more jobs for a time, he wouldn't have been beaten by Sephira's men, and he would still have the money Corbett had paid him the night before.

He knew, though, that he could not have refused Abner Berson's offer. "Do you have to work every job that calls for a conjurer?" Kannice had asked him. And the truth was that he did. There was no one else. He had tried to explain as much to Kannice that morning, but they had been at odds over the riots and both of them had been angry. Ethan owed it to her to explain again.

Tonight, though, he couldn't bring himself to face that conversation or her inevitable questions about his injuries. In the end, Ethan chose to walk home. He had some cheese and bread there, and even a small flask of Madeira that Diver had gotten for him—Ethan knew better than to ask where. He didn't have a lot of any of it, but there was enough to make a meal. And then he could sleep.

As he walked through the lanes he tried to concentrate on what he had learned thus far about Jennifer Berson and the final hours of her life. A good deal of it struck him as odd. He sensed, though, that he had heard much of importance in his encounters with Berson and Derne, and even Sephira Pryce, if only he could sift through it all. But the day's events had finally caught up with him. He was tired and sore, and he felt like his brain was moving slower than usual.

Still, his senses remained sharp. As he stepped onto Cooper's Alley he felt the back of his neck prickle. He was being watched again. It wasn't his conjuring ability that told him this. At least not exactly. There were protection spells a conjurer could use to ward himself, even to make himself blend into his surroundings, though these worked better in crowds than in empty lanes. A speller with enough skill might even cast spells that could alert him to the presence of certain enemies.

But Ethan hadn't used any such conjurings. He merely sensed the presence of *something*, or more precisely, *someone*. He couldn't always perceive conjuring ability in others, but when he did, the feeling was unmistakable, as though an ethereal tether bound him to that person, charging the air between them as during an electrical storm. He felt that way now. And a moment later, he also sensed a conjuring. The feeling was vague; either the spell was weak or the conjurer was casting at a great distance. He couldn't say for certain. But he had no doubt that someone was working a spell. The air around him vibrated, like a plucked string on a harp.

He slowed and turned a full circle, looking for a conjurer, thinking it strange that he should feel the person so acutely, but not the spell. He saw no one on the street. Candlelight from the windows of homes along the lane spilled weak pools of light onto the cobblestones, and the moon shone overhead, only a night or two shy of full and gleaming white.

Ethan eased his knife from his belt. "Who's there?"

He expected to see a conjurer emerge from the shadows. He couldn't have been more surprised to see a girl of no more than eight or nine years step into the street, her clothes in rags, her dark, lank hair hanging to her shoulders. Without realizing it, he had lowered himself into a fighter's crouch, his weapon held ready. He straightened now, allowing his blade hand to drop to his side, though he didn't put the knife away.

He slowly walked toward the girl, glancing from side to side, expecting at any moment to see Sephira Pryce and her men charging at him. The girl watched him with large pale eyes, but she didn't back away or show any sign of fear. She looked half starved, her cheeks sunken, her skin sallow, bare wrists as thin as sticks.

"Who are you?" Ethan asked, stopping a few paces short of the girl.

"Anna," she said in a small voice. "Are you Kaille?"

Ethan nodded. Where was the conjurer he had sensed moments before? "Are you here alone?"

"You're working for the Bersons," the girl said. "Is that right?"

Ethan scanned the street again, taking care to check the nearest windows. "Someone sent you, is that it?"

"Are you working for the Bersons?"

He stared at the girl briefly. Perhaps by answering her questions he might learn something of whoever had sent her. "Yes, the Bersons hired me."

"You seek a piece of jewelry," Anna said. "A brooch. Rubies and diamonds."

"That's right. You know a great deal about me."

"I know enough," she said calmly, looking up at him.

"And yet I know nothing about you except your name." Ethan smiled. "That's not fair, is it?"

"My name's Anna. I live here. What more do you want to know?"

"Here?" Ethan repeated. "You mean in the South End?"

"Here, in the streets."

That wiped the smile from his face. "You have no home?"

She gazed back at him, saying nothing.

"Who takes care of you?"

"I don't need anyone taking care of me."

"But where do you sleep? Where do you get your food?"

"I get what I need," she said, still with that maddening air of calm. "I get along fine without anyone helping me."

"But you must have some family."

"I want to talk about the brooch," she said.

Ethan shook his head. "No. What's your last name?"

Anna started to walk away. "Fine," she said, tossing the word over her shoulder. "Then you'll never find it."

She didn't walk quickly, and in turning her back on him she showed no fear. But neither did she give any indication that she was doing this for effect. If he let her go, she would leave.

"Wait!" Ethan called in surrender, as she reached the next illuminated window. "Come back. Please."

She had halted beneath the window at his first word. Now she started back toward him. There was something odd about her, though Ethan couldn't quite figure out what it was.

"No more questions about my family," she said, as she drew nigh again. "Or I'll leave."

"All right," Ethan agreed reluctantly. "Can you at least tell me who sent you?" He glanced around again, his unease growing by the moment. He still sensed someone conjuring, closer now. But where?

She frowned, then shook her head. "I don't think so."

Ethan took a step toward her, and then another. She didn't flinch, but he didn't want to risk scaring her off. He squatted down so that he was looking her in the eye. "Listen to me, Anna. Whoever sent you could be dangerous. That brooch—it was taken from a girl—"

"Jennifer Berson."

"That's right," Ethan said. "She's . . ." He hesitated. He didn't want to frighten the girl, but she needed to understand her peril. "She's dead now."

"I know," the girl said solemnly.

"Whoever sent you—whoever has that brooch—might well have been the person who killed her."

"You're a thieftaker," she said. "Isn't that right?"

He nodded, frowning. "Yes, but—"

"Then all that matters to you is the brooch. If you find that and give it back to her family, you'll be paid."

"How is it you know so much about thieftaking?"

"Am I right?" she asked.

Ethan stared at her. He wasn't just talking to the girl, he knew. This was a negotiation with the person who had sent her, who might well be close enough to hear everything they said. In the end, he decided to treat it that way. "It's not that easy," he told her. "Jennifer Berson is dead, and her family is entitled to know why, and who's responsible."

The girl shook her head. "You're a thieftaker. The brooch is all that matters. And I can get it for you. I know where it is."

"Can you take me there now?" Ethan asked.

"I can get it for you."

Ethan shook his head. "No. The person who has it now—"

"Is none of your concern," the girl said sternly. "Meet me tomorrow at this time, right here. I'll take you to it. You can give it to Berson and get your money."

"There's more to this than the brooch," Ethan said. "Even if you don't understand that, the person who sent you does."

He was still squatting, and his knees were starting to ache. Ten years ago, he could have stayed thus for longer. But not anymore. He straightened his legs slowly, stiffly. His stomach and sides ached from the beating.

As he stood he realized two things simultaneously. First, the girl had said nothing about the bruises on his face. And second, standing in a dark portion of the street, Ethan could see his shadow cast on the cobblestone lane by the glow of the moon.

The girl cast no shadow. That was why she had looked so strange before, when she had walked away and then faced him again. She had cast no shadow then, either. Not from the moon; not from the window. And the light on her face hadn't changed in the least.

"What are you?" Ethan asked, in a breathless voice.

A faint smile touched the girl's lips. "Tomorrow night," she said. "I'll take you to the brooch. Or else you're a dead man."

With that, she vanished, like a candle flame extinguished in a sudden wind. Ethan spun around, searching for the conjurer who had created her, summoned her from the air, much as Ethan had summoned that white horse the night before. An elemental spell. An illusion. That was why he had felt a casting, but not a potent one. And yet this spell went so far beyond any he was capable of wielding, it struck him dumb.

The vision Ethan had conjured to scare Daniel the previous night had lasted mere moments, and Ethan hadn't even managed to make the horse's hooves click on the wharf fill. But this conjurer had sustained his illusion—or hers—for several minutes. The girl had spoken to him, asked him questions, responded to Ethan's words. She had been . . . alive, or as close to alive as a creature of a conjurer's art could be.

And she had warned him, too. *Tomorrow night . . . Or else you're a dead man.* He knew better than to dismiss this as an idle threat. A conjurer who could summon an illusion like this one could probably overcome even Ethan's most powerful wardings.

Chapter
EIGHT

Ethan remained utterly still, listening for a footfall
or the scrape of a boot sole on cobblestone. Anything that
might reveal the whereabouts of the conjurer who had summoned that little girl out of the mist. A horse-drawn chaise rattled by
in the distance, and a dog barked. Closer, a man sang "Rail No More,
Ye Learned Asses," loudly and off pitch, the familiar lyrics slurred together. But Ethan heard nothing of the conjurer.

"Damn," he whispered. He realized that he was crouching again, and
clutching his blade so tightly that his hand had begun to ache. Slowly, he
straightened up. After another moment, he sheathed his knife.

He started walking again, watchful, still straining his ears. He halted
every few steps, to make certain that the conjurer wasn't using Ethan's
footsteps to mask his or her own. But he was sure that the other conjurer
had already managed to steal away. As he came within sight of Henry's
shop, Pitch and Shelly came bounding out of the darkness to greet him.
He knelt and allowed them to lick his ears and face.

"Where were you two when I was talking to the ghost girl?"

They wagged their tails, regarding him with curiosity. Then they
began to lick him again.

"All right," he said, standing. "You'll get no food from me. Go find
Henry."

At the mention of Henry's name, they wheeled and ran back to the shop. Ethan followed and walked around back to the stairway that led to his room.

Pausing at the bottom of the stairs, Ethan listened once more and scanned the stairway and the alleys on either side of the building for any sign that he had more visitors. The last thing he wanted was to end his day with another beating at the hands of Sephira's men. Convinced that no one else was there, he started up toward his door, his legs heavy.

As he reached the first turn in the stairway, though, he saw a shadow move above him. He grabbed his knife, slashed it across the back of his hand, and shouted the first thing that came to mind.

"*Pugnus ex cruore evocatus!*" Fist, conjured from blood!

He heard a man grunt, then stumble. The fatigue in his legs forgotten, Ethan took the steps between himself and the shadow two at a time. The man was still doubled over when he reached him, and Ethan wasted no time. From a step below, he threw a hard punch that caught the man square in the jaw. The stranger crashed into the banister, making the wood creak dangerously. Then he toppled forward onto Ethan, who shoved the lurker back so that he sprawled on the stairs.

"Mister Kaille, please!" the man croaked.

Ethan leaped forward, grabbing the stranger by his hair and pressing the edge of his knife against the man's neck.

"Who are you?" Ethan demanded. Before the man could answer, Ethan nicked his throat with the knife, drawing a trickle of blood.

"*Lux ex cruore evocatus!*" Light, conjured from blood!

A brilliant golden light burst forth above them, as if Ethan had conjured a small sun.

"Well, I'll be damned!" Ethan muttered, heedless of what he was saying, and to whom.

Staring up at him, his face pale and his eyes wide, a bruise darkening on his jaw, was Mr. Pell.

"You shouldn't curse in front of a minister," the man said in a shaky voice.

Ethan actually laughed. "No, I don't suppose I should. What are you doing here, Mister Pell?"

"I came to speak with you. I didn't mean to startle you so." He hesitated. Then, "May I get up?"

"Yes, of course." Ethan released him and sheathed his knife before helping the minister to his feet. "I'm sorry, but—"

"Mercy! What happened to your face?"

Ethan smiled ruefully. "As I was about to say, I've already had visitors today. I thought you might be one of them, and that you had in mind to finish me off."

"Who did this to you?"

"It doesn't matter," Ethan said, with a small shake of his head.

He stepped past Pell, unlocked his door, and motioned the minister inside. Leaving the door open for the moment, so that the light he had conjured flooded his room along with the cool night air, he lit a pair of candles and gestured for the minister to have a seat. He closed the door and faced the man, frowning at the swelling of Pell's jaw.

"I can heal that if you like."

"By conjuring, you mean." The minister shook his head. "I would rather you didn't." After a moment he added, "Thank you, though."

"Of course. May I offer you something to eat or drink? I don't have much, but I believe I at least owe you a bit of wine."

Pell grinned at that, then winced. He raised a hand to his jaw. "No, thank you. Anyway, it's my own fault. I should know better than to surprise a man in your line of work."

"Maybe. What do you want with me that couldn't wait until morning?"

The minister looked away, gently touching his bruise again, and then dabbing at the cut on his neck and checking his fingers for blood. There was none.

"I needed to speak with you about Jennifer Berson," he said.

Ethan eyed him with interest. "What about her?"

"Well, not about her exactly. But about what happened to her."

The thieftaker lowered himself onto his bed, eyeing the minister closely. "Do you know something about her murder?"

Pell sat staring at the floor, absently touching the cut skin on his throat. Several times he opened his mouth as if intending to speak, only to close it again, frowning each time.

"Mister Pell?"

"I don't know who killed her," Pell said at last. "Obviously if I did, I would tell you. I . . . I'd like to see this person stopped."

"Then what?"

Pell's eyes, pale blue and shining with candlelight, met Ethan's. "I lied to you today. When I said that I had never seen someone who had been murdered. That . . . that wasn't true. I should have told you earlier, but I wasn't . . ." He shook his head. "There was another child who died. It was some time ago now, on Pope's Day of last year. And I thought at the time that he couldn't have died the way people said he did. I asked you about your conjurings because as I told you already, I have speller blood in me, too. I've forsworn witchery for the Lord, but if ever I see another child killed this way . . ." He shook his head and swallowed. "I need to know how to do what you did today. I need to know how to determine whether spells have been used to kill."

Ethan stared at the man, not sure where to begin. He had so many questions he wanted to ask, not least among them, whether the minister had mentioned any of this to Troutbeck or Caner, or, for that matter, to Ethan's sister.

"How do you even know about this?" Ethan finally asked. "Was he taken down to the crypts as well?"

"Hardly," the man said, a note of bitterness in his voice. "He died near the chapel and was carried there by the men who found him. Mister Troutbeck tasked me with sending them elsewhere. The boy's family—Brown was the surname—they weren't members of our congregation. I said a prayer over the lad, and then sent them to South Meeting House."

Ethan wasn't sure what to say.

"Mister Caner wouldn't have approved," Pell said. "But he wasn't there that night."

"Can you tell me more about the boy?" Ethan asked after a short silence. "How old was he?"

"Very young. Five or so, I think."

"Was he from a wealthy family?"

Pell shook his head. "No. A very poor family, in fact. I didn't say anything earlier because he had so little in common with Jennifer

Berson that I thought I was looking for similarities where none existed. But—"

Ethan raised a hand, cutting him off. It was coming to him now. He remembered hearing of this boy. "You say this was Pope's Day?"

The minister nodded.

"I assume there was the usual nonsense?"

"Naturally," Pell said.

Every year on Pope's Day—November 5—gangs of toughs from the North and South Ends paraded through the streets to mark the anniversary of Old Guy Fawkes's Papist plot to blow up Parliament. These gangs met each year near the center of the city and fought pitched battles in the streets, bloodying themselves and anyone who got in their way.

Many of those who took to the streets on Pope's Day would have also been mixed in with the rabble responsible for the previous night's devilry. In fact . . .

"Who was leading the South Enders that day?" Ethan asked.

"Well, that's just it," the minister said. "They were led by Ebenezer Mackintosh. He and the North End man were arrested for the boy's death. But both were let go. It went to trial sometime later, but they were never convicted."

"Mackintosh," Ethan repeated. The same scoundrel who had led the rioters on their rampage through Boston the night before.

"Was anything stolen from the boy?" Ethan asked.

"Aside from his life, you mean." Pell shook his head. "I doubt he or his family had any property worth stealing."

"But you say he died like Jennifer Berson? There were no marks on him?"

"No, it wasn't that. He bore terrible marks. But he was said to have died from being run over by a cart. That's not what killed him."

Ethan frowned. "Mister Pell—"

"My father was a surgeon, Mister Kaille. I didn't train as one myself, but I learned plenty from him. This boy was dead before the cart struck him."

"How can you know that?"

Pell took a breath. "His head was crushed. That was the injury that was said to have killed him. But he had another wound: a break in his arm." The minister pointed to the upper portion of his own arm. "Here. The jagged end of the bone pierced the skin from within."

Ethan had been in battle, and had seen such wounds before. He nodded for the man to go on.

"I examined the wound when he was brought to us," Pell said. "It was terrible. The boy's skin had been ripped, as if he was mauled by a feral dog, and I could see that the blood vessels in his arm had been torn. Now, I saw my father do surgeries. I know what happens when a vessel in one of the limbs is broken that way. There should have been blood everywhere. Forgive me for being crude, but it would have gushed from that wound as long as his heart continued to labor. The boy should have bled his life away before his other injuries killed him. But there was hardly any blood on his clothing, and when I asked the men who brought him to us, they said that there was little more on the street. The poor child had to have been dead before the bone shattered."

Ethan pondered this for several moments. He couldn't deny that every fracture of this sort he had seen bled profusely. "Have you mentioned this other incident to anyone else?" he finally asked.

"You don't believe me."

"I didn't say that. I'm merely asking if you've spoken of the boy's death in the past day or two."

"No. I didn't make the connection until I watched you examine the Berson girl. That's when I started thinking about the boy, and how strange his death had been."

"Why didn't you say something while we were in the crypt?"

Pell shrugged, his brow creasing. Suddenly, he looked terribly young. "I wasn't sure my memory of the boy's death was reliable, and . . . and I feared you would think me foolish for mentioning it. But tonight, as I was readying myself for bed and I was supposed to be praying, I couldn't get the two of them out of my head. That's when I decided to find you."

"Where do you live, Mister Pell?"

"Mister Caner has been kind enough to let me a room in his home. For a most reasonable fee," he added.

"Did anyone see you leave his house?"

That brought a smile to the minister's face. "No. Back in my youth, before I was sent to study for the ministry, I was something of a rascal. I became quite adept at slipping from my home and back in again without my parents' knowledge." His eyes danced. "Until, of course, I got caught and wound up reading for Orders."

Ethan decided in that moment that he liked Pell. "And is it this same penchant for mischief that makes you want to learn a spell you're forbidden to use, a spell that could get you banished from the Church, and possibly even burned as a witch?"

The minister blushed and grew pale at the same time, so that the only points of color on his face were bright red spots high on each cheek. "I'm no fool, Mister Kaille. I wouldn't get myself banished or burned or hanged. And I've been thinking that I've spent too long denying this part of my ancestry."

"I can appreciate that. But I'm not willing to risk your life by teaching you spells. And if by some chance my sister were to learn that I had so much as mentioned such things to you, she would have my head." Ethan paused, looking at the minister. "Then again, if you hope to return to the Chapel without anyone knowing that you left, you had best let me heal that bruise on your jaw."

Pell probed it gingerly with his fingers, frowning again. "I could say that I fell."

"Yes, you could," Ethan said, keeping his expression neutral.

"You don't think that would fool anyone."

Ethan couldn't hide his amusement any longer. "No, I don't."

Pell's frown deepened, and for several moments he sat, seeming to wrestle with his conscience. "All right then," Pell finally said. "Go ahead."

Ethan reached for his knife, cut his forearm, and gently dabbed a bit of his blood on the minister's jaw. *Remedium ex cruore evocatum.*" Healing, conjured from blood.

Ethan felt that familiar pulse of power, and Pell shuddered as if from a sudden chill. Reg blinked into view at Ethan's side. His sudden appearance drew a quick intake of breath from the minister.

"What is that?" Pell asked, recoiling.

"I'm not sure there's time to explain right now. He's basically a ghost."

Reg scowled.

"All right. He's a guide who helps me draw on the power I need for conjurings. Better?" he asked the ghost.

The glowing old man nodded.

"Does he appear every time you conjure?"

"Aye," Ethan said. "Without him the spell wouldn't work."

Pell watched the ghost warily. "I don't think he likes me."

"I'd be surprised if he did," Ethan told him. "He doesn't even like me."

The minister raised a hand to his jaw again. Already the swelling was going down.

"The air around me, it . . . it buzzed, when you cast the spell. Does it always feel like that?"

"It does to you, because the blood of a conjurer flows in your veins. Others who have no history of spellmaking in their families wouldn't feel a thing. Except for the healing, that is."

The minister touched the bruise again, more boldly this time. The discoloration had faded. By the time Pell was back at Caner's house, there would be no sign that Ethan had hit him.

"Why don't you heal your own wounds?" Pell asked. "Surely you could do for yourself what you've done for me."

"I could," Ethan said. "Other than me, no one saw your bruise. But after I was beaten, I was found by the cooper whose shop is below. He lets this room to me. He's a decent man and a friend, but he doesn't know I'm a conjurer. I'm not sure how he would feel about me living here if he did."

"Of course," Pell said. "I should have known."

Ethan shrugged. "You don't live the life of a speller. There's no reason you should have to think as I do." After a moment, he looked up and found the minister watching him. "Go back home, Mister Pell, before you're missed."

Pell stood. "All right." He stepped to the door. "You'll let me know what you find out about these killings?"

"Of course. Thank you for telling me all of this. And my apologies for assaulting you."

Pell smiled and pulled the door open. "It wasn't too bad. To be honest this night's been more of an adventure than I've had in some time. I rather enjoyed it."

He stepped out of the room and quietly pulled the door shut behind him. Ethan could hear the man descending the stairs, but only just. It seemed Pell remembered much from his mischief-making days.

It had grown late and Ethan's appetite had long since vanished in a haze of fatigue and pain. He locked his door, and then as an afterthought, propped a chair against it, jamming the back of the chair firmly against the base of the doorknob: a little extra protection in case Sephira and her men tried to pay him another visit.

He undressed and fell into bed, and he was asleep within moments of closing his eyes.

Immediately upon awaking, Ethan knew that he had slept far longer than he intended. The daylight streaming into his room through the one window was far too bright, and he could hear Henry in the shop below hammering away at the stays of some new barrel.

He sat up quickly—too quickly. The pain in his head, his neck, his sides and back actually ripped a gasp from his lips. He sat still for a long time, allowing the agony to drain away while he cursed Sephira Pryce with a vehemence that would have shocked Mr. Pell. When at last he could move again, he did so with great care.

Once he was dressed and had managed to pull on his boots, Ethan left the room for a nearby grocer, intending to buy some food, tea, and molasses for his long-neglected larder—on credit, of course, since Sephira and her men had taken all of his coin. As if sensing his purpose, Pitch and Shelly met him at the bottom of the steps and fell in alongside him as he walked.

"You two are shameless," he said. Pitch looked up at him, tail wagging, clearly pleased with himself.

After purchasing some food—he had to endure stares from the grocer and his wife, as well as their children—and returning with it to his room, Ethan had some tea and buttered bread for his breakfast. Then he set out again for the waterfront. Perhaps the boys working the warehouses knew something about the Dernes, and the Bersons as well. Eventually he would wind up back in the Dowsing Rod; whatever he couldn't learn on the wharves he could find out there. Boston had its share of newspapers, but half of what their publishers printed they learned in Boston's taverns.

Halfway to the Dowser, Ethan spotted Diver. His friend walked with his hands deep in his pockets, his shoulders hunched, his eyes scanning the street. Ethan came up beside him and laid a hand on his shoulder.

Diver jumped as if he had seen a snake and reached for his blade. Ethan took a step back, holding up his hands for his friend to see.

"Ethan!" he said. "Don't do that, mate! You scared me half . . ." He stopped, gaping at Ethan's face. "Damn! What happened to you?"

"Had a visit from Sephira and her men."

Diver's eyes went wide. "When?"

"Yesterday." He dropped his voice. "I just took on a new job—Abner Berson—and Sephira doesn't like me taking away her rich clients."

"I thought you weren't working for a while."

"So did I," Ethan said. "But this job is different."

"I would think it is," Diver said pointedly, "with Berson paying."

"Speaking of jobs, why aren't you at the wharf?"

The younger man's expression soured. "Why d'you think?" he said. "I showed up this morning and no one was working. Mister Woodman was there himself turning boys away. 'We don't want any rabble working here today,' he said. 'And not for a while to come, either.'" Diver shook his head, his expression dark. "He wasn't the only one, either. Merchants seem to think that every grub in Boston was with that mob. So I left and decided to go to the Dowser. But there's talk of some of these merchants hiring toughs to walk the streets. 'Keep the rabble at bay.' That's what they're sayin' anyway. Thought you were one of them, for a moment."

"I figured it must be something like that," Ethan said. "But you might want to think twice about reaching for your blade every time someone puts a hand on you."

"It's this deal with the French," Diver said, his voice falling to a whisper as he glanced around to see that no one could hear. "Has me on edge, you know?"

"I figured that, too." Ethan put his hand on the man's shoulder again, and they started walking toward the tavern. "Come on. We'll get a bite to eat."

"You buying?" Diver asked.

"No, you are. Sephira took all my money."

Diver frowned. "Hope you're not too hungry."

"Starved," Ethan said with a grin.

The Dowser was as crowded as Ethan had ever seen it so early in the day. Nearly everyone turned as Ethan and Diver stepped inside. A few people stared hard at Ethan's bruised face, but the rest quickly looked away again. The place fairly buzzed with conversation, though there was little of the boisterous laughter Ethan was used to hearing within these walls. On the other hand, the tavern smelled of good food and ale, as it always did. Some of the Dowser's patrons stood at the bar eating oysters and drinking ale. Others sat at tables, eating creamed fish stew—chowder, as it had come to be known in Boston in recent years.

"Y'all right, Ethan?" Kelf said, running the words together, as Ethan and Diver crossed to the bar.

"Aye, thank you, Kelf. Where's Kannice?"

" 'N back. I'll get her."

"She seen you since . . . ?" Diver gestured at Ethan's face.

Ethan shook his head. "No." But he was thinking more about the cross words they had exchanged before he left the previous morning. He should have known better.

She emerged from the kitchen wearing an icy expression, but as soon as she saw him it melted away. "God have mercy!" she said, her brow furrowing. "What happened?"

"I'm fine," Ethan said.

"Yes, I can see that." Her voice dripped with sarcasm. "You've never looked better. Tell me what happened."

"I will, later," he said, softening the words with a smile. "First, though, have you heard anything about merchants shutting down their wharves?"

She frowned and shook her head. "No. Not that it would surprise me, but I've heard nothing."

"It might just be a few in the South End," Ethan said to Diver. "Friends of Hallowell or Story, maybe."

"We'll be lucky if that's all that comes of last night's nonsense," Kannice said, casting an accusing glare at Diver. "Wait until news of this reaches the king. And Grenville. Then there'll be trouble."

To his credit, Diver ignored her. "What about the wharves?" he asked. "How long do you think they'll be sending us away?"

"Not long," Ethan said. "The merchants will want to make it clear that they don't like being at the mercy of street gangs and mobs. But they have ships to unload and goods to sell. That's what they care about. I'd wager that you'll be working the wharves again in a day or two."

"I hope you're right," his friend said with so much relief that Ethan knew he was thinking about the rum and wine. Never in his life had Diver complained about a day off from work.

Kannice ran a hand through her hair, shaking her head and looking grim. "Frankly, if this is the worst of it—a bit of inconvenience for Diver and his friends—we should count ourselves lucky and keep our mouths shut."

Ethan was inclined to agree, but before he could say so, Diver responded.

"It's Grenville and his lot who should count themselves lucky," he said. "Everything they do is meant to help them that are rich and leave the rest of us scuffling for a shilling and a meal. If that's what they have in mind for us, we'd be just as well off on our own."

Kannice whirled on him. "I won't have seditious talk in this bar, Devren Jervis! Shouting in the lanes is one thing; treason is quite another! If you're going to carry on about things you know nothing about, you had best be leaving!"

Diver took a step back, blinking. "I didn't mean anything by it, Kannice. I was just speaking as a—"

"As a what? A fool? I knew that already!"

"As a man who's got business in the streets," Diver said, a wounded expression on his face.

Kannice drew herself up. "Well—"

"I need him to stay, Kannice," Ethan broke in quietly. "He's promised to buy me a bit of supper."

She impaled Ethan with her glare. He knew what she was thinking: She would gladly have fed Ethan for free if it meant banishing Diver from her tavern. But after a moment, she relented.

"Fine then," she said. She stared hard at Diver. "No more of that talk."

"I promise," Diver said.

She waved a hand toward their usual table at the back of the tavern and started toward the kitchen. "Sit down, both of you. I'll bring some stew."

Ethan and Diver seated themselves at the table. A moment later, Kannice brought them two bowls of chowder. She set the bowls in front of them and sat beside Ethan.

"Now," she said, "about your face."

Ethan took a spoonful of stew. It was as delicious as he remembered. Rich, slightly sweet, with just a hint of dill.

"Sephira Pryce," he said quietly, after swallowing. "She wanted to impress upon me that I wasn't to grow accustomed to working for men of Abner Berson's means."

"How is it that she's still allowed to walk the streets of this city? Maybe if Sheriff Greenleaf had an ounce of courage he could find a way to keep the peace without relying on her kind."

"I'm her kind," Ethan said. "If Greenleaf had an ounce of courage, I might be out of a job."

"You'd find another, and a better one at that." She eyed his bruises again and her frown returned. "You're lucky she didn't kill you."

"She doesn't want me dead," Ethan said between mouthfuls. "She as much as said so. She needs me to take jobs she can't handle."

"Ones that involve conjuring, you mean."

"Aye. But it bothers her that this time being a conjurer got me a job on Beacon Street. She considers that her domain, and she wanted me to know it. She made her point and then she left."

She took his hand. "She belongs in gaol rather than out on the streets."

"I won't argue."

He took another spoonful of soup, and as he did the door to the tavern opened. Several men stepped inside, led by an imposing man with a large hook nose and hard pale eyes. He wore a white wig and a black hat, which he removed upon entering the tavern. Even from his table at the other side of the room, Ethan recognized him immediately; he and Kannice had been speaking of him mere seconds before.

"What now?" she muttered. Her gaze flicked in Diver's direction.

Ethan, though, had a feeling that Sheriff Stephen Greenleaf hadn't come looking for Diver. He recognized two of the men with Greenleaf as members of the night watch; he thought it likely that the third man was with the watch as well. The sheriff would have brought them along only if he expected trouble. And since he knew that Ethan was a convicted mutineer, Greenleaf would have wanted men at his back when he came to speak with him.

Ethan laid his spoon on the table and watched as Kannice stood and walked across the tavern to the doorway where the men were standing. She looked like a waif next to them, but that wasn't likely to bother her.

"What can I do for you boys?" she asked in a cheery voice, stopping in front of the sheriff. "Are you hungry?"

Greenleaf hardly spared her a glance. "We're looking for Ethan Kaille," he said. "We know he's here."

Even in the dingy light of the tavern, Ethan saw the color drain from Kannice's face. To her credit, she didn't immediately glance his way, but neither did she manage to say anything.

"What do you need, Sheriff?" Ethan said, standing.

Greenleaf smiled thinly and stepped past Kannice. His men followed. "Good day, Mister Kaille," he said, his voice echoing.

The sheriff wasn't a bad sort. He didn't like Ethan, and Ethan felt the same way about him. But the man had a nearly impossible job. As sheriff of Suffolk County he was expected to keep the peace throughout Boston and the surrounding countryside. But he had no soldiers, no guards, no militia. Even the men of the watch standing behind him answered to city authorities. He would have had to borrow them for this excursion.

Greenleaf stopped a few feet from the table and nodded in Ethan's direction.

"He has a knife on his belt," he said calmly to the men of the watch. "Take it from him."

One of the men came up behind Ethan, a pistol in hand, while another stepped in front of him, also holding a gun, this one at waist level, so that its barrel pointed at Ethan's gut. Ethan held up his hands, making it clear that he had no intention of resisting. The man behind him took his knife.

"Is that all you have?" Greenleaf asked.

"Yes, sir."

The man in front of Ethan lowered his weapon. The one behind Ethan shoved him toward the door hard enough that Ethan stumbled and nearly fell to the floor. Instantly Diver was on his feet, his own blade in hand. Just as quickly, Greenleaf's men rounded on him, all with their pistols held ready.

"Diver, no!" Ethan said quickly, even as Kannice also hissed a warning.

Seeing that he was outmanned, Diver tossed his knife onto the table and raised his hands as Ethan had done. One of the men knocked the blade out of Diver's reach. When Diver started to lower his hands, the man hit him hard in the gut with the butt of his weapon. Diver doubled over, and the man drove his face into the table. Blood spurted from Diver's nose and he dropped to the floor, hands clutched to his face.

"No!" Ethan cried, taking a step toward Diver. Another man blocked his way, his gun raised.

"Enough," the sheriff said loudly.

Ethan stopped, raising his hands again in surrender. "There's no need to involve him in this."

Greenleaf glared down at Diver, a frown on his broad face. Kannice had rushed to Diver's side with a cloth to stanch the bleeding.

"The pup involved himself," the sheriff said.

"He's young, and a fool. He wasn't thinking. I'm the one you came for, and you've got me. Let's leave it at that."

Greenleaf eyed Diver for another moment before finally dismissing him with a shake of his head. "Fine," he said to Ethan. "Come along, then. No more trouble."

The man behind Ethan pushed him again, though with less force than before. Ethan glanced briefly at Kannice, who looked as frightened as he had ever seen her. He gave her what he hoped was a reassuring smile, but her expression didn't change.

"Take care of him," Ethan said. "I'll come back as soon as they let me go."

She nodded.

The man at his back pushed him again, not that it was necessary. Ethan reached the door and stepped out into the street.

"This way," the sheriff said without looking back at him. And they began to march him toward Boston's prison.

he sheriff and his men were silent as they led him through the lanes. None of the men so much as looked at him, at least not that Ethan could see. They also didn't shackle his wrists or ankles; he had feared that they might.

He tried to stay calm. He had done nothing wrong. Even if they put him in a prison cell, they couldn't hold him for long. That's what he told himself.

But still his limbs trembled, and he had broken out in a cold sweat that had nothing to do with the hot August sun hanging over the city.

The last time men working for the British government had come for him, they had locked him away for more than thirteen years, first in a filthy cell in Charleston, then on a barely seaworthy ship bound for London and in a second filthy cell, and finally on the sugar plantation in Barbados. Just thinking of the island made the scars on his back itch with the memory of too many floggings. He had lived in a hovel with other prisoners: cutthroats, thieves, deserters. He labored in the cane fields from dawn to dusk, under a scorching sun and in air so damp he felt that he was drowning with every breath. At night, he slept on a vermin-infested pile of straw and covered himself with a threadbare, moth-eaten blanket.

He was allowed two meals each day: water, hardtack, and a morsel of cheese at midday, and much the same in the evening, with the occasional bit of rancid meat thrown in. Their one delicacy was a small piece of sweet, red fruit they were given every second or third day to keep scurvy at bay. The fruit was usually half rotted, but it was so much better than everything else they ate that it tasted ambrosial.

But even with this treat, Ethan recalled constantly being hungry. When it became more than he could bear, he ate roaches, beetles, and moths. Once he caught and killed a rat behind the hovel and ate it raw, but it made him violently ill and he never tried that again. He prayed for rainy days, not because they offered a respite from the labor—they didn't—but because working in the rain was so much less onerous than working under the sun.

Harvests were the worst: backbreaking work, endless days. One year, a stray blow from an old man wielding a cane knife left a bloody gash on Ethan's left foot. At this time, he had forsworn conjuring the way a reformed drunk rejects spirits. Spells, he decided, had robbed him of his reason, and thus of his freedom and his love. But even had he still been casting, he would not have dared attempt to heal himself while living in such close proximity with his guards and fellow prisoners. Within two days, the wound was infected. Within four, Ethan's entire leg from the knee down was bloated and hot to the touch. The overseers managed to save the leg, but they had to cut off three of his toes to do it.

Memories of the plantation pounded at him. Ethan didn't know why Greenleaf had come for him, but he decided in that moment that he would die before he allowed himself to be transported again.

"I've done nothing wrong," he muttered to himself, trying once more to calm his nerves.

One man of the watch walking beside him laughed. Ethan glowered, but the man just stared back at him, obviously enjoying himself, knowing all too well that Ethan could do nothing to wipe the grin from his face.

The people they passed in the streets eyed Ethan with unconcealed curiosity. A few shouted at him, and though he couldn't make out all they said, he gathered they thought him part of the mob that attacked Hutchinson's home. Hearing their remarks, Ethan wondered if the sheriff thought this as well.

Leading him from the Dowsing Rod to the Boston prison, the men had to march him down Queen Street, past the ruined home of William Story. Story's yard had been cleaned up since the day before, and there were fewer gawkers now. Still, as they walked by, the sheriff's men eyed him keenly. Ethan refused to look directly at any of them.

Boston's prison stood opposite Story's home, where Brattle Street intersected Queen. It was an odd spot for a prison, set in the midst of some of the nicer houses in Boston and within hailing distance of the First Church. The prison itself was a simple building, notable only for its ancient, ponderous oak door and the heavily rusted iron hardware that held it in place. Its windows were small, the stonework plain and homely. It was no more or less inviting than any other gaol. Yet, as they approached it, Ethan couldn't help but quail. Too many memories; too many years lost.

Then they were past that massive door and the shadow of the building itself, still walking eastward on Queen Street. Relief washed over him, followed immediately by a new kind of fear. If they didn't intend to place him in the prison, what was this about?

"Where are you taking me?" Ethan asked.

Greenleaf glanced back at him, amused. "I was wondering when you would ask." He waved a hand vaguely in the direction of the prison. "You assumed we were taking you there. A guilty conscience, perhaps?"

Ethan ignored the gibe. "Where are we going?"

"The Town House," the man said, facing forward again.

Ethan couldn't have been more surprised if the man had said that he was being taken to the governor's mansion.

"Why?" he asked.

The sheriff didn't answer, and they walked the rest of the way in silence.

The people of Boston referred to the brick building on King Street as the Second Town House. The first structure built on the site had burned to the ground at the beginning of the century. The Town House that stood before Ethan now had also burned, back in the 1740s. The brick exterior survived, but everything within its walls was gutted and had to be rebuilt yet again.

Ethan had been in the Town House countless times before. As a thieftaker he was often interested in the proceedings that took place in the courtrooms at the west end of the second floor.

That was where Greenleaf and his men led Ethan now. They entered the building, crossed the great hall to the nearer of two broad stone stairways, and began to make their way up to the second floor. As they climbed the stairs, Ethan thought he saw a shock of bright yellow hair that reminded him strongly of Sephira's tough. But when he paused on the stairs and tried to get a better look, the man vanished from view.

"Come along, Mister Kaille," the sheriff said.

Ethan searched for another few seconds, but he didn't see the man again. He would have liked to go back down and find him. If Sephira's henchman was here, Ethan wanted to know why. But the men of the watch stood with him, and Greenleaf was waiting. Ethan followed him up to the second floor.

They turned at the top of the stairway and walked to a pair of polished wooden doors: the entrance to the chambers of the Superior Court. The sheriff halted.

"Wait here," he said.

He opened one of the doors and slipped inside.

For several moments, Ethan and the rest of his escort stood together in the broad corridor, saying nothing. Outside the representatives' chamber, in the middle of the second floor, men in wigs and suits spoke in groups of three and four, their voices echoing and blending into an incoherent din. None of them took much notice of Ethan and the men with him.

At last, the door to the court opened again and the sheriff peered out into the corridor.

"The chief justice will see you now," Greenleaf said.

Ethan didn't move. "The chief justice?"

"He asked to speak with you."

"What about?"

"Just get in here. He isn't a man to be kept waiting." He motioned Ethan into the chamber.

Taking a long, steadying breath, Ethan entered.

The chamber was empty save for the sheriff and a man who sat behind the grand, dark wood court's bench at the far end of the chamber. Seeing the man, Ethan understood at last, and he chided himself for not reasoning it out sooner. The chief justice of the province also happened to be the lieutenant governor. Thomas Hutchinson.

Ethan walked to the bench and stopped in front of Hutchinson. The man regarded him appraisingly for a moment.

"That's all, Sheriff," Hutchinson said. "Thank you."

Greenleaf let himself out of the chamber, closing the door behind him.

Hutchinson faced Ethan once more, and for what felt like several minutes, as their eyes remained locked, they were like foes in a card game, each taking the measure of the other. Hutchinson was a tall man and he sat forward in his chair, his shoulders thrust back slightly, which gave him a barrel-chested look despite his slender build. He had large, dark eyes, a high forehead, and a long, prominent nose. The curls of his powdered wig framed his face. His clothes were simple, but immaculate: a black suit with a white shirt and cravat. His eyes were bloodshot and there were dark rings under them. He looked to Ethan like he hadn't slept in days.

"I hope you weren't inconvenienced much by my summons," Hutchinson finally said. He didn't ask Ethan to sit, so Ethan remained as he was and answered.

"No, Your Honor."

"I understand there was an incident."

"Sir?"

"At the tavern, where they found you. A man was injured. A friend of yours."

Ethan didn't know what to say. Had the sheriff told Hutchinson about the attack on Diver? And if so, how had he explained what happened?

"Well?" the lieutenant governor said, sounding impatient.

"There was, Your Honor. One of the sheriff's men . . . my friend thought that he meant to hurt me, and he—"

"The man shoved you from behind," Hutchinson said, his tone brusque.

"That's right."

The lieutenant governor nodded once. "The sheriff will speak with him." He cleared his throat. "I take it you've heard of what was done to my home two nights ago."

Hutchinson was a strange sort. On the one hand, his manner was haughty—abrasively so. And yet he had just shown Ethan, and Diver as well, more consideration than Ethan would have expected from a man of his station, particularly one whose home had recently been wrecked by the very people he was expected to govern.

"Yes, Your Honor," Ethan said. "I walked by there yesterday. I'm sorry for how you and your family have suffered."

The corners of Hutchinson's mouth quirked upward into a fleeting, bitter smile. "Seeing it from the street, you would have no idea of how we've suffered. The damage to the exterior was nothing compared to what those devils did to the inside. They demolished every wall and every door in the house, leaving it nothing more than a shell. They left not a single piece of furniture whole. They stole my wife's jewels, took every bit of clothing any of us owned, took every book in my library. They shattered or stole our plates and glasses, they walked off with our food and drink. They stole nine hundred pounds, and pieces of silver that had belonged to my father, and his father before him."

The litany came easily to the man; Ethan had the feeling that he had recited it many times in the last two days.

"They left me nothing," Hutchinson went on. "And had I remained, rather than fleeing my own home like a thief in the night, I would have lost far more. As it is, I fear to show my face in the streets. I will be leaving Boston for our home in Milton in another day or so, and I'll be taking my wife and children. I fear for their safety even more than I do for my own."

"Again, Your Honor, you have my deepest sympathy," Ethan said. "No one should be treated so. But if you believe that I—"

"I don't," Hutchinson broke in. "You've been hired by Abner Berson. Is that right?"

"Yes, sir," Ethan said, narrowing his eyes. Why would the lieutenant governor of Massachusetts take an interest in his business dealings? And what else did Hutchinson know about him?

"You wonder how I heard of this."

"I assume you have it from Mister Berson himself, or from a mutual acquaintance," Ethan said. "What I wonder is why the inquiries of a common thieftaker should draw the notice of a man of your importance."

Hutchinson frowned, which served to give his face a fearsome aspect. "If you need to ask, Mister Kaille, I must recommend to Berson that he reconsider the faith he's placed in you. Isn't it obvious? The same villains who abused my family and me with such violence are responsible for the death of Berson's daughter."

"You know this as fact, Your Honor?"

"I know it from what I've seen, from what was done to me. This mob was whipped to a frenzy, not just that night, but over the course of weeks. It was bad enough what was done to Oliver's properties. But then to compound it like this." He had been speaking very quickly and he paused now, pulled a handkerchief from his pocket, and dabbed at his upper lip with a shaking hand. "They were exhorted to these acts of barbarism by James Otis and Peter Darrow and Samuel Adams, and every other carnival barker who claims to be a champion of . . . of *liberty*." He said the word as if it were an imprecation. "And then they were directed through the streets by that cutthroat, Ebenezer Mackintosh." He dabbed again at his lip, folded the handkerchief, and stuffed it back in his pocket. "If you want to find Jennifer Berson's killer, I would suggest you start with him."

"With Mackintosh, sir?"

"He is being held down the street at the gaol. At least for the moment. Already his brethren are agitating for his release, as if he had been arrested merely for being drunk. They revere him so. What is it the rabble call him? The Commander of the South End, or some such nonsense? And Captain Mackintosh. As if such a man could be captain of anything."

"Yes, sir."

Hutchinson regarded him briefly, suspicion in his gaze. "Do you know Mackintosh, Mister Kaille?"

"Only by reputation."

"And what reputation would that be?"

"Merely that he has a following among those who march on Pope's Day, and that whatever his faults, he's respected by the men in the street."

"I see." Hutchinson considered Ethan for several seconds. "Perhaps I should have asked this earlier. Are you one of these so-called Sons of Liberty?"

"I'm a son of the British Empire, Your Honor. I sailed in the Mediterranean under Admiral Matthews and would have fought the French in Canada if I'd had the opportunity."

Hutchinson looked impressed. "You sailed with Matthews?" he asked.

"Yes, sir."

"Who was your captain?"

"Thomas Cooper, sir."

Hutchinson's eyebrows went up. "You were on the *Stirling Castle*? At Toulon?"

"Yes, sir."

The lieutenant governor actually smiled. "Well, then perhaps it is I who should reconsider my first impression. You must understand; a man hears things, and it's not always easy to know what to make of them."

"I do understand, sir. I'm sure much of what you've heard about me is true."

Hutchinson's smile faded slowly. "I see. Well, Mister Kaille, I merely wished to tell you what I knew about the events of two nights past. The mob that attacked my home showed utter disregard for both our personal well-being and our property. I have it from Abner Berson himself that his daughter was not only murdered, she was also robbed. The similarity between these incidents is obvious to me, and I would hope it is to you, as well."

"I understand, Your Honor." He tried to keep his voice level, but apparently he failed.

"What is it you think you understand?" Hutchinson demanded.

"Merely what you told me, sir."

The man continued to stare at him. "No. You think I wish to fix the blame for Jennifer Berson's murder on those who destroyed my home."

"You did just tell me that they were guilty of both crimes."

"Because they are! This isn't a matter of vengeance! It's simple logic!"

"Yes, Your Honor. And if my own logic leads me to the same conclusion, I assure you I won't rest until these men are punished."

"I think I see," Hutchinson said. "Perhaps you would like me to hire you, too. For a fee, you can find my silver and my money. Is that it?"

Ethan bristled at the insinuation, but he kept his voice even as he said, "No, sir. I only work for a single client at any one time. If you need to hire a thieftaker, you'll have to go to Sephira Pryce."

Apparently the lieutenant governor hadn't expected him to respond as he did. The man regarded Ethan for another moment. "Very well, Mister Kaille. You may go."

"Thank you, sir." Ethan strode toward the door.

"I'll be interested to hear how your inquiry progresses."

Ethan didn't face Hutchinson again, but he did pause at the door. "Yes, sir," he said, and let himself out of the chamber.

Greenleaf and the men of the watch were there in the corridor. The sheriff nodded to him, and one of his men, perhaps the one who had shoved Ethan, glowered, but none of them tried to keep Ethan from leaving. They even returned his knife.

He exited the building, and started back toward his home, still seething at what Hutchinson had implied. He hadn't gone far, though, when he spotted that same shock of yellow hair that he had seen in the Town House. He ducked behind a carriage that was rattling by, and, crouching low, jogged along beside it, keeping himself hidden until he could see this man more clearly.

A well-dressed gentleman sitting in the carriage leaned out over the door and stared hard at Ethan. Ethan ignored him, keeping to the side of the vehicle until at last he reached a narrow alley between a tavern and a storefront. He ducked into the shadows, and then, once the carriage had passed, peered back toward where he had seen that blond hair.

It was still midafternoon and the streets were crowded. The lanes stank of horse piss and flies buzzed around piles of droppings. It took Ethan a moment to spot the man again, but as soon as he did, he recognized him. Yellow-hair. Sephira's tough. The bruises on Ethan's face and body throbbed with remembered pain.

Another carriage rumbled down the street, harnesses creaking, the dry clop of unshod hooves echoing off nearby buidlings, and as it rolled past Ethan stepped out of the alley and walked with it, again taking care to keep the carriage between himself and Yellow-hair. If he could keep out of sight long enough to reach Leverett's Lane, he could cut back to Water Street and make it home without being seen. That was the plan, anyway.

He hadn't gone far, however, when he caught sight of another familiar face. Thick features, a ruddy complexion, widely spaced eyes and a wide mouth. Gordon. Another of Sephira's men. And this time Ethan had no chance to hide. The man spotted him, a broad grin splitting his face to reveal crooked, yellow teeth.

Ethan halted, glanced back over his shoulder, and saw Yellow-hair walking his way, though the man hadn't seen him yet. Gordon whistled sharply, no doubt to point out Ethan to his friend. Ethan didn't wait to see what Yellow-hair did.

His route home was blocked, so he went north instead, dashing up a small lane—he thought it was called Pierce's Alley—toward Faneuil Hall. He could hear footsteps behind him, and so knew that both men were after him. He assumed that Sephira's other henchmen were close by.

It didn't take long for his bad leg to start aching, but he couldn't allow his limp to slow him down. Emerging from the shadows of the alley into the afternoon sun, still at a full run, Ethan chose to cut through Dock Square toward the Dowser.

Before he had gotten far, however, he spotted two more of Sephira's men. One of them, another brute, stood at the southwest end of the square, blocking his access to Cornhill Street and Hillier's Lane. The fourth man—Ethan remembered once hearing Sephira call him Nap— stood opposite this other, guarding the corner of Union Street. Nap was muscular and tall and Ethan had no doubt that he was a competent fighter—better than Gordon and the brute, probably. But he was the smallest of Sephira's crew, and, like the other man, he hadn't yet caught sight of Ethan.

That wouldn't be true for long.

He ran hard toward Nap, sweat soaking his face, his limp worsening. Another shrill whistle cut across the normal street noise of the square. Gordon, no doubt. Nap whirled at the sound, searching for its source. A moment later, he looked directly at Ethan, recognition making his eyes widen. He reached frantically for his blade, but by then Ethan was bearing down on him.

Lowering his shoulder, Ethan rammed into the man, hitting him full in the chest. Nap and Ethan were about the same size, but Nap hadn't managed to brace himself. He flew off his feet and crashed into a group of ladies wearing fine linen dresses. All of them wound up in a heap on the cobblestones. Ethan stumbled, but kept his feet and ran on, his shoulder screaming agony.

He was on Union Street now. He had no doubt that the others were right behind him. Rather than continue toward the Dowsing Rod and risk leading Yellow-hair and the others right to Kannice, Ethan followed Ann Street eastward, down along the wharves and warehouses.

His leg was growing worse by the moment, and his lungs burned. He didn't slacken his pace, but he knew he couldn't outrun Sephira's men forever. They were younger than he was, stronger. He scanned the street for somewhere he might hide, even as he continued to run. Too late he realized that the lanes were less crowded here, that he was more alone than he would have been had he taken a different route.

At the next corner, he turned, intending to head up into the central part of the North End. But he halted immediately, his chest heaving with every breath.

"Damnit!" he said.

A single man stood at the corner of the next street, waiting. . . . *For him.* Seeing him, the man smirked and started in his direction. Ethan backed away, and then ran back onto Ann Street, still heading north.

"Kaille!"

Ethan spun. Yellow-hair was behind him with Nap, who didn't look at all pleased to see him. Yellow-hair was grinning, though, standing in the middle of the lane, a pistol held loosely in his right hand.

Ethan started away again, but a moment later, two more men

emerged onto the street a block in front of him. He slowed. Gordon and the brute who had been with Nap stepped onto the lane from Cross Street, joining the two other toughs who had blocked his way.

They had herded him to this spot, like wolves nipping at his heels. And he had let them do it. He had been too quick to run, too predictable.

Ethan stopped and positioned himself so that he could watch Gordon and the men approaching from the north while also keeping an eye on Yellow-hair and Nap.

"What does Sephira want with me now?" he asked, still breathing hard. "She's not satisfied with having you beat me to a bloody mess . . . now she wants you to finish the job?"

"If only," Yellow-hair said. "She wants us t' deliver a message. Tha's all."

Ethan cast a quick look toward Gordon. He and the brute were closer than Ethan expected.

"Stop there," Ethan called to them, pulling out his knife.

Gordon laughed. "Ya think ya kin kill us all with tha' blade?"

"He's a speller, fool!" Yellow-hair said. "He doesn' have t' kill us with th' knife."

Gordon halted in his tracks, throwing out a hand to stop the other men. His face had gone white.

"I'll conjure if I have to," Ethan told them, looking first at Yellow-hair and then at the rest. He pushed his sleeve up, exposing his scarred forearm. "I could kill all of you, and there would be nothing you could do to stop me."

"Easy, Kaille," Yellow-hair said. He had stopped, too, and now he raised his pistol for Ethan to see and then slipped it back into his coat pocket. He opened his hands. "Ya see? I jus' wanna talk t' ya."

"All right," Ethan said. "Talk."

Sephira's man beckoned to him with a wave. "In private. Come with me."

Ethan didn't move. "I don't think so."

Yellow-hair frowned, but said, "Miss Pryce heard tha' ya'd been offer'd Jennifer Berson's missin' brooch."

Ethan stared at him, at last letting out a small, breathless laugh. "Where did she hear that?"

"Is it true?"

"Retrieving the brooch means nothing if I don't find her killer."

"Miss Pryce disagrees," he said. "Ya're a thieftaker. Yar job is t' retrieve stolen goods."

Ethan was fast tiring of Sephira and her men always being a step ahead of him.

"Is it true?" Yellow-hair asked again. "Have ya been offer'd th' brooch?"

"Yes."

The man smiled. "Tha's good, Kaille. Miss Pryce says tha' ya'd be wise t' take it, return it t' Berson, an' be done with this bus'ness." His smile widened. "She also said tha' this time ya can keep whatever he pays ya."

"That's generous of her. But why should she care? I happen to know that this is one crime you and your friends didn't commit." Ethan glanced back at Gordon, who had started to creep forward again. Immediately he raised his blade to his bared forearm. Gordon froze. Ethan gestured with the knife, and the man took a few steps back.

Yellow-hair beckoned once more for Ethan to join him. "Come on, Kaille. There's somethin' she wanted me t' show ya. These others'll stay here. It'll jus' be th' two of us, an' ya can keep yar knife."

Ethan eyed the other men. He didn't trust any of them, but he had a better chance of escaping if he was only with Yellow-hair. He walked to where the man stood and indicated that he should lead the way. Yellow-hair grinned and started down a narrow alley that ran parallel to the waterfront. Ethan followed.

They walked a short distance in silence, before Ethan asked, "What's her interest in this? Do you even know?"

"She has an interest in ev'rythin' tha' happens in this city. Ya should know tha' by now."

Ethan glanced back to make sure none of the other men had followed them. He saw no one.

"She wanted me t' tell ya tha' this is no time for ya t' try an' be some sorta hero. Ya should take th' brooch an' be done. Ya've had a taste o' workin' for th' Beacon Street crowd—th' Abner Bersons an' their kind. Ya could make a lot o' money. This is no time for ya t' do somethin' stupid."

"Yesterday she told me that I was never again to work for the Abner Bersons of the world. Now she's trying to tempt me with their silver? Tell Sephira she should make up her mind."

They crossed Fish Street and entered another alley. It seemed that they were headed toward the North Battery.

"Where are we going, Yellow-hair?"

The man looked at him. "Yellow-hair?"

Ethan shrugged. "That's what I call you. I don't know your name."

The man shook his head and laughed. "It's Nigel."

"All right. Where are we going, Nigel?"

"Not much longer now."

They fell into another brief silence.

"Ya're wastin yar time, ya know," Nigel said at length.

"It's a waste of time to learn who killed Jennifer Berson?"

"We already know who killed her. Ya're not helpin' th' Bersons, an' ya're not helpin' yarself."

"That's crazy!" Ethan said. "You don't think Berson and his wife want to find out who killed their daughter and why?"

"Ya're no' listenin', Kaille! He'll be satisfied when he gets his jewel back, an' when he knows for certain tha' she's dead 'cuz o' tha' mob. Whoever killed her was takin' orders from Ebenezer Mackintosh. He's gonna hang for this, an' when he does, justice'll be done."

He sounded too sure of himself. Ethan felt uneasy. He slowed, then halted. "Where are we going? What is this all about?"

Nigel didn't stop. "Jus' a bit farther."

Ethan began to follow again, his grip on his knife tightening. He said nothing more to the man, and Nigel seemed content to walk in silence. Eventually they reached the North Battery and turned onto Battery Alley. They hadn't gone far on the narrow lane when Nigel stopped.

Ethan looked around warily. "What are we doing here?"

"Miss Pryce had one more message for ya," Nigel said. He paused, his brow creasing. "It went like this: Ya owe me a word o' thanks for cleanin' up yar mess."

"What the hell does that mean?"

"Yar mess, Kaille. Daniel Folter."

Ethan felt the blood drain from his face. "What about him?"

"Miss Pryce is sure it was an oversight. Ya were supposed t' hand him over t' th' sheriff, or failin' that, take care o' him yarself. But ya didn'. Th' people o' Boston have t' feel safe. They have t' know tha' th' men who steal from them will be dealt with. Mercy is weakness, she told me t' say, an' she thinks ya're weak."

"That . . . demon." It came out as a whisper.

Nigel grinned. "Ya shoulda taken care o' it yarself. We only did wha' *you* had been hired t' do."

He turned his head slowly and looked into an alley. Following the line of his gaze, Ethan saw a form lying in the shadows. He couldn't see a face, but what he did see—long legs, torn breeches, a worn, blood-stained waistcoat, and more blood staining the cobblestones—told him all he needed to know.

"I should kill you where you stand," Ethan said, raising his knife to his forearm.

Nigel grabbed his pistol from his pocket and leveled it at Ethan's chest.

"Ethan?"

They turned at the same time to stare at the boy who had stepped onto the street from another small alley leading off toward the wharves.

Holin Harper, the oldest child of Marielle, Ethan's former be-trothed, stood at the corner, flanked by Pitch and Shelly. Ethan had no idea what the boy was doing here or how he had found them, but he could not allow Marielle's child to come to harm. Yellow-hair appeared to sense this, like a wolf smelling fear in its prey. His eyes flicked in Ethan's direction, and there was a grin on his lips.

Both dogs growled deep in their throats, their hackles rising.

"Don't even think about it," Ethan said, his voice low.

This had to be done carefully. Neither Holin nor his sister knew that Ethan was a conjurer and Elli would have his head if they found out. Worse, she would forbid them to see Ethan again.

"Leave us now," he told Sephira's man. "Or I swear I won't care at all what happens to me."

Fear flashed in the man's dark eyes. But his grin returned quickly, even as he put the pistol back in his pocket. "Fine, Kaille." He looked at the boy again and chuckled. "But ya better give a thought t' Miss Pryce's message." He nodded toward the alley where lay Daniel's body. "Tha' could be you." He smiled at Holin and started back the way he and Ethan had come.

Ethan stood silently, his forearm itching, his blade hand shaking. He wanted to feel hot blood running over his skin. He wanted to draw upon the power coursing through his body and reduce the smug bastard to a pile of ash.

But he merely stood there, feeling utterly helpless as he watched Sephira's man walk away.

e works for Sephira Pryce!"

Ethan felt ill. He'd had few dealings with Folter; like Kannice, he thought him a fool. But he had chosen to let the pup go, to spare him years in prison or worse. Corbett wouldn't have approved, but the merchant had hired him to deal with the matter, and Ethan had done so, in his own way. There had been no harm in it. Corbett had his jewels back, and Folter would still be alive if he had left the city as Ethan told him to. The fool. The poor, dead fool.

"Ethan?"

He should do something for Daniel. He should cover the body, or at least get word to the sheriff. But right now, he was more concerned with keeping Holin out of that bloodied alley.

Mercy is weakness.

He refused to believe that. He was a mutineer and a conjurer. The members of the Admiralty Court had known this when they sent Ethan to labor in the cane fields rather than sentencing him to swing from the gallows. That had been an act of mercy, an acknowledgment that while Ethan had done wrong, he had been young and stupid rather than truly wicked. Where was the weakness in what the court had done?

"Ethan?"

Holin stood with his hands buried in his pockets, his eyes following Yellow-hair, who was still on Ann Street, though out of earshot.

"That man works for Sephira Pryce, doesn't he? He even mentioned her."

Every time Ethan saw Holin he thought the boy must have grown by half a foot or more. He had nearly reached Ethan's height and would probably grow another six inches before he was done. Still, his face was that of a boy, and he remained gangly. He looked like he was never sure of the whereabouts of all four limbs at once. His skin was fair, his hair the color of wheat, his eyes like the sky on a clear autumn morning. His features were so fine as to be girlish and he still had no hint of his first beard.

The boy turned to him. "Are you all right? Your face . . ."

"I'm fine," Ethan said, making himself smile. "It looks worse than it feels."

"It looks pretty bad."

Shelly nudged Ethan's hand with her snout; he scratched her head absently. "I know. And yes, that man works for Sephira Pryce."

"It looked like you two were fighting."

"Sephira and I are both thieftakers," Ethan said, as if that explained everything. "It's natural that we should be rivals." He frowned, noticing for the first time where they were, and where the boy had been. "What are you doing down here, Holin? The wharves are no place for . . ." He had been about to say "for a boy," but he stopped himself. "For someone your age," he said instead.

Holin laughed, his blue eyes dancing. "That was well done. Mother never catches herself in time."

"She doesn't have to; she's your mother. Now answer the question."

"I've started working at Hunt's Wharf," Holin told him, standing just a bit straighter. "Loading and unloading for one-and-six a day."

Ethan frowned again. If Holin was working on the waterfront, he had no choice but to cross through this part of the city every day. Ethan had half a mind to tell Elli to keep the boy at home, at least until he had found this sorcerer. But Holin would be angry with him, and chances were that Elli wouldn't listen anyway.

"How old are you now?" Ethan asked. "Fourteen?"

"Fifteen!" Holin said, indignant.

"Fifteen." Ethan nodded. "That's decent money for a . . . a young man your age."

Holin laughed. "Aye, you're much better at that than Mother is."

"Come on, I'll walk you home," Ethan said, glancing in the direction Nigel had gone. He didn't see the man anymore. He started to put away his blade, but then thought better of it. His leg still ached and he felt sweat trickling down his temples, but his pulse was slowing.

"I offered to give the money to Mother," Holin said, as they began to walk, the dogs trotting ahead of them. "But she's letting me keep it. She says we have enough and that grandfather will help us if we need more."

"That's kind of her," Ethan said absently, still watchful.

The truth was Elli didn't need the money. Her father, Van Taylor, was still one of the wealthiest shipbuilders in Boston. And John Harper, Elli's husband, had been a successful merchant. When he died, he left her a spacious stone house in the North End. And if that wasn't enough, she owned a small shop just around the corner from their residence, where she sold lace and ribbons, silk and satin, catering to the finer tastes of Boston's wealthier women.

Ethan was a prisoner when Elli married Harper; he was still in the cane fields when John died of pleurisy eight years ago. He could convince himself that during his years on the plantation he had wished Elli happiness, knowing that she would not wait for him. But he couldn't deny that upon returning to Boston, and learning that she had been widowed, he immediately began to wonder if he might win back his first and only love.

At first, he refrained from contacting her, knowing that there was no point so long as he remained a pauper, a wretched convict without prospects. But once he had established himself as a thieftaker, he sought her out. The first several times he showed up at her door, Elli sent him away. He had concealed from her the fact that he was a conjurer and had humiliated her by being part of the *Ruby Blade* mutiny. She wanted nothing to do with him.

But one day, nearly a year after his return to Boston, he encountered Elli and her children in Faneuil Hall. It was the first warm day of spring, and Ethan was enjoying the sights, smells, and flavors of the market. His imprisonment felt like a distant memory. He greeted Elli jovially, but she remained distant and cold.

The children, however, eyed him with unconcealed fascination. They had no man in their lives save their aging grandfather; as far as they knew, neither did their mother. And yet, here was this strange man who spoke to their mother as if they were old friends. He bought them sweets over Elli's objections—thinking back on the day, he took no pride in this, but he had been alone in the city for too long and was desperate to insinuate himself into Elli's life. Before the day was over, he had wheedled an invitation to dinner—another memory that made him wince.

But by the time their meal together had ended, it was clear to both Ethan and Elli that the children adored him. What was more, Ethan was taken with them as well. He had always dreamed of having a boy, of raising a son the way he wished his father had raised him. And Clara, Holin's younger sister, was as beautiful, clever, and serious as her mother. How could Ethan not see in her the daughter he and Elli might have had together?

He and Elli struck a bargain. She would let him into their lives, allow him to be a friend to the children, but under two conditions. First, he was never to reveal to either child that he was a conjurer. And second, he was to forswear forever his love for her.

The first was a trifle; the second was almost more than he could bear. In the end, though, he decided that having this small role in their lives was preferable to having none at all.

Since that time, he had visited with them often. And if being with the children meant he could spend a few hours with Elli, too, all the better. But until this day, his friendship with them had never endangered Clara's life or Holin's.

As they walked the boy prattled on, relating some story one of his friends had told him. Ethan barely listened, his mind still churning over his latest encounter with Sephira's toughs. That is, until something the boy mentioned caught his attention.

". . . Both of them dead like that. One of them still as could be, the other kicking like an Irishman doing a jig. Had to be a ghost."

"Wait," Ethan said, halting. They were standing in the shadow of the Old North Meeting House, not far from the ruin of Thomas Hutchinson's home. The dogs had abandoned them; probably they were heading back to Henry's shop. A few people still milled about in front of the lieutenant governor's house, but otherwise the street was relatively empty. "Two people dead? This was today?"

Holin stared back at him as if he were a madman. "No! This was a long time ago. I told you: that couple who were hanged for mistreating their children."

"The Richardsons?"

Holin's face brightened. "Aye, that was the name. The Richardsons."

"And why were you telling me about them?"

The boy's expression hardened once more in a way that reminded Ethan of Marielle. "Like I said, their son just started working the wharf with Rory and me."

"And this boy was telling you about the hangings . . . ?"

Holin looked as if he might smack Ethan in the middle of the forehead. "Of course not! Rory was. He was there the day John's parents swung. He saw it. Said the man danced and danced when the rope went tight, but she didn't move at all."

Ethan nodded. He had no idea who Rory was, but he didn't dare risk angering the boy further by asking. At least now, what Holin was telling him made sense. He started walking again, and Holin joined him.

"You get it now?" the boy demanded, plainly still irritated.

"Yes," Ethan said quietly. "I'm sorry. I was distracted."

"You're so much like Mother it . . ." He broke off, his face flushing. Elli would never have mentioned to either child that she and Ethan had ever been anything more than acquaintances, and out of respect for what he assumed her wishes to be, Ethan, too, had said nothing about their past. But Holin and Clara both were intelligent and observant. They had to know.

"I'm sorry," Ethan said, breaking an awkward silence. "I should have been listening more closely."

"You were still thinking about Sephira Pryce?"

"Aye."

"That man killed a friend of yours, didn't he?"

Ethan faltered, falling behind the boy for just an instant. "What makes you say that?"

"I overheard what you were saying. I'm sorry, Ethan." Holin kept his gaze fixed on the cobblestones, as if fearful of looking up and finding Ethan's eyes upon him. "I knew what he was telling you, and I saw how you reacted."

Ethan wasn't sure what to say. Elli wouldn't want him to tell Holin the truth, but the boy was right. He was fifteen. By showing up when he did, he might well have saved Ethan's life, either by keeping Nigel from killing him, or by preventing Ethan from dooming himself with a killing burst of power. He deserved an honest answer.

"They killed a man whose life I had spared," Ethan finally said. "He had stolen some jewels, and the merchant who hired me wanted me to have him arrested when I got the gems back. Failing that, he wanted me to kill him."

"Why didn't you?"

Ethan glanced his way. The boy was watching him, looking pale and young, and a bit frightened.

"British justice can be hard—harder than I felt this man deserved. And it's no trifle taking a life. I didn't think he deserved to die. I took the jewels, I took his weapons, and I told him to leave the city." Ethan shrugged. "He didn't. Not in time, at least."

"So Miss Pryce killed him to make the merchant happy?"

"Sephira killed him because she knew it would make me angry, and because she wanted me to know that she's watching what I do."

Holin said nothing.

"Your mother wouldn't have wanted me to tell you that. She would have preferred that I lie to you this one time, tell you something that would be less likely to . . . to trouble you."

"You mean scare me."

"Are you scared?" Ethan asked. By now they were on Charter Street, approaching Elli's house. But they stopped short of it and stood facing each other.

Holin considered this. "I'm afraid for you," he said at length. "It sounds like Sephira Pryce is your enemy, and I think that could be dangerous."

Ethan smiled, thinking in that moment that Holin would grow up to be a wise man. "It probably is," he admitted. "But that ship's long since put out to sea."

"Well," Holin said, "you don't have to worry about me telling Mother."

"Thank you."

Holin hesitated a moment. Then, "You ever seen a man hang?"

Too many times. He had seen prisoners hanged in the West Indies, and he had seen enemy soldiers hanged during the war. "More than once," he said. "And I can tell you that some dance, and some don't. It's all in the way the rope snaps tight. It's nothing to do with spirits."

"You're sure?"

Ethan gently laid a hand on the boy's shoulder. "I'm sure."

The door to the house opened and Clara stepped outside, her dark hair tied back from her face to reveal a smooth high forehead.

"It *is* Holin," she called over her shoulder. "And Ethan's with him."

"Good evening, Clara," Ethan said, smiling at her, even as he surreptitiously sheathed his blade.

She smiled back but didn't say anything. A moment later, her mother appeared behind her, her expression severe. Elli wore her hair just as Clara did, so that it accentuated her high cheekbones and the graceful curve of her neck.

"Why are you with him?" she asked, her voice as cold as her eyes. "Has something happened?" And then, before he could answer, "Where did you get all those bruises? What have the two of you been doing?"

"I'm fine," Ethan said pointedly. "Thank you for asking." He paused, hoping to see some sign that she regretted speaking to him as she had. He was surprised to see a bit of color warm her cheeks. "The bruises are from yesterday," he said. "They had nothing to do with your son. Holin and I ran into each other down by the harbor, and I offered to walk him home."

"Mother and I have made a pudding," Clara said. "There's plenty."

The look Elli gave her daughter would have made King George flinch, but the girl showed no sign of noticing.

"Thank you, Clara," Ethan said, his eyes flicking to Elli's face. "But I can't stay long."

Elli scowled, understanding from his words and quick glance that he wanted to speak with her. It had been years since they had been in love, but still she knew him as few people did. "All right then," she said, sighing. "You can come in for a moment or two."

Holin and Ethan ascended the low steps leading to the door and entered the house. It had been warm out on the street, but it was cooler inside. Candle flames reflected off the polished wood floor of the sitting room and the warm scent of that pudding Clara had mentioned made Ethan's stomach growl. He crossed to the empty hearth to wait for Elli.

"Holin, get out of those clothes," she said. "And Clara, darling, why don't you check on the pudding again."

"But, Mother, it's done."

"Yes, well, you can make certain it's still warm."

"Yes, Mother," Clara said in a flat voice.

Elli walked into the room but halted several feet from him. Ethan silently cursed himself for wishing that she would come closer. She had always been stunning—black hair, green eyes, olive skin—and the years had done nothing to diminish her beauty. But through all the time he had spent in the cane fields she had remained frozen in his mind as the young woman he had left at the wharves when the *Ruby Blade* sailed. To this day that memory lingered. When he dreamed of her, as he still did, though with ever less frequency, she looked just as she had that day twenty years ago.

Even now, after five years in Boston, he was still mildly surprised each time he saw her, though not by the small lines in the skin around her mouth and eyes, or the few narrow streaks of silver shining in her hair. Rather, it was the hardening of her beauty that gave him pause. He had to remind himself that she had borne these two children and a third who had died at birth; that she had lost a husband; and yes, that she had lost him as well. Difficult as it was to credit now, he knew that had pained her once.

She had always been reserved, slow to smile, and slower still to laugh. But the years had left her grave, and as remote as the moon.

"You look awful," she said, crossing her arms over her chest.

"I know."

He thought she might say more about his bruises, but she merely regarded him for another moment before saying, "You wanted to speak with me."

"It's about Holin. He tells me he's working at Hunt's Wharf."

"What of it?"

"I've learned of two murders that have been committed in the streets over the past several months," Ethan said, lowering his voice. "Both victims were young—one was older than the boy, the other younger. I think they're connected in some way, though I don't know how. But the point is, I want him to have a care as he walks through the city."

All the color drained from Elli's face. "You don't know who's doing it?"

"No. They've been killed with powerful spells, but beyond that I know nothing."

"God have mercy," she whispered.

"He mentioned a boy to me," Ethan said. "Rory?"

"Rory Harren," Elli said. "His father's a sailor on a merchant ship. Rory's a bit older, and he started at the wharf first; I didn't want to let Holin go down there at all, but with Rory working, too, I thought it would be all right."

"If they could walk home together in the evenings, I think they would be fine."

"But if this . . . this conjurer—"

"It would be harder to attack two." He hesitated, his mind going back over what he knew of Jennifer Berson, and what Pell had told him about the Brown boy. Two victims, both alone, but in the vicinity of large crowds. "He wants his victims isolated," Ethan said. "It's easier that way." He couldn't say how the insight came to him, but as soon as he spoke the words he knew it was true.

"All right," Elli said. "I'll make sure he goes down there with Rory."

"And comes back with him, too. Dusk is the more dangerous time."

"Of course." She still sounded frightened, but her cheeks had regained some of their color.

They stood in silence for a moment or two, until Ethan looked away, smiling self-consciously. "Your pudding is getting cold."

"Probably." She started to say something, stopped, biting her lip. "Clara is right," she told him at last. "There is plenty."

"Thank you," Ethan said. "But I think I should go. I'm . . . I'm working on something."

She nodded.

After another awkward moment, Ethan said, "Good-bye, Elli," and walked past her back toward the door.

Elli didn't turn, but as he pulled the door open she called, "Thank you for telling me."

"Tell them I said good-bye."

Then he was outside, descending the steps and striding back down the lane, eager to be out of the North End. The warm evening air felt good on his face, and he was breathing easier now that he was out of Elli's house.

He didn't love her anymore. He grew more certain of that every time he saw her. But he did desperately miss being in love with her. He had been happiest in those months before the *Ruby Blade* sailed, and during his years as a prisoner he had clung to the memory of that happiness the way a sailor lost amid the swells of an angry sea clings to a scrap of wood. There was a part of him that still feared letting go.

In that moment he wanted nothing so much as to go to the Dowser and see Kannice. He needed to tell her that he was fine and no longer being held by the sheriff. But with night falling, he had an engagement to keep with the illusory little girl of this conjurer he pursued. He started back toward the South End, drawing his knife once more and pushing up his sleeve. He didn't know what kind of spell might work against a conjurer as skilled as this one, but he wanted to be ready to try anything.

Ethan had faced skilled conjurers before, a few here in Boston in the years since his release from the plantation, and one or two from before his imprisonment. Only two years ago, he had tried and failed to bring to justice a speller who killed two merchants and attempted to murder another. The speller, Nate Ramsey, had sought to avenge his father, whom the merchants had cheated out of ship and fortune. Ramsey had been as potent a speller as any he had known; Ethan still dreaded the day when he might have to face the man again. But he was starting to believe that this conjurer who had summoned the ghostly girl Anna from thin air was even more skilled than Ramsey.

He cut himself and whispered, *"Veni ad me."* Come to me. The night air pulsed, and an instant later, Uncle Reg was striding beside him, grave and resolved.

They crossed over Mill Creek and cut south at Dock Square. Soon they were in the narrow lanes of the South End not far from the waterfront. The air had grown cooler, and a fine mist crept over the city from the harbor. Still Ethan walked, the ghost with him, and still he saw no sign of the little girl. The moon hung low in the east, nearly full, its glow muted by the haze.

They were less than a block from Ethan's home when he felt at last that same vague awareness of spellmaking. A moment later, he spotted her, standing in the street next to a darkened storefront. This time he noticed immediately all that had eluded him the previous night. The moonlight touched her clothing, but she cast no shadow, and her face glowed faintly as if lit from within. On the one hand this reassured him: There were limits to this conjurer's power and skill. On the other hand, seeing these flaws in the illusion made him wonder anew how he could have failed to notice them during their first encounter.

The girl marked his approach, a mischievous smile on her grimy face. "You came," she said, when he was within a few paces of her. "That was smart, Kaille." She gazed at the ghost beside him, looking him up and down for a moment before dismissing him with a flip of her hair. "He won't be of much use to you."

Uncle Reg bared his teeth at the girl, like a feral dog, but she didn't spare him another glance.

Ethan looked around, though he didn't expect the conjurer to allow himself to be seen.

"We're quite alone," the girl told him.

"I'll have to take your word on that."

"It's better this way, you know. You'll get the brooch, you'll get your money, and no one else will be harmed."

"I'm not sure that's true," he told her, still glancing up and down the street. The conjurer had to be watching them; perhaps if he could figure out his or her vantage point . . . "Abner Berson wants to see someone punished for his daughter's murder. He shouldn't be denied that comfort."

She smiled. "I agree."

"You agree?" She had his full attention now.

The smile lingered as she gestured for him to follow her. "Come with me. I'll take you to the brooch."

He didn't move. "What should I call you?" he asked.

"I told you last night," she said over her shoulder. "I'm Anna."

"I'm not talking to the illusion," he said, raising his voice and turning a slow circle in the lane. His gaze flicked from one darkened window to the next. "I'm talking to you. I'm talking to the person conjuring this child. I'm here, I'm ready to take the brooch. But I want to see you."

At last his eyes came to rest on the girl again. She was regarding him grimly, shaking her head. "I don't think so. Call me Anna, and leave it at that."

She started walking away again. Ethan and Uncle Reg had no choice but to follow. Walking after her, listening for footsteps other than hers—for the conjurer had managed to make her steps heard— Ethan began to wonder if his foe was so powerful that he could not only communicate through the girl, but also see and hear through her. If so, walking behind her gave him a moment's advantage.

His knife still in hand, Ethan cut his forearm, and muttered, "*Locus magi ex cruore evocatus.*" Location of conjurer, conjured from blood.

He felt the blood being drawn from the wound he had made. He felt power flowing through his veins and then out of his body. And then an instant later, he felt that same power whip back at him like the lash of a plantation driver. The force of it knocked Ethan back off his feet. He landed hard on the cobblestones, the air leaving his body as if someone had stepped on his chest.

The little girl didn't even break stride as she said, "Don't do that again, or you'll get worse."

So much for catching this conjurer off guard. Ethan got to his feet slowly, took a long breath, and followed her once more.

She led him southward, navigating the streets of the South End with the certainty of a chaise driver, until at last they were clear of the smaller streets and were walking past the pastureland at the southern edge of the city. They followed a lonely stretch of road past Rowe's Field, with its long, thick grass and old dried piles of cow dung.

"Where are we going?" Ethan asked.

The girl didn't answer. She didn't slow or glance back, but instead led him down Orange Street toward the Neck. Ethan wiped a sweaty palm on his breeches, wondering how he had been so foolish as to let her lure him out this far.

What truly amazed him, though, was that here in the open, where it would have been much more difficult for the conjurer to keep himself hidden, Ethan still saw no sign of anyone save the little girl. Her movements weren't as fluid or as natural; she looked less like a child and more like a puppet. It seemed this other speller found it harder to maintain control of the illusion from a distance. But Ethan took the fact that he could maintain it at all as further proof of just how deep his powers ran.

Anna didn't stop until they neared the town gate, at the end of the Neck. There were few houses or buildings. The breeze off the harbor had stiffened and the moon was higher, its glow brighter.

The girl stepped off the road and cut through the empty fields that lined the lane. The grass was wispy here, the ground more sand than soil. Anna led Ethan to the fortified wall that guarded this end of the Neck and pointed to a small bundle lying on the ground at the wall's base. "There," she said, her voice sounding as thin and hollow as a ghost's.

Ethan glanced around again, then stepped past her and bent to pick up the ball of cloth. It felt light, but he could tell right away that something substantial lay at its center. Peeling away the material, Ethan found a small jewel. He pulled a few strands of grass from the ground at their feet, but then paused, eyeing the girl.

"I'm going to summon a light," he said. "A simple living spell. Is that all right?"

Uncle Reg eyed him avidly, pleading with him to try a stronger spell against the girl. Ethan knew better than to make the attempt.

Anna nodded jerkily. "Just light. Nothing else."

"Right." Ethan held the grass in his hand and said, *"Lux ex gramine evocatus."* Light, conjured from grass.

A bright light, faintly tinged with green, kindled in the palm of his hand, consuming the grass as if it were a flame, but causing Ethan no pain. He held the light closer to the jewel and saw that it was oval in shape, rubies and diamonds set in gold, just as Jennifer Berson's servant had described. Turning it over, he saw the initials—CN—carved into the back.

"Well?" Anna asked him.

"It looks like the brooch Abner Berson hired me to find."

"That's because it is."

"How did you come by it?"

The girl smiled, or at least that was what Ethan thought the conjurer intended. The image wavered as though reflected on river waters, distorting her features.

"You have the brooch," she said. "Your inquiry is at an end."

Ethan shook his head. "I was hired to find this jewel. But I was also hired to find the person who took it and see to it that he or she is punished, for thieving and for murder."

"It is over, Kaille. Accept that, or die."

"It can't be over until—"

"Until the murderer is punished," the girl said, sounding bored. "I know. What you don't understand is that he has been punished. This matter is closed."

"Punished how?" Ethan demanded.

"He's dead."

Ethan shivered, feeling that cool wind wrap itself around his throat. "Who are you blaming for this?" he asked. "Who's dead?"

But of course he already knew what she would say.

This time her smile was unmistakable, and cruel. "Daniel Folter."

Ethan took a step back from her and found himself pressed against the rough stone of the town wall. "Folter couldn't have killed her."

"You don't know that. And neither will Berson."

"I do know it. Folter wasn't a conjurer."

She wavered again. After a moment Ethan realized it had been meant as a shrug. "So?" she said. "Why does that matter?"

"Jennifer Berson was killed by a spell!" Ethan said, his voice rising. "You can't blame Folter for this!"

"Prove it," the girl said, grinning like a demon.

"I will! I'll—" He stopped, realization crashing over him like a breaker in a winter storm.

Ethan let the light die away, wrapped his fist around the brooch, and strode past the girl.

"You're too late, Kaille," Anna called after him. "Folter is dead, and Berson will be all too willing to believe that he killed his daughter. There are even witnesses who saw him with Mackintosh's mob later that night."

Ethan spun around to look at her. "That's a lie! There couldn't be!"

The girl merely smiled.

Ethan started walking again. After a few more strides he broke into a run, though he knew it was no use. His limp would slow him, and the distance was too great.

She had lured him to the Neck not to kill him, but to keep him as far from King's Chapel as possible.

Chapter
ELEVEN

y the time he reached the gate to the chapel grounds, he was barely running at all. Pain from his bad leg radiated up into his groin and gut, and his breath came in great aching gasps. He stumbled up the path to the chapel entrance, pounded on the door with his fist, turned and slumped back against the wall of the building to wait for a response.

Before long the door opened.

"Yes, who's there?" A head poked out from the doorway, illuminated from below by a candle. The play of light and shadow exaggerated the size of his nose, the boniness of his face, and the sallow hue of his skin.

Ethan forced himself to stand and stepped out where the man could see him. Troutbeck started and backed away, his eyes growing wide.

"Who are you?"

"It's Ethan Kaille, Mister Troutbeck," he said, still breathing hard. "I'm sorry to have startled you."

"Mister Kaille," the minister said, the fear in his voice giving way to petulance. "What could you possibly want at this hour?"

"I need to speak with Mister Pell. Is he inside?"

Troutbeck's brow knitted, and for a moment Ethan thought the man would send him away. But then he walked back into the church, muttering "This way" as he went.

Ethan limped after him.

Candles placed at regular intervals illuminated the sanctuary, and several more had been lit on a sconce beside the altar, giving the interior of the chapel a welcoming glow much at odds with Troutbeck's demeanor. Ethan hadn't made it far into the church before the minister halted, forcing him to stop as well.

"Wait here. I'll summon him."

Ethan nodded, and as the curate hurried back toward the vestry, Ethan lowered himself gingerly onto the nearest pew. Leaning back, he closed his eyes, wishing he had thought to ask for a drink of water.

Moments later, he heard footsteps. Opening his eyes, he saw Pell striding toward him, concern etched on his young face. Troutbeck lurked at the back of the chapel, behind the pulpit. Ethan had no doubt that he would try to eavesdrop on their conversation.

"Mister Kaille," Pell said, licking his lips nervously. He glanced back at the curate. "I didn't expect to see you here. Certainly not at this hour."

"I know," Ethan said. He stood, tentatively putting weight on his bad leg. It very nearly gave out under him. He grabbed at the back of the pew in front of him to keep from toppling to the floor. "I need to see the body of Jennifer Berson again."

Pell shook his head. "You can't. She was buried this afternoon."

He couldn't say that he was surprised; Anna had all but told him as much. Still, he had to resist an overpowering desire to scream at the top of his lungs every curse he knew.

"Why?" he asked after a moment. "I thought it was customary to wait four days."

Pell glanced at Troutbeck again. "It is," he said. He motioned for Ethan to follow him and started toward the chapel entrance.

Ethan pushed away from the pew, stepped out into the central aisle, and hobbled after him, wincing with every step.

Pell waited for Ethan to catch up with him. "What have you done to your leg?"

"It's an old wound."

They walked out of the chapel into the cool night air and the silver glow of the moon, and made their way down the path into the churchyard. Ethan checked the street and the grounds, expecting to see the conjurer's girl or Sephira's henchmen. But aside from a pair of gentlemen walking past in earnest conversation, their shoes clicking on the cobblestones, the street was empty.

"Tell me about the girl," Ethan said.

Pell grimaced. "There's not much to tell. Her family demanded the funeral. We couldn't refuse. You didn't expect us to keep her here forever."

"No. But another day would have helped."

"Why?" the minister asked, dropping his voice. "What's happened?"

"What hasn't happened? I've been beaten, threatened, I've even been summoned to speak with Thomas Hutchinson himself."

"Hutchinson!" Pell repeated, sounding impressed. "What interest does he have in this?"

"He believes Jennifer Berson was killed by the same mob that destroyed his home."

"Is he right?"

Ethan shook his head. "It doesn't matter. The important thing is I have the brooch."

Pell's eyes widened. "You do? That's remarkable!"

"Actually, it's not. The conjurer who killed her wanted me to have it. He or she is assuming that once I've given it to the Bersons, they'll be satisfied."

"I don't understand," Pell said, shaking his head. "You've got the brooch, but you don't know who gave it to you?"

"Essentially, yes. It's too much to explain right now. But the conjurer wants me to believe that Berson's daughter was killed by a petty thief named Daniel Folter, who allegedly was part of the mob."

The minister frowned. "Folter," he repeated. "Why is that name so familiar?"

Could he really be this fortunate? "Is it possible," Ethan asked, "that you know his name because his body is lying in your crypt right now?"

"Yes!" Pell said. "I mean, no, he's not there. But that is how I know about him. He was brought here earlier this evening. Mister Troutbeck had me send the men who carried him to another church."

"Do you know which one?"

Pell shook his head. "No. But I can tell you there's no doubt as to how he died. He had been beaten and then stabbed several times. He looked a mess."

Of course. Sephira and her men had killed Folter; the conjurer was merely using his death to mask his own crimes.

"You don't believe Folter killed Jennifer Berson?" Pell asked.

"I know he didn't. He wasn't a conjurer. But now I can't prove it to anyone else, not even her father."

Before Pell could respond, Ethan heard someone approaching along the lane. He reached for his blade.

"It's all right," Pell said quietly. Then, in a louder voice, he called, "Good evening, Mister Caner."

The man walking toward the chapel paused in midstep, but then walked on. "Is that you, Trevor?"

"Yes, Reverend, sir."

"And who is that with you?"

"This is Ethan Kaille. He's the thieftaker Mister Troutbeck mentioned to you yesterday."

"Ah, yes," the rector said. By now he had joined them in the church-yard. Stopping before them, he extended a fleshy hand to Ethan. "A pleasure to make your acquaintance, Mister Kaille."

Ethan gripped the man's hand. "And yours, Mister Caner."

The rector was short and round, and even in the moonlight Ethan could see that he had a pleasant face. His mouth was shaped like a small bow and his eyebrows were bushy. He wore a wig of thick white curls in a style that had been current before Ethan sailed with the *Ruby Blade*, but not since.

"You've been looking into the matter of the Berson girl, is that right?" Caner asked.

"Yes, Reverend, sir."

"How goes your inquiry?"

"I believe I'm making some progress," Ethan said, choosing his words with care.

"Fine, fine. Glad to hear it. Terrible business." Caner stood a moment shaking his head slowly, his lips pursed, a frown creasing his brow. "Trevor," he said rather abruptly, "I wonder if you wouldn't mind leaving us, so that I might have a word in private with Mister Kaille."

Ethan saw his own surprise mirrored in the young minister's expression.

"Of course." He raised his eyebrows for just an instant. "Good night, Mister Kaille. I wish you continued success with your inquiry."

"Thank you, Mister Pell," Ethan said. "Good night."

After watching Pell enter the chapel, Caner faced Ethan again, his expression far less pleasant than it had been when first he joined them in the yard.

"Walk with me," he said, moonlight shining in his heavy-lidded eyes.

He didn't wait for Ethan to answer, but walked out of the chapel yard and up Treamount Street. Ethan followed.

"You're a danger to him," Caner said quietly, as Ethan caught up with him.

"Excuse me?"

"Don't look so surprised, Mister Kaille. I know who you are, and what you are. I know Trevor quite well. And you're a danger to him. What is more, you know this to be true."

"Mister Pell—"

"Mister Pell is hardly more than a boy. He sees you—a thieftaker—and he is intrigued, as any young man would be. But Trevor sees more than that. He sees a man who is known to have used the dark arts to solve mysteries. What could be more fascinating?"

They walked in silence for several moments, Ethan marshaling his thoughts, Caner watching him keenly.

"You know a great deal about me," Ethan said at last. "May I ask why that is?"

The minister smiled reflexively. "I remember the *Ruby Blade*, and as a man of God, I take note of the devil wherever he appears, no matter his guise."

"You believe me a servant of the devil?"

"An unwitting one, perhaps. A dupe, if you will. But yes. Through you, Satan would lure Trevor Pell into his service, and thus gain a foothold in our church."

"You don't seem to be afraid of me."

"I have faith in the Lord, and in His faith in me."

Ethan kept his eyes fixed on the road before him. "So do you intend to have me hanged for a witch?"

Caner shook his head. "No, Mister Kaille. I am at war with the forces of Hell, as is every man of God. As I say, I don't believe you to be a willing ally of Satan, and I see that you are doing work for good. If you can find Jennifer Berson's killer, that will be an act of mercy for her family. I see no need to destroy you." He paused. "That is, unless you insist upon bringing the devil into my church. Leave Trevor Pell alone, and you have nothing to fear from me."

"I think you exaggerate the influence I have over Mister Pell. He and I have spoken only a few times. And I assure you that I wish him no ill."

Caner halted, as did Ethan.

"I lease Mister Pell a room," the rector said. "Late last night he left our house, doing his best to go undetected. He came home sometime later. Do you know anything about where he might have gone?"

Ethan met the man's gaze. "Did you ask him?"

"I did not. To be honest, I think I already know. You may roam this city day and night, exposing yourself to every sort of wickedness, but men of the Church do not." He took a breath, straightened. "I'm telling you to leave him alone. I don't want him having anything to do with you."

"I've already told you that I have no control over Mister Pell. I've done nothing to corrupt him or put him in danger, and I never would."

"And his whereabouts last night?"

"You'll have to ask Pell."

Caner said nothing. After a moment, Ethan said, "Good night, Mister Caner," and turned to go.

"What were you doing at my chapel?" the minister asked.

Ethan faced the man once more, and sighed. "I heard a rumor that

Jennifer Berson had been buried. I was hoping I would find it wasn't true."

Caner's brow furrowed. "Why?"

"Because now I can't prove that she was killed by a conjuring, and the wrong man is going to be blamed for her murder."

The rector raised a hand to his mouth. "He's to be hanged?"

Ethan shook his head. "He's dead already."

Caner's forehead wrinkled again with puzzlement, but Ethan didn't bother to explain. He turned and hobbled away, leaving the minister to ponder what he had said.

This late in the evening, the streets of Boston were largely deserted. Ethan did cross paths with a man of the watch who called out the time and eyed Ethan warily as he walked past. But other than this fellow, and a few men far gone with drink, he saw no one.

When at last he entered the Dowser, he found it practically empty. Diver sat alone in the far corner, a cup of ale resting on the table in front of him. His nose was swollen and discolored, and his eyes were ringed with dark purple bruises. Seeing Ethan, he stood so quickly that he toppled his chair.

"Thank goodness!" Ethan heard from the bar.

Kannice stepped out into the great room, crossed to where he stood, and put her arms around him.

"I've been worried sick," she said.

"I'm fine," he told her, breathing in the scent of her hair. "They took me to see Hutchinson."

"Hutchinson?" Diver said, sounding impressed. "What did he want with you?"

"He wanted to make sure I knew that the same people who wrecked his house would have been capable of killing Jennifer Berson."

"Surely you haven't been with him all this time," Kannice said.

"No. After I left the Town House, I had another encounter with Sephira's men."

Diver walked toward them, looking from Ethan to Kannice. "And what did they want?"

"Sephira would like me to finish my inquiry and leave matters as they are," Ethan said. "Aside from that though, it was mostly the usual bluster." He should have told Diver about Folter, but he didn't want to speak of the matter in the middle of the tavern. "I would have come back here after speaking to Hutchinson, but her men chased me into the North End. And then Holin found me."

"Holin?" Kannice asked, her tone hardening a bit. "Marielle's boy?"

"I saw him home, and then kept an appointment with an illusion." He held her gaze, until finally he coaxed a reluctant smile. "If you feed me, I'll tell you all about it."

"I'm sure you will." But she was still smiling.

She went into the kitchen and reemerged a moment later with a bowl of dark stew that smelled of venison and red wine. She had bread for him as well.

He took the bowl from her, and after Kannice filled a tankard of ale for him, the three of them walked back to Diver's table. Ethan began to eat, and in between mouthfuls he told them about Anna and the brooch. He also told them of the other killing he had learned about from Pell. And finally, he told them about Daniel.

"Daniel was no conjurer," Diver said grimly, when Ethan had finally finished his tale. "He wasn't the smartest of men, and I wouldn't have lent him tuppence, but he wasn't a murderer, either."

Ethan sipped from his second ale. "I know. I won't allow him to be blamed for Jennifer's murder."

Diver stared back at him, his face a mess, his dark eyes demanding more.

"You have my word, Diver. I won't allow it."

His friend nodded at last, stood, and drained his ale. "I'll be going then," he said. "I'm glad you're all right, Ethan. I was worried about you." He chanced a look at Kannice. "Both of us were." And with that, he left.

Kannice and Ethan said nothing. Eventually Kannice took one of Ethan's hands in hers, but she just watched him, her eyes shining with the light of a dozen candles.

"I didn't intend to go to Marielle's home," Ethan finally said. "But with children being murdered in the streets, I wasn't about to let Holin walk home alone."

Kannice dropped her gaze to their hands, a sad smile on her face.

"You don't believe me."

"I believe you didn't intend to go there. But I also think that you'll find any excuse to see her."

She looked up at him once more, still smiling, as if she wished to soften what she had said.

"I don't love her," Ethan said. "I did once, but I don't anymore."

"Do you love me?"

The question hung between them. Ethan started to answer, then stopped himself. He wanted to tell her that he did. He knew that he cared about her more than he did anyone else in the world, and he wanted to tell her that. But it wasn't what she had asked.

The truth was Ethan didn't know if he could love anyone anymore. He had loved once and that love had been ripped from him, along with his freedom and his pride and his ambition. His heart had been lashed day after day, month after month, for more years than he cared to count. The scars remained; they had grown hard, like calluses on a worker's palm. He didn't think they would ever soften.

"What I feel for Marielle is similar to what I feel for my father," Ethan said.

Kannice raised an eyebrow.

"That sounded stranger coming out of my mouth than it did in my head," he told her, grinning briefly. "I have something to prove to her. I want her to see that I'm more than the young fool who got himself transported to the Indies. Just as I would want my father to see that if he was still alive."

Kannice shrugged. After a moment she nodded. "I can understand that. But I find it hard to believe that's all you feel when you're with her."

"You're right. I feel regret, and loss. Maybe I see the life that I might have led had things been different. But I don't care for her the way I care for you. I don't want to be with her."

"Well, that's the stew talking. And maybe the ale as well."

Ethan shook his head. "No," he said earnestly. "It's me."

She squeezed his hand gently, but said nothing.

Seeing the sadness that lingered in her eyes, Ethan cursed himself for not being able to say what she wanted to hear, for his inability to stay away from Elli and the children, even for his refusal to lie to Kannice by telling her that he did love her. At that moment he would have done just about anything to drive that pained look from her lovely face. But he knew her well enough to understand that the best thing he could do was tell her the truth and let her decide what she wanted.

"It's getting late," he said. "I should probably go."

"Probably." She still held his hand, and now she met his gaze. "You have too many people angry with you, Ethan. Sephira, this conjurer. Hutchinson will be angry if you don't do what he expects of you. Don't do anything stupid."

"You mean like take on a job for Abner Berson?"

Kannice didn't smile. "Just watch yourself. And don't be shy about showing your face here and letting me see that you're still alive."

He lifted her hand to his lips. "All right."

A short time later, Ethan left the tavern. The moon had vanished behind a bank of clouds and the wind off the harbor had freshened. Dressed only in his breeches, shirt, and waistcoat, he hunched his shoulders against the chill. He kept his hands thrust in the pockets of his breeches, one fist wrapped around Jennifer Berson's brooch.

With the moon hidden, the streets had grown dark and forbidding. Ethan couldn't keep himself from flinching at every vague shadow, every creak of a wooden door, every sudden gust of wind. He expected at any moment to see Yellow-hair or Greenleaf, or some conjured horror, emerging from the murky darkness. He strode through the streets as swiftly as his leg would allow, and only began to breathe easily again when he was back behind Henry's shop, stepping over the dogs who lay together at the base of his stairway. As soon as he was in his room he locked the door and lit several candles.

He undressed quickly, fell into bed without bothering to darken the room, and bundled himself in a woolen blanket. Exhausted as he was, he slept fitfully, and was awakened in the middle of the night by strange dreams of Sephira Pryce that left him both shaken and aroused. Eventually he fell asleep once more and didn't awake again until morning. But he felt no more rested than he had when he went to bed.

He climbed out of bed, still sore; relieved himself, ate a small breakfast—bread, cheese, some water—and dressed. A light rain was falling as he left his room, so he threw on his coat and made his way out onto Water Street. There were still an unusual number of laborers and wharf men in the lanes, and Ethan wondered if Diver had again been turned away from work.

He didn't ponder this for long, though. He had come to a decision overnight. He needed help. He had no intention of ending his inquiry, but for now Sephira and the conjurer who had summoned Anna out of air and light didn't know that for certain. He could evade them for a time, but eventually—probably within a day or two—they would figure out what he was doing and track him down. He had to find Jennifer Berson's murderer. To do that he needed to know more about the spell that had been used to kill her and, if Mister Pell was right, to kill that child who died on Pope's Day.

There were perhaps thirty other active conjurers in Boston. No doubt there were far more than that who had conjurers' blood in their veins, but many of his kind did all they could to avoid notice. People were still burned and hanged as witches throughout New England; fear of discovery ran deep among conjurers, and those who didn't have access to power tended to shun those who did. Because of his profession and because of the *Ruby Blade* mutiny, Ethan might well have been the second-best-known conjurer in Boston. The most famous of the city's spellers was an old woman named Tarijanna Windcatcher, who made her living as a tavernkeeper and a self-described marriage smith.

She ran a bar that catered to the few sorcerers who openly roamed the streets of Boston, and she found matches for men and women who despaired of ever finding love on their own. Janna made no secret of the fact that she was a conjurer, and those who paid for her services assumed that she used her powers to find matches for them. Ethan had once asked her if this was in fact true. Janna refused to answer.

She came from one of the islands of the Caribbean—Ethan didn't know which one. She was orphaned at sea as a small girl and rescued by a ship that had sailed from Newport. Janna was African, and Ethan didn't know how she managed to avoid being taken as a slave. He had heard rumors of a romance, years before, between Janna and a wealthy

Newport shipbuilder who couldn't marry her because of her race, but did provide for her so as to secure her freedom for the rest of her life. He didn't know how much of this was true, but she had managed to remain free and eventually, after finding her way to Boston, to buy herself the tavern, such as it was. At some point, having no memory of her family name, she took the name Windcatcher. She claimed there was no significance to it; she just liked the way it sounded.

She sold the usual drinks in her tavern, as well as stews, meat, and bread—nothing compared with Kannice's fare, but passable. But she also sold herbs and oils, rare stones and talismans, ancient texts about spellmaking and blades, incense, and spirits used in rituals. In short, anything that sorcerers might find useful for conjuring. Ethan usually fueled his spells with blood or leaves found here in the city. But on those few occasions when he needed something different, he always went to Janna.

Ethan followed Orange Street out past the pastures and fields, and overgrown paddocks that seemed to have been neglected for years. None of the houses out this way looked particularly sturdy, though few looked as fragile as Janna's. Gulls sat atop the town gate in the distance, ghostly forms in the silvery mist, their cries echoing off stone and wood.

Janna's tavern, the Fat Spider, stood at the corner of Orange and Castle Streets, within sight of Amory's Stillhouse, and not far from where Anna had taken him the night before. The building always appeared to Ethan to be one strong gust of wind away from toppling over. It leaned heavily to one side and its roof sagged dangerously in the middle. The placard on her door read, "T. Windcatcher, Marriage Smith. Love is Magick." Ethan laughed every time he saw it. Janna might as well have climbed on to the roof of her tavern and screamed "I'm a conjurer!" as loud as she could.

The Spider was warm within, and it smelled of woodsmoke and roasted fowl, clove and cinnamon. The stub of a single candle burned on the bar, but the place was empty. Ethan walked to the middle of the room and called Janna's name. After a moment, he heard the scrape of a chair on the floor overhead, and slow footsteps leading to the top of the stairway.

"Who that?" a woman's voice called.

"It's Ethan Kaille, Janna."

The woman muttered something that he couldn't hear, though he could tell from her voice that she wasn't happy he had come. Still, she descended the stairs, which creaked loudly with each step she took.

She wore a simple linen dress of ivory and a brown woolen shawl wrapped around her bony shoulders. Her skin was the color of dark rum; her hair, which she wore so short that it barely concealed her scalp, was as white as the moon on a winter night. She had a thin, wrinkled face, and dark eyes that were as alert and fierce as a hawk's. As always, she carried a cup of Madeira wine; Ethan had never seen her without one.

"Kaille," she said, scowling at the sight of him. "Thought you was a customer."

"Sorry, Janna."

Her expression didn't change but she waved him toward the bar. "Well, you here, so you might as well sit an' drink with me."

She poured him a cup of Madeira, and then he followed her to the hearth, where a fire burned. They sat at a small table and Ethan sipped his wine, which Janna had watered quite a bit. He shouldn't have been surprised. Given how much she drank, undiluted Madeira would have left her broke and soused.

"You come for a healin' tonic?" she asked, sitting forward in her chair and eyeing his battered face.

Ethan chuckled, though once more he wished that he could have healed himself without raising the suspicions of Henry, Derne, and others. "No."

"Who did that t' you?"

"Who do you think?"

Her expression turned stony. "Sephira Pryce."

Janna didn't really like anybody. She tolerated Ethan because he was a conjurer, and she could be charming at times when her work demanded it. But she treated strangers with contempt, and wasn't much nicer to people she knew. Aside from a scrawny black dog that occasionally came by her place, she had no friends that Ethan knew of. Still, there was no one in the world she hated more than Sephira Pryce. That she and Ethan shared this probably explained why she helped him with his work, despite knowing there was little profit in it for her.

Ethan wasn't sure why she hated the Empress of the South End so much. He had no reason to think that the two had ever met, much less had dealings. A year or two before, Janna mentioned that Sephira had once cost her a substantial amount of money. Ethan never learned exactly what happened, but he knew that if he managed to convince Janna that she could hurt Pryce by helping him, she would tell him whatever he wanted to know, regardless of whether he paid her.

"She's a wicked woman," Janna said, shaking her head and sounding so bitter one might have thought that Sephira had beaten her.

"You'll get no argument from me."

Janna shook her head a second time and leaned back in her chair. "So, no healin' tonic. You finally gonna let me fix you a love tonic for that woman o' yours?"

Ethan shook his head, knowing that she meant Elli. "No, thank you."

"Wouldn' take much. Where there's a past, th' love is easier t' coax back."

"What I need is information, Janna."

She dismissed him with a wave of her thin hand. "You always need information. There's no coin in that for me."

Usually this was where Ethan pulled out a few shillings and put them on Janna's table. Already she was casting furtive looks his way. Ethan took another sip of wine and returned her stare.

"You're right," he said. "This time there's no money. Maybe there will be if you're able to help me, but I haven't got any right now. Sephira took every coin I had."

"Why she so mad at you all o' sudden?"

"A rich man hired me, and she wanted the job for herself."

Janna laughed delightedly, exposing sharp yellow teeth. "Good for you, Kaille!" She laughed some more, shaking her head slowly.

"I need your help, Janna. There's a conjurer in the lanes who's killed twice now: a young woman a few nights ago, and a little boy last fall."

Her expression grew serious. "I heard talk o' this."

"What did you hear?"

"Not much. I heard o' th' killin's. That's all."

"His latest victim was Jennifer Berson."

"Her father's th' rich man?"

Ethan nodded, reached into his coat pocket, and pulled out the small bundle containing Jennifer's brooch. "This is what was taken from her."

Janna took the bundle and unwrapped it, whistling at the gem. "Nice," she said. "Cut yourself, an' put some blood on it."

Ethan hesitated.

"I'm too old t' be cuttin' myself for your jobs."

He did as she instructed.

Janna muttered something under her breath and an instant later, there was a small flash of blue light round the brooch. But that was all. The glow vanished as quickly as it had come. Ethan thought he glimpsed a pale blue figure standing off to the side, but by the time he turned to look, it had vanished. Janna stared at the gem for a moment, and then frowned.

"Nothin'," she said, handing the brooch back to him. "You have somethin' else?"

"No. But I saw her body. There wasn't a mark on her. I knew that a conjuring had killed her, and so I tried a revealing spell."

"And?"

He frowned. "And I didn't learn anything. I thought the glow would pool at the spot where the spell struck her, and I thought it would reveal the color of the conjurer's power, but . . ." He shook his head. "I suppose my spell didn't work, or whoever killed her managed to conceal his conjuring."

Janna sat forward once more. "Why? What did you see?"

"Her entire body glowed. The effect of the conjuring didn't seem to be concentrated anywhere."

Her dark eyes narrowed. "And what color did you see?"

"Silver, like starlight. There was really no color at all."

"Damn," Janna muttered. She sat back again, scratching her forehead.

"What is it, Janna?"

"This speller might o' concealed th' color o' his power, but tha's all. You saw just what you were supposed t' see."

"I don't understand."

"That 'cause you're not thinkin', Kaille. You're assumin' that she was killed by a spell." Janna shook her head. "She wasn't. She was killed *for* a spell."

It made so much sense that Ethan's first reaction was to be furious with himself for not realizing this on his own. His second was to be horrified.

Conjurers generally spoke of three kinds of casting. Elemental spells, the simplest, were fueled by one of the elements—fire, water, earth, even air. Living spells, which were more difficult and more potent, demanded blood or hair, leaves or bark—anything that came from a living creature or plant. All the conjurers Ethan knew relied exclusively on elemental and living spells.

But there was a third kind of conjuring, though some said it was merely a type of living spell taken to its most dangerous extreme: killing spells. Some called such conjurings sacrifice spells, but it was the same thing. A killing spell had to be fueled by the death of a living creature; any creature, though most powerfully by the death of a human. For a conjurer willing to take a human life there were few limits to what castings could accomplish. A living spell might draw a cup of water from the ground. A death spell could bring rainstorms to an entire countryside. A living spell could be used to murder a man. A killing spell could wipe out hundreds.

The real question, though, as Janna would have been the first to remind him, was not what *could* killing spells do, but what *had* they done in these two instances?

"This conjurer would have t' be workin' some mighty spells," Janna said, breaking a lengthy silence. "Somebody'd notice."

"You would think. You ever used a killing spell, Janna?"

"Killed a goat once. For a love spell, I think it was. Some wealthy man wanted a girl, an' she didn' wan' him. Took all th' power I've got."

"Did it work?" Ethan asked.

Janna glared at him. "All my spells work." After a moment, she gave a small jerk of her head, pointing at him with her chin. "What about you? You ever use a killin' spell?"

Ethan shook his head. "No, never. I went a long time without conjuring at all—when I was a prisoner—and I'm not as accomplished at casting as I should be. To be honest, the more powerful conjurings scare me."

"They should. Spellmakin's nothin' t' play at."

"Have you heard anything? You usually know what's going on in the lanes, especially if there's conjuring involved."

She regarded him sourly. "You still not offering money?"

"I still don't have any," he said, chuckling. He quickly grew serious again. "You said it yourself, Janna. This conjurer would have to be casting some pretty potent spells. Dangerous ones, and not just for the people he's killing. If you know anything, you need to tell me."

It was like getting a street urchin to admit that he had stolen from a peddler. "It's not much," she said after a long time, sounding annoyed that he was making her tell. "Might not be anythin' at all."

"Let me be the judge of that."

"It's been a while now. This was back in the fall."

"On Pope's Day?" Ethan asked.

"Before then," she said, clearly irritated by the interruption. "It was th' day those two people got themselves hanged."

"The Richardsons?"

"Yeah, that's them. The ones who didn' take care o' their little ones."

For close to a year, since their hanging in October, Ethan hadn't given a thought to Ann and John Richardson. Now they had come up in conversation twice in two days. Odd. And perhaps important.

Janna pointed toward the southern end of the Fat Spider. "Their hangin' was right over there," she went on. "Right by th' town gate. Big crowd came t' watch. An' that day, right in th' middle o' the hangin' I felt a spell. A strong one," she said, her brow wrinkling. "Stronger even than I can do. I'd bet everything I got that it was another killin' spell. Nothin' else feels like that."

"And the victim?" Ethan asked.

"That's just it," Janna said, shaking her head. "They never found one. I didn' tell anyone, 'cause I don' need that kind o' trouble, if you know what I mean. But so far as I know, they never found anyone."

"Maybe it wasn't a person."

"Thought o' that," Janna said. "But a spell that strong . . ." She shrugged.

"So you think he's killed three times, not two."

"And tha' means he's cast three powerful spells. You find out wha' those spells did, an' you'll find your speller."

Ethan considered this. There had been times when he'd wondered if Janna wasn't a bit mad, but there could be no disputing her logic in this instance. She was right; the spells were everything.

He drank a bit more of the watery Madeira, then placed his cup on the table and stood.

"Thank you, Janna," he said. "Next time I come I'll make sure to have a few shillings in my pocket."

"You do that," she said without a trace of humor.

He started for the door.

"Wait." Janna stood, walked behind the bar, and stepped into a back room. Ethan peered into the small room, wondering what she wanted with him. When at last she reemerged, she carried a small cloth pouch, which she handed to him.

It was light, and held some sort of leaf, an herb of some kind, with a sharp, unpleasant smell.

"That's mullein," Janna said. "Powerful protection."

It was more than that. Mullein might have been the most potent of all warding herbs used by conjurers. It strengthened all spells, but it was especially effective as a shield against hostile conjurings. It could also be added in small amounts to tonics for coughs and fevers, and in poultices for wounds. This was as generous a gift as he had seen Janna give to anyone. Perhaps she liked him more than he thought.

"Thank you, Janna," Ethan said. "I owe you. When I have some money . . ."

She shook her head.

"Never mind that. You watch yourself, Kaille," she said. "Between this speller and Sephira Pryce, you got some nasty folk wishin' you harm."

As if I need Janna to tell me that. "Again, thank you."

"Now, go. I got things t' do." She softened the words with a rare smile.

Ethan grinned back and let himself out.

TWELVE

E than stepped onto the filthy, rain-slicked lane and started back toward the center of the city. He needed to return the brooch to Abner Berson and ask the merchant if he wanted Ethan to continue his inquiry. Ethan didn't wish to end it before he found Jennifer's killer, but Berson hired him to find the brooch, as both Yellow-hair and the ghostly girl, Anna, had reminded him. He had done that. It was up to Berson to tell him to continue or desist.

As he walked, he tried to think of what connections might exist between the Richardson hanging, the Pope's Day parades, and the assault on Thomas Hutchinson's house. All three events had drawn large crowds, many of them, no doubt, the "rabble" of which Hutchinson had spoken.

Ebenezer Mackintosh had led the South Enders on Pope's Day, and he also had incited the mob to riot two nights ago. Ethan wouldn't have been surprised to learn that he had been at the hanging, too. Hundreds had converged on the Neck that day to watch the notorious pair swing, and many had pelted the Richardsons with stones before the couple died. It was, he thought, just the sort of event to which Mackintosh and his faithful would have flocked. But he had never heard anything to indicate that the self-styled Commander of the South End was a conjurer, much less one as skilled as the speller who had created Anna.

Janna was right. It wasn't enough simply to know that these killing spells had been cast. He needed to know what the conjurings had done, what evil the lives of this villain's victims had purchased.

For that much he did know. Whatever power the killer had drawn from Jennifer Berson's death and the deaths of his other two victims must have been dark. Such was the nature of killing spells, Janna's "love spell" not withstanding. A conjurer willing to murder for a casting would do anything, destroy anyone, in pursuit of whatever wicked purpose drove him. This conjurer had to be found and destroyed.

Sephira wouldn't be happy; unless somehow Ebenezer Mackintosh proved to be the greatest conjurer in all the colonies, neither would Thomas Hutchinson. And once the conjurer realized that Ethan hadn't ended his inquiry, he would come after him, too. Ethan didn't care. He knew that no one else could stand against this monster.

So resolved, Ethan arrived at the Berson home. William greeted him at the door and had him wait, dripping wet, in the entrance hall while he fetched the master of the house. A few moments later, Berson strode into the hall and led Ethan back to the study where they had spoken a few days before. Berson looked much the same as he had during their previous meeting, although perhaps the rings under his eyes were a bit more pronounced, his wig powdered with slightly less care. These past few days would have taken their toll on the man and his family.

"You have news for me?" the merchant asked when he and Ethan were seated by the hearth.

Ethan pulled the bundle containing the brooch from his pocket and held it out for Berson to take. The man hesitated, his gaze flitting from Ethan's face to the package in his hand. Taking it at last, he unwrapped it with trembling hands. He let out a soft cry at the sight of the brooch and took a ragged breath. Tears ran down his cheeks.

"Thank you, Mister Kaille. You probably think me foolish, but I take some comfort in seeing this again."

"I think I understand, sir," Ethan said softly, keeping his gaze lowered.

"You've found the person who killed her, then?"

"No, sir."

"But you know who did it. You must."

Ethan shook his head.

"I don't understand," Berson said, staring down at the jewel lying in his thick palm. "How did you come by this?"

Ethan wasn't sure how much to tell the merchant. It was one thing to tell Janna about the spells he had cast and the conjurer he had been pursuing. It was quite another explaining this to someone who wasn't a conjurer himself, who probably feared such power and wanted nothing to do with those who wielded it. But in the end he decided that Berson deserved to hear everything. He told the man about both of his encounters with Anna, even going so far as to repeat her claim that Daniel Folter had killed Jennifer.

"And you're quite sure that this Folter fellow didn't kill her?" Berson asked when Ethan had finished.

"That's right. I know for a fact that Daniel wasn't a conjurer."

Berson looked up from the brooch. "You say he 'wasn't' a speller. Does that mean . . . he's . . . ?"

"He's dead. He was killed just yesterday. This conjurer told me—speaking through the girl I mentioned—that he wants me to stop looking for your daughter's killer. He threatened to kill me if I don't."

"I understand, Mister Kaille. I'm grateful to you for retrieving her brooch. You told me the other night that you didn't usually take jobs that involved murder. You've done more than I could have expected." He pushed himself out of his chair with a great effort. "I'll pay you, and you can be free of this matter."

"Actually, sir," Ethan said, standing as well, "I don't think you do understand. I'm not asking your permission to end my inquiry. I'm asking that you allow me to continue it."

The merchant couldn't have looked more surprised if Ethan had asked to lease a room in the house. "You want to go on with this?"

"I believe your daughter was killed for a larger, even more sinister purpose. I won't burden you with details about conjuring and how my kind do what we do, except to say that there are spells so evil they require power drawn from human sacrifice. I believe your daughter died so that this conjurer could cast such a spell."

"May God save us all," the man whispered, actually recoiling from Ethan. "Can you prove this?"

Ethan shook his head. "No."

"But then how——?"

For several moments, Ethan refused to look at the merchant. At last, chancing a quick glance, he saw that Berson's face had drained of all color.

"You needed . . . you needed her . . . her corpse, didn't you?"

"Yes, sir," Ethan said, his voice low.

"Damn. I didn't consider that. I just . . . the thought of her lying there in the crypt . . . My wife couldn't take it anymore. The customary four days just felt like too long a time."

"I understand, sir."

"You're kind, Mister Kaille. But I've made this harder for you. So, what can I do to make up for it?"

"You can refrain from telling anyone what I'm doing," Ethan said. "If someone asks, even a member of your household, tell them you're satisfied that I've learned everything I can about Jennifer's murder, that Daniel Folter is responsible for her death, and that as far as you're concerned the matter is closed."

"Even people within my home?" Berson asked. "Surely my wife——"

Ethan raised a hand. "Please, sir. I'm not going to lie to you. I fear this conjurer, not least because I don't know who he is. I'm sure your wife wouldn't knowingly do anything to jeopardize the inquiry or my life. But I would feel safer if we could keep this matter between the two of us."

"All right," Berson said soberly. "Can I do anything else?"

Ethan felt heat rising in his cheeks. "To be honest, you can." He gestured at his face. "The people who gave me these bruises took every coin I had, including the money you gave me. I managed to pay for my lodgings before they got to me, but I have no coin for food or anything else."

Berson smiled and dug into his pocket for the change purse Ethan had seen the other day. "Of course, Mister Kaille. Will five pounds be enough?"

"Two would be enough, sir."

"Well, I'll give you five anyway." The merchant handed him the coins. "Considering all you've done on our behalf and what you have endured to retrieve the brooch, it's the least I can do."

Berson led him back to the entrance hall and pulled open the door. He glanced behind him and said in a booming voice, no doubt so the others would hear, "Well, Mister Kaille, I'm grateful to you for finding my daughter's brooch and putting this matter to rest. Best of luck to you."

"Thank you, sir," Ethan said, gripping the merchant's proffered hand.

Berson winked at him and said in a low voice. "May the Lord keep you safe, Mister Kaille. I'll look forward to our next conversation."

Ethan nodded and left the house, thinking that for all the complaining he heard in the Dowser about wealthy men and their ways, Abner Berson struck him as no less kind or honorable than anyone living in one of Boston's more modest quarters.

Reaching the end of the broad stone path in front of Berson's house, Ethan stepped out into Beacon Street, and immediately found himself face-to-face with Nigel, who looked as wet and bedraggled as an over-large hound. Ethan took a step back, intending to run, but then thought better of it. If there was one of them, there were probably five. Ethan had no doubt that Sephira's toughs had him trapped. Instead, he pulled out his blade and pushed up the sleeve of his coat.

"No need for that," Nigel said in a low drawl. "She jus' wants a word."

"Right," Ethan said. "If you don't mind, I'll keep my blade out anyway."

Nigel merely shrugged and started walking away. "Follow me," he said, not even bothering to look back.

Ethan hesitated, then followed. Gordon and Nap fell in step beside him, seeming to materialize out of nowhere. He heard footsteps trailing him as well.

"Do you all live together, too?" Ethan asked, glancing at the two men walking with him.

Gordon glowered at him but said nothing. Nap chuckled.

The toughs escorted him east and then south, past King's Chapel and the Old South Church toward the more open lands around d'Acosta's Pasture. At last, they came to a large house on Summer Street that stood only a short distance from the soaring wooden steeple of the New South Church. This wasn't considered the most desirable place to live in Boston—that would have been back where the Bersons had their home. It wasn't even the best street of the South End. But it was a good neighborhood nevertheless, and far better than Sephira Pryce deserved.

The house, Ethan had to admit, appeared from the street to be tasteful and elegant. It was large and constructed of the same white marble used to build the Berson home, but it wasn't as ostentatious as Ethan would have expected the Empress of the South End's home to be.

The men escorted Ethan up a cobbled path to the door. Nigel knocked once, and at a faint response from within pushed the door open. Ethan started to enter, but Nigel put out a massive arm to block his way.

"Yar knife," he said, holding out his other hand.

Without his blade, Ethan would be at a distinct disadvantage in any confrontation with Sephira and her men. "I don't think so."

"Then ya're not goin' in."

"Fine with me."

"You have my word, Ethan," came Sephira's voice from within the house. "You'll be safe. Maybe not the next time we meet, but for now, no harm will come to you."

He had to admit that he was now curious. He took a breath, handed Nigel the knife, and stepped inside.

The interior of the house was far more ornate than the exterior, though again Ethan was surprised and a little disappointed to discover that Sephira had refined taste. A small entrance hall with a white tile floor and colorful wall tapestries led into a vast common room that was well furnished and brightly lit with bay-scented candles. The rugs covering the dark wooden floor were colorful without being tawdry, and they matched the tapestries. Ethan thought it likely that the rugs and tapestries came from the Orient. Everywhere he looked he saw paintings and sculptures, and though he didn't pretend to know much of such things, he couldn't help but be impressed by the quality of every piece.

"In here," she called to him from a chamber to the left of the common room.

He followed her voice into a study that was similar in size to the

Berson library. But where Abner Berson's room had been filled with volumes, this chamber was filled with blades. Swords of every imaginable shape and size hung from the walls. There were scimitars from the Holy Land, their hilts studded with a galaxy of gems, and austere bastard swords that might well have come from the Scottish Highlands. There were fine long blades that had to have been made on the Iberian Peninsula, and one short sword that appeared to have been forged entirely from solid gold.

"That one was made by the Turks," Sephira said, seeing where his gaze lingered. "Would you like to hold it?"

Ethan shook his head, glancing her way before crossing to a small glass case at the far end of the room. This was filled with a variety of firearms. They were all hand weapons, mostly of the flintlock variety, but there were older pistols as well—wheel locks and at least one matchlock that might also have been from the Orient. Each was as unique as the blades adorning the walls. One had a grip of carved ivory, another of some polished, light-grained wood Ethan didn't recognize, and still another of what Ethan guessed was solid silver.

Beside this case stood yet another that held daggers and dirks. As with the swords and pistols, Ethan could scarcely believe the diversity of Sephira's collection. Forced to guess, he would have said that there were blades and firearms in this room from every continent, and from nearly every country in Europe.

After gazing at the smaller blades for some time, Ethan turned to Sephira, a thousand questions on his tongue. But seeing how she watched him, the calculation in those cold blue eyes, Ethan swallowed them all and chided himself for allowing her to distract him in this way. He was like a little boy, too easily enthralled with sweets and shiny toys.

Looking at Sephira—at how she was dressed and how her hair had been styled—he also understood that the blades and pistols hadn't been the only things meant to entice. Ethan had never seen her in a gown, and he doubted he ever would. But while she was still dressed in the garb of the streets, her clothes this day were more feminine than usual. Instead of breeches, she wore a long black skirt. Her silk blouse, open at the neck, and the black silk waistcoat she wore over it both fit her closely, accentuating the curves of her body. A sapphire pendant hung from a silver necklace, drawing Ethan's eyes where they already wished to go. Her hair spilled down her back in dark ringlets, and even from across the room, Ethan could smell her perfume.

She smiled, perhaps seeing more in his gaze than he wished to reveal. "You like my collection?" she said, sauntering over to where he stood.

"I have to admit I do. That curved blade near the back, the one with the ebony hilt, that's from India, isn't it?"

"Why, Ethan, I had no idea you knew so much about knives." She sounded genuinely surprised.

"I once had a small collection myself. Nothing like this, but I spent a number of years as a sailor and a soldier, and I traded for a few keepsakes along the way."

"And where is this collection now?"

"I have no idea. I haven't seen them since I was taken to Barbados nineteen years ago." He faced her, his eyes locking on hers. "Why am I here, Sephira?"

"You're my guest," she said, laughing and purring at the same time. She took his hand. "What would you like to do?"

He disentangled his fingers from hers. "I'd like to leave."

She offered that same little pout he had seen in his room a few days before. He glanced around quickly, half expecting Nigel to be there, his fist raised.

"So soon?" she asked. "At least do me the courtesy of supping with me."

She left the room before he could refuse. Ethan followed reluctantly, stepping into the common room once more. Seeing no sign of her, he faltered, tensing. He even went so far as to begin speaking an illusion spell, just in case her toughs showed up.

"In here," she called from another chamber at the rear of the house.

Ethan followed Sephira's voice and found her seated at the head of a long table. Several platters of cheese, bread, fowl, and fruit sat before her, and a place had been set for him at her right hand. Sephira held a flask of red wine, and she poured out two goblets.

"Sit, Ethan. Join me. There's plenty for both of us."

"I haven't time for this."

She regarded him mildly. "You haven't time to eat?"

He started to say that he needed to get on with his inquiry, but he managed to stop himself. He had just asked Berson to help him maintain the fiction that his investigation was at an end, and here he nearly revealed the truth to the most dangerous person in Boston.

"Come." She flashed that charming smile. "I promise we'll only speak of important matters. No more nonsense about my collections or anything like that."

"How do I know it's not poisoned?" he asked, taking the seat beside hers and pointing to his wineglass.

"You don't," she said. "But that makes it all the more exciting." She lifted her goblet and held it before her. Ethan lifted his as well. "To friendly rivals," she said, touching her glass to his.

Ethan had to laugh. He sipped the wine, which was excellent, and not watered at all. After a moment, he took some cheese, bread, and fowl. He left the fruit, though, because she took none. He didn't really believe that she intended to poison him, but he made a point of eating only the same foods as she.

She nodded approvingly as he began to eat, and then said, "You've been to see Abner Berson."

He eyed her for a moment before answering. "I have."

"And what did you two discuss?"

Apparently when Sephira said that they would "speak of important matters" she meant that he would answer her questions about his business.

"I'm not sure that's any of your concern, Sephira."

"So you're not going to tell me."

He chuckled and shook his head. "You keep forgetting that I don't work for you."

She let out an exasperated sigh. "Not this foolishness again."

"I know that you have it in your head that I'm just another man in your employ, but I'm not. I never will be."

"We'll see about that last point," she said. "But even if we are rivals, don't you think that when Berson and, say, Fergus Derne sit down to-gether for a meal, they discuss trade?"

"Maybe," Ethan conceded. "But I'm pretty certain that Derne never sends his toughs to Berson's home to beat the man within an inch of his life."

"Oh, it wasn't that bad," she said, waving the comment away. She studied his face briefly. "You're healing quite nicely. A few more days and no one will ever know it happened."

"What did you mean a minute ago? Are you suggesting that I should come and work for you?"

She smiled again, leaning closer to him. "What do you think I meant?"

"I think that I must have scared some people while I was working for Abner Berson. Nobody wanted me to find out too much, and now you've gone so far as to offer me employment."

"I haven't offered you anything, yet. Tell me what you discussed with Abner Berson."

"No."

She had started to sip her wine again, but she stopped herself and carefully placed the goblet back on the table. "There are other ways for me to find out, you know."

"Are you planning to ask Berson?"

Sephira smiled thinly, but didn't answer.

A part of him enjoyed goading her, perhaps too much. Her kind manners and beguiling smiles notwithstanding, she hated him. The last time they met she had threatened to kill him, and she might well follow through on that threat the next time. Usually, the fact that she wanted information from him was enough to convince Ethan that he ought to keep to himself whatever he knew. In this instance, however, he could help himself by telling her the truth, or at least part of it.

"I gave him Jennifer's brooch," Ethan said at last.

"Her brooch?" Sephira repeated. "Really?"

"Yes, and he paid me." Ethan patted his pocket, making the few coins Berson had given him jingle. "You're not going to steal these from me, too, are you?"

She raised an eyebrow and gestured vaguely at their surroundings. "Do you really think I need to? I took those other coins to make a point," she went on before he could respond.

"Right. Because the beating wouldn't have been enough."

She ignored that. "So, you're no longer working for Berson?"

"Why? Do you have a job for me?"

"Answer the question."

"I found the brooch, which is what I was hired to do. And I was paid for my trouble. You may not think much of my business sense, but I know better than to work for free."

She laughed, low in her throat. "Very good, Ethan. I didn't know if you were smart enough to do the right thing. I suppose, I under-estimated you."

His shrug was meant to reveal little. "Now will you answer a question for me?"

She picked up her cup and drank a bit of wine, her eyes never leav-ing his. "Perhaps," she said, replacing the goblet.

"Who first told you that I was working for Berson?"

"As I've explained to you before, Ethan, very little happens in this city without my knowledge."

"But you knew everything, and quickly. You knew I had been hired, you knew why, and somehow you even knew when I had been to King's Chapel and when I intended to meet with Berson himself. I'm wondering how you learned all of this."

"I have sources," she said coyly, enjoying herself too much for his taste.

"I'm sure—" He stopped, still staring at her. *I have sources,* she had said. And what was it Berson had told him during their first conversa-tion. Ethan asked him why he had been hired instead of Sephira, and Berson said that he had considered Pryce but that she would have ad-mitted herself that she knew little about conjurings. *And so we . . . we asked around,* Berson had said. *I've always known there were spellers in Bos-ton. A person just needed to know where to look. And when I heard that there was a thieftaker who was also a speller . . .*

Who had he meant when he said "we"? His wife? Ethan couldn't imagine that he had consulted her in this matter. She had been too distraught to see Ethan that night. Berson wouldn't have spoken to her about hiring a thieftaker. His younger daughter? That made no sense. William or another servant? Ethan couldn't imagine Berson asking for their advice, either. Which left Cyrus Derne.

"Ethan?" Sephira said, her eyes narrowing.

"Yes," he said. He forced himself to concentrate. It wouldn't do for him to lose himself thinking about an inquiry he claimed already to have concluded. "I'm sure you do have sources, Sephira, and they must be the envy of any thieftaker in Boston."

If it turned out that Berson had spoken to Derne, how would the young merchant have known that Ethan was a conjurer? Unless Derne had gone to another thieftaker first—Sephira, of course—and she had steered him to Ethan when she realized that Jennifer was killed by a conjuring. After speaking with Derne two nights before, Ethan had assumed that the man knew nothing of his abilities. Perhaps Cyrus Derne was a better liar than Ethan had thought.

"Tell me," she said. "Did Berson ask you who was responsible for the murder of his daughter?" Her tone remained light, but she watched him keenly.

"Of course he did."

"And?" Her patience had started to wear thin. "What did you tell him?"

"What should I have told him?"

She started to answer, and Ethan would have wagered every coin in his pocket that she was going to name poor Daniel Folter as Jennifer's killer. But she caught herself in time, smiling once more and inclining her head. "I would like to know how you answered the man," she said eventually.

"I told him I didn't know, that I heard a name mentioned in connection with the crime, but that I couldn't say for certain that this individual was her killer."

She frowned. "And he was satisfied by that?"

"Satisfied? No. But I told him that I had done what I could."

Sephira's brow remained creased, and she continued to stare at him so intently one might have supposed that she had the power to read his thoughts. "I don't believe you," she said after some time.

Ethan reached for his wine and took a sip, his hand as steady as an offshore wind. "What don't you believe?"

"Any of this. Any of what you've said." She shook her head, a small, disbelieving laugh escaping her. "Here I thought I might learn something of value from you, and you've been lying to me the whole time!"

"No, I haven't." She started to argue and he lifted a finger, silencing her. "I've barely lied to you at all."

"But you admit that you have lied."

"Of course I have. Just as you've lied to me. You and I are never going to be friends, Sephira. This entire encounter has been founded on a lie. And because I've proven a match for you in this little game, you're suddenly indignant."

She stared at him.

Ethan drained his cup and set it down on the table. "I'm disappointed in you." He stood and sketched a small bow. "My thanks for a lovely supper."

He stepped away from the table and started toward the door.

"You have no intention of leaving this matter alone, do you?"

Ethan paused momentarily in midstride, but didn't look back at her. He was reaching for the door handle when she called his name.

Against his better judgment he stopped and faced her.

"I don't have to let you leave," she said. "My men are just outside that door. At a word from me . . ." She shrugged. "No one would miss you. No one of consequence."

He had been expecting this. He didn't have his knife, but there were other ways. Pushing up his sleeve, he dragged his fingernails along the underside of his forearm, leaving three raw streaks that quickly began to seep blood.

Sephira opened her mouth.

"Don't!" Ethan said. "I'm leaving. Your men are going to give me my knife and let me go. Or I'm going to burn this magnificent house of yours to the ground."

She looked angry enough to kill him with her bare hands.

"Call in Nigel and tell him to hand over my blade."

"This isn't over, Ethan."

"It's never over between us, is it?"

His calm only seemed to goad her further. "This is no longer amusing! I've warned you about pursuing the Berson matter, and you've ignored those warnings time and again. Well, fine. I'm done talking about it."

"How convenient for both of us, because I'm done listening."

She shook her head slowly, her cheeks flushed, her blue eyes wide with anger. Even now as she was threatening his life, she was as beautiful as any woman he had ever seen.

"You think your damned witchcraft will keep you safe?"

"It has in the past."

"There are other ways," she said. "You have a friend—a lovely woman. She owns a small tavern called the Dowsing Rod. It would be a tragedy if something were to happen to her or her establishment."

The spell was on his lips before he could consider what he was doing. "*Discuti ex cruore evocatum!*" Shatter, conjured from blood! Power pulsed through the chamber, making the hairs on his arm prickle. Uncle Reg appeared beside him, glowing bloodred, grinning like a ghoul. In his rage, Ethan aimed the spell at Sephira, but he managed to steer it away from her at the last moment.

There was a sudden rending of wood, and the small table next to where she was standing exploded as if torn apart from within. Scraps of timber were strewn over the rug on which she stood, and flecks of wood dust coated her skirt. Sephira stared at what he had done, her mouth agape.

Ethan had already scraped his arm again, lest he need more blood to fight his way out of her house.

"If you or your men go anywhere near Kannice or the Dowsing Rod, I'll kill you all. I don't care if I hang for your murder. I'll rip you apart just like I did that table. Now call in Nigel. I'm ready to leave."

Sephira raised her eyes to his. At last, she called, "Nigel!"

A moment later, the door opened. Nigel paused on the threshold, noted Ethan's bloody arm and the mess in the middle of the common room, then entered the house, though he left the door wide open.

"Give him his knife."

Nigel pulled the weapon from his coat pocket and took a step in Ethan's direction.

"Just leave it on the arm of that chair," Ethan said, pointing with a bloodstained finger.

Nigel glanced at Sephira, who hesitated, then nodded.

The big man did as Ethan had told him.

"Now go stand with her."

The man crossed to Sephira. Ethan retrieved his knife and walked to the door.

"Watch your back, Ethan," Sephira said. "Don't sleep. Don't even blink."

He returned the blade to his belt, his hand trembling now, though with rage or with fear he couldn't say. He glanced back at her once more and left the house, Uncle Reg stalking beside him.

Chapter
THIRTEEN

*S*ephira and her toughs didn't come after him right away, though as he made his way back through the South End Ethan looked over his shoulder often, expecting at any moment to see them bearing down on him. Once he was away from her house the pounding of his heart subsided, and he began to wonder what in the name of all that was holy he had been thinking. Casting a spell in Sephira Pryce's home? Destroying her furniture? Threatening to kill her? He might as well have stolen money from her purse as she watched, or called her a whore in front of her men.

If he needed any more incentive to find Jennifer Berson's killer and be done with her father and the conjurer, he now had it. Sephira would never stop hating him; as long as he insisted on thieftaking in Boston, she would begrudge every coin he made. But if he could conclude this inquiry perhaps her desire to see him dead would diminish.

He decided to begin by speaking with Cyrus Derne. If Derne had lied to him the first time they spoke, Ethan wanted to know why.

It was midafternoon, and he knew better than to think that Derne would be at his home. Instead, he began the long walk across the city to Derne's Wharf and Warehouse on Ship Street in the North End. He turned up his coat collar and hunched his shoulders against the rain. He walked at the edge of the road, keeping the iron posts that lined the thoroughfare between himself and the carriages and chaises. Rivulets of rank water ran between the cobblestones, gathering in the shallow trough in the middle of the lane and draining at intervals along the way. Carts and horses splashed him as they passed, chilling him, staining his clothes.

Derne's Wharf jutted out into the harbor beside others belonging to merchants of similar means. Abner Berson's wharf was only a short distance down Ship Street. Hancock's Wharf, the longest in the North End, second in the entire city only to Long Wharf, sat just to the south of them both. All these wharves had large wooden warehouses where the merchants stored diverse goods and prepared them for market.

Two formidable men stood guard at the base of their wharf, and one of them stopped Ethan as he tried to set foot on the dock.

"Who're you?" he asked, studying Ethan's bruised face.

"Ethan Kaille. I'm here to see Cyrus Derne."

The man eyed him dubiously.

"I work for Abner Berson," he added.

That convinced him. "Aye, all right," he said, and waved Ethan onto the wharf.

Ethan made his way down the dock past shops and storage buildings, until he came to the largest of the warehouses. A sign over the door read "Fergus Derne and Son, Boston. Established 1715."

Dockworkers were carrying crates, burlap sacks, and cloth-wrapped parcels into the building. A few rolled barrels, and others worked in tandem to carry timber. Ethan waited until several of the men had entered, and then followed them inside, pausing by the door to give his eyes a chance to adjust to the dim light. Shouted conversations echoed through the building, an incomprehensible din that made the space feel smaller than it was.

Wares were stacked everywhere, and in addition to the workers who off-loaded the ship, a host of others sorted items into different areas, supervised by a number of foremen. At first it struck Ethan as chaotic, but it didn't take him long to discern a rhythm and pattern to what everyone was doing.

He began to walk through the building, taking care to stay out of the way, even as he searched for Cyrus Derne. He didn't see either

Derne or his father, and he wondered if perhaps they were elsewhere on the wharf. But as he reached the back of the warehouse, he spotted both merchants in a small office.

They were speaking in low voices to a man of medium build who couldn't have been much older than Ethan's thirty-nine years. After a moment, Ethan recognized him as Gilbert Deblois, the brother of a wealthy merchant and a successful dealer of firearms in his own right. Ethan wouldn't have been surprised to learn that Sephira had purchased some of the weapons in her collection from him.

He walked to the door leading into the office, smiling benignly as he stood watching the three men, his hands clasped behind his back.

Cyrus Derne barely spared him a glance. "Yes, what is it?" he demanded.

"Good afternoon, Mister Derne."

Derne looked at Ethan again, more closely this time. At last, after several seconds, the man recognized him.

"Mister Kaille!" he said, making no effort to mask his surprise.

"It's a pleasure to see you again, sir," Ethan said, offering a hand.

Derne stepped forward and gripped it, still looking perplexed. "What are you doing here?"

"I was hoping for a word with you."

Derne released his hand and cast a self-conscious look at Deblois and then at his father. Fergus Derne had paused to watch Ethan and his son, an expression of deepest disapproval on his broad face. No doubt he believed Ethan had committed an inexcusable breach of decorum by coming here. Deblois merely seemed annoyed at having his business dealings interrupted.

"This isn't the best time for me, Mister Kaille," the younger Derne said, facing Ethan again. "If you could come by my home later, some time this evening perhaps—"

"No, sir. I'd like a word with you now."

"Now, see here, Kaille," the elder Derne said. "This is a place of commerce. My son is occupied with—"

"A girl is dead, sir!" Ethan said, raising his voice enough to draw stares from the closest of the workmen in the warehouse. Deblois frowned, but he directed his gaze at Fergus Derne rather than at Ethan. "A girl your son loved and intended to marry," Ethan went on, lowering his voice slightly. "Surely you weren't about to tell me that whatever business you're conducting is more important than finding her killer."

So much for keeping secret the fact that he was still looking into Jennifer's murder. But Sephira already knew, which meant that everyone else who mattered soon would as well. Besides, he wouldn't have traded the look on Fergus Derne's face for anything.

"Well . . . I . . ." The older man turned to his son for help, his cheeks crimson.

"Can we speak of this outside, Mister Kaille?" Cyrus asked, indicating a door at the back of the warehouse that opened onto the wharf.

"That would be fine."

"I shouldn't be long," the younger Derne told Deblois. He gestured for Ethan to follow and led him to the door.

Once outside, they walked a short distance from the building so that they would be beyond the hearing of anyone standing by the door. Derne pulled his coat tighter around his shoulders and glowered at Ethan.

"Now then," he said, halting and drawing himself up to his full height. "What's so important that it couldn't wait until this evening?"

"I want to know why you lied to me the other night."

"I don't know what you're talking about!" Derne said. He sounded indignant, but his gaze slid away.

"You told me that you had no idea why Berson had hired me, and you said that you had no idea how Jennifer died. The truth is you knew she had been killed by a conjuring, and you recommended to her father that he give me the job."

Derne didn't answer at first. He stared out across the harbor at a vessel putting to sea, a mist-laden wind stirring his dark hair. Two workers lingered in the doorway to the warehouse watching Ethan and Derne.

"Who told you?" Derne finally asked. "Was it Abner?"

"No. I worked it out for myself. I would guess that he asked you who he ought to hire and you offered to find someone for him. You went to Sephira Pryce first, but once she realized that a speller was involved, she sent you to me."

The young merchant twisted his mouth sourly. "I suppose I shouldn't be surprised that you reasoned it out." He took a breath and faced Ethan. "I'm sure deception comes naturally to men in your line of work."

Ethan ignored the remark. "Why not tell me the truth from the beginning?" he asked.

"That was Miss Pryce's idea. She indicated that the two of you are rivals and she suggested that if you knew the idea had come from her, you would refuse the job."

Sephira knew him well; he would have done just that. But why had she been so eager for him to take a job she claimed she didn't want him to have? Unless she knew from the start just how dangerous the conjurer who killed Jennifer was. That might have made her wary of taking the job herself, and all the more eager for Ethan to take it, particularly if she thought that the conjurer would eventually kill him. But then why go to the trouble of having him beaten, of following him through the marketplace? Too much of this still didn't make any sense.

Derne was growing more impatient by the moment. "Are we done?" he asked. "There are other matters that require my attention."

"What reason did Seph—did Miss Pryce give for refusing to take the job herself?"

"It was just as you said. She realized that witchcraft was involved and told me that we would want a speller. She mentioned your name right off. I hadn't heard of you, but later, when I told Abner, he knew who you were."

"Who else have you told?" Ethan asked.

"Told what?"

"That I'm a conjurer?"

"No one," Derne said. "Not even my father."

"Good," Ethan said. "I asked you other questions that night, about when you had last seen Jennifer, about whether you had been abroad in the city the evening she died, about other suitors she might have had. How many other lies did you tell me?"

"You have no right to speak to me this way!" the merchant said, contempt in his voice.

Ethan knew that he should have kept his temper in check. But after all he had endured the past few days, hearing this man complain about being spoken to rudely pushed him over the edge. He grabbed Derne by the collar and yanked him forward, nearly pulling him off his feet. Out of the corner of his eye, he saw the two workers start in their direction.

"Call them off," he said, his voice low. "Now!"

"It's all right," Derne called to the men, a sickly smile on his face. "Just . . . talking."

The men hesitated, looked at each other. Finally, one of them shrugged, and they resumed their positions just inside the door.

"Now listen to me," Ethan said, keeping his voice down. "Since this began I have been beaten, robbed, threatened, chased, and lied to." He waved his free hand in the direction of the city. "Jennifer's murderer is out there somewhere, hunting me, just as I'm hunting him. The difference is he knows my name and what I look like and where I live. And he has every intention of killing me. So do you really think I give a damn how you'd like me to speak to you?"

Derne shook his head, his eyes wide. It occurred to Ethan that in all likelihood no one, with the possible exception of his father, had ever manhandled the young man this way.

"I'm going to ask you again: Did you lie to me about anything else the other night?"

The merchant licked his lips. "Yes. I was abroad in the city that night. Jennifer wasn't with me. I swear she wasn't. I won't tell you what I was doing there. But it had nothing to do with her or her murder. You must believe me."

Ethan glared at him a moment longer before releasing him and shoving him away. "You don't know that," he said. "You idiot! I'm sure you would like to believe that whatever you did there had nothing to do with her death, but you don't know it."

"Of course I—"

"Listen to me!" Ethan closed his eyes briefly and dragged a hand over his face. "Why would she have gone into the streets at such an hour unless it was to follow you?"

Derne just stared back at him.

"What was it you were doing there?" Ethan demanded.

"I'm not telling you that."

"You may not believe that her death has anything to do with your foray into the city, but if she did follow you—if she was curious about your dealings there, or wondered if you had a woman—" Derne started to object, but Ethan didn't give him the chance. "If she followed you for any reason, then she might have stumbled upon something she wasn't supposed to. Her murder could have everything to do with your business. Now you must tell me what you were doing that night!"

Derne shook his head. "No." He shook his head again. His face was pale and his tongue flicked nervously over his lips. "No, I won't. You don't know what you're talking about. You know nothing of my business and I'm not about to tell you. But I know you're wrong."

Ethan lunged for the man again, but Derne jumped back more nimbly than Ethan had expected he could.

Derne raised a finger in warning. "You'll not touch me again, Mister Kaille! If you come near me now, I'll call for those men. And if I see you at my home, you'll have my father's hired men to deal with. Not to mention Sheriff Greenleaf." He grimaced. It took Ethan a moment to realize that he had intended to smile. "Perhaps the sheriff would be interested to know that you're a witch as well as a thieftaker."

He started to back away, as if expecting Ethan to attack him at any moment. Ethan would have liked nothing more, but the two men by the door were still watching, and Ethan thought they looked eager for an excuse to intervene.

"Abner Berson won't be happy to learn that you've refused to help me," Ethan said.

Derne actually laughed at that, a high-pitched nervous bark. "Not that I care, but you're wrong. Abner would understand completely. He's a merchant."

Ethan wanted to argue, but he wasn't entirely sure that the man wasn't right. Berson had far more in common with the Dernes of the world than he did with Ethan.

At last, Derne reached the door, still walking backward. He groped for the doorframe, found it, and quickly slipped into the warehouse.

"Stupid bastard," Ethan muttered. But he felt sick to his stomach. Shivering at another raw gust of wind, he walked back along the wharf toward the street.

Just as he reached the thoroughfare, he saw Diver walking toward him, his eyes scanning the street warily and his hands in his pockets. He didn't notice Ethan until the thieftaker stepped right in front of him, blocking his way.

"Ethan!" Diver said, halting and looking around again. "What are you doing here?"

"Had to speak with someone back there," he said, nodding his head toward the warehouses. "Though for all the good it did me, I could have gone to the Dowser instead and had an ale or two. You coming up from work?"

Diver had halted in front of Derne's Wharf. He glanced toward the storage buildings and the guards standing outside them. "That's right. I got off early today. You were talking to someone down here? Berson was it?"

"Actually, no," Ethan said quietly. "Cyrus Derne."

"Derne?" Diver laughed, but Ethan could see something was bothering him. "Damn, Ethan! Pretty soon you won't want anything to do with us poor folk."

"Actually, Derne's the least of it. Sephira Pryce had me to supper today."

Diver had been eyeing the wharf again, but at this his gaze snapped back to Ethan. "You're not serious!"

"I am. She showed me her collection of blades and pistols, she poured me wine, she even hinted at offering me work." He took a step, intending to walk back toward the Dowser. "Come on, I'll tell you about it on the way."

Diver hesitated, though only for an instant. Still, that was enough.

"What's the matter with you?" Ethan asked. "You're acting like I was the last person in the world you wanted to see."

"I am not," Diver said unconvincingly. "I was . . . I was headed home. I'm tired; it's been a long day. But . . . but sure, I'll come to the Dowser with you." His voice sounded falsely bright.

Ethan eyed him curiously as they began to walk.

"What were you talking to Derne about?"

Ethan hadn't expected Diver to ask about Derne before hearing of his latest encounter with Sephira. But he recounted his conversation with the merchant as they headed up to Middle Street and across Mill Creek into the center of the city.

When Ethan had finished, Diver said, "I didn't know that he and Berson's daughter were engaged."

"You wouldn't have known it to listen to him today, either."

"Do you really think she was killed because of something Derne was doing?"

"I don't know," Ethan said. "I can't think of any other reason she would have been out on the streets alone at night. And I can't imagine why a conjurer would have chosen to kill her unless it had something to do with her father or Derne."

"But maybe she was taken into the streets after she was killed. Or maybe someone made her go there. They could even have used a spell on her."

Ethan shook his head. "No, that's too powerful a con—"

He stopped in the middle of the street, swaying slightly, his head spinning. "I'm an idiot!" he whispered.

"What? Are you all right?" Diver laid a hand on Ethan's back and peered into his face.

Ethan barely noticed. It was right there in front of him, like a trail of blood on an empty lane. All he had to do was follow the drops and they would lead right where he needed to go. And he had been too blind to do even that much.

You find out what those spells did and you'll find your killer. That's what Janna had told him. But even after hearing this, and recognizing the wisdom in her words, he hadn't altered his approach to his inquiry. Ethan had been assuming that the murderer killed Jennifer Berson because of who she was or who she knew. But what if she was killed simply because she was there, in the streets of Boston, at precisely the wrong time? What if her murderer had never intended to kill the daughter of a wealthy merchant, but had been looking merely for someone—anyone—who was alone in the city and young enough to provide, through her death, the power necessary for an ambitious conjuring? Rather than trying to link the killer to Jennifer Berson, Ethan should have been searching for the object of his spell.

Janna had given him another clue as well, though he hadn't realized it at the time; he was sure she hadn't either. She told him that she had used a killing spell to compel someone to love a wealthy man. This wasn't surprising, really; control spells were among the most difficult castings known to the conjuring world. They were also among the most frequently used dark conjurings.

"Ethan!"

He realized that Diver had been speaking to him for some moments, repeating his name and asking him if he was all right. A few people had gathered around them in the street and were eyeing Ethan the way they would a drunk or a madman.

"I'm all right." He glanced around. "Really," he said loudly enough for the others to hear. "I'm fine."

The strangers around him appeared unconvinced, and he could hardly blame them. Though the bruises on his face weren't as tender as they had been a day or two before, they had begun to color, leaving him looking worse than ever. He was wet and bedraggled; his clothes were sodden. It was no wonder they thought him insane.

"Come on, then," Diver said, tugging gently at his coat sleeve.

They started walking again, but Ethan no longer had any intention of going to the Dowser. Night would be falling in another hour or two, and he didn't want to be abroad in the city after dark if he could help it. He would get to the tavern eventually, but first he needed more information. And it was about time that he spoke with those who he knew had been in the streets the night Jennifer Berson died.

"What was that all about, anyway?" Diver asked.

"I can't tell you right now." Ethan halted again. "Look, Diver, you go on without me. There's something else I have to do."

"Go on without you? But we're just about there!"

"I know. I'm sorry."

Diver threw his hands wide. "I wasn't even going to the Dowser until you came along. What am I supposed to do now?"

"I don't know," Ethan said, starting away from him. "I said I was sorry."

"Well can you at least tell me where you're going?" his friend called after him.

"I have to speak with someone at another tavern."

"What other tavern?"

He made no reply, though as he hurried back up Hanover Street he glanced over his shoulder one last time. Diver still stood in the road, his hands on his hips.

≈≈≈

The Green Dragon Tavern was located on Union Street, just off of Hanover. It was a plain, two-story building with a pitched roof and a brick façade. There was nothing remarkable about it, save for the cast-iron rod that projected over the front door, serving as the perch for an iron sculpture of a crouching dragon, its wings raised, its mouth open in a fiery roar.

The first floor of the building had for years been used as a meeting house by the Freemasons. The tavern itself was located in the basement of the building. It was open to all, but since the passage of the first Grenville Act, the year before, it had gained a reputation as a gathering place for those who opposed Parliament's actions. Ethan did not doubt that these same men had organized the Stamp Act riots.

A few men in workmen's clothes milled about in the narrow street in front of the building, seemingly oblivious of the rain. Another man stood in the doorway, and he watched Ethan as he approached the tavern. But no one stopped him or offered a word of greeting. Ethan paused just inside the door, shook the rain off his coat like a hound, and then descended the stairs to the basement.

Halfway down, the smells reached him: pipe smoke and musty ale, roasted meat and freshly baked bread. Ethan paused at the bottom of the stairs. A fire burned in a large stone hearth on the far side of the room and candles flickered on every table. Light and shadows danced capriciously along the uneven wood planking on the floor and the dingy walls. A few men stood at the bar, mugs of ale in their hands. Ethan had heard conversations while coming down to the pub, but all of them ceased when he walked in. The men simply stared at him, their expressions far from welcoming.

Ethan stared back. Up on the street, in the light of day, he had considered this a fine idea. Down here in the inconstant gloom, he was having second thoughts.

"My name is Ethan Kaille," he finally said. "I want to speak with those who led the demonstrations of three nights past."

At first, no one answered. But then a single figure stepped away from the bar, a tankard of ale in his hand. He was about Ethan's height and age, and he stood straight-backed, his pale blue eyes meeting and holding Ethan's gaze. He wore a simple white shirt and black breeches, a red waistcoat, and a powdered tie wig.

"Good day, Mister Kaille," he said in a ringing voice. "We've been expecting you. My name is Samuel Adams."

Chapter
FOURTEEN

Adams walked to where Ethan stood, and proffered a hand, which Ethan gripped.

"I'm pleased to meet you, Mister Kaille," he said, a disarming smile on his ruddy face. "I've heard a good deal about you."

"And every man in Boston hears a good deal about Samuel Adams."

"Yes, well, not all one hears can be credited." His smile had turned brittle, and Ethan noticed that his head shook slightly, even as the man continued to hold his gaze. "My colleagues and I have been wishing to speak with you. We had every intention of inviting you here. We're grateful to you for saving us the trouble."

He caught the eye of a man standing by the bar. "James, would you be so kind as to fetch Mister Kaille an ale? Then you and Peter can join us at the table." Adams faced Ethan again. "This way," he said.

Ethan followed the man to a table by the fireplace and sat, his back to the far wall. Adams took the seat across from him and lifted his tankard to his lips with a trembling hand. Seeing that Ethan had noticed his tremor, he smiled once more, faintly this time.

"Palsy," he said. "I've been plagued by it all my life, mild though it is."

Ethan nodded, not knowing what to say.

A moment later, they were joined by two men. One of them, a portly man with a broad, heavy face, thin lips, and somewhat protuberant eyes, carried an extra ale, which he placed in front of Ethan before sitting beside him. The other man was as handsome as his companion was odd-looking. His face was square; his eyes were brown. He wore his hair long and in a plait, and he powdered it white.

"Allow me to introduce my friends," Adams said. He indicated the portly man with an open hand. "This is James Otis." Gesturing toward the other man, he said, "And this is Peter Darrow."

Otis nodded. Darrow flashed a smile and proffered his hand.

"Pleased to meet you, Mister Kaille."

Ethan shook the man's hand before facing Adams again. "You said you had been expecting me. Then you know why I've come."

"I believe we do, yes," Adams said. "You've been hired by Abner Berson in the matter of his daughter's death. Isn't that right?"

"It is, sir. And nearly everyone I've spoken to about it believes that your friends were involved."

Adams narrowed his eyes. "Our friends?"

"And who is it you've spoken to?" Otis broke in. "Berson's friends, no doubt. Tories, every one."

"He has a point," Adams said. "Berson is well acquainted with those who administer the province. So is Cyrus Derne, who I believe was to marry Jennifer Berson."

"So is Mister Kaille."

"Meaning what?" Ethan demanded of Darrow, who had spoken.

The look in Darrow's eyes had hardened. "The obvious. Your sister is married to a customs official, a friend of Andrew Oliver no less."

"Geoffrey Brower? I barely speak to the man, much less consult with him during my inquiries."

"Nevertheless, Mister Kaille," Adams said, drawing Ethan's gaze once more. "We know that you served in the British navy, and that your family is firmly tied to the Crown."

"What else do you think you know about me?" Ethan asked. He tried to sound indifferent, but he wondered if they knew how he came to be working for Berson.

"That you were a prisoner for many years. That you're a thieftaker." Adams paused, glancing at Otis and Darrow. "And that thus far, your inquiry has taken you to those who wish my colleagues and me ill."

Ethan looked at each man. "Well," he said, "if you're willing to cast your lot with men like Ebenezer Mackintosh, you shouldn't be surprised to find others treating you like rabble."

"You go too far, sir!" Otis said. "We have no more cast our lot with that charlatan than you have!" He waved a shaking finger in Ethan's face. "And for you to say so—"

"It's all right, James," Darrow said, reaching across the table to lay a hand on Otis's other arm. "They blame Mackintosh for the Berson murder?" he asked Ethan.

"Shouldn't they? Mister Hutchinson believes that he incited that mob to riot. And I wouldn't be surprised if he was right. With everything else Mackintosh and his mob did that night, it's not so great a leap of logic to believe the rest. You know what kind of man Mackintosh is."

"Yes, we know," Adams told him. "Better than most, actually. Peter here won his release after the Brown boy was killed on Pope's Day last year. He also defended Mackintosh at his trial."

Darrow frowned. "Samuel—"

"*You* defended him?" Ethan could scarcely believe it. "You know this man—you see the way he incites his South End rabble—and still you choose to associate yourself with him?"

"The charges brought against him were for disturbing the peace," Darrow said. "He was never charged in the matter of the Brown boy's death. And with good reason. The child was killed when he was run over by a cart carrying one of the effigies. And Mackintosh wasn't anywhere near the cart or the boy when it happened. You may not approve of the man's tactics—neither do I—but he didn't deserve to hang for the boy's death."

Ethan was less sure of this than was Darrow. But he kept to himself his doubts about Mackintosh as well as his knowledge of what really killed the child.

"So you'll tolerate vandalism and violence from your allies," he said instead. "Just not murder. Is that it?"

Otis bristled. "Again, sir, you speak of matters you don't understand."

"Don't I? Two weeks ago, Mackintosh and his mob destroyed the property of Andrew Oliver for no other reason than because Oliver happens to be distributor of stamps. Where was your outrage then, Mister Otis? Where were your cries for justice?"

Otis's face reddened and his eyes widened, so that he looked apoplectic.

But it was Adams who responded. "The assault on Oliver's house, while regrettable, was necessary to convey to Parliament, and to the Crown's representatives here in the colonies, that we are not their slaves, but rather their loyal subjects. Perhaps you've heard men speak of 'liberty and property.' That is what we are trying to protect. You have to understand, Mister Kaille, that we colonists hold a unique place in the Empire. We are subjects of His Majesty the king, but being remote from England, and having no representation in Parliament, we have the right—nay, the responsibility—to decide for ourselves what taxes and fees are appropriate for this land. The attempts by Parliament to burden the people of America with fees like this new stamp tax, and to ignore our rights as a free and self-governing people, cannot and shall not go unanswered."

Ethan had heard some of this before, and he wasn't sure he believed that Adams and his friends had the right to define for themselves what it meant to be British subjects, particularly if their definition was this self-serving. "And what of Oliver's liberty and property?" he asked. "What of his right to live free and unmolested?"

Adams shrugged, his head and hands still shaking. "As I say, the attacks on his home and office were regrettable. Still, he is but one, and I speak of the liberties of every man in the colonies."

"I assume then, that you justify the attacks on Hutchinson, Story, and Hallowell the same way."

"Hallowell and Story, perhaps," Adams said. "But Hutchinson?" He shook his head. "Not at all. What happened two nights ago was something entirely different. There was no control, no discipline. I believe in liberty, not lawlessness, not licentiousness. And I have no desire to see all of our labors undone by a mob of ruffians and fools."

"You see, Mister Kaille," Otis said, his voice calm, at least for the moment, "we have no desire to protect Ebenezer Mackintosh. Far from it. The man is a scourge upon our cause. He's been placed in gaol, and

I, for one, hope he remains precisely where he is. If I could see him hanged tomorrow for the injuries he and his rabble inflicted upon Thomas Hutchinson, I would."

Ethan stared for a moment at Otis, then at the other two. They weren't working with Mackintosh. They wished to use the man as their sacrificial lamb.

"You think he killed Jennifer Berson," Ethan said.

Adams and Otis looked at Darrow.

"We doubt he killed her himself," Darrow said. "But as you say, he led the mob that doubtless was responsible for her death. And unlike the death of the Browns' child on Pope's Day, this might well have been a deliberate act of murder. That's what Abner Berson is saying, anyway. And what's more, this mob, also unlike the one in November, engaged in other violent and aggressive acts against innocents. He might well swing for this killing."

"And that would please you," Ethan said. "All of you."

"It will please us to see justice done," said Otis.

"Do you know that you sound exactly like Hutchinson? And Berson? And Derne? All those who you dismiss as Tories, they want the same thing you do. Somehow, you've all decided that Ebenezer Mackintosh is guilty of murder, and that your lives would be easier if he were to be arrested, convicted, and executed."

"That's nonsense!" Otis said, his voice rising, his mood as changeable as a summer afternoon in New England.

"It's true," Adams broke in. Otis glared at him, but Adams kept his eyes fixed on Ethan. "You're right: We've decided precisely that. James here called Mackintosh a scourge. That's about right. He is a threat to all we hope to accomplish. In one night, his rabble did more to damn the cause of liberty than Parliament has managed in the last two years. And that is saying something." He shook his head. "It's our fault, really. We enlisted the man as an ally some while ago, hoping that he and his followers could help us."

"Help you how?" Ethan asked.

"The Sons of Liberty," Darrow said. "The Loyal Nine—whatever you wish to call those of us who oppose the Acts—we're lawyers, craftsmen, shopkeepers, even merchants, though few of us are as well fixed as the Bersons of the world. But we also need the support of laborers, wharf workers, seamen—precisely the kind of men Mackintosh leads in the South End. We'll never win the support of the wealthy—their ties to the Crown and Parliament remain too strong. But if we have the men in the street and those of us who, like Samuel and James and myself, work at crafts and at the law, we just might prevail. We need Ebenezer and his friends. We need them in the streets. We need their help with non-importation, we need—"

"Wait," Ethan said. "What was that?"

"Non-importation," Adams said. "Agreements among tradesmen, merchants, and others to stop buying goods made in England. It began after the Sugar Act was passed. Mackintosh spoke of ending his feud with the North Enders and uniting in support of the non-importation movement. But that didn't last long.

"The point is, Mister Kaille, Mackintosh was working with us. But now he's out of control. He's hurting our cause far more than he's helping it, and he's creating havoc in the streets of Boston. We thought that he and the men he commands would strengthen our cause, and instead they have, unwittingly no doubt, become perhaps our greatest liability. If I didn't know better, I might wonder if he was taking direction from the Crown itself." He paused, sipping his ale. "I don't know who killed the Berson girl. That's what you came to find out, is it not? And in truth, none of us knows for certain what happened to her. But we know that Mackintosh incited that mob, that had it not been for his exhortations, the excesses of August twenty-six would never have occurred. For that alone, the man deserves to be punished."

Ethan shook his head slowly. He hadn't come for a lesson in politics, and he wanted nothing to do with the Sons of Liberty or, for that matter, those arrayed against them. He had hoped to learn something of value about Jennifer Berson from these men. Perhaps he should have known better. "Were any of you in the streets that night?" he asked. "Did you actually see anything that might help me in my inquiry?"

They looked at one another, shaking their heads.

"No," Darrow said. "Samuel has told you the truth. The Sons of Liberty had nothing to do with what happened that night. We did not condone the riot at North Square. We had word that Mackintosh intended to do to the Story and Hallowell homes what had been done to Andrew Oliver's house. But that was to be all. And we ourselves wanted no part of it."

"Of course you didn't." Ethan stood. "I don't consider myself a proponent of liberty, gentlemen. At least not by your definition. But still, I would have expected more from men such as yourselves." His gaze lingered for a moment on Adams, who stared back at him, unfazed by his words. "Good day."

He left the tavern, climbed the steep stairway, and stepped out onto Union Street once more. A soft rain still fell over the city, blown in off the harbor by a stiff, cool wind. Ethan began to make his way toward the Dowser. When he was halfway there, he changed his mind and continued south toward King's Chapel. Henry Caner's objections notwithstanding, Ethan needed to speak one last time with Mr. Pell. Probably the minister wouldn't be able to help him, but there was always a chance.

Treamount Street was crowded with people making their way home from the market and from their work. Carriages rattled past, and Ethan had to twist his body one way and then another to avoid others walking along the side of the lane.

As he walked, he spotted Mr. Caner walking in his direction. He lowered his gaze, hoping that the rector hadn't seen him. The last thing he needed was for the minister to inquire as to where he was headed. He walked quickly, his head down, occasionally sending furtive glances in Caner's direction.

And so at first he didn't notice the carriage that halted just ahead of him. But then the door swung open and he heard a familiar voice speak his name.

"Kaille."

Ethan stopped and looked into the carriage. Nigel leaned forward from his seat, staring out at him, smiling. He held a pistol, its hammer pulled back, its barrel aimed directly at Ethan's heart.

Firearms were crude weapons, not known for their accuracy or reliability. But Nigel was only a few feet from him, and not for a moment did Ethan doubt that he would shoot if Ethan gave him the opportunity. No doubt only the crowd around them had kept him from pulling the trigger already.

"Go for yar knife, an' ya're dead," the man drawled.

Ethan took a step back, then stopped, feeling something sharp pressed against his lower back. He glanced over his shoulder. Nap was behind him, knife in hand.

He took Ethan's blade from its sheath, and said "Get in," in a low voice.

People on the lane had started to take notice of them, and Caner had to be close by. For a moment Ethan considered shouting for help. But these were Sephira's men; some on the street already seemed to have recognized them as such. No one would come to his aid if they thought for a moment that it might mean incurring the Great Lady's wrath.

He searched again for anyone who might help him. But there was no one. He didn't even see Caner anymore. Perhaps the minister had walked past without Ethan knowing it. Having no choice, he climbed into the carriage.

"Tha's smart that is," Nigel said, as Ethan took the seat opposite his. "It's too bad y'arn't always tha' smart."

Nap climbed in after him and sat beside his comrade.

Nigel pulled the door closed and rapped twice on the outside of the door. Immediately the carriage lurched forward.

"Where are we going?" Ethan asked.

The two men stared out their respective windows, saying nothing.

They followed the one lane a long way, until Ethan wondered if they intended to take him over the Neck, through the town gate and out into the country along the road toward Roxbury. If they intended to kill him and leave his body, that would be as convenient a place as any. But they turned to the west off Orange Street before they reached the gate, and turned a second time soon after. At last, they rolled to a stop. Nigel got out first and motioned with his gun for Ethan to follow him. Nap simply grinned, toying with Ethan's knife.

A light rain still fell on the city, and the sky had begun to darken. "Hello, Ethan."

He knew that voice, too. Herself.

Ethan ignored her for the moment, and tried to get his bearings. In the gathering gloom, it took him a few seconds to figure out where they were. He could make out Beacon Hill in the distance, shrouded in mist, and closer he saw the Common Burying Ground. He thought they must be at the end of Pleasant Street, a deserted stretch of road that jutted into Boston Common. He noticed lines of ropewalks in the distance, but the workers had abandoned them for the night. Aside from a few cattle, there wasn't another soul in sight. This, he realized, would also be a pretty convenient place for them to kill him.

At last, he looked at Sephira. She stood in the lane, flanked by eight men, including Gordon and the brute he had seen on the street the day before. Ethan glanced back and saw four more men standing with Yellow-hair and Nap.

"Sephira. We should really stop meeting like this."

"Oh, I assure you," she said, without even a hint of a smile, "this is the last time."

Ethan stared back at her and pushed up his sleeves, knowing that he could scratch at his arms enough to hold off a few of her toughs, but not all of them. He heard Sephira laugh.

"You going to claw at yourself again, Ethan?"

"If I have to."

"Oh, you'll have to." She held two fingers to her lips and whistled loudly.

Immediately her men stepped in front of her and spread to form a broad arc. Nigel and his men had done the same. Within moments Ethan would be surrounded. He searched for anything he might use against them, but didn't see much. Although . . .

Deserted as it was, this part of the lane was rough and overgrown with weeds. Stooping quickly, Ethan grabbed two handfuls of grass, straightened, and scattered the stalks in a wide circle all around him.

"*Ignis,*" he said in a low voice. "*Ex gramine evocatus.*" Fire, conjured from grass.

Uncle Reg appeared, shining like the rising moon, his teeth bared.

Flames shot up around Ethan and the old ghost, throwing off enough heat to warm Ethan's face and hands. There were a few spots where the grass hadn't spread evenly, but Ethan pulled some more from the ground

THIEFTAKER

and filled the gaps, muttering the spell to himself. He would have to keep feeding it; the spell wouldn't last forever. But it offered him some protection from Sephira and her men.

"We can wait," she said. "You can't keep that fire burning forever."

"Can't I?" he shouted back. But Sephira was right. His circle wasn't wide enough to encompass that much grass, and what he had wouldn't last more than an hour or two. And the more he pulled up, the closer he would have to venture to the ring of flame the next time he needed some.

He stooped again, picked up a stone that fit comfortably in his fist, and dropped it into his pocket, just in case. He also pulled up more stalks of grass, and watched for any slackening of the flames around him. Sephira and her men lurked just beyond the ring of fire, their faces glowing with the blaze, the heat making their features swim, so that they looked like Hell's demons.

"You should have listened to me, Ethan," Sephira called to him, sounding bored. She still wore the sapphire around her neck, and it glittered in the firelight. "You should have taken your money and found another Ezra Corbett to occupy your time."

"I would have," Ethan said. "But Berson asked me to continue my inquiry. He won't be happy to hear that you're trying to stop me."

"You said you were done working for him!"

"Did I?" Ethan asked innocently. "I must have lied."

He couldn't see her well, but there could be no mistaking the hard set of her jaw, or the widening of her eyes. She said something to the man closest to her and immediately he began walking around the fire ring, speaking in low tones to the others.

Ethan realized that the flames were burning down in some places. He scattered more grass and spoke the spell again. Even as did this, though, two men suddenly burst through the ring from opposite sides, both of them shielding their faces with their coats.

One of them came through unscathed; the tail of the other's coat caught fire. Making his decision in an instant, Ethan charged the first man, pulling the stone from his pocket as he closed the distance between them.

This first man had drawn a blade, and as Ethan stepped closer, he swiped the knife at Ethan's neck, forcing him to duck. The man lashed out with his foot, aiming his kick at Ethan's lowered head. Ethan threw up both arms to block the man's foot, but was staggered by the force of the blow. He righted himself, noticing out of the corner of his eye that the second man had stripped off his burning coat and was now stalking him as well.

Ethan was in the middle of the lane now, too far from either edge to get at the grass. He tried to sidle to the right. But the man in front of Ethan cut him off and closed on him.

Glancing behind him, Ethan saw that the other man was coming closer, too. Again he had to choose. This time he went for the tough whose coat had burned. He took a step toward the man, spun swiftly on his good leg, and kicked out with the bad one, which couldn't take the weight of such a move, but worked fine as a club. His kick caught Sephira's man in the chest, knocking him backward.

Ethan spun again, trying the same kick against the first man. Sephira's tough was ready, though. He dropped to the ground and kicked at Ethan's pivot leg, sweeping it out from under him. Ethan fell hard, landing on his back and cracking his head against cobblestone. Shaking his head to clear his mind, Ethan saw that Uncle Reg stood nearby, watching it all, a disapproving scowl on his glowing face.

"It's not as easy as it looks!" Ethan growled at the ghost.

In the next instant, the first man dove at him, his knife raised.

Ethan managed to roll away from the blade, though the man still landed on him. He raised his knife a second time, but before he could stab down with it, Ethan hit him hard in the mouth with the stone he still held. The man dropped his knife, one hand clutching his face, the other grabbing for the stone. Ethan hit him again, and this time he heard the bone in the man's nose break. Blood poured from the man's face as he rolled away.

But before Ethan could get to his feet, or even catch his breath, the other tough kicked him in the side, in the same spot where Nigel and his friends had broken his rib a few days before. Ethan retched. A second kick to the head addled him. He saw the man lift his blade, and knew that he wouldn't have the strength to block the blow.

"*Discuti,*" he said quickly. "*Ex cruore evocatum.*" Shatter, conjured from blood.

The ground pulsated. There was a terrible crackling sound, as if someone had stepped on dried leaves or brittle wood, and the man looming over Ethan collapsed, screaming in agony.

Ethan rolled onto his knees. Blood still flowed from the other man's nose, though Ethan's spell had wiped away much of it. He eyed Ethan, clearly terrified, and backed away from him toward the fire, which was dying down again.

"*Ignis!*" Ethan said. "*Ex cruore evocatus!*" Fire, conjured from blood!

Again the blood vanished from the man's face. At the same time, the flames leaped higher than they had when fed by the grass.

The man dabbed at his face with his fingers and then stared at them. "Wha'd ya do?" he asked in a trembling voice.

"Just used a bit of your blood. Hope you don't mind."

The tough gaped at him.

"Take him," Ethan said, gesturing at the other man, who writhed on the cobbled lane. "And go."

"But . . . but th' fire!"

"You'll have to move quickly then, won't you? Now go!"

The man walked slowly to his friend, watching Ethan the entire way. For his part, Ethan kept his eyes fixed on the tough, more than willing to draw upon the man's blood again if he had to.

In fact . . . He waited while the man lifted his friend and began to drag him toward the wall of flames. And at the moment the tough reached the fire, as he gathered himself for a rush through the blaze, Ethan began to speak another spell.

"*Dormite omnes, evocatum—*" Slumber, all of them, conjured—

The phrasing slowed him down, made him stumble over the Latin. Not a lot, but just enough. It was the difference between putting one man to sleep and putting all of them to sleep. And somehow Sephira knew this. Even as he spoke, he heard her cry out something unintelligible. Whirling, Ethan saw Nigel raise his pistol. He dove to the side, just as he heard a loud report that echoed across the Common. He hit the cobblestones hard, scraping his hands and bruising his knees and elbows. He also felt a burning pain in his upper arm. Looking down, he saw blood spreading over his coat sleeve and glistening in the glow of the fire.

He had been lucky. An inch to the right and the bullet would have shattered his shoulder. A few inches more and it might have hit his neck, likely killing him. As it was, the bullet had merely grazed his arm.

Ethan started to push himself up, but as he did, he saw something glinting on the road before him. The knife dropped by the man he had hit with his stone. First things first, though. He spoke another fire spell, using the blood on his shoulder to build up the flames once more. Then he cast a second fire spell, and directed it at Nigel's pistol. He knew it would have taken Yellow-hair some time to reload, but he didn't want to risk being shot at again.

Finally, he picked up the knife and climbed slowly to his feet. Blood had started to flow once more from the bullet wound. "*Remedium ex cruore evocatum,*" he said. Healing, conjured from blood.

"We're back where we began, Ethan!" Sephira said, walking slowly around his fire.

"Aye. Why don't you send a couple of more men over? I'm sure I can make good use of their blood, too. Or maybe I'll just kill them and be done with it. I can take all of you, two at a time."

"Or we can all fight our way through the flames at once. What will you do then?"

Ethan held up the knife. "Anything I want," he said. "One of your men has been kind enough to give me a blade."

Her face fell and he saw her spit a curse, though he couldn't hear what she said.

"You should leave now, Sephira. I can do far more with blood than I can with grass."

"Maybe. But you can't bleed yourself forever, and you don't want to do anything that will draw attention to yourself."

"I'm standing in a ring of conjured fire. Killing you with a spell won't draw more attention than that."

She smiled at him through the blaze. "Then you had better do it quickly." She glanced right and left. "Now!"

On her word, every one of her men who remained standing rushed the flames and leaped through them, landing within the ring, their knives ready. Nigel grinned at him, as did several of the others.

Ethan pushed up his sleeve and slashed his forearm. "Who wants to die first?" he asked, turning slowly to look at all of them. "You?" he asked the brute. "You, Nigel? I probably can't kill all of you. But I guarantee you that the first one to take a step toward me will die in more agony than he can imagine."

None of the toughs moved, and not one of them was grinning anymore.

"*Ignis ex cruore evocatus!*" Fire, conjured from blood!

He said it as quickly as he could, felt power pass through him like a shaft of lightning. The man next to Yellow-hair exploded in flame. Ethan had been aiming for Nigel himself, but he was in motion as he cast the spell, and conjurings weren't always as precise as he wanted. The burning man staggered, then dropped to the ground, flailing at his clothes and hair. Nigel and a few of the others also beat at the fire with their hands or their coats until at last they extinguished the flames. Several of the men had shied away from the one Ethan attacked, but now they faced Ethan again and started to advance on him. Ethan had already cut himself again and he lifted his bleeding arm for all of them to see.

"Who's next, eh?" he said. "One step more, and you'll be burning, too. Or maybe I'll just snap your necks. I can do that, as well."

Again the men faltered.

"Get him already!" Sephira shouted from beyond the ring of flame, which had burned down so low that she could have stepped over it. Ethan noticed, however, that she remained exactly where she was.

Looking beyond her, though, Ethan saw something that struck him dumb. He couldn't decide whether to be terrified or elated. Two men were walking toward him, one slight and in black robes, the other taller, brawny, in a dark suit, his hair topped by a powdered wig. The first man he recognized immediately as Mr. Pell. And the man with the wig was none other than Sheriff Greenleaf.

"Stop where you are!" the sheriff called to them, his voice carrying, even here in open country.

Sephira spun around, as did her men.

"Miss Pryce!" Pell said. "I have to warn you that you're in grave danger." He pointed at Ethan. "That man is suspected of being a witch! He is a threat to you, your men, and all who live in Boston."

Sephira glanced back at Ethan, confusion knitting her brow. "Well . . . yes," she finally said, facing the minister again. "I've actually wondered about him."

Pell pointed again. "That fire—did he do that?"

Sephira nodded, her face a mask of innocence. "Yes, he did. He also wounded two of my employees. He attacked them, unprovoked. That's why my men have him surrounded now. We can deal with this for you, if you like."

The minister shook his head gravely. "No, I'm afraid that won't do, Miss Pryce. I was sent by the Reverend Henry Caner, and he was quite precise with his instructions. This is a Church matter. If we determine that this man is, in fact, a witch and that he has been casting foul spells and working his devilry, then he'll be dealt with."

Sephira's expression had soured. Even she couldn't murder a man with a minister and the sheriff of Suffolk County watching.

She eyed Ethan briefly, then made a small, sharp gesture. Immediately, Nigel and the other men started back toward her. Two of them carried the man Ethan had burned, and when the men reached the one whose bones he had broken, two more stooped to pick him up.

Greenleaf watched Sephira, looking almost embarrassed, and she glared back at him. As she stepped past him, Greenleaf whispered something to her. Ethan couldn't hear what the man said, but he would have wagered everything he owned that the sheriff had apologized for meddling in her affairs.

Pell, on the other hand, appeared frightened, his face ghostly pale in the firelight. He kept a wary eye on Sephira as she walked past, but then turned back to Ethan. A moment later, he spotted Uncle Reg and his eyes widened slightly. The ghost leered at him.

Sephira looked from the minister to Ethan, perhaps sensing their friendship. Her expression darkened. At last, though, helpless to do anything about the fact that she had been robbed of her prey, she turned once more to follow her men. Then she stopped and turned again to face Ethan.

"I'll take that blade," she said to him.

"And I'll take mine."

She smirked, held a hand out to Nap. He pulled Ethan's knife from his pocket and handed it to her. Sephira walked to where Ethan stood, her hips swaying provocatively, no doubt for Pell's benefit. Stopping in front of him, she lifted Ethan's blade, staring at him. After a moment, she flipped it over and handed it to him, hilt first. Ethan gave her the blade he had taken.

Sephira slipped the weapon into her pocket and looked into Ethan's eyes. "You were fortunate tonight," she said, her voice barely more than a whisper. Her breath smelled of wine.

"Being taken by the Church is fortunate? You know less about conjurers than I thought."

"You're not fooling me, and neither is your friend the minister."

"He's—"

She touched a finger to his lips. "Shhh. You're my Grail, Ethan. I quest for you. You may have escaped me again, but you'll be mine eventually. And before I'm through with you you'll wish you were back laboring in the Indies." She flashed a radiant smile and turned from him. "He's yours tonight, Reverend, sir," she said, walking past Pell without so much as a glance in his direction. "But all you've done is delay the inevitable."

FIFTEEN

onjurers in the American colonies and back in England and the rest of Europe had for centuries been persecuted
as witches. Hangings and burnings had occurred in just about
every country Ethan could name. Women had been executed as witches
in Massachusetts within the last century, and to this day ministers
throughout the colonies railed against the dangers of witchcraft, claim-
ing that those who conjured were in league with Satan.

It probably didn't help that in order to conjure, a speller had to
bridge the gap between the living world and the domain of the dead,
the ethereal realm of spirit and soul. That was why a speller needed a
guide in the form of a ghost; it was why Ethan needed Uncle Reg.

Accusations of witchcraft often began within a family or a small
circle of friends, and Ethan wondered if those who made the accusations were people like Bett, who themselves had forsworn conjuring, but saw those they loved, or were supposed to love, casting spells
and communing with ghosts. Whatever the source of such accusations, he felt certain that even in Boston, even in 1765, a man such
as himself, who was known to have conjured—who bore scars that
proved as much—lived in constant danger of being accused, tried,
and executed.

Ethan trusted Pell as much as a conjurer could ever trust a minister, but he felt little more at ease in the company of Stephen Greenleaf

than he had when Sephira's toughs had him trapped. The sheriff had yet to produce a gun, but Ethan did not doubt that he carried one.

"Twice in as many days, Mister Kaille," he said at last. "This time it seems that I'll be taking you into custody."

Pell had been standing in the same spot, watching Sephira as she followed her men down the lane. Upon hearing what Greenleaf said, though, he strode over to Ethan. Uncle Reg started to fade as the minister approached, casting one last glance Ethan's way.

"We'll be taking him to King's Chapel, Sheriff," Pell said.

Ethan could tell that he was trying to sound authoritative, but Greenleaf showed no sign of being impressed.

"I don't work for you or the Reverend Caner, Mister Pell," he said. "If Mister Kaille has broken laws in this county, it falls to me to see that he's punished."

"I was defending myself against Sephira Pryce and her men," Ethan said. "They outnumbered me twelve to one! And you're worried about me breaking the law?"

"Miss Pryce's reputation is unimpeachable," Greenleaf said, raising his chin. Ethan noticed that the sheriff had yet to come close to where Ethan stood. "Mister Pell says that you used . . . witchcraft against them. Is this true?"

"No," Ethan told him, his eyes meeting the sheriff's. "I don't engage in witchcraft."

This was true in the strictest sense. Conjurers weren't witches. Like most spellers, Ethan believed that witches were the stuff of legend—an imagined threat dreamt up by overzealous ministers. Conjurers were as real as the flames he had just summoned.

Greenleaf didn't seem to know what to make of Ethan's denial, but he continued to keep his distance.

"Are you hurt?" Pell asked. His gaze fell to Ethan's bloody shoulder. "Is that a knife wound?"

"A bullet wound, actually. What are you doing here?"

Pell glanced quickly at the sheriff and swallowed. "Arresting you, as ordered by the Reverend Henry Caner of King's Chapel, Boston. We're to take you back to the church."

Greenleaf shook his head. "As I've already told you, I don't answer to Mister Caner."

"We all answer to the Lord, Sheriff," Pell said. "Or do you deny His authority as well?"

The sheriff opened his mouth, but then snapped it shut again. The sky had dimmed almost to black, but Ethan could see that his cheeks burned red.

"Mister Kaille," Pell said, turning to face him. "May I have your blade please?"

Ethan hesitated, but only for a brief moment. Even without his blade, there was enough blood on his clothes for a conjuring. He handed the knife to his friend.

"Very good," Pell said, slipping it into a pocket within his robe. "As long as you cooperate, there'll be no need for us to use force. At the first sign of resistance, we'll have no choice but to resort to harsher means of controlling you. Do you understand?"

"Of course."

"We'll see to your wounds when we reach the church. Then you'll be apprised of the charges against you."

"All right."

"Lead the way, Sheriff," Pell said to Greenleaf.

It was cleverly done. The sheriff couldn't object to being offered the lead, and this way Ethan and Pell could walk together and keep an eye on the man.

A small frown wrinkled Greenleaf's brow, but a moment later, he started leading them back toward the chapel. Ethan and the minister followed him up the deserted lane, onto Hollis Street, and then onto Clough. They skirted the edge of the Common, following a narrow country lane toward the Granary and King's Chapel. Pell said nothing, and Ethan thought it best to follow his example.

At this hour the lanes of Boston were far less crowded than when Sephira's men had forced him into their carriage. Still, the few people who were abroad stared at him as the sheriff marched him past. A few gave him a second, closer look.

Ethan's side ached when he inhaled, his head hurt from where

Sephira's man had kicked him, and his shoulder throbbed. He had been bloodied and beaten more in the past few days than at any time since the beatings he had been given upon arriving at the plantation in Barbados so many years ago. It hadn't escaped him that every time he learned something new, something that moved him closer to discovering the identity of Jennifer Berson's killer, Sephira showed up to threaten him, or that ghostly little girl confronted him in the streets around his home. He knew this was no mere coincidence.

Before long they reached the chapel grounds. They entered the yard through the gate on Treamount Street, and Pell stepped past Greenleaf, leading the sheriff and Ethan up the steps and into the sanctuary. The minister indicated that Ethan should sit in one of the pews.

"I'll stay with Kaille, Mister Pell," the sheriff said. "You can inform the rector that we're here."

"Actually, Sheriff, I prefer to remain here with Mister Kaille. Mister Caner can be found at his home across the burying ground. Would you be so kind as to tell him what's happened."

Greenleaf's frown was more pronounced this time. "Forgive me, but I'm not sure that would be wise. If Kaille tries to escape you won't be able to stop him."

A look of annoyance crossed Pell's face. "Of course. You're right, Sheriff." He cast an uncertain look Ethan's way, but then left the chapel.

For several moments neither Ethan nor the sheriff said a word. Greenleaf watched him, though, his pale eyes narrowed.

"If you're not a witch where did those flames come from?" he asked at last.

Ethan kept his eyes trained on the chapel floor. "Don't you think Sephira is capable of lighting a fire?"

"Of course, but why would she?"

"You should ask her."

Greenleaf came closer, so that he loomed over Ethan. "I'm asking you."

Ethan looked up at him serenely. "You might wish to consider, Sheriff, that if I am a witch, and I have all this blood on my clothes, I can reduce you to a pile of ash with little more than a thought."

"But . . . but you said . . ."

"I know exactly what I said. I also know that you didn't believe me. Do you believe me now?"

Before the sheriff could answer, the chapel door opened again and Pell entered. "Mister Caner will join us shortly," he said. He looked from Greenleaf to Ethan, a question in his eyes.

Ethan gave a small shake of his head. Greenleaf moved away again.

Pell came over to stand by Ethan, as if protecting him. Silence descended on the chapel once more, save for the patter of rain on the sanctuary windows.

"Does the bullet wound hurt much?" the minister asked after some time, his voice low.

Ethan kept his gaze fixed on the sheriff. "It still hurts, yes," he said in a whisper.

"There's a welt on your temple, too."

"One of Sephira Pryce's men kicked me there, and in the side. I may have a broken rib." He glanced up at the minister. "Again."

Pell's eyes danced with mischief. "I'm beginning to think that you're not as good at thieftaking as I first thought."

Any other time, Ethan would have laughed. But they were waiting for Caner. Pell might have trusted Caner to help them with this pretense, but Ethan had his doubts. The rector hated him. Regardless of any friendship Ethan and Pell had built these last few days, Caner might well see in this night's events the perfect opportunity to rid himself and his church of what he saw as a dark threat.

Seconds later, the door to the chapel opened once more, and Caner entered the building.

"It will be all right," Pell mouthed.

Ethan merely shook his head.

The rector strode down the central aisle of the sanctuary to where Pell waited for him. With some effort, Ethan stood. Caner looked Ethan over, his eyes lingering on the welt on his head and the bloody hole in his coat. Then he turned to Greenleaf.

"What is all this, Sheriff? Why have you brought this man into my chapel?"

Greenleaf blinked. "Mister Pell didn't tell you?"

"I'm not speaking to Mister Pell, am I?" the rector said. "I asked you a question. What is this man doing here?"

"We . . . we found him with Miss Pryce. He was . . . he was standing at the center of a ring of flame that I believe he started with some kind of . . . witchcraft. And two of Miss Pryce's men had been wounded. One had been burned. I believe the other had broken bones in both legs. I expect those injuries also were the result of some devilry." He turned to Pell, looking for help. "Don't you agree, Mister Pell?"

"He's wounded, too," the rector said, before Pell could respond. "Did you notice that?"

Greenleaf shifted his weight from one foot to the other. "Well . . . um . . . yes. Yes, I did."

"Do you believe that those injuries also came from witchcraft?"

"No, Reverend, sir."

"Why not?"

"Well, because one of Miss Pryce's men had a pistol that might have been used to shoot his arm."

"I see," Caner said. "And what about that bruise on his head?"

"I don't know how he got that, Mister Caner," Greenleaf answered. "I suppose one of Pryce's men could have done that, too."

"Did you actually see this man cast any sort of . . . spell?"

The sheriff rubbed a hand over his mouth. "No, Reverend, sir. But Miss Pryce said—"

"They were fighting—this man, and Miss Pryce's men. Is that not so?" Caner's expression was severe.

"Well, yes, it is. But—"

"I understand that Miss Pryce enjoys some renown in this city, but for all she does on behalf of the people of Boston, we must remember that she is a creature of the streets, just as Mister Kaille is. Did it never occur to you that she might have made the accusations she did to bring injury to an enemy?"

"Well—"

Caner regarded Ethan dismissively. "You've got the wrong man."

"But, the fires—" Greenleaf began.

"The fires must have been set by Pryce's men," Pell said. "As you say, Sheriff, we found Mister Kaille standing in the center of the ring, and

Miss Pryce's men were all around him. It retrospect it seems that he was the one most at risk from those flames."

The sheriff gaped at Pell. "But you said that he—"

"I'm afraid I might have been mistaken," the young minister said. "My apologies."

Caner laid a hand on Pell's shoulder and offered an indulgent smile. "Mister Pell is new to the ministry and is still subject to some of the foibles of youth. I'm sure you understand."

Greenleaf straightened and glowered at Caner and the minister. "I think I do, Mister Caner," he said pointedly. He eyed Ethan again.

"You did all that you could under the circumstances," Caner told him. "You have my deepest gratitude."

"Yes, I'm sure," the sheriff said. The rector's words were a clear dismissal. He regarded Ethan once more. "I'm sure our paths will cross again, Kaille. I, for one, will be looking forward to it." He nodded to Pell, cast one last dark look Ethan's way, and left the chapel.

Even after the door closed, Ethan waited several moments before asking Caner, "Why would you do that?"

The rector shrugged, opened his hands. "I saw you taken. Under normal circumstances I wouldn't have thought to intervene. A dispute between two thieftakers is no concern of the Church. But in this case, I thought to make an exception. Not for your sake, but for that of Abner and Catherine Berson."

"Well, thank you. I'm in your debt."

"A debt you can repay by renouncing witchery, turning to God, and vowing never to let the words of a conjuring pass your lips again."

Ethan stared at the man. He opened his mouth, closed it again. He glanced at Pell, whose eyes were trained on the floor, his lips pursed.

At last, Ethan faced the rector once more. "I'm afraid I can't do that, Mister Caner."

He expected the man to pursue the point. Instead, Caner's mouth quirked to the side. "No, I don't suppose you can. But the Lord wouldn't forgive me if I didn't try." He started toward the door of the chapel. "I won't always be so tolerant, Mister Kaille. Don't let me hear of you conjuring again."

"I'll do my best."

"Trevor, I expect you to retire shortly. You have your studies, and I won't have you wandering the city at all hours."

"Yes, Mister Caner." When the rector was gone, Pell beckoned to Ethan. "Come. We'll get you to a surgeon."

"I can heal myself. I've already done a bit on the bullet wound."

Pell eyed him sternly, although the effect was muted somewhat by the youthfulness of his face. "I don't care. Mister Caner and I just lied to Sheriff Greenleaf in order to keep him from imprisoning you as a witch! You will not heal yourself of these wounds!"

Ethan didn't argue. He gestured for the minister to lead the way. "How did you know where to find me?" he asked as they walked out of the chapel and onto Treamount.

"Mister Caner said they had taken you toward the Neck," Pell said. "So we started in that direction. When I heard the pistol, I thought it might be aimed at you, so we followed the sound of the report."

"Well," Ethan said, "you saved my life. You and Mister Caner. I couldn't have fought off Sephira and her men much longer."

"I thought you were doing pretty well."

"You mean aside from the bullet wound and the bruise and that dented rib I mentioned."

Pell grinned. "Well, yes, aside from all of that."

They had turned down Winter Street and were approaching Newbury Street, and the pasture lands.

"Where are we going?" Ethan asked.

"To the home of a doctor I know."

"A member of the congregation?"

Pell shook his head. "Someone I met when I first came to Boston. I'd come from western Connecticut, and had been taken with a fever. Doctor Church got me well."

They stopped at a modest house with a gabled roof and a welcoming glow of candles shining from within. Pell knocked once, and after a short wait the door opened, revealing a tall man with stooped shoulders and long, powdered hair. His eyes were deep-set, his nose strong, his chin somewhat weak.

"Mister Pell," the man said, sounding genuinely surprised and pleased to see the minister.

"Good evening, Doctor Church," Pell said. "Forgive us for impos-ing on your time so late in the evening. I bring you a patient; a friend of mine who is in need of your skills."

The doctor looked at Ethan, his eyes lingering briefly on the bruise on Ethan's temple and the bloodstains on his coat.

"Of course," the man said. He stepped aside and waved them into the house.

The door opened onto a comfortable sitting room, illuminated by spermaceti candles and warmed by a fire in the hearth.

"Doctor Benjamin Church," Pell said, "may I introduce, Ethan Kaille. Ethan, Doctor Church."

Ethan and the doctor shook hands.

"Who is it, Benjamin?" came a woman's voice from another room.

"A patient, Hannah," the doctor called. "No need to trouble yourself." He eyed Ethan again. "This way, gentlemen," he said, and led them to a back room.

He lit several candles, their glow building gradually to reveal a chamber that was far more austere than the previous one. Jars and bottles jostled for room atop of a cabinet against one wall. Next to it, a table held a number of steel surgical instruments. Ethan glanced at them before quickly looking away. Healing himself with conjurings was one thing; surgeons made him queasy.

Dr. Church pulled a chair to the middle of the room. "Sit," he said. Ethan did as he was told.

"We'll start with the shoulder," the doctor said, stepping to a wash-basin and scrubbing his hands. "I'd say that's the worst of it."

Ethan cast a quick self-conscious look at Pell. He had already healed that wound, at least enough to stop the bleeding.

Pell misunderstood. Or else he was as squeamish as Ethan. "Perhaps I'll wait in the other room," he said, a wan smile flitting across his pale features.

"All right," Church said absently. "Take off your coat if you can manage it," he told Ethan. "Your waistcoat and shirt, too."

Reluctantly, Ethan peeled off the bloodstained coat, removed his waistcoat, and pulled his shirt over his head. The doctor stepped around him and leaned over to peer at the bullet wound, which was still badly discolored, despite Ethan's spell. After a moment, he straightened again.

"I see," Church muttered. "I take it the bullet never actually entered your body."

"No, sir. I was fortunate."

"Indeed, you were. Still, it would have better if you had cleaned that wound before healing it."

Ethan stared at him, his mouth hanging open. He had expected questions, even accusations; not this blithe acceptance of his healing spell.

"Come now," the doctor said. "You can't believe that you are the first of your kind I've encountered."

"No, sir," Ethan said, recovering from his surprise. "I had to heal it when I did. I couldn't afford to lose too much blood."

"At least not that way."

Ethan chuckled. "That's right."

"The bruise at your temple is new. The rest are a few days old."

"Yes, and I think I might have a broken rib." He pointed to the spot where Sephira's man kicked him.

The doctor began to probe Ethan's rib with deft fingers.

"It isn't broken," he said after a few moments. "Though one of these ribs feels like it's healed from a previous break." When Ethan didn't respond, the doctor went on. "You've had a rough time of it. Perhaps you should consider finding another line of work."

"Pell would agree with you."

"I'm sure." The doctor examined his shoulder again, then straightened once more, shaking his head. "Well, Mister Kaille, I'm afraid there isn't much I can do for you. Your bruises will heal on their own. The bullet wound should as well. If it becomes fevered or if there is discharge of any sort, come back and see me."

"I will, Doctor. Thank you."

Church crossed to the door. "Get dressed. I'll be with Mister Pell."

The doctor left him and Ethan pulled his clothes back on with care, inhaling sharply through his teeth whenever he moved his shoulder too quickly or twisted his torso too suddenly. When at last he was dressed again, he joined Pell and Church in the sitting room.

Pell turned at the sound of Ethan's approach. The minister looked relieved to see him. "Doctor Church was just asking me what you've been doing that would lead to so many injuries. I didn't know what to tell him."

"It's all right," Ethan told the minister. To Church he said, "I'm looking into the death of Jennifer Berson."

The doctor's expression sobered. "I see. Forgive me for asking."

"It's all right," Ethan said, remembering at last something that should have come to him long ago. "You know, before Sephira Pryce's men invited me into their carriage, I was on my way to King's Chapel to ask you a question, Mister Pell. But perhaps I would be best served asking both of you. The day Ann and John Richardson were hanged, were there any other unexplained deaths in the city?"

Both men considered the question for a few moments.

At last, Pell shook his head. "Not so far as I know."

"I don't recall hearing of any, either," the doctor said. "Why do you ask?"

"Something I heard," Ethan said. Another thought came to him; a recollection of his conversation with Holin the previous day.

"Did either of you see the Richardsons' corpses after their hanging?"

"No," Pell said. "I believe they were cut down and thrown in a shallow grave."

"And good riddance to them," the doctor added.

Many people, Ethan knew, shared this view of the Richardsons. He himself did.

Pell was watching him. "There's no doubt as to how they died, Ethan."

"No, of course not." Ethan started to say more, but then stopped himself. "Doctor, we've taken up enough of your time. What do I owe you?"

The doctor shook his head. "Nothing. Which is about what I did for you."

"We've intruded upon your evening, bothered you at your home—"

"Thank you, Mister Kaille. Perhaps, in the future, if I have need of a thieftaker, you'll do a favor for me."

"It would be my honor, sir," Ethan said.

Church walked them to the door. "You know, if you're looking for someone who might have had something to do with Jennifer Berson's death—"

"Let me guess," Ethan said. "Ebenezer Mackintosh."

"You know of him."

"How could I not? Every person I meet wants to blame him for the girl's murder. It may be the only point of agreement between Thomas Hutchinson and Samuel Adams."

"You've spoken with Samuel?"

"Yes. James Otis and Peter Darrow, as well. Do you know them?"

Apparently Church found the question amusing. "We're acquainted, yes." His tone said much more. Ethan thought it likely that Benjamin Church was allied with Adams and the others.

"I found it interesting," Ethan said, "that Mister Darrow should help Mackintosh escape punishment for one death, and then accuse the man of complicity in another."

The doctor's shrug was noncommittal. "Peter knows Mackintosh better than most. And I, for one, trust his judgment in such matters."

They stood eyeing each other for another moment. Then Ethan forced a smile. "Well, good evening, Doctor. Thank you for your care and your time."

"You're welcome, Mister Kaille." Church nodded to the minister. "Mister Pell."

Ethan and Pell left the house and started walking back to King's Chapel, their collars raised against the rain.

"Where will you go next?" Pell asked after a lengthy silence.

"Why? Are you planning to follow me around the city with the sheriff or men of the watch?"

"That's not a bad idea."

Actually, Ethan reflected, it wasn't.

"I'm going to the Dowsing Rod," Ethan said. "And then home, I would imagine. I've had a long day. Another one."

Pell said nothing for several moments. "Why were you asking about the Richardsons?" he finally asked.

"Something a friend told me, about feeling a spell that day." He

raised his shoulders, then immediately winced at the pain. "I've wondered if this conjurer might be responsible for a third killing, in addition to Jennifer Berson, and the Brown boy on Pope's Day."

They had reached King's Chapel, and they stopped in front of it.
Pell wore a thoughtful look, his brow creased, his hair wet with rain.
"I was at the hanging," he said, his voice low.

"Did you feel a spell?" Ethan asked.

"I don't know. I remember being uneasy. Something about that day
wasn't right. But even now I can't put a name to it." Pell took a breath.
"Did I feel a spell? At the time I wouldn't have known. I've only come
to recognize the feeling these past few days, watching you conjure." He
shook his head. "This is all too new."

"It's all right," Ethan said. He put out his hand, and Pell grasped
it. "Thank you."

"For what?"

Ethan laughed. "For saving my life. For taking me to see Doctor
Church. For helping me find Jennifer Berson's killer."

"I've helped?"

"I think so."

"I don't understand any of it."

"I'm not certain that I do either," Ethan said. "Not entirely, at
least. But if I'm right, there's a conjurer out there who's using spells,
fueled by these deaths, to make others do his bidding."

Pell's eyes went wide. "A conjurer can do that?"

"Absolutely. Conjurings can do most anything, if the person casting them is willing to pay a high enough cost. I could make you take
your own life, but I would have to take the life of another to do it. I
could destroy this entire city, but I'd probably have to bleed myself to
death."

"So this conjurer—"

"This conjurer is skilled and powerful, and entirely willing to spend
the lives of others in pursuit of his aims, whatever they may be. I can't
think of anything more dangerous."

"How will you stop him?" Pell asked.

Ethan smiled wryly. "I haven't the faintest idea. Good night, Mister Pell."

He left the minister beside the chapel gate and began to make his way through the streets to the Dowser, nervously surveying storefronts and alleys. He felt vulnerable; for the second time in as many days, he was forced to admit to himself that the simple act of walking through the city had him frightened. He had survived battles at sea and years as a prisoner. He had been wounded and beaten and had gone to sleep many nights wondering if he would live long enough to win his freedom. And here he was, scared of shadows on a deserted lane. A part of him wished that on that first day in the Dowser he'd had the sense to send away Abner Berson's man. . . .

"No." He said it aloud, startling an elderly man who hurried along through the darkness and mist in the opposite direction.

This is what Sephira and the conjurer want, he told himself. The beatings and the threats were intended to make him give up. Or to kill him. They weren't going to succeed at either. This conjurer had to be stopped. As Ethan had told Pell, spells cast without regard for life were a threat to every person in Boston. No one would be safe as long as this conjurer walked the streets.

Ethan forced himself to slow down, to stop peering over his shoulder every other moment. By the time he reached the Dowser, he felt better.

Stepping inside the tavern, he took a long steadying breath. This one place never really changed. The same people sat at the bar or crowded around tables, arguing over the same matters, laughing at the same jokes. As always the Dowser was warm and bright, and it smelled of pipe smoke and ale and stew. And as always, stepping inside and being greeted by those aromas made Ethan realize that he was famished.

He walked to the bar, searching for Kannice.

"HiEthan," the burly barkeep said, running the words together as always.

"Hi, Kelf."

"Kannice's in back. Wan' me t' get her?"

"Actually, no." Ethan felt around in his pocket for a pair of shillings and handed them to the man. "She didn't let me pay a couple of nights ago, and she won't tonight, either. So this is just between the two of us, all right?"

"Course. What'll ya have?"

"What's the stew tonight?" Immediately he raised his good hand, forestalling an answer. "Doesn't matter. I'll have a bowl and an ale."

"I'll bring it t' ya."

"My thanks, Kelf." Ethan walked to the back of the tavern, winding his way past the usual crowd. Diver wasn't there, so he sat alone, as he often did, at an empty table far from the door.

A few moments later, Kannice arrived at his table with a bowl of mutton stew and a tankard of pale ale. She placed them in front of him and kissed the top of his head.

"I'm glad to see you," she said, hovering behind him.

He took hold of her hands and kissed them both. "And I you."

"I hate to . . ." She faltered. Ethan twisted around in his chair to look at her, taking care not to let her see his newest bruise. She still stood behind him, chewing her lip. "I'm sorry, Ethan. I know things have been hard for you the past few days. But I can't . . . well . . . I need you to pay for the food and drink. I hope you understand."

Ethan hesitated, but only for a moment. She had given him more free food than he cared to remember. He could afford to pay twice this one night. "Of course, I understand," he said. He dug into his pocket again, searching for another coin.

Kannice stared down at him, an odd expression on her face, as if . . . He stopped searching for the coin just as she burst out laughing.

"You would have paid me again, wouldn't you?" she said breathlessly.

Ethan looked back at Kelf, who grinned at him from behind the bar. Ethan leveled a finger at him and the man threw back his head and laughed.

"He promised me he would keep that quiet," Ethan said as Kannice sat down across from him.

"Kelf works for me, not for you. Besides, I saw him putting the coins in the till and . . ." She trailed off, her smile vanishing as she noticed the welt on his head. "What's happened now?"

"Sephira and her men."

"They beat you again?" Her eyes fell to his shoulder. "And is that blood on your coat?"

He nodded.

"A knife?"

"A bullet, actually."

"A bullet!" she repeated, so loudly that others paused in their conversations.

"It just grazed me," he said, speaking softly.

"Does it hurt?"

"Some." *A lot, actually.* "I've seen a doctor. I'm fine."

She frowned. "Is that right?"

He held her gaze. "Aye."

"All right, then let's go back to Sephira for a minute. She's not content with beatings and threats anymore?"

"No, I think she intended to kill me this time, but I got away with help from a minister and Sheriff Greenleaf." He smiled self-consciously. "That sounds a little strange, doesn't it?"

She blinked. After several moments, she shook her head, allowing herself a small, breathless laugh. "The crazy thing is I believe you."

"Well, I should hope so."

"And I should hope that after all this you would give up your inquiry and keep yourself alive. But that's probably too much to ask, isn't it?"

"Do I even have to answer that?"

She took a breath, her blue eyes never leaving his. "No," she finally said. "So then why don't you tell me what you know so far?"

He smiled and she took his hand. He began to tell her what he had learned from Janna and Pell about killing spells and the death of the boy. He also told her about his conversations with Hutchinson and Derne, and with Adams and his friends.

"This conjurer is really that strong?" she asked when he was done.

"Do you remember Nate Ramsey, the speller who escaped me a couple of years ago?"

Kannice nodded.

"This man makes Ramsey seem weak."

She took a long breath, her cheeks blanching. But her voice remained steady as she said, "And now you think he's used the lives of this boy and Jennifer Berson to cast his spells."

"He may have used a third person, too. I'm not sure. And they're not just any spells. They're control spells. I think he's using the deaths to get others to do his bidding."

"Do you think that he's using them for whatever he needs done at the time, or do you think there's a larger purpose behind the murders and the spells?"

Ethan considered this. It was a fine question, one he himself hadn't thought to ask. Kannice did this for him: She forced him to see things differently. Talking to her about his jobs was often like playing a game of chess and in the middle of it, rotating the board and looking at the pieces from his opponent's perspective.

"I think they are connected," Ethan finally said. "I couldn't tell you how, though, or even why I think so. I've been trying to put myself in this conjurer's mind, but I can't get myself to think as he does."

"I would have been surprised if you could." She gave his hand a squeeze and got up from the table. "Eat. I'll come by again later."

"Hey, wait," he said, stopping her. "Did Diver say if he would be coming by tonight?"

"Do you mean when he was here last night?"

"No, today. This afternoon."

"He wasn't here today."

"Well, of course—" He stopped, narrowing his eyes. He hadn't actually seen Diver enter the Dowser; they hadn't reached it yet. And Diver told him at the time he hadn't intended to come to the tavern at all. Still, his friend had acted strangely throughout their encounter.

"Are you worried about him?" Kannice asked.

"This is Diver we're talking about. I'm always worried about him. But I'm sure it's nothing."

She went back to the kitchen, and Ethan finished his ale and bowl of stew. Kelf brought him seconds of both, and Ethan finished these as well, sopping up the last of the stew with an end of fresh bread.

As he ate, he considered what Ebenezer Mackintosh might gain by committing these murders and making enemies of men on both sides of the Stamp Act conflict. So many believed that Mackintosh was guilty; perhaps it was time that Ethan spoke with the Commander of the South End, not only to hear what Mackintosh might say in his own defense, but also to see if he could determine whether the man was a conjurer. He was still pondering this sometime later when Kannice joined him at his table.

"Feeling better?" she asked.

"I am, thank you."

She stared at her hands. "Are you going to stay?"

"I'd like to," he said. "But I shouldn't. Not while this conjurer is after me."

"You're here now."

"Yes, now, when the tavern's crowded with people. But staying the night could be dangerous." He brushed the hair from her forehead. "If something happened to you because of what I'm doing . . ." He shook his head. "I probably shouldn't stay until all this is over."

"Wouldn't you be safer here?" she asked. "Sephira and her toughs beat you in your home. You said the conjurer found you in the lane not far from Henry's shop. They know where you live."

"I'm not worried about me."

She leaned forward and gently touched her lips to the bump on his temple. "I know," she whispered. "That's probably why you look such a mess."

Ethan cupped her cheek in his hand and they both smiled. He kissed her lips and she returned the kiss hungrily.

Eventually Ethan pulled away. "I want to stay," he said again. "But I think I have to go. Now. Before you convince me not to."

Again she smiled. "All right. Come see me tomorrow."

"Of course."

Ethan stood and kissed her brow before leaving the table. He raised a hand as he passed Kelf on his way to the door, and pulling his coat tighter around his shoulders, stepped out into the street. The rain was falling harder now, though the air was warmer and the wind had died down.

He walked swiftly through the center of the city toward the South End, passing the prison, the Town House, and the Old Meeting House. Tense, watchful, he started at every sound he heard. The closer he got to his home, the more uneasy he grew, until he felt that every muscle in his body was coiled, ready for a fight. Still walking, he reached for the pouch of mullein leaves Janna had given him. He pulled out three leaves and a few dried flowers, and held them ready.

"*Veni ad me.*" Come to me.

The air hummed and Uncle Reg appeared beside him, his expression grim, his fists clenched. Not a good sign.

They turned onto Cooper's Alley, and Ethan froze, the blood draining from his face.

All the windows on his street were dark; with the sky covered over and the rain falling there was precious little light. But Anna stood in the middle of the street, blocking his way, glowing faintly in the darkness, her hair clinging to her forehead as if soaked, a hard look in her pale, overlarge eyes.

Ethan backed away, knowing that he couldn't fight her. He had the mullein, but that wouldn't be enough against the conjurer.

But before he could flee, the girl shook her head. "Stay where you are."

"So you can kill me? No, thank you."

"I think you will."

Light flared so brightly that he had to shield his eyes. When he looked again, he saw that a flame hung over the street just behind her, as if suspended by some unseen hand. Beneath it, in the dancing golden glow of the fire, something lay on the rain-soaked cobblestones.

Not something, someone.

Holin.

than's first thought was that the boy was dead, murdered just as Jennifer Berson and the Brown child had been. Holin didn't move. His face was deathly pale, his mouth locked in what Ethan feared was a permanent grimace, his eyes squeezed shut as if he was in pain. Rain ran over his cheeks like tears. His hands were rigid and clawed. One might have thought that he was struggling to move, to break free of whatever spell the conjurer had placed on him.

But Anna—the conjurer—had wanted Ethan to stay. She—he?— was using Holin as bait, to lure Ethan to the wraith so that she could use the full weight of her power to destroy him. It was the only hope Ethan had for the boy; Holin had to be alive.

"You didn't listen," Anna said, walking toward him slowly. "You didn't . . ." She cocked her head to the side and sniffed the air. A moment later, she laughed. "Mullein!" she said, sounding delighted. "You think that a few leaves of speller's herb will help you stand against me?" She shook her head, her mirth vanishing as quickly as it had come. "You're a fool, Kaille."

"*Tegimen!*" Ethan barely even breathed the word. "*Ex verbasco evocatum!*" Warding, conjured from mullein!

The leaves and flowers in his hand melted away, like sand in seawater, and the cobblestones beneath his feet sang with power. He felt the warding coil up his legs like twin snakes, wrapping itself around him, enveloping him.

"A warding," the girl said, as the protection reached his waist, his midriff, his chest. "How quaint. I could kill you where you stand, despite your spell and your herbs and whatever else you might think to try against me." She leaned her head to the side, the glow of her skin ghoulish. "But I'll give you one more chance before I do that."

"What spell did you use on him?" Ethan demanded.

The little girl smiled. "One of my own, one that you could never do."

Ethan pushed up his sleeve, intending to cut himself and try to revive the boy with a spell.

"Don't," the girl said. She didn't raise her voice at all, but Ethan stopped with his blade poised over his forearm. "If you try to free him, I'll kill you both. There's only one way you can save his life, and you already know what that is."

Ethan glared at her, finally responding with one curt nod. "You want me to forget about Jennifer Berson."

"I've told you as much before. You should have listened to me. I would be within my rights to kill the boy as punishment for what you've done."

"Punish me. Not the boy. He's done nothing to you."

"But what if I can punish you by hurting the boy? That accomplishes much for me. I would like to kill you, Kaille. I'm tempted to kill you right now. But if I do, it will raise suspicions. Berson knows what you're doing. He'll wonder if your death has something to do with his daughter." She shook her head. "No, I need for you to go back and tell him that it was Folter all along, that he was working for Ebenezer Mackintosh. I need you to say that you were wrong, that Folter was a speller after all, that there was no one else who could have done it. And when you've done that, I'll release the boy."

"No," Ethan said. "You'll release him now. Or I swear to God, I'll find you and I'll tear you apart with my bare hands."

Anna laughed, a high tinkling sound, like the laughter of any small girl. "Fool," she said.

He felt the pulse of the conjuring an instant before it slammed into him.

The next thing he knew he was on the ground, writhing so violently that he could feel his head and hands and arms flailing painfully against the cobblestones. He could do nothing to stop himself. It felt as if someone had sliced him open from sternum to gut and poured molten iron into his body. He heard a scream echoing off the buildings around him, realized it was his own. But there was nothing he could do to stop that, either.

She had laughed at his warding, at the mullein, at his empty threat. Now Ethan understood why. He had never before sensed such power; he had never felt so helpless, so utterly betrayed by his own conjuring abilities.

And then it was over. Ethan lay on the stone, panting, rain washing over his face. In that moment he would have done anything the conjurer asked for a simple promise that he would never endure such blazing agony again. He was sure that was exactly what the bastard wanted.

He forced himself up, staggered, but quickly righted himself. His ghost watched him. Normally Reg would have been laughing at his failure, or shaking his head in disappointment. Not this time. The ghost actually looked scared.

"If you think," Ethan said to Anna, "that I'm going to let you have him just because you managed to hurt me a little, you're—"

Gods! Weren't mullein and a warding worth anything? Ethan was on the ground again, his back arched, his teeth clenched so tight he thought they would shatter. Red-hot iron flowed like blood through his limbs, his body, his head. He wanted to scream again, but couldn't. He wanted to tear his skin open to get the iron out, to let that rainwater cool him. He could imagine it sizzling, turning instantly to vapor. He could—

Breathe. He could breathe, again. He opened his mouth to let in a few drops of rain, coughed, and sat up too quickly. When his head stopped spinning he climbed to his feet once more.

Tegimen, he thought. *Ex verbasco evocatum.* Warding, conjured from mullein. He used more of the leaves this time, hoping for a more potent casting.

"Another warding won't help you," the girl said. "It doesn't matter how many leaves you use. My power flows too deep for the likes of you."

More than anything in the world just then, Ethan would have liked to punch this conjurer in the mouth. Obviously he was enormously powerful. But how did he know so much about Ethan's gift? The conjurer had to be close. The last time Ethan had seen the little girl—far from here at the town gate—the conjurer had barely been able to maintain the illusion. That wasn't the case tonight. In fact, the conjurer had managed to attack Ethan with one spell while maintaining that image of Anna. Ethan couldn't have done that; he wouldn't even have known how to make the attempt.

"Then you'll have to kill me," Ethan said, stalling now. "Because I won't let you have Holin."

Too often during these encounters with the girl, Ethan allowed himself to think about the conjurer's power, and how weak he was by comparison. The time had come to consider what he could do, not what he couldn't. He had tried a finding spell the second time he saw the girl, and it had failed. But why did he need a finding spell at all? Why not let an attack spell find the conjurer for him?

He still had his knife in hand and now he held it up for the girl to see. She gazed back at him, frowning in confusion. As she watched, Ethan fitted the blade back into its sheath, guiding it in with the other hand. But as the knife slid in, he allowed it to cut the skin between his thumb and forefinger.

Discuti! Shatter! The word echoed in his mind as blood began to flow from the wound on his hand. *Ex cruore evocatum!* Conjured from blood!

Again, Ethan felt the conjuring, and he knew that the conjurer had as well. But he hoped that the conjurer wouldn't be expecting an attack when Ethan had yet to try a finding spell, and that watching him through Anna's eyes, the man hadn't noticed the blood on his hand and so would be expecting a weaker spell.

For once, fortune was on Ethan's side. He heard a sound—half cry, half snarl. A man's voice, beyond doubt, colored in equal measure by rage and shock and pain. At the same time, Anna disappeared, as if snatched away by demons. Ethan sprinted to Holin's side as quickly as his leg would allow.

The boy yet breathed, though only just, his chest rising and falling in a shallow, irregular rhythm. The rain had soaked through his clothes. His skin felt cold and his lips were a pale shade of blue.

Ethan slid his arms under the lad, knowing that Holin wouldn't survive much longer without a fire, dry clothes, and warm blankets.

"You shouldn't have done that!" He knew without looking that Anna was back and standing behind him. She didn't sound like a child anymore. Her voice was taut and harsh; a little girl's voice blended with that of a grown man.

In the next instant, Ethan pitched forward over Holin, landed hard on his shoulder, and rolled onto his back. The molten iron seared his entire body from the inside, filling every inch of him, to the very tips of his fingers. He opened his mouth to scream, felt himself vomit instead. But still the anguish continued to build until he feared that his mind would melt or explode or simply cease to function.

He won't stop until I'm dead. Ethan didn't need Anna to tell him this. He knew it, and for an instant he welcomed the idea. No more life; no more pain.

As soon as he formed this thought, the agony ceased, and again Ethan wondered if this conjurer could read his mind.

"Fine, Kaille."

Ethan stared up at the illusion. She still looked like a little girl, even if she sounded like some creature from beyond the living world.

"You leave me no choice but to end this matter. You'll watch the boy die, and then in the morning you'll go to the sheriff, and you'll tell him that you're the one who killed Jennifer Berson, and that little boy last fall, and this one as well. You'll admit that you're a conjurer; you'll tell him you used your 'witchery' to commit these murders so that you could cast control spells. I'm sure he'll piece together the rest."

"I'll go to him tonight! I'll tell him what's really happened."

"You won't remember what's really happened. By the time I'm done with my spell, you'll be passed out in the lane. You'll wake, find your-self next to the boy's body, and you'll know, as you do your own name, that you killed him."

Ethan reached for his blade, but before his hand even found the hilt, the same burning agony poured into his veins again. His body went rigid; his stomach heaved again. He would have clawed out his own eyes to make it stop.

"I can do this all night, Kaille. I can make you suffer in ways you never imagined, and well before my power is exhausted you'll beg me to kill the boy and cast my spell. Or you can accept that you've lost, and be spared that torment. It's your choice."

"Yes!" he rasped. "Just stop! Please!"

As soon as Ethan spoke the words, his pain drained away, leaving him spent and limp, his heart laboring. He forced his eyes open, saw the girl standing over him, tiny, luminescent, a fierce grin on her waif-like face.

"Good, Kaille," she said. "A wise choice, for once."

Ethan turned away from her, and doing so caught a glimpse of movement on the other side of the lane. Briefly—the span of a heart-beat; no more—he thought that someone had come to help him. But the form was too small, too dark. It took him a moment to recognize Pitch, his dark eyes shining with the distant glow of Anna's conjured fire.

Alarm crossed Anna's face and she glanced quickly in the direction Ethan was looking. Seeing the dog, however, her face relaxed back into that triumphant grin.

"It's a simple spell, really," she began, her voice easing back toward the normal tone of a small girl. "You speak it just the way you would any other. Strange, isn't it? There should be something different about a spell that kills. Don't you agree?"

Ethan barely listened to her. Pitch stood staring at him, his head canted to the side. Ethan stared back, his heart aching. What could he do to save Holin, to save himself? Nothing on his own. He couldn't match the conjurer's power or skill or cunning. Not alone. But he wasn't alone anymore.

"Pitch."

He mouthed the word, nothing more. But Pitch raised his ears and gave a tentative wag of his tail. Ethan felt hot tears mingle with the rain on his cheeks.

"Forgive me."

A different kind of pain clawed at Ethan from within, as potent as that caused by the conjurer's attacks, and more damning. For if he survived the night, this pain would never go away.

Anna had paused in what she was saying. Ethan sensed that she was watching him. He could imagine the confusion on the girl's face, but he didn't look up at her. He kept his eyes locked on Pitch's. And he spoke the words in his mind.

Caecitas ex vita huiusce canis—ex Pitch—evocata. Blindness, conjured from the life of this dog—from Pitch.

Instantly he felt the power of the spell thrumming along his entire body, like tens of thousands of tiny needle points tickling his skin. The cobblestones trembled with it. The entire city pulsed. Surely every conjurer in Boston felt it. Yet Pitch didn't shudder or flinch. He didn't make any sound at all. His legs gave way; he toppled onto his side and lay still.

Ethan realized that he was alone, save for Holin. Anna had vanished once more. He could hear the man—the conjurer—screaming again, fury and pain in the inarticulate cries. Probably he could have tracked him by the sounds, learned who he was. Under the circumstances, he might have prevailed in a battle of spells.

He didn't make the attempt. Struggling to his knees, he crawled to where Pitch lay, knowing that he ought to do something to honor the creature; knowing just as surely that he couldn't. As he ran trembling fingers over the wet fur of Pitch's head he tried to say again that he was sorry. The words caught in his throat. He climbed to his feet, staggered to Holin's side, and lifted the boy into his arms. Pausing once more to look at Pitch, he hurried down the lane, past Henry's shop and his room. At the next corner, he turned northward and bore the boy back into the North End to Elli's house.

By the time he reached her street he was exhausted and weak. The houses here were as dark as they had been on Cooper's Alley. All except Elli's. She would be panicked, unable to sleep or eat, unsure of whether to wait there with Clara or venture into the dark streets in search of her son. Even from down the lane, Ethan could see that candles shone in her windows, so that pale shafts of light cut across the street, making the rain sparkle. He saw her peer out into the night from the nearer of the two.

She must have seen him coming. In the next moment, her door flew open and she ran down the steps, heedless of the rain.

"What's happened to him?" she asked, her voice high and strained. "Is he hurt?"

"I don't know," Ethan told her, breathing hard, his leg aching.

He stepped past her, entered her house, and went immediately to the sitting room, where a fire blazed. He laid Holin on a sofa and began pulling off the boy's wet clothes.

"He looks half dead!" Elli said, hovering at Ethan's shoulder. "How did this happen? What mischief did you get him into now?"

He whirled on her so quickly that she fell back several steps. Grief and guilt and the memory of pain flared in his chest like conjured fire. But though a thousand angry replies leaped to mind, he bit them all back. There were tears in Elli's eyes, and her cheeks were every bit as ashen as her son's.

"I didn't do this," he said, struggling to keep his voice level. He could feel Pitch's wet fur under his fingertips. His chest burned with guilt, with grief, with the remembered pain of the conjurer's relentless attacks. "And I just . . . did something to save him—to save both of us—that I'll regret for the rest of my days."

She said nothing, but nodded.

Ethan turned his attention back to the boy's soaked clothes. "Get blankets, as many as you can find. And throw another log on that fire."

"Of course."

She hurried from the room, and Ethan finished undressing the boy. He moved the sofa so that it faced the hearth, and when Elli entered the room with an armful of blankets, he took several from her and together they laid them over the boy.

"Some soup or tea would help him," Ethan said.

"All right." She started to leave. "For you, too?"

He glanced back at her, their eyes meeting briefly. "Thank you."

Once more she left the room. Ethan knelt beside the sofa and studied Holin's face, head, and neck. He saw nothing to indicate that the boy had been injured, which meant that this stupor had been induced by a spell. Elli would kill him if she learned that he had conjured in her home, even if he cast the spell for Holin's benefit. So quickly, while she remained occupied in the kitchen, he pulled out a single mullein leaf.

"*Suscitatio ex verbasco evocata.*" Awaken, conjured from mullein.

At first nothing happened. Ethan considered trying the spell again with more leaves. But then the boy's eyelids fluttered, and he let out a low groan.

Instantly, Elli was by Ethan's side. "I thought I heard him."

"You did," Ethan said. "He should be awake before long."

Holin moaned again, opened his eyes and then closed them. A moment later, he shifted beneath the blankets, looking and sounding far more like a sleeping boy than like a child caught in the thrall of a conjurer.

"The Lord be praised," Elli said. Tears flowed freely down her face, and for once she made no effort to hide them from Ethan.

"He looks like he'll be all right now," Ethan said. He climbed to his feet, feeling old and sore and wearier than he would have thought possible. His clothes were as soaked as Holin's had been, and he realized that he was shivering. "I should go."

"The tea is almost ready," Elli said. "And there are some clothes in the back room that belonged to John. They should fit you. Get yourself changed. I want to know what happened tonight."

Ethan knew better than to argue. He limped to the back room and found an old chest filled with men's clothes, all of them far nicer—and no doubt far more expensive—than anything he owned. He rummaged through the chest until he found what had to be the oldest, most threadbare shirt and breeches John Harper had owned. He stripped off his wet clothes and put these on. The breeches were too long for him, though they fit around his middle, and he had to roll back the shirt-sleeves. But putting on the dry clothes made him feel far better. He returned to the sitting room, arranged his damp clothes before the hearth, and took a seat beside the fire. Soon, he had stopped shivering.

Elli had already settled into a chair by the hearth. She held a cup of steaming tea in one hand and was stroking Holin's wheat-colored hair with the other. As Ethan sat, she straightened a bit in her chair. A second cup of tea sat on a small table beside him. Elli pointed to it.

"Thank you," he said, picking up the cup and holding it under his nose. It smelled of apple and mint, and warmed his hands.

"Can you tell me what happened?" Elli asked. He could hear the effort she was making to keep any hint of accusation from seeping into the question. "Do you know why this was done to my boy?"

He hadn't even considered the question of why. He had seen Holin lying there in the lane, and had focused every subsequent thought on finding a way to save the boy's life. But as soon as Elli asked him, the answer became obvious. Sephira Pryce.

Sephira's men killed Daniel Folter, and Anna tried to convince Ethan that Daniel had killed Jennifer. Holin had seen Nigel and Ethan in the street, and now the conjurer had taken Holin and tried to use him for another killing spell. Sephira and this man were working together. But to what end?

"Ethan?"

His eyes snapped up to hers. "I'm sorry. I was . . . The short answer to your question is that Holin was taken because of me. Because someone saw us together yesterday, when I walked him home."

"Who?" she asked, as if intent on killing whoever it was herself.

"I shouldn't—"

"Who, Ethan?"

"Sephira Pryce," he said.

Elli blinked once, but offered no other response.

"You remember the conjurer I mentioned yesterday?"

She nodded, growing pale once more.

"He's the one who had Holin. But I think he and Sephira are working together. I think that's how he knew to go after Holin in the first place."

"Was he going to—?" She broke off, seeing the look on Ethan's face. "Holin could have died, just like those others."

"He's fine now. We were fortunate."

She stared at him for a long time, until at last Ethan looked away and sipped his tea.

"You weren't fortunate," she said. "You saved him. You told me you did something that you'll regret."

"Let it go, Elli." He said it softly, but he knew she wouldn't argue.

"Well, thank you," she said at length. "For whatever you did."

"Don't let him go to work tomorrow."

"Don't worry," she answered, falling into the stern tone he had heard her use with Holin and Clara. "What about the next day?"

"It'll be over by then." Speaking the words, he knew it was true. He could scarcely believe that his confrontation with Nigel had been only yesterday, that he had spoken with Janna this very morning. Tomorrow night was still a lifetime away, in more ways than one.

"You think you can defeat this conjurer so soon?"

Ethan shrugged, staring fixedly at the fire.

"Ethan?"

"If it takes longer than a day, and I think Holin is still in danger, I'll let you know."

He glanced Elli's way and found her watching him, her green eyes seeing right through the placid expression he had imposed on his features.

"That's not what you meant, is it?"

"Before I go, I need to wake him, and ask him some questions. Is that all right?"

He was sure she would object, that after all that had happened she would want to protect Holin even from this. But she surprised him. "Yes, but I'm staying right here."

"Of course." He put down his tea cup and shifted to the sofa so that he was sitting beside the boy. He gently shook Holin and spoke his name. At first Holin merely stirred without waking, but Ethan shook him again and called to him a second time. After another moment, the boy rolled over, his eyes open. He looked at Ethan and then his mother before lying back and staring up at the ceiling.

"How are you feeling, Holin?" Ethan asked.

The boy swallowed. "Confused." His voice sounded weak.

"Are you in any pain? Do you feel sick?"

He shook his head and cleared his throat. "No, nothing like that. I don't remember . . . How did I get here?"

"I brought you home. What's the last thing you do remember?"

"Walking up from the wharf. It was light still. What time is it now?"

"It's late," Ethan said. "Past midnight."

"Why weren't you with Rory?" Elli asked in that same stern voice.

"He and some friends were going to a tavern." He looked at his mother. "I didn't think you'd want me going with them."

In spite of everything, Ethan smiled, turning away so that Elli wouldn't see.

Elli started to say more, then stopped and just stared at Holin. The boy had rendered her speechless. Ethan wished he had been taking notes.

"Do you remember seeing anyone?" Ethan asked, facing Holin once more. "Did you stop to speak with someone, or pass anyone in the street?"

"I don't think so." An instant later, he shook his head and frowned. "No," he said with more certainty. "In fact, I remember thinking that the city seemed deserted. I didn't see anyone, and I thought it was strange. That's the last thing I remember: thinking that there should have been more people on the street. Then . . ." He shrugged. "Then you woke me up."

Ethan and Elli shared a look.

"All right then," Elli said, standing. "It's time for you to get to bed. Can you make it to your room?"

"I think so," Holin said. But he didn't move. "What happened to me?" he asked Ethan. "Why are you here so late?"

Ethan glanced at Elli again, but she said nothing.

"I'm afraid I got you mixed up in some of my dealings, Holin. I'm sorry for that. I won't let it happen again."

The boy stared hard at him, obviously dissatisfied with that answer.

"It's nothing you need to worry about," Ethan said. "Nothing you should be involved in. And I think you had better get yourself to bed before your mother forbids me to ever come here again."

"All right," Holin said, sounding tired. He stood too quickly, swayed dangerously, and might have fallen had Ethan not reached out to steady him. "Whoa," the boy breathed.

"Perhaps I should walk you up," Ethan said.

With Ethan supporting the boy, they made their way up the narrow stairway to Holin's chamber. There, Ethan and Elli helped the boy into his bed before descending the stairs once more and returning to the sitting room.

Ethan began to gather his clothes, which were warmer but still damp.

"You should stay here," Elli said, surprising him again. "You can sleep on the sofa, by the fire."

"Thank you, but that's not—"

"They'll find you if you go home."

"Elli—"

"Look at me and tell me that you wouldn't be safer here."

Ethan stared back at her, but he couldn't argue. The conjurer would want revenge for what Ethan had done to him this night, and he had little doubt that Sephira was after him, too. His room above the cooperage was the first place they would look. The Dowser would be second, and at that thought he very nearly sprinted from the house and back to the tavern without saying another word to Elli. Hearing Sephira threaten to hurt Kannice was one thing; knowing that this conjurer might go after her was something else entirely.

"Besides," Elli went on after a brief pause, "you're wearing John's clothes, and I don't want you leaving with them."

He chuckled and shook his head.

"You're laughing at me."

"No," he said. Then, "A little, yes. You understand that if I were to stay here, I would be putting you and the children in danger. I would have to set a warding on the house, and that would mean spilling blood for a conjuring."

Elli flinched at the last word, but then she gathered herself. "That's fine. Whatever you need to do to make it safe for us."

She was full of surprises this night.

"Thank you, Elli," he said, and meant it. "It's a kind offer. But there's somewhere else I need to be."

"At this hour?"

"Yes. You're right: They might be looking for me. And if they are, I want to be there. Better they find me than someone else."

"The woman. The one who owns that tavern."

He had never mentioned Kannice to her, in large part because she had made it clear that she didn't want to know any more about his life than she absolutely had to. She must have heard about Kannice from Holin and Clara.

"Her name's Kannice." They stood there for several moments, saying nothing. Ethan felt his cheeks reddening and he wasn't sure why. "Well," he said, bending to pick up the rest of his clothes. "I'll change back into these and be on my way."

"Don't be a fool," she said, scowling at him and sounding much more like the Elli he had grown used to these past few years. "They can't be dry yet. Wear what you have on. You can bring them back later. Clean."

He smiled. "Again, thank you." He pulled on his wet hose and boots, and walked to the door. "I can still put a warding on the house. You'd all be safer."

"No," she said. "Thank you." Their eyes met again. "May God keep you safe."

"And you."

He pulled on his damp coat, opened the door, and stepped once more into the rain and darkness.

SEVENTEEN

As soon as he was outside, Ethan pulled his knife free, forced up his coat sleeve and the shirtsleeve beneath, and cut his forearm.

"*Velamentum ex cruore evocatum.*" Concealment, conjured from blood.

He didn't need to feel the resonance of the spell in his body and in the street beneath him to know that he was taking a great risk. The spell would allow him to walk the lanes without being seen. Sephira and her toughs could walk right past him without knowing he was there. But if the conjurer was still hunting him, the casting of the spell might well alert him to Ethan's whereabouts. And Ethan suspected that a man of such power would see right through a concealment charm.

Nor was he done taking risks. He strode back to Cooper's Alley, where Pitch still lay. He couldn't bury the dog without then telling Henry what he had done and why. But he could at least honor Pitch by placing his body where it belonged. He lifted the creature into his arms and bore him to the front of the cooperage. Kneeling, he laid him just outside Henry's door, taking a moment to stroke the dog's fur one last time. He didn't dare do more.

Ethan stood and struck out for the Dowsing Rod. He still had his sleeves pushed up and he drew his knife again, in case he encountered the conjurer. He kept to narrower streets, even though it meant taking a longer route, and he did his best to move silently. Somehow he managed to make it to the Dowser without running across any of the people who wanted him dead. A minor miracle.

He tested the door of the tavern, expecting that he might have to use a spell on the lock. It was unbolted. Ethan let himself inside, pulling the door closed behind him. He was careful not to let the door close loudly, but at the click of the door handle, he heard Kelf call out from the kitchen "Who's there?" in a voice that would have given Sephira pause.

He quickly cut himself again, and cast a second spell to remove the concealment charm.

The barkeep emerged from behind the bar carrying a large cleaver and guardedly peering toward the door. It was dark in the great room. The fire in the hearth had burned low, and all but a few of the candles had been extinguished, so it would have been hard for him to see Ethan anyway. And concealment spells didn't wear off instantaneously.

"It's me. Ethan." As an afterthought, he pushed down his sleeve to hide the raw skin on his forearm.

Kelf lowered his weapon, still squinting at the shadows. "Ethan?" He shook his head. "Ya near t' scared me t' death."

Ethan walked to the bar and sat on one of the stools. "I'm sorry, Kelf. I didn't want to wake Kannice."

"Ya didn't?" Kelf asked, sounding confused.

"Long story." When Kelf continued to gaze back at him, Ethan said, "I'm in a bit of trouble, and I didn't want to go home. So I thought I'd come here and sleep downstairs; keep watch on the door."

Kelf hefted the cleaver again. "Ya need me t' stay? Nothin' personal, Ethan, bu' ya're not exactly th' biggest fella in Boston. I can help ya."

"That's a kind offer, Kelf. But I can take care of myself better than you might think from looking at me."

"Aye, I don' doubt it," the barkeep said. "Ya wiry types are like that."

Ethan said nothing.

"Righ' then. I'll be on my way. I've jus' finished up in there." He grabbed his coat off the bar and started for the door. "Ya wan' me t' lock it?"

"Please," Ethan said. "Good night, Kelf."

"G'night, Ethan."

Once Kelf had left the tavern, Ethan walked back to the door, cut his forearm once more, and placed a warding spell on the door. Reg appeared once again, glowing brightly in the dark room. The spell made the air hum; probably it sang through the streets. But as with the concealment spell, he believed the warding to be worth the risk.

Satisfied that the Dowser was secure for the night, he threw another log onto the fire, moved a pair of chairs in front of the hearth, and arranged them into a sort of bed. He hadn't any blankets, and just about everything he had on was damp, but he thought the fire would cast enough warmth to let him sleep.

Just as he got himself settled, however, he heard the floorboards above him creak, and a moment later, footfalls on the stairway.

"Kelf?" Kannice's voice.

"No, it's me."

"Ethan?" She came down the stairs, wrapped in a robe. "Are you all right?"

"Aye, I'm fine. It's been a long night."

"I don't like the sound of that. I thought you couldn't stay here until your work for Berson was finished."

"That was before. Now I'd rather not leave you alone."

She frowned. "I don't like the sound of that, either."

He nodded, thinking of Pitch and feeling his throat tighten. "The conjurer took Holin. I was able to get him back, and get away myself, but . . . but I had to do something terrible. After, I was afraid to go home, and I was afraid that if I didn't come here, whoever this person is would take you next."

"Why didn't you come up?"

"I didn't want to wake you. Also, I set a warding on the door. I want to make sure it holds, and I want to be able to take it off in the morning before Kelf gets here."

"So you were with Elli tonight." She offered it as a statement.

"I was. I had to get Holin home and—"

"I understand. I assume that's where you got those clothes."

Ethan felt his cheeks burn. "I was soaked, Kannice. I—"

She held up her hand, silencing him. Then she stooped quickly and kissed his lips. "I said I understand," she whispered. "You were with Elli, and rather than stay there, you came here."

"Yes, well, her stew is awful."

Kannice punched his good arm, glaring and smiling at the same time. "Your clothes are wet," she said, tugging gently at his shirt. "Come upstairs and we'll take them off."

He held her gaze. "That's not why I came back here."

"I know." She took his hand and pulled him again.

Still, he didn't stand. "All right. But ask me first."

Her smile faded, though she continued to hold his hand. "What was the terrible thing you did?"

A tear rolled down his cheek, and then another. "I had to use a killing spell to get away; I had no choice. I had to . . . to kill Pitch." He looked away, a sob escaping him. "He showed up just in time. It was like he knew I needed him." He covered his face with his hand, unable to keep from weeping.

"Oh, Ethan," she said, her voice breaking on his name. She knelt beside him and ran her free hand through his hair. He knew she was casting about for something to say, and just as surely he knew there was nothing she could say to heal this wound.

They remained thus for several moments as Ethan gathered himself. At last, he took a long breath, feeling too weary to climb the steps to Kannice's room. Had the conjurer broken through his warding at that moment, he would have been helpless to fight the man off.

"Come on," Kannice said, standing and tugging at his hand again. "You need sleep."

He nodded and let her lead him up the stairs to her bed.

He slept poorly, troubled by strange, dark visions. At one point he dreamed that he battled the conjurer again, the hot pain in his chest and head so severe that he cried out, waking himself and Kannice. She put her arms around him and sang to him, until at last he fell asleep again. The worst dream, though, came later. He was in Cooper's Alley, walking toward Henry's shop. Shelly stood in the middle of the street, her pale eyes fixed on him, her teeth bared. Ethan called her name and squatted down, holding out a hand for her to sniff. But she growled, the fur on her neck and back standing on end. And then she turned and trotted away.

Ethan woke from that dream with an ache in his chest that he feared would never go away. He was alone, though he could hear Kannice moving around downstairs. Daylight seeped around the edges of the window shutters, and the smell of cooked bacon wafted up from below. He knew he had to get up; he had slept too long already. But he couldn't bring himself to move until the door opened and Kannice stuck her head in the room.

"I wanted to let you sleep, but Kelf's here and he can't get in. I told him that the door is stuck and that I'm working on it, but he's going to start getting suspicious."

Ethan sat up, ran a hand through his hair. "I'll be right down. What's the time?"

"It's early yet. Just an hour or so past dawn. I'm sorry."

"Don't be. I have things to do, things that can't wait."

Ethan had gotten in the habit of leaving a change of clothes in Kannice's wardrobe and after she went back down to the tavern, he dug them out: a pair of breeches, a white shirt and brown waistcoat, even a pair of hose. His boots were still damp, but they were the only pair he had. He examined his arm, which was covered with fresh scars from all the conjuring he had done the past few days, and lamented having charmed the door. Remembering Janna's mullein, he retrieved the pouch from a pocket of his wet clothes, which lay in a pile on the floor by Kannice's door. Then he went down to the tavern.

"... Break it down an' fix it later!" he heard Kelf shouting through the door as he reached the bottom of the stairs.

Kannice glanced back at him, eyes wide.

"No, Kelf!" Ethan called. "I think I can get it!"

"Ethan!" the barkeep said. "Wha'd ya do t' this blasted thing?"

"I'm not sure, give me a minute." He hated to use even a single leaf of the mullein for this, but he didn't want to have to explain to Kelf why he had his sleeve up and his knife out. *Extegimen ex verbasco evocatum.*

End warding, conjured from mullein. Feeling the hum of power, seeing Reg, he looked self-consciously at Kannice, though of course she hadn't noticed anything.

For Kelf's benefit, he tinkered with the door handle and key for a few moments, before opening the door.

"The tumbler must have gotten stuck," he said, as Kelf stalked into the tavern, scowling at him, at the lock, at Kannice.

The barman shook his head, eyeing the door. "Never happens when I lock up." He shook his head again and stomped off into the kitchen.

A grin flashed across Kannice's face and was gone. She walked over to Ethan and kissed him, her brow knitting. "You didn't sleep well."

"No, but I slept. That's something."

"Eat something before you go."

He followed her to the bar, where a platter of fried bread, eggs, and bacon waited for him. He ate quickly and fished in his pocket for a shilling.

"Don't you dare," Kannice said.

Ethan smiled. "Thank you."

"Where are you going now?" she asked, her expression deadly serious.

"Are you going to follow me around, and make sure I'm safe?"

"If I have to."

He leaned forward to kiss her. But she put a hand on his chest, stopping him.

"Tell me, Ethan."

"What good do you think it'll do? Do you really think you can save me from the—"

Kelf emerged from the kitchen, a barrel of ale on his great shoulder. He put it down with a thud, looked from one of them to the other, and returned to the kitchen, muttering to himself.

"I know I can't save you from anyone," Kannice said earnestly. "But maybe I can get word to someone who can."

"I'm not sure there is anyone, not against this conjurer. But for what it's worth, I'll be speaking with Cyrus Derne this morning. And then Ebenezer Mackintosh. After that I'm not sure."

"All right. Is there any point in telling you to be careful?"

He stood, kissed her, and picked up his coat off the bar. "Probably not," he said, making his way to the door.

The rain had stopped, but dark clouds still scudded low over the city and puddles of befouled water filled the lanes. The air had cooled again, and a sharp wind rattled the door and windows of the tavern. Turning up his collar, he walked north into the teeth of the gale, crossing into the North End and continuing toward Bennet's Street.

He wasn't sure what to expect when he reached the Derne mansion. It was early still, and he felt reasonably sure that both Cyrus and his father wouldn't have left yet for their wharf.

As Ethan approached the house, though, he was surprised to see Sephira Pryce and her men standing out front. Nigel grinned when he spotted Ethan, and he said something to Sephira, alerting her to Ethan's arrival. She waved, a rapacious smile on her face. Ethan faltered a step, but then continued on toward the house, hoping that Sephira wouldn't be so bold as to murder him here in the wealthiest part of the North End, in the light of day. As he had told Kannice, there was no point in telling him to be careful.

As Ethan approached the Derne house, Nigel and two of his friends stepped in front of him, blocking his way. Ethan halted, and the toughs remained where they were. But the grin on Yellow-hair's face told Ethan that he would have been grateful for any opportunity to pick up right where things had left off the previous evening, before Pell and the sheriff interrupted them.

"You're not welcome here, Ethan," Sephira said, stepping out from behind her men and walking to him.

She was dressed in her street clothes again—a long coat over the usual breeches, shirt, and waistcoat—but her lilac perfume smelled stronger than usual. Maybe Ethan wasn't used to seeing her so early in the day, or maybe she put on extra scent when visiting men as wealthy as the Dernes. Either way, it was too much; no one as hateful as this woman ought to have worn anything that smelled so sweet.

"Are you and your boys the Dernes' personal guards now, Sephira?" Ethan asked. "Have things gotten that difficult for you since I started taking away your wealthy clientele?"

She laughed. "You really are an idiot, aren't you? Do you think you're safe now because it's daytime and we're surrounded by nice houses?"

"Actually, yes, I do," he said, keeping his voice low. "Because of that, and because I have sources for conjuring that don't require me to spill blood. Just as I did last night when I used a little bit of grass to hold off a dozen of your men. I could kill you where you stand without drawing a blade or making a sound. It would just look like I scared you to death."

Her face fell a bit and Ethan was certain that he saw fear in her eyes. She would recover quickly; she always did. But he enjoyed the moment.

"What do you want?" she asked.

"I came to speak with Cyrus Derne. But I wouldn't mind knowing what you're doing here."

Sephira smoothed her waistcoat. "Well, I have no intention of telling you anything, and Derne asked us to keep you away from him."

"You really are his guards," Ethan said. "Why is Derne so afraid of me?" He knew the answer, of course, but he wanted to know what the merchant had told Sephira. Not that he really expected her to say.

"He's not afraid of you. No one's afraid of you, Ethan. He just doesn't want to see you. Apparently you disturbed him in the middle of a negotiation yesterday at his place of business." She shook her head. "That was foolish of you. But then again, you have a habit of making enemies of the wrong people."

"I find it hard to believe that you would come to the North End just to keep away a conjurer who might or might not show up at Cyrus Derne's door. What are you doing here, Sephira? What business do you have with him?"

"Ethan," she purred. She came closer to him and leaned forward so that her face was only inches from his. "You sound jealous."

"I imagine he and his father have connections with merchants throughout the British Empire," he said, piecing it together as he spoke. "I'm sure that they pay very well, and would find value in an ally with your knowledge of the city and its shadier side. They might even look to someone like you to help them in a dispute with a man as influential as Abner Berson. Did Cyrus Derne really love Jennifer Berson, or was that a ruse, a way of getting close to her father?"

She regarded him with an odd mixture of amusement and alarm. Finally, she laughed and shook her head. "Go home, Ethan, before you get yourself hurt. You're meddling in matters you can't possibly understand." She turned to her men. "We're done here." Glancing back at Ethan, she laughed again, and then led Nigel and the rest of her men back down Middle Street, toward the South End.

Ethan watched them go before making his way up the path to the Dernes' door. Two chaises waited outside the house, their horses standing with their heads bowed. Derne was home. Ethan knocked once, and the door opened immediately. The same hulking servant Ethan remembered from his first visit to the house stood in the doorway, staring down at him, his expression no more welcoming than Nigel's had been.

"Ethan Kaille to see Cyrus Derne," Ethan said.

"Mister Derne doesn't wish to speak with you, Ethan."

Ethan frowned. The servant hadn't opened his mouth. He glared at Ethan a moment longer and then stepped aside, revealing the last person Ethan had expected to see here: Geoffrey Brower—Bett's husband, his brother-in-law.

As always, Geoffrey was impeccably dressed and perfectly groomed. He wore a suit of pale green silk, and his hair was pulled back and powdered. Geoffrey had a high forehead, a hook nose, and dark eyes, and he was as thin as a blade and uncommonly tall. He towered over Ethan, who had once remarked to Bett that her husband spoke down to everyone he met in more ways than one. She hadn't seen the humor.

Geoffrey eyed Ethan briefly, apparently waiting for some sort of greeting. When Ethan offered none, he walked past him out of the house, saying, "Please, come with me."

Ethan considered ignoring the man. But Derne's servant hadn't moved and hadn't gotten any smaller. With one last glance at him, Ethan followed his brother-in-law.

"Mister Derne believes that you're harrying him," Geoffrey said, as Ethan caught up with him. His expression was grave. "Are you?"

"I don't believe so. I came here the night Abner Berson hired me to look for his daughter's brooch, and I asked Mister Derne a few questions. And then I asked him a few more questions yesterday at his wharf."

"And here you are again today."

"Yes. Here I am."

Geoffrey raised an eyebrow. "Cyrus Derne is a wealthy man. And we both know that wealth buys far more than a fine house and nice things. He has impressed upon representatives of the Crown that he wants you kept away from him and his family."

"So you came to his house as a representative of the Crown?" Ethan asked.

"I came to him as a friend. I shouldn't have to tell you that the events of the past few days have alarmed those of us who still profess loyalty to His Majesty King George the Third." He looked sidelong at Ethan. "I also should not have to tell you that you would be wise to avoid men like Samuel Adams and Peter Darrow."

Ethan stared at him. "Am I being followed, Geoffrey?"

Brower laughed. "Don't be ridiculous. Adams and Darrow and James Otis are being watched, as are a host of others who are believed to be threats to the peace."

Of course. "Well then," Ethan said, "it might interest you to know that I'll be visiting Ebenezer Mackintosh next. I'm sure that will raise some eyebrows."

"Actually, I believe most will wonder why it took you so long to confront the scoundrel." Geoffrey stopped walking. "But out of respect for Bett, I'll trust you to conduct the rest of your inquiry as you see fit. My concern is that you keep away from Mister Derne. Do that, and you'll have nothing to fear from me."

Ethan nearly laughed out loud. He had never been afraid of Geoffrey. But as he faced him, he kept his expression neutral. "That's Christian of you, Geoffrey," he said. "Tell me though: Don't you worry about the appearance of a customs man going to such lengths to protect a merchant like Derne?"

The color drained from Geoffrey's cheeks, even as he forced a weak smile onto his thin lips.

"For that matter," Ethan continued, "doesn't it bother you to work so closely with a woman like Sephira Pryce? Does Bett know that you have dealings with her?"

"I do not!" Geoffrey said. But his denial seemed to lack conviction.

"Of course not." Ethan started to walk away, then turned to face Brower again. "I've never had anything to fear from you, Geoffrey. But if you dare get in my way again, I'll have a conversation with my sister that I believe she'll find quite illuminating."

He didn't wait for a response. Nor did he return to the Derne house. This had nothing to do with Geoffrey Brower, or with Sephira Pryce for that matter. If Derne had made up his mind not to speak with him, Ethan could do little to force the matter. At least as long as Derne remained in his home.

Instead, Ethan headed back to the center of the city, to the Boston Prison. The time had come for him to speak with Ebenezer Mackintosh.

Thomas Hutchinson had mentioned to Ethan that Mackintosh's friends were working to get the cordwainer released from gaol, but Ethan had put little stock in this, thinking it the bitter imaginings of a wronged man. As he approached the prison, though, he saw no less a personage than Peter Darrow exiting the building leading a slight young man in laborer's clothes. Ethan had no doubt that this was Mackintosh.

He approached them. Mackintosh took no notice of him, but Darrow spotted him from a distance and momentarily faltered, his expression difficult to read. He appeared tired and he moved stiffly. His eyes were red, his cheeks blotchy. Ethan wondered if he had been drinking the night before.

"Mister Kaille," the lawyer said. "I suppose I should have expected this. Have you met Ebenezer Mackintosh?"

Ethan stopped in front of the two men. "No, I haven't."

"Ebenezer Mackintosh, this is Ethan Kaille. Mister Kaille, Ebenezer Mackintosh."

They shook hands and Ethan actually winced. The shoemaker had a crushing grip, as well as a winning smile. His face was angular and thin, his eyes small and widely spaced, so that he vaguely resembled a fox. His nose was crooked and his hair hung to his shoulders in brown waves. Ethan wouldn't have called him conventionally handsome—not like Darrow, with his square chin and almond-shaped eyes. But there was, he was forced to admit, something compelling about the man. Mackintosh had uttered not a word, and already Ethan could see why people were drawn to him.

"Nice t' meet you, Mister Kaille. You a friend o' Mister Darrow?"

"Not really, no."

Mackintosh's face fell, puzzlement furrowing his brow. Already people on the street had recognized the cordwainer and were crowding around them, hoping to shake the hand of the Commander of the South End and congratulate him on his release from prison.

Mackintosh turned to Darrow, perhaps hoping that the lawyer would steer him away from Ethan. But Darrow didn't move. He was watching Ethan, wearing that same bland expression.

"I need to speak with you, Mister Mackintosh," Ethan said. "And I'm afraid it can't wait."

The man glanced at Darrow again. "Well, I don' know tha'—"

"I'm investigating the murder of Jennifer Berson, which occurred the night of the twenty-sixth. There are those in the city, many of them in positions of power, who would like to see you blamed for her death."

A hard look came into Mackintosh's eyes, offering Ethan a glimpse of the street fighter lurking within.

"Aye," the man said. "All righ'. Where?"

"Come with me," Darrow said to both of them, and started away.

It didn't take Ethan long to figure out that the man was leading them back to the Green Dragon. He didn't relish the idea of having this conversation with Adams, Otis, and Darrow listening in, but he would deal with that when they reached the tavern.

As they walked, a number of people approached Mackintosh offering words of support, or merely hoping to shake hands with him. And the cordwainer had a smile for every one of them. Ethan was amazed at the number of well-wishers he could greet by name. Thomas Hutchinson might have thought Mackintosh a common street tough, but Ethan thought he underestimated him. Watching Mackintosh exchange pleasantries with his people, Ethan realized that he had skills as a politician that Hutchinson simply did not possess.

But his renown had a dark side as well. Here on Brattle Street,

they were as close to the North End as to the South, and for every South
Ender who saw Mackintosh as a hero, there was a North Ender who
glared at him with murder in his eyes, clearly incensed to see him walking the streets again.

Mackintosh, though, was oblivious of these others, or at least pre-
tended to be. He seemed to bask in the adulation of his fellow South
Enders, and he strode along the avenue like a conquering hero.

Turning onto Hanover Street, they walked past the Hallowell house.
Ethan watched Mackintosh for some sign of remorse or shame or even
pride in what he had wrought the night of the riots. But he gave no sign
of realizing where he was. He walked and waved and smiled, and he allowed Darrow to lead him to the Green Dragon.

Once they were inside, though, some of Mackintosh's swagger fell
away. His smile vanished, leaving a wary, nervous stare. He might have
trusted Darrow, but he also seemed to understand that he had few allies
in the Dragon.

"We can take a table in the back of the tavern," Darrow said,
glancing back at Mackintosh and Ethan as they descended the stairs.
"I'll get you both ales, if you like."

"Tha's f—"

"No," Ethan said, cutting off Mackintosh.

Darrow halted at the bottom of the stairs. Mackintosh stopped as
well.

"What's the problem, Mister Kaille?" Darrow asked sourly.

"I want to speak with him in private, without you and Adams and
Otis listening to what we say." *He thinks you're his friends,* Ethan wanted
to add. *But you and I know better.*

Darrow's jaw muscles bunched. Mackintosh eyed them, seeming
to grow more confused and nervous by the moment.

"I wan' Mister Darrow with me," he said at last.

Ethan sighed, but he could hardly blame the man. Mackintosh
had known Darrow for a year and Ethan for ten minutes. To Darrow's
credit, he didn't gloat at all. Rather he turned to Ethan again, a question in his eyes.

"All right, then," Ethan said. "If that's what he wants, you should
join us."

Darrow nodded and led them the rest of the way down the stairs to the tavern. While he crossed to the bar, Ethan and Mackintosh took a table by the hearth.

"You don' trust Darrow?" the cordwainer asked as they sat.

"I wouldn't say that I don't trust him. But I'm not sure that he has your best interests at heart."

Mackintosh laughed. "An' you do, is tha' right?"

"No," Ethan said. "I couldn't care less about your best interests. But you never would have thought to trust me, so that hardly matters."

Mackintosh frowned. "Darrow helped me out some time back. He helped get me off after we sacked Oliver's house, an' jus' this mornin' he got Sheriff Greenleaf t' let me go. You might not think he has my interests at heart, but he's done me a good turn time an' again. I know him. I trust him. You . . ." He shrugged.

"I understand."

Before they could say more, Darrow came to the table with two ales. He placed one in front of each of them, and then sat.

Mackintosh still looked troubled.

"Is everything all right?" Darrow asked.

"Mister Mackintosh was explaining that he trusts you and not me," Ethan said.

"I see," Darrow said. "And were you telling him why he's wrong to put his faith in me?"

"I merely told him I didn't think you were concerned first and foremost with his welfare."

"What do you think of that, Ebenezer?" Darrow asked.

"You've helped me out o' some tough spots, Mister Darrow. Tha's wha' I told him." But Mackintosh didn't meet the man's gaze.

Darrow regarded him for another moment before facing Ethan again.

"Perhaps you should ask your questions, Mister Kaille. Ebenezer has had several long and trying days."

"Of course," Ethan said. He faced Mackintosh. "As I already told you, I've been hired by Abner Berson to inquire into the death of his elder daughter, Jennifer. She died the night of August twenty-sixth, around the time you and your followers were abroad in the city ransacking the homes of Benjamin Hallowell, William Story, and Thomas Hutchinson."

"And there's folk who think I'm t' blame?"

"Aye," Ethan said, resisting the impulse to glance Darrow's way. "She wore a brooch that night, and it was stolen from her. And since her father is wealthy, and a friend of the lieutenant governor, Hallowell, and Story, some have suggested there may be a connection between the attack on Hutchinson's house and her death."

"How did she die?" Mackintosh asked.

How indeed? They had come to the crux of the matter, and to the one thing Ethan least wished to discuss in front of Darrow. He didn't know how to answer, or how to determine if Mackintosh was a conjurer. In the end, he decided that he had little choice but to dissemble, at least until he could contrive to speak privately with the man.

"No one knows for certain," he said. "There are some who claim that her killer used dark powers against her."

Mackintosh stared at him for the span of a heartbeat. Then he let out a loud, nervous laugh. "Dark powers. You're havin' a bit o' fun with me, right?"

Ethan said nothing.

"Is he makin' a joke?" Mackintosh asked Darrow. "Are you two havin' th' run on me?"

"I don't know what Mister Kaille is up to," Darrow said in a hard voice. "I was led to believe that yours was a serious inquiry, Mister Kaille," he said. "What is this foolishness?"

"I'm only repeating what others have said," Ethan told him.

"Wha' others?"

"That I won't say."

"Well, it's madness!" Mackintosh said, sounding truly shaken. "They wan' me t' hang for a murderer, an' if tha' don' work, they'll hang me for a witch instead!"

"Nobody is going to hang you, Ebenezer," Darrow said. He frowned at Ethan. "I thought better of you, Mister Kaille."

Ethan made no answer to Darrow, but asked Mackintosh, "Do you remember seeing a lone young woman in the streets that night?"

The cordwainer shook his head. "Do you know how many of us

there were? Hundreds. Maybe more. I know tha' most o' my South End boys were there, an' a fair number from th' North End, too. But askin' me t' remember one girl . . . Obviously you weren' there, or you'd know better."

"Did your men stay with you the entire time?"

He shook his head a second time. "No, we split up. Some wen' t' pay a visit t' Hallowell, th' rest wen' t' see Story. We met up again an' then wen' on t' Hutchinson's house. An' before you ask, I wen' back an' forth between th' two—kept an eye on both groups."

Ethan nodded, unable to hide his disappointment. When he met with Adams, Darrow, and Otis, the men had blamed Mackintosh for the girl's death, and Ethan had no doubt that they could convince the Crown authorities that he was responsible. He had led the mob, controlled it even. He admitted as much, and that might well be enough for a court, particularly if they could also blame Daniel. But Ethan wasn't interested in holding Mackintosh responsible. He wanted to know who had actually killed Jennifer Berson. And he sensed that Mackintosh was right: There was no way to know this for certain, short of speaking to every person who had been in that crowd.

"Can I see your forearms, Mister Mackintosh?"

The other man regarded him as if he was mad. "Wha'?"

"Please," Ethan said. He could hear the weariness in his own voice. "Humor me. I need to see your forearms."

Mackintosh looked to Darrow, who hesitated but then nodded. The cordwainer pushed up his sleeves and held out his arms for Ethan to see. There was a single long scar on one of them, which might have come from a knife fight. But otherwise, unlike Ethan's own arms, which were scored with a lattice of scars old and new, Mackintosh's were unmarked. If he was a conjurer, he had found some other way to draw upon his blood for spells.

"Wha' are you lookin' for?" Mackintosh asked.

"It doesn't matter," Ethan said. He stood, drank a bit of the ale Darrow had bought him, and started toward the stairway. "It isn't there."

Chapter

EIGHTEEN

As much as he didn't wish to see Mackintosh sacrificed by Darrow, Adams, and the others, Ethan was disappointed to learn that the man wasn't a sorcerer. Everyone he had talked to thought that Mackintosh was responsible for Jennifer Berson's death, and though he mistrusted them and questioned their motives, he had also come to hope that they might be right.

Now he knew they weren't. And with the cordwainer eliminated as a suspect, Ethan's suspicions fell once more on Cyrus Derne. He thought it likely that whatever dealings the merchant had in the city the night of the riots had gotten his betrothed killed. Whether that had been his intent remained open to question.

He didn't think that Derne or his friends would allow him to get close enough to the merchant to question him, so he needed to think of another strategy. He went back to the Dowser.

As soon as he entered the tavern, Kelf called for Kannice, who emerged from the kitchen clutching a scrap of parchment in her hand. She stepped out from behind the bar and handed it to Ethan.

"This came a short while after you left," she said.

Ethan unfolded it. It read simply "Come quickly." It was signed by Mister Pell.

"Did Pell himself bring it?" Ethan asked.

Kannice shook her head. "A boy. No one I recognized."

"All right. Thank you."

"How did it go with Derne and Mackintosh?"

Ethan shrugged. "Derne wouldn't see me; Mackintosh couldn't tell me much." He held up the note from Pell. "Maybe this will be something."

She nodded, and Ethan left, hurrying down Treamount to King's Chapel.

When he reached the church he found Mr. Troutbeck in the sanctuary. The curate looked pale and seemed agitated. Ethan expected the man to order him off the premises, but Troutbeck acted genuinely relieved to see him.

"Mister Kaille! Thank goodness you're here."

"What's happened?"

"It's Trevor—I mean, Mister Pell. He's in the crypt. There was another body brought in, and he insisted on showing you. The mother has come to claim the girl, but he won't let anyone take her. He merely says again and again that you have to see the girl first." Troutbeck frowned and glanced back toward the stairs leading to the crypt. When he spoke again, he had lowered his voice. "He's gone so far as to arm himself. He actually has an old sword down there."

Any other time, Ethan would have laughed at the thought of Pell holding off Caner and Troutbeck with a blade. But at the mention of this newest death, he had been gripped by terror. A girl was dead. Her mother had come. Had he saved Holin's life the night before only to lose Clara today?

"He's waiting for me?" Ethan demanded, already striding across the sanctuary toward the stairway.

"Yes," Troutbeck called after him. "Is this about the Berson murder?"

"I'll tell you when I know."

Then he was on the stairs, running down them so quickly that he nearly fell. Emerging into the candlelit corridor, Ethan saw the body lying on the same stone table that had held Jennifer Berson's body only days before. Long, dark hair. A slight form.

Pell stood, the sword held loosely in his hand.

"Thank God you've come," the minister said. "I didn't know how much longer I could hold them off."

Ethan barely glanced at him, but walked quickly to the table, his heart hammering. But when he was close enough to see the girl's features, he exhaled, realizing that he had been holding his breath. Her coloring was similar to Clara's, but it wasn't her. He braced his hands on the stone table, closed his eyes for a moment, and took a long, shuddering breath.

"You were afraid you knew her," the young minister said.

"Terrified is more like it."

"Someone dear to you?"

"As close to a daughter as I'm ever likely to have."

The girl had a pleasant round face and had just barely come into womanhood. She should have been wandering through shops with her mother, or perhaps with a suitor. She should have been anywhere but here, in this cold, dim chamber. But all Ethan could think as he looked at her was *Thank God it's not Clara.*

He bent closer to the girl's neck and face. He lifted her head, probing with his fingers for a lump or dried blood. But he found nothing. Like Jennifer, she was unmarked. "Where was she found?" he asked.

"Near the wharves again," Pell said. After a brief silence, he asked, "Was she killed by the same man?"

"I believe so. But there's only one way I can be certain she was killed by a spell."

The minister winced, tight-lipped. "I thought that might be the case."

"Do you want to leave?"

Pell drew himself up to his full height. "No. I'll stay here."

"Caner is worried about you," Ethan said. "He fears that I'm going to ruin you."

"I know. I don't share his concern, and neither should you. I was ruined a long time ago." He said it with a straight face, and for a moment Ethan wondered if some dark truth lay beneath his words. But then a small grin flitted across his features.

Ethan laughed. "Have you ever considered the possibility, Mister Pell, that you would make a better thieftaker than you do a minister?"

"I hadn't until I met you," Pell said. "Now, get on with it."

Ethan drew his blade and stared at the girl for some time, wondering which spell he ought to cast. Either of the spells he had used on

Jennifer Berson the last time he was in this building—reveal power, or reveal source of power—would tell him whether she had been killed by a conjurer. But Ethan wanted to find some way to learn more about the conjurer who killed her. Chances were he had masked his power, just as he had with the spell that killed Jennifer. Ethan needed some way to overcome whatever precautions the conjurer had taken. But how?

When at last it came to him, the idea struck him as so simple that Ethan laughed out loud.

"What?" Pell asked.

"I think I've thought of a way to overcome the concealing spells this conjurer's been using."

"And that's funny?"

"It's simple, and one of the oldest spells I know. I should have thought of it days ago." He pushed up his sleeve and cut his arm. Then, as he had with Jennifer, he dabbed his blood onto her face, neck, and chest. *"Revela omnias magias ex cruore evocatas."* Reveal all magicks, conjured from blood.

Pell inhaled sharply at the sight of Uncle Reg, whose glowing form suddenly appeared beside Ethan.

At the same time, the entire chamber came to life, as if Ethan's blood flowed through the walls, the ceiling, the stone beneath his feet. The torchlight flickered, though the air remained still, and Ethan shuddered, as from a sudden chill.

"I felt that," Pell said in a hushed voice.

Ethan didn't answer. He kept his eyes fixed on the girl, saw the blood vanish from her skin. And then he caught just a glimpse of what he had been hoping for. The light spread from her chest, as it had when he cast the spell on Jennifer's body. In mere moments, she was sheathed in that same silver light that had enveloped the Berson girl. But in the instant between the first glimmer of light, and the spread of that silver glow, Ethan saw a flash of color.

It was a rich golden yellow, the color of the sun's first rays on the sands of a beach or the last glimpse of daylight in the western sky. Ethan's first thought was that a color that beautiful should never have been used for killing spells.

"Did it work?"

"You didn't see it?" Ethan asked.

"I see how she's glowing," Pell said. "Is that how she's supposed to look?"

He frowned. "That's how Jennifer looked after I did a similar spell." He beckoned the man forward with a wave of his hand. "You saw the way the light spread over her body, beginning over her heart."

Pell nodded.

"The spell I cast is supposed to reveal the nature of all conjurings that have been set upon her. That silver light . . ." Ethan shook his head. "That's not a natural color for this kind of power. The silver is a masking spell, something the conjurer used to conceal his first casting. The first spell was yellow. I saw just a hint of it before the silver covered it over. That was the true color of his casting. It spread from her heart as well, and I think it would have covered her entire body, just as the silver does. She was used as the source for another killing spell."

"By a conjurer whose power is yellow?" the minister asked, clearly trying to follow what Ethan was telling him.

"Basically."

"But I didn't see any color from your spell."

Ethan smiled. "That's because you haven't cast a revealing spell. What I saw with that yellow was not really his conjuring, but the residue of it. All spells leave behind some trace of the conjurer's power. They also leave some trace of the source used by the conjurer to make the spell work. There's a spell to reveal that, as well."

Pell rubbed his forehead. "Of course there is."

"If someone were to cast another revealing spell on her now, my spell would show up as well." He paused, then, anticipating the minister's next question, "The residue from my conjurings is rust-colored."

"Like your ghost?"

"My guide," Ethan said. "Yes, like him."

"But if the color doesn't show up without a . . . a revealing spell, what's the use of knowing that? Why does it matter what color this conjurer's power is?"

Ethan looked at the dead girl. "That's an excellent question. The truth is, it doesn't mean much unless I find the conjurer and see his guide. As you've pointed out, the color will be the same."

"Is there a spell that reveals what another conjuring was intended to do?"

"No," Ethan said. "I'm afraid not."

"So, you don't know what the conjurer did with this girl's life. Or with Jennifer Berson's."

"Not yet."

But even as he said this, Ethan felt something tugging at his mind, taunting him, remaining just beyond his reach. He did know; the answer was right there in front of him. But he couldn't remember what it was.

"Ethan?"

"There's something . . ." Ethan said, shaking his head slowly.

Before Pell could question him further, they both heard footsteps on the stairs. The minister stared at Ethan, the look on his face like that of a child caught in a lie.

"Can you do anything about that glow?" Pell asked.

"I'd have to cast another spell," Ethan told him. "And it would work too slowly."

"Damn!" the minister said, sounding very unministerlike.

A moment later, Henry Caner entered the corridor. He was alone—a small grace—but judging from the look on his face, Ethan guessed that the rector would have ordered him hanged had there been men of the watch with him.

"What is this?" Caner demanded, his words echoing loudly in the crypt. "What have you done to her?"

Ethan didn't flinch from his glare. "I've cast a revealing spell, Reverend, sir."

"In my church? How dare you!"

"He had no choice, Mister Caner," Pell said. "I gave him leave to do it."

"You had no right, Trevor! And your decision might well get you dismissed from this church, perhaps from the ministry!"

"It's not Mister Pell's fault," Ethan said. "I would have cast the spell even if he had demanded that I leave. To be honest with you, Mister Caner, the sanctity of your church was the least of my concerns. And it should be the least of yours, too."

"Meaning what?"

Ethan pointed at the stone table. "She was murdered by a conjurer, the same man who killed Jennifer Berson and quite possibly two other people."

"That doesn't excuse what you've done here. One act of evil can't justify another."

"Evil?" Ethan repeated.

"I warned you when last we spoke that I wouldn't continue to tolerate your . . . black arts. I ought to give you over to the sheriff. In actuality this time."

"I won't let you do that, Mister Caner."

"What did you say?" the rector demanded of Pell, his chins quivering.

"You heard me, Reverend, sir. Mister Kaille is trying to find a murderer, a conjurer who uses spells to kill. If you can't see the difference between his conjurings and those of this monster, then perhaps I should find another church in which to serve God."

Caner glared at him, and then at Ethan. "You see? You've poisoned his mind, set him against me, and against the Lord."

"I don't believe I have. You heard him. He still wishes to serve God. Just not necessarily here."

"What are you doing, Trevor?" Caner asked, as if he hadn't heard Ethan. "Don't you see that he's a threat to all that you believe? Don't you understand that his very presence here is an affront to the Lord?"

"I don't believe that's true, Mister Caner," Pell said.

Caner recoiled. "You don't believe that Mister Kaille has desecrated these grounds with his witchcraft?"

"I believe that the circumstances justify what he did." The minister hesitated, but only for a moment. "And I believe it's possible that his gifts come not from Satan, but from our Lord God."

The rector gaped at him, his small mouth hanging open.

"We can discuss theology later," Ethan said. "For now, I need to know as much about this girl as you can tell me."

Caner continued to stare at Pell, his expression more sad than angry, his heavy-lidded eyes making him look weary.

"Mister Caner?" Ethan said.

"There's not much to tell," the rector said, still eyeing the young minister. "She was found near the wharves in the South End, by a man and woman who were . . ." He paused, shook his head. "Well, in any case, they found her and sought out a member of the watch. The girl's mother is a widow, and they have little money. I fear the girl was working in the streets, if you follow."

Ethan winced. She was too young to have been leading such a hard life.

"You say there have been four murders?" Caner asked.

"I believe so. This girl, Jennifer Berson, the young boy who died on Pope's Day—Brown was his name—and another who was killed the day that Ann and John Richardson were hanged."

"The boy was killed by witchery? I thought he was run over by a cart."

"He was," Pell said. "But after he died."

Caner's brow creased. "I don't understand any of this."

"I know you don't," Ethan said, feeling sympathy for the rector in spite of all that had passed between them. "These people were killed by a conjurer, who used their lives to lend strength to his spells. And these spells, I believe, were intended to control the behavior of others."

To his credit, the minister didn't dismiss these claims out of hand. But neither did he sound convinced as he asked, "Do you know this for certain, or is it conjecture?"

"I have some proof," Ethan said. He indicated the girl. "You see that glow—"

"You did that," Caner said.

"Yes, I did. I cast a revealing spell. What you see there is the mark of the conjurer who killed her. If this man had killed her with an attack, the silver glow would be concentrated wherever his spell struck her. Instead, it covers her entire body, because instead of hitting her, like a conjured weapon, the spell drew the life out of her. It used her to bend the will of another. Killing her wasn't the aim of the spell; her death was the means to another end."

"This is sorcerous nonsense!" Caner said. "For all I know, you're concocting all of this to confound me!"

Ethan shook his head. "You're wise enough to know I'm not. I can take that spell off of her. It would take another casting, but I could do it. Then you would be free to examine her for yourself and see that there isn't a single physical mark on her. But I don't think I have to. You've already seen her. You know that a conjuring killed her. And now you know what kind of a spell it was."

The rector regarded him grimly, his lips pressed thin. "The only conjurer that I know of in this city is you, Mister Kaille," he finally said, the word "conjurer" sounding awkward coming from his mouth. "If she was killed by witchery, chances are you're the one who did it. I should call for Sheriff Greenleaf right now."

"Then do," Ethan told him. "If you really believe I did it, then you're right: You should have me hanged. A killing spell . . ." He faltered, his eyes stinging at the thought of Pitch. "It's a relatively painless way to die, but it's murder nevertheless. If I had done this, I would deserve whatever punishment you could imagine. But I didn't."

Caner shook his head fiercely. "You offer no proof! Your denials mean nothing to me. You're a witch!"

"I'm a speller who is trying to prevent another tragedy. Consider what I'm telling you, Mister Caner. This girl's murder had an even darker purpose, just like the other murders this conjurer committed. He used her death to cast another spell. And while I don't know for sure, I believe that all these murders are connected, that they have some larger purpose. That's why you must trust me, even though I'm a conjurer. I'm the only person who can stop him."

Again the minister stared at him; he looked thoroughly unnerved. Which did he fear more: Ethan, or his own ignorance in matters relating to "witchery"?

"What is it you want me to do?" Caner finally asked, surrender in his voice.

"Well, you can start by promising that you won't have me hanged."

Caner waved a meaty hand, either dismissing the notion, or accepting it without argument, Ethan wasn't sure which. "What else?" the rector asked.

Ethan started to answer, but then stopped, the memory coming to him at last. It hadn't been his imagination; there had been something. "I need to borrow Mister Pell," he said.

Caner narrowed his eyes. "What for?"

"Yes," Pell said, his eyes wide with surprise. "What for?"

Ethan grinned at his friend. "I need to watch two people, and I'm but one man. I told you before that you might make a fine thieftaker. If Mister Caner will grant his permission, we can put that notion to a test."

Caner scowled at them both. Pell fairly beamed.

Chapter NINETEEN

Ethan was more eager than ever to speak with Cyrus Derne, eager enough that he had abandoned any hope of contriving another meeting between himself and the merchant. Derne had decided to use his money and influence to protect himself from Ethan's questions; Ethan would use his conjuring skill to slip past the men Derne had hired as guards.

From King's Chapel, Ethan made his way back to the Derne house on Bennet's Street to confirm what he already suspected. The chaises were gone. Derne had probably returned to his wharf. Ethan went there next. Along the way, he stopped in a deserted alley and cast the same concealment spell he had used the previous evening while walking from Elli's house to the Dowsing Rod. Once more he knew that he risked alerting the conjurer to his whereabouts, and if Derne was Jennifer Berson's killer, the merchant would have no trouble seeing through Ethan's spell. But he would deal with that when the time came. The casting would at least allow him to get past the guards at the base of Derne's Wharf, and whatever others the merchant had positioned between the street and the warehouse where he had his office.

As Ethan walked, he took care to tread softly. This was easy enough on the cobblestones of Boston's streets, but when Ethan reached Derne's Wharf, it became far more difficult. Like most of Boston's wharves, this one was made of fill: solid refuse from shops and homes piled into wooden cribs and covered over with a blend of dirt and sand, of crushed seashells and rock. There wasn't a man alive who could walk on fill without leaving an imprint with every step. Even after he slipped past the first guards onto the wharf, he had to creep along its edge, constantly watching for anyone who might come too close. Late in the day, he might have been able to reach Derne's office quickly, but in the middle of the afternoon the wharf was crowded enough that people were constantly walking past in one direction or the other.

Halfway to Derne's office he stopped, realizing once more that he had been foolish. He didn't have to risk venturing farther out onto the wharf. Derne would take care of that for him. The merchant wouldn't remain in his warehouse forever, and if he had dealings in the city that he wanted to keep from Ethan, chances were he wouldn't want many others knowing about them, either. Eventually he would leave the building and abandon his escort. There was nothing for Ethan to do but wait.

He wondered if he might be best off waiting back at the street, where he could pick up Derne's trail on the cobblestone rather than on this treacherous fill. He had even gone so far as to turn back when he spotted a familiar face coming in his direction. Diver.

Ethan frowned at the sight of him, wondering whether he would be better off letting his friend pass by, or enlisting Diver's aid. Diver could go where Ethan could not. He could find out what Derne was doing and who was with him. Except that Diver shouldn't have been here at all. What business did he have on Derne's Wharf? He usually worked Greenough's Shipyard or Thornton's. If he had been working for Derne he would have told Ethan as much several nights before, when Ethan told him about Jennifer Berson.

What was more, his friend was behaving oddly. He walked slowly, repeatedly glancing back toward the street, and warily eyeing the hired men ahead of him.

The memory hit him like Yellow-hair's fist. The last time Ethan had seen Diver, they had been here, at Derne's Wharf, or at least on the street just beside it. Ethan had come to question Derne; Diver, he assumed at the time, was merely passing by on his way home from work.

Diver had acted strangely then, too. At the time, Ethan had been too preoccupied with Jennifer Berson's murder and his conversation with Derne to give Diver's behavior much thought, but now it all came back to him: how uncomfortable Diver had been at seeing Ethan there, how reluctant he had been to go to the Dowser, even how interested he had been in Ethan's conversation with Derne. Was it possible that Diver had business with the merchant?

He watched as his friend strode past him, and then he set out after him, moving with as much stealth as possible. When Diver reached Derne's warehouse, he slowed. But then he squared his shoulders, took a breath, and approached the building's entrance. The men there stopped him and said something Ethan couldn't hear. Ethan thought for certain that they would keep Diver out. He was dressed in his usual work clothes and he looked far more like a South End tough than he did a merchant.

After a brief discussion, though, Derne's men let him pass, and Diver entered the warehouse.

Ethan was so overcome with curiosity that he started forward to follow his friend inside. What business could Diver—Diver!—have with one of the most influential merchants in Boston? It actually took his glowing ghost throwing out a hand in front of him to keep Ethan from giving himself away.

"Right," he whispered. "My thanks."

Moments later, his interest in Diver's affairs took on a far darker urgency. His friend emerged onto the wharf once more, accompanied by none other than Cyrus Derne. The two of them headed back toward the street and several of Derne's guards fell in behind them. They walked this way for a short distance, but then Derne halted and spoke to one of the men. Their conversation lasted only a few seconds, and when Derne and Diver started away again, none of the others followed.

Ethan trailed them, walking with some care, but unwilling to risk losing sight of the pair. A few heads turned at the sound of his footsteps, but of course no one could see him. As they came to the end of the wharf, Ethan spotted Derne's chaise, and he had to bite his tongue to keep from cursing aloud. If they traveled somewhere by carriage, he would have little chance of keeping up.

But Derne and Diver turned northward onto Ship Street and walked past the chaise. Relieved, Ethan followed. Now that they were back on paved lanes, he could get closer to them. But though he thought he was near enough to hear anything the two men said, they exchanged no words. Ethan had the distinct impression that Derne barely tolerated Diver's company.

At the north end of Ship Street, they headed west on another lane. Though his bad leg was starting to ache, Ethan walked quickly to the corner. Carefully he peered around the side of a wheelwright's shop. Derne and Diver were several strides ahead of him, still unaware of his pursuit. Waiting until they had gone some distance up this new street, Ethan continued after them.

They hadn't gone far when two more people turned onto the street some distance ahead of them and started walking in their direction. Ethan slowed, then halted. Uncle Reg stopped as well, watching him, his expression wary. Ethan's pulse suddenly was racing. Fear, rage, confusion—his emotions were as roiled as a stormy sea. One of the people approaching Derne and Diver was dressed as a merchant, though Ethan didn't recognize him. He looked a little older than Derne, and he wore a black suit and a tricorn hat. Ethan should have been curious about this man; learning his name or trade might have helped him with his inquiry. But he barely spared the merchant a glance. His eyes were drawn to his companion. Sephira Pryce.

Diver and Derne had halted. When Pryce and her companion reached them, they stopped as well, and the four of them stood speaking, their voices low enough that Ethan couldn't hear any of what they said.

He knew there were spells that allowed conjurers to see in the dark and hear far beyond their normal abilities, but he hadn't learned them. He didn't even know if they could be cast with blood or if they needed some other source. But at that moment he would have given everything he owned to know how to cast such a spell.

What was Diver doing with these people? What business did Derne have with Sephira? He reached for his blade, thinking that he might try that spell after all. If it failed, no one would be the wiser.

And that was when he felt the pulse of a conjuring radiating up through the stones of the lane. A spell that was directed at him.

He braced himself, expecting an attack. But there was no pain, at least not yet. The spell gently coiled itself around him, like a vine climbing the trunk of a tree. He couldn't be certain, but forced to guess he would have said that this was a finding spell. And he felt certain that if he were to cast a revealing spell he would see that golden yellow light he had glimpsed in the King's Chapel crypt. The conjurer had found him.

Knowing that he hadn't much time, he ducked back around the corner, away from Diver and the others, and then found a narrow byway. If the conjurer struck at him with the right spell, it would overmaster his concealment charm. The last thing he needed was for Sephira and the conjurer to attack him at the same time.

Once he was out of sight, he pulled his knife from his belt and pushed up his sleeve. Before he cut himself, though, he remembered the mullein leaves that Janna had given him. Pulling out the pouch he quickly counted out how many remained. Eleven. Three spells, if the castings were to amount to anything. After that he would have nothing but blood to use as a source for his conjurings. He pulled three leaves from the pouch.

"*Tegimen ex verbasco evocatum.*" Warding, conjured from mullein.

He felt the stone tremble, and he knew that the conjurer had felt it, too. But immediately that ethereal vine released him. Not that it mattered. If the finding spell hadn't told the conjurer where he was, Ethan's own spell had.

For his part, Ethan had some idea of the conjurer's location. That finding spell had been double-edged. The conjurer had used it to locate him, but in doing so had revealed his whereabouts to Ethan. He was close, no more than a city block or two away. To the west and south. If Sephira hadn't been on the street, and if Ethan hadn't been so sure that her men were close by, he would have run. But whether by design or sheer coincidence, his two most dangerous enemies had him trapped. One might have thought that Diver and Derne had lured him here. He didn't want to believe that Diver would have any part of such a plan, but at that moment he didn't know what to think.

"There you are!"

He knew the voice. Anna.

She stood in the narrow, dark space behind him, glowing faintly, her expression cross, as if she were a parent and he a wayward child. She ignored Uncle Reg, but the ghost bared his teeth at her. Ethan could almost hear the old man hiss, like a feral cat.

"You shouldn't have done that last night," Anna said. "You shouldn't have hurt me like that. You shouldn't have killed that poor dog. There are a lot of things you shouldn't have done."

Ethan wondered if Diver and the others could hear her. At that moment he would have preferred Yellow-hair and every tough who had ever worked for Sephira Pryce to this little girl and the man who had conjured her.

He opened his mouth to shout for help, but Anna raised a finger to silence him.

Agony. Pain so sudden, so excruciating, that it banished all other thought from his mind. It felt as if someone had driven a spike through his right eye. Clutching his face, Ethan crumpled to the cobblestone. He drew breath, an anguished scream building in his chest.

"Shhh," Anna whispered from just beside him.

As abruptly as it had come, the pain was gone.

"Don't make a sound," the little girl said, bending over him. "I'll have to kill them all. And while you might want a few of them dead, I know that at least one is your friend."

Diver. The conjurer knew that Diver was his friend. But far more important, the conjurer couldn't be Derne. Whoever he was, Ethan had grown pretty sick of him.

The remaining mullein leaves were in the pouch hanging on his belt, and now he racked his brain for a spell to fire back. He could preserve the leaves for two spells, or he could use all the rest of them for one powerful assault.

"When they're gone," Anna said, staring down at him, "which should be just another moment or two, you're going to get up and walk north on this lane."

"Why not just kill me here?"

Her smile was so innocent, so normal, that Ethan shuddered. "Other plans," she said, in a singsong voice.

He thought about asking what would happen if he refused, just to keep her talking and perhaps to distract the conjurer so that Ethan's attack would have a better chance of success. But he knew what would happen if he asked, and he flinched away from the idea of it. He thought that years of forced labor and brutal floggings as a prisoner had inured him to pain. Apparently they hadn't. At least not the type of pain this man was capable of conjuring.

Anna smiled again. "Smart, Kaille. I thought you would fight me, but you're learning."

Pain or no, this was too much.

Ambure ex verbasco evocatum. Scald, conjured from mullein.

At the thrum of power Anna straightened, then vanished. Ethan thought he heard a voice cry out. Not wasting these precious moments, he pulled out his knife and cut himself.

Discuti ex cruore evocatum! Shatter, conjured from blood!

Another pulse, another cry—this time he was certain. But still Ethan didn't stop. Cutting himself again, he struggled to his feet. *Ignis ex cruore evocatus!* Fire, conjured from blood! The street felt alive with the power of his spell. Another cut, more blood, which he spread on his face, like some warrior from the realm of the dead.

Tegimen ex cruore evocatum! Warding, conjured from blood!

It was remarkable to him that so few people could feel this spell, that they could be unaware of the power rippling through the city lanes. Never had he cast so many spells in quick succession.

The last conjuring, the warding, continued to tingle along his skin—a shield that covered his entire body.

He left the narrow lane and strode around the north corner of Ship Street, intending to call to Diver. Derne and Sephira be damned. But they were gone. He ran to where they had been standing and scanned the street for any sign of them. Nothing.

"Damn!"

And then he was on the ground again, his body rigid, molten iron in his veins, blades impaling him through the eyes, a taloned claw raking his heart. He couldn't scream or breathe. He couldn't even curl up into a ball and die. Torment pinned him to the cobblestone, obliterating all else.

Except her voice—Anna's voice—which somehow managed to reach him through his suffering. "You are a fool, and you will endure agonies you can scarcely imagine before you die!"

He had managed not to drop his knife, and even as the assault on his mind and body continued, Ethan tried to move his hand, tried to cut his arm one more time.

The conjurer didn't like that at all. Ethan hadn't believed that anything could hurt more than what the man had already done to him. He was wrong. He heard a cracking sound. Several of them. Bones. In his hand. The knife fell free. Pain crashed over him like a storm-driven breaker. He rolled onto his side and vomited on the cobblestone lane.

"No more spells!" Anna said severely.

He would die before he would agree to that. Through all that he had suffered, he realized that the conjurer was coming nearer. He was still to the south, but closer, perhaps less than the distance between lanes. Useful information.

Desperation could prompt a man to do strange things, things he had never even considered before. It wouldn't sustain another fire or a shattering spell, but perhaps something less violent would also prove less expected.

Scabies ex vomitu meo evocata. Itch, conjured from my sick.

The foul mess vanished from beneath his face, and the stone street hummed along the length of his body. He didn't hear a scream this time, but the image of the little girl vanished again. Ethan assumed that meant his spell had worked. He would have preferred to cause the man pain; he wanted desperately to kill him. But the idea of such a powerful conjurer convulsing at what would have felt like ten thousand flea bites, and scratching his skin raw, gave Ethan a certain amount of satisfaction. And if he could find a man on the street madly scratching himself, he would know at last who this conjurer was.

He picked up his blade and sheathed it. Then he struggled to his feet, cradling his ruined hand against his gut and clenching his teeth against another wave of nausea. He fell against the side of the nearest building, his head spinning, his body aching in every joint and muscle. He felt the way he had after Sephira's men beat him in his room, except worse. Much worse. He pushed himself away from the wall and staggered across the lane, heading north, away from the conjurer. The man's abilities went deep—the power he wielded dwarfed that of any other conjurer Ethan had encountered—but he was still subject to the laws governing spellmaking. The greater the distance between them, the less effective his spells would be. The same could be said of Ethan's spells, of course, but at this point that was a trade Ethan was happy to make.

Each step jarred his aching bones, especially the painful jumble of bone shards in his hand. Still, he forced himself to keep moving. Earlier in the day he had all but sworn that he would kill the conjurer. Now he cared only about getting as far away from him as possible, about living to fight this battle another day.

He hobbled to the next corner, pausing briefly to get his bearings. He had reached North Street. He could head south, toward the residences of the North End, but that would take him too close to the conjurer. His choice, though, was to head north, to Lynn Street, another lane of wharves and warehouses. Beyond them lay the harbor. He had allowed the conjurer to corner him here. He was hurt, weakened, exposed. And he expected at any moment to be attacked again.

He decided to turn south, hoping that the conjurer wouldn't expect that. He hurried to the next corner—Charter Street—and turned westward.

There were people on the streets here, but they took no notice of him. Apparently his concealment spell was still intact. Not good. He needed help. He lifted his knife again, intending to cut himself and remove the concealment charm.

But before he could draw blood, he felt a pulse of power, sensed it rushing toward him, speeding beneath the stone, seeking him out. An instant later, it found him, coiled around him again. *Another finding spell.* The conjurer was still to the south, but Ethan could feel him approaching.

A second surge of power followed closely on the heels of the first, and before this one hit Ethan knew it was different. He tried to flee, but he could no more outrun this conjuring than a ship at sea could sail clear of the dawn.

It struck at his legs, like steel barbs ripping through the muscles in his calves. He stumbled, fell forward, crashing heavily on his maimed hand and splitting his lip on the cobble.

The pain in his hand threatened to overwhelm him. He was drowning in it; he felt consciousness slipping away, and a part of him welcomed the darkness.

But not the strongest part. Forcing his eyes open, Ethan willed himself up, onto his side, and to his hand and knees. He staggered to his feet and managed all of three strides before stopping again.

Anna stood just in front of him, murder in her large, pale eyes.

Ethan and Uncle Reg faced her, the ghost's eyes blazing like cannon fire. People and carriages passed by, oblivious. Ethan opened his mouth to shout for help.

But Anna made a small gesture with her hand and the bone in Ethan's bad leg gave way. He managed not to fall on his wounded hand again, but he landed awkwardly on the shattered leg, which hurt every bit as much.

The girl loomed over him, shaking her head, fury on her thin face.

Ethan heard footsteps approaching.

Anna looked up at the sound and smiled. Then she bent down and with one finger reached toward the center of Ethan's brow. He hadn't even the strength to shy away from her.

"Enough," she whispered, touching her finger to his forehead.

The blackness took him after all.

Chapter
TWENTY

onsciousness came to him slowly, like an advancing
tide.

At first Ethan retreated from it. There was no pain here,
no fear. Only rest. He was sleeping. How long had it been since he had
slept this deeply, this comfortably? Just a few more hours, he whispered. Did he really? Did he say it out loud?

"It can't wait. You have to wake up now."

Anna's voice. He was really starting to hate her.

He opened his eyes slowly, blinking against the glare of a fire.
Night had fallen; except for the gleaming white full moon above him,
he could see little beyond the blaze and the glowing little girl. A warm
breeze touched his face, smelling faintly of fish and the low tide.

He was manacled at the wrists and ankles, his back pressed against
the bark of a large tree, his arms pulled back, leading him to guess
that the chain joining the manacles circled around the trunk. He was
also gagged. And yet, though his circumstances were dire, he also realized that he was no longer in pain. Carefully he flexed the hand the
conjurer had crushed. Then he wiggled his fingers more boldly. The
hand was fully healed.

Both legs also felt whole again, although the chains were tight
enough that he could barely move them. Yet another chain led to a
metal cuff around his neck, to keep him from moving his head more
than a few inches. Predictably, all the manacles—those at his wrists

and ankles, as well as the one around his neck—were cushioned, wrapped in cloth, from the look and feel of them. He couldn't chafe his wrists, ankles, or neck on the metal cuffs. The conjurer had left him with no way to draw blood; even the cloth in his mouth kept him from biting his tongue or his cheek.

His coat, which still bore bloodstains from Nigel's bullet, was gone. The rest of his clothes had nothing on them that he could use to fuel a spell, except the cloth itself, which was too far from its living form to be suitable for a conjuring. He didn't have to check to know that his knife had been taken.

The tree itself, on the other hand, offered him plenty of material for a spell. Either the conjurer hadn't thought of this, or he didn't think that a spell that drew upon anything less than Ethan's blood would be strong enough to harm him. Ethan had little doubt as to which of these was the case.

He could feel the conjurer; he was near. The power he used to create the illusion of Anna coursed through the ground and the body of the tree like blood through veins. It seemed the night itself was alive with it. Ethan should have been frightened. Chances were, he would be dead in another few moments. But he felt strangely calm. His battle with this conjurer had gone on long enough. For better or worse it would end here, tonight.

"You're more than I thought you were, Kaille," Anna said. "You have some talent with conjuring, and more than a bit of courage. I had hoped to find a way to spare you."

Unable to speak because of the cloth in his mouth, Ethan raised his eyebrows, feigning surprise.

She cocked her head to the side and smiled. "You don't believe me." Even now, a long figure in the firelight, she acted and sounded so much like a child that Ethan had to look away. He could have learned something about spelling from this conjurer had they met under different circumstances.

But if he was going to die here, he wouldn't do so talking to this illusion of a little girl. He wanted to face the conjurer; he wanted to know who had bested him.

"No response, Kaille?"

He shook his head, still refusing to look at her.

"I can make you answer me. You know I can."

He shrugged, gazing off into the darkness, trying to figure out where exactly he was. Candles shone in the windows of a few distant houses, but he was far from the crowded lanes of Cornhill or the North End.

Ethan could tell that the girl was staring at him; he could imagine the annoyance on her face.

"I think I understand," she said. "You want to see . . . him."

Ethan nodded. Anna glanced to the side. Then she grinned at Ethan once more.

"All right." A man's voice, one Ethan thought he recognized.

An instant later, Anna disappeared. Ethan heard the scrape of a boot on cobblestone, and Peter Darrow stepped into the firelight. He was dressed as he had been earlier that day: a dark blue silk suit, an ivory-colored shirt, a tricorn hat nestled on his perfectly groomed and powdered hair. He looked every bit the country gentleman. Even if Ethan managed to get away, there wasn't a person in Boston who would believe that this handsome, dapper man was in fact a conjurer and a murderer.

Because they wouldn't be able to see the ghost walking next to him, the guide who made his conjurings possible. Remarkably, it was a little girl who could have been Anna's twin, except for the golden yellow glow that suffused her form, and the bright yellow eyes that stared back at him, as if she were some otherworldly owl. Seeing her, the calm Ethan had enjoyed only moments before began to give way to despair.

"You should have listened to us, Mister Kaille," Darrow said. "Samuel, James, and I tried to tell you that Mackintosh was your man. You should have gone along."

Ethan stared at him, knowing that he shouldn't have been so surprised. Darrow had looked terrible that morning. His eyes had been bloodshot, and he had been hobbling much the way Ethan did when his leg bothered him. Were these the results of the spells Ethan had used to attack him the night before? The shattering spell and the blindness casting that had cost Pitch his life?

"Because of you, I've had to spill a lot of blood for healing spells. On both of us." He pointed to a red mark on his arm. "This one proved particularly troublesome. That scalding spell was quite effective. I hadn't faced it before. Well done. And as for *your* wounds." He shook his head. "You were a mess. As I say, it took a lot of blood."

Ethan gave the man a puzzled look. *Why heal me if you're going to kill me?*

The lawyer smiled again. "You're wondering why I would go to all that trouble. Anna already told you: other plans."

Ethan didn't like the sound of that at all. He twisted his neck and raised his chin, trying to fight free of the gag. The chain and cuff at his neck restricted his movement too much.

"Now, now, Kaille. None of that. I've gone to a great deal of trouble to keep you from conjuring. I won't have you biting your tongue for blood." He walked to Ethan and tightened the cloth. While he was there, he also checked the manacles and their cloth linings. Finally, he stepped back, apparently reassured that his prisoner wasn't going anywhere.

"I really did have some hope that it wouldn't come to this," he said. "You impressed me last night with your resourcefulness. A killing spell. I hadn't expected that."

Ethan glared back at him.

"This may surprise you, but I think you and I could have worked well together, if only you had proven yourself a bit more malleable. I'm sure I could have convinced the others. Even Sephira Pryce would have had to admit that you would make a valuable ally."

"Th' uhthahs?" Ethan managed to say past the gag, hoping the man would understand. "Ah-hams? Oh-his?"

Darrow laughed and shook his head. "No. The others aren't Adams and Otis. They're men you don't know, men who don't approve of these self-proclaimed Sons of Liberty, or the so-called Loyal Nine."

Ethan's eyes went wide.

"You're surprised. Don't be. Without me, there might have been more of this. More riots, more lost property, more protests. Adams and Otis and their rabble might not seem like much now. Samuel is always one shilling away from debtor's prison, and James is half mad. But they have talents as well. Adams is a visionary, and Otis has a silver tongue, and they're both good with a pen. They've drawn the attention of men in London. Powerful men who wish to see these disturbances ended now, before they grow into something more.

"This was why I had some hope that you and I might one day work together. That first day you came to the Dragon, you made it clear that you didn't approve of what Adams has been up to. And I thought, Here is a man I could work with, a partner perhaps. You and I have a lot in common. Not just conjuring. Like you, I was born in England and served in the British navy. And like you, I find Adams and Otis and the rest of their ilk worthy of contempt."

He shook his head. "But you refused to accept that Mackintosh was responsible for Jennifer Berson's death. And somehow you fixed on Derne as her killer. We couldn't have that."

Darrow started to say more, but then stopped, staring intently into the darkness, like a hawk when he spots his next meal. Ethan gazed in the same direction and strained his ears, but he neither saw nor heard anything. It occurred to him that even now, while speaking to Ethan, Darrow might be using Anna as a lookout.

"He's coming," Darrow said crisply, facing Ethan again. "Finally." He grinned. "Not much longer now." He threw another log onto the fire.

"Whoh?" Ethan asked through the cloth in his mouth.

The lawyer raised an eyebrow with obvious amusement. "Did you just ask me who it is that's coming?"

Ethan nodded.

Darrow frowned. "Come now, Kaille. With all you've learned in the past several days, you can piece this together yourself. I've come to respect you as a foe. Please don't tell me that respect has been misplaced."

He was right. Ethan knew who was on his way here. Ebenezer Mackintosh. But he still didn't understand what Darrow hoped to accomplish. And he would have done just about anything to keep him talking. He had no idea how he might win his freedom, but as long as Darrow was speaking to him, he had a chance.

He wasn't about to try saying "Mackintosh" with a gag in his mouth. Instead, he nodded.

"You know?" Darrow said.

He nodded again. "Buh whyh?"

Darrow's eyes narrowed. "All right. I suppose you deserve to know that much. What is it that makes Adams so effective?" He didn't pause for an answer. "I assure you it's nothing he does himself. The man is naïve to a fault, and Otis is worse. But somehow they have managed to win the trust of laborers, men in the street. Just the sort of fools who would follow 'Captain' Mackintosh into the flames of Hell. Together, Adams and Mackintosh are formidable, or at least they could be in time." His eyes glittered in the firelight. "So I found a way to drive them apart, to make certain that the men in the street, and the sort that keep their hands clean while drinking ales in the Green Dragon, never trust each other again. You heard Adams in the Green Dragon the other day. Already he had come to regret this alliance with Mackintosh. He could see that it was harming his precious cause. That was just what I wanted."

Ethan shook his head. "Whyh?" he asked again, more stridently.

Darrow pressed his lips thin, his patience apparently on the wane. "Why, what? Why wouldn't they trust each other?"

Ethan shook his head, holding the man's gaze.

Darrow's bearing changed; he understood what Ethan wanted to know. He walked back to where Ethan leaned against the tree and drew a knife from his belt. Ethan's knife.

Darrow laid the tip of the blade beside Ethan's eye, pressing it lightly against the skin. "I would prefer you whole," the man said quietly, his breath on Ethan's cheek. "But you understand that if you do anything to anger me—anything at all—I'll take out your eye."

"Yesh."

Darrow reached up and tugged the gag away from Ethan's mouth.

Ethan opened his mouth wide, then closed it and swallowed. His jaw hurt and his throat was parched.

"What is it you want to know?" Darrow demanded, still pressing the knife against Ethan's flesh.

"Why kill Jennifer Berson?" Ethan asked, sounding hoarse.

"I thought that was what you were asking," Darrow said. "You might say that the Berson girl was my one mistake, except that in the end she won't matter very much. The truth is I didn't know it was her until after I had killed her. I needed someone for the spell, and I found her. She was dressed plainly, wandering the streets near Mackintosh's mob. She had no business being there, and I simply didn't recognize her." He shrugged. "I realized who she was only after she was dead and the spell was cast."

"And that's when you stole the brooch," Ethan said.

"I needed to make her murder into something that her family would understand. If there were questions, I would have trouble. Make it about their riches, and they would grieve, they would want their jewel back, but they would blame the brutish rabble. It would be a terrible loss, of course, but it would make sense in their view of the world." He opened his hands, as if the logic of all he had done was beyond question. "And it would fit perfectly with what I wanted to do. I just didn't count on you being so damned inquisitive."

"What was the spell for?"

"What do you think?"

Ethan considered this, and as he did, he remembered something Adams had told him in the Green Dragon. "The attack on Hutchinson's house," he said, meeting Darrow's gaze. "The Sons of Liberty approved of the rest of what Mackintosh did. They probably put him up to it. But not that."

"Well done, Kaille."

"And the girl you killed this morning—you used her death to compel Sheriff Greenleaf to release Mackintosh."

Darrow's expression darkened. "That was your fault. Ideally, I would have left him in prison. Adams and Otis would have left him there, too, and that would have angered Mackintosh's followers. But now Mackintosh has another murder to commit."

Comprehension hit Ethan like a fist to the gut. He leaned his head back against the tree and stared up at the moon through a tangle of leaves and branches. He had kept Darrow from using Holin's death to control him, but now, very likely, he would be used for a casting that would control Mackintosh.

"I'll use your death to convince poor Ebenezer that he killed you. You were an agent of the Sons of Liberty, you see. And you were intent on seeing him punished for the Berson murder. It all fits together rather nicely, don't you think?" After a brief pause, he added, "Don't worry, Kaille. It's not a bad way to go, actually. You'll hardly feel a thing. Given how much I've wanted to hurt you at various times over the past several days, you could have come to a much worse end."

"You're working for the Crown?" Ethan asked, facing him again. "The king's men know what you're doing?"

"I serve His Majesty," Darrow said. Ethan thought he heard a note of defensiveness in his voice. "His men don't have to know all that I do. They trust me. They know that I'll do all in my power to guard the empire."

Ethan wasn't sure he believed this, but he didn't dare challenge the man. "So Jennifer Berson was a mistake," he said. "What about the others?"

"What others?" But Ethan could tell that he knew.

"The boy on Pope's Day," Ethan said. "And whoever it was you killed the day the Richardsons swung."

Darrow regarded him for several moments. "I *am* impressed."

Before Ethan could respond, Darrow sheathed the knife and retied Ethan's gag, making it even tighter than it had been. Still leaning close to him, Darrow whispered. "I needed the boy in November for the same reason I needed the girl this morning. As to the other . . ." He opened his hands. "Adams already told you: Mackintosh and his counterpart in the North End were speaking of a truce, of ending their Pope's Day feud in order to strengthen the non-importation agreements against the Grenville Acts. We couldn't have that." Darrow smiled. "And as it happens, no one died that day who wasn't going to die anyway." He stepped back. "And now, I really must go greet Ebenezer. But don't worry, we'll be back shortly."

He checked Ethan one last time. Then he walked away, his shoes scraping on cobblestone as his form was swallowed by the night.

As soon as Ethan could no longer hear Darrow's footsteps, he turned his attention to escaping, or at least finding a way to draw blood. Biting his tongue or cheek would have been ideal, since Darrow wouldn't have noticed that he bled. But the lawyer had made that impossible when he retied the gag so tightly.

The bark of the tree—an elm from the look of it—was rough enough to have scraped his skin, but his chains didn't allow him enough freedom of movement to do much more than rub his coat sleeve until it was threadbare.

The manacles, however, might be another matter. If he could remove some of the cloth covering the metal at his wrist or ankle he could cut his skin on its edge. Pulling his hand as far out of the cuff as he could, so that the ring pressed into his flesh, and then bracing the cuff and hand against the tree, Ethan was able to reach the cloth covering with his fingers. He couldn't grip it well, but this covering hadn't been firmly attached to the metal.

He worked it methodically with his fingers, rubbing at it again and again. The cloth came away slowly, bunching beneath his fingers, until at last he could feel cold iron. The manacle was smoother than he had hoped it would be. Worse, its edge had been rounded, so that it offered him little chance to cut his skin. Still he tried. Shifting his hand again, bracing the cuff differently, this time against the tension of the chain, he was able to push that exposed edge against his skin, just below his thumb.

He began to scrape his wrist against the edge, working as quickly as he could, knowing that Darrow would be back before long. But though his hand grew sore and began to redden, nothing he did scraped away any skin. He would eventually have a bruise, if he lived long enough, but this wasn't going to draw blood.

As far as he could tell, there was no way he could use the cuffs and chains at his ankles. But toying once more with the chains that held his arms, Ethan realized that by lifting his arm a little and keeping it close to the trunk he could create enough slack in the chain to get his fingers into the links.

It wasn't something he wanted to do. Pell and Kannice might have challenged him on this after the week he'd had, but Ethan really didn't enjoy pain. But there would be blood, and in this circumstance nothing else mattered. The trick would be concealing the wound from Darrow.

He heard footsteps, then distant voices approaching.

". . . Hurt me?"

"He's a thieftaker, Ebenezer. A mercenary. He was hired to do this. What he wants or doesn't want is beside the point."

"Bu' who hired him?"

"That is the most difficult part of this, at least for me. I suppose I bear some of the blame for not anticipating where all of this would lead. But it was Adams and Otis."

The footsteps ceased.

"Mister Adams an' Mister Otis hired him so tha' he could bloody me an' then send me back t' th' prison?"

"I'm afraid so."

Ethan placed the pointing finger of his right hand into a chain link and then tried to wrench it out. It didn't work the first time, or the next. And with the second attempt, the chain rattled against the tree with a chiming sound.

Darrow and Mackintosh had started walking again, but they halted a second time at a sharp "shhh!" from the lawyer.

Ethan had one last chance. He placed his finger back in the link and twisted it out again. This time it did what he had hoped it would. It tore the nail away from his finger.

He inhaled sharply through his teeth, hoping that Darrow wouldn't hear. He felt warm blood pour from the finger and he cupped his hand around it, catching the blood. At the same time, he lowered his arm as carefully and as quickly as he could, this time doing his best to keep the chain silent.

There was enough blood flowing that he feared it would drip and catch Darrow's eye, so he wiped his hand on the tree bark as close to his body as possible. He then shifted his feet enough so that he could at least partially block the stain from Darrow's view.

All of this took him but a few seconds, which was fortunate because just as he lowered his hand and assumed as casual a stance as he could manage, Darrow and Mackintosh stepped into the firelight. The cordwainer had been speaking again, but now he fell silent, halting at the edge of the fire glow and eyeing Ethan warily.

Ethan gazed back at them both, trying to keep his expression neutral. He had blood for a conjuring. Now he needed to find the right spell.

Darrow came forward, his eyes narrowed. "What have you been up to?"

Ethan was sure he intended to check his manacles, chains, and gag to make sure they were still secure. Doing so, he was certain to see the blood on Ethan's hand, and all would be lost.

But Mackintosh, after glaring at him for a few seconds, drew a knife from his belt and started toward Ethan, murder in his eyes.

Darrow blocked his path. "No, Ebenezer! That's the last thing you want to do. Believe me. I assure you, you'll have your vengeance soon enough."

Mackintosh still glowered at Ethan. For an instant, Ethan thought that he might try to push his way past Darrow. But he nodded and reluctantly put away his knife.

"That's a good lad," Darrow said. He glanced back at Ethan, flashing a quick, amused smile, as if he and Ethan had shared some great jest. For the moment, he seemed to have forgotten that he wanted to check Ethan's shackles.

"Why d' you have him chained up like tha'?" the cordwainer asked. "You'd think he was strong as a bear, with all that iron on him. An' why wrap his manacles?"

Darrow eyed Mackintosh for a moment. The blood still flowed from Ethan's finger, and he took this opportunity to wipe it on the tree bark behind him, watching Darrow the whole time.

"That's a fine question," the lawyer said, facing Ethan again. "Can you think of a reason not to tell him?"

"Tell me wha'?" Mackintosh asked.

"That he's a conjurer."

The cordwainer's brow furrowed. "A wha'?"

"What you and I would call a witch. He can cast spells."

Mackintosh's frown deepened. "You're mad."

"No, I'm not. That's the reason I have him chained this way. We can't let him have access to any blood. Blood for a conjurer is like whiskey for a drunk: He should be denied it at all costs." He crossed to Ethan and looked him over carefully. "Now what were you up to before?"

Knowing that any motion on his part would draw Darrow's attention, Ethan tried to hide his wounded hand, but in a way that would make the man think he was concealing the raw spot on his wrist.

Darrow grabbed his forearm, and lifted Ethan's hand so that the firelight could reach it. Ethan kept his hand fisted, hiding the bloody finger, and just as he had hoped, Darrow immediately noticed the exposed metal on the manacle.

"Ethan," he said in a stern voice. "You shouldn't have done that." He ran a finger over the darkening bruise on Ethan's wrist. "Didn't amount to much, did it?"

Ethan shook his head.

"Wha' is it he's done?"

Darrow glanced back at Mackintosh. "He tried to cut his wrist on the metal cuff." He smoothed out the cloth, making certain that all of the metal was covered once more. "We're fortunate that he didn't succeed. I promise you he wouldn't have hesitated to kill us both with his witchery." As he spoke, he checked the other manacles. Apparently satisfied that Ethan was still powerless to escape, he returned to the cordwainer's side.

"So you wan' me t' believe tha' he's a witch—a real witch, who can make spells an' tha' sort o' thing?"

"That's right. More, I think it's possible that he killed Jennifer Berson himself, and has been trying to blame you for the murder, all at the behest of Samuel Adams, James Otis, and the Loyal Nine."

"But why?"

"Because you're a dangerous man, Ebenezer. Adams and the others think of themselves as leaders, but you really are one. They want to control you, and failing that, they'll eliminate you and control the men you lead."

Ethan shook his head, making the chain at his neck ring.

"I think he's tryin' t' say tha' you're wrong."

Darrow laughed convincingly. "Of course he is. Would you expect him to do anything else?"

"He'hsh lhying!" Ethan said through the gag.

"Wha' was tha'?" Mackintosh asked.

Darrow turned toward Ethan, a sly look on his handsome face. "I believe he said that I'm lying."

"Take out his gag. I want t' hear wha' he has t' say."

"I can't do that, Ebenezer. Without the gag in his mouth he can bite down on his tongue, make himself bleed, and kill us both."

"Barrowh's a wihs fhoo!" Ethan said, staring hard at Mackintosh, hoping that he would hear "Darrow's a witch, too," in the sound he had made.

Rage flashed in Darrow's eyes. Clearly he had understood.

"What'd he say tha' time?"

Darrow shook his head. "I'm not sure. And it doesn't matter."

Mackintosh watched Ethan, clearly troubled by all that he had heard. "Well, so he's a witch. Wha' are we going t' do with him?"

"He's not just a witch. He's a killer. There's only one thing we can do to him. He tried to blame you for the Berson killing; I thought you would want to be here to see him die. In a way, you could say that I'm killing him for you."

Ethan felt sure that Darrow was but moments away from casting the killing spell. He had to do something, and he knew better than to think that any blood spell he cast right now would work. It might force Darrow to reveal that he was a conjurer, but whatever spell the lawyer cast on Mackintosh using Ethan's life would erase that memory. He needed more time.

Imago ex igne evocata. Illusion, conjured from fire.

He felt the power of the spell pulse in the tree against his back and under his feet. The old ghost appeared next to him, his bright eyes fixed on Darrow, who glowered back at both of them. Mackintosh gave no indication that he had noticed anything, at least at first.

Ethan saw the image of Stephen Greenleaf step into the firelight. He wore the same dark suit he had been wearing the last time Ethan saw him, and he looked as substantial as any illusion Ethan had ever conjured. But that wouldn't be enough. Closing his eyes, he drew on the fire a second time, feeling the ground vibrate once more.

"He's lying to you, Mackintosh," the illusion said in a thin, wraith-like voice.

The cordwainer gaped and even took a step back from the image. "Tha's Greenleaf!"

"No, it's not. Not really, anyway. It's merely an illusion conjured by Kaille."

"Darrow is a conjurer, too," Ethan made the sheriff say, amazed that he had succeeded in getting his illusion to speak. "He killed Jenni—"

Pain exploded in his shoulder. Ethan cried out, his knees buckling. Opening his eyes, Ethan saw that Darrow hadn't moved, although his golden ghost had returned. He had shattered the bones in Ethan's shoulder with a spell, probably drawing on a few of the leaves fluttering above them.

Darrow glared at him, the threat of more pain in his eyes.

"Wha' happened t' him?" Mackintosh asked, confusion and fear chasing each other across his angular features.

"I have no idea," Darrow said.

The image of Greenleaf had wavered, like a flame sputtering in a sudden wind. But Ethan managed somehow to maintain the illusion through his pain, and now he drew on the flames again.

"Darrow did that to me," he made the sheriff say. "He used witchery to—"

Molten steel coursed through his veins, silencing his illusion, stealing his breath, numbing his senses. He writhed against the tree, his chains thrashing, his head bucking against the bark.

At the same time, Darrow shouted, "Stop it!"

That proved to be a mistake.

Ethan couldn't hold the image of Greenleaf anymore. But the illusion spell had served its purpose.

Mackintosh was gaping at Darrow now, terror on his face. "You're doin' somethin' t' him! You're hurtin' him! Bu' you haven' touched him! He's right, isn' he? You're a witch, too! Th' two o' you are usin' witchcraft on each other!"

Darrow's face contorted with rage, but only for an instant. With a visible effort he calmed himself. He even forced a smile. "Enough," he said, his voice level.

As abruptly as it had begun, the torment ceased. Ethan sagged against the tree; had it not been for the chains, he would have crumpled to the ground, although hanging from them made the pain in his shattered shoulder unbearable.

He wanted to curl up into a ball and sleep. A part of him wanted to relent and die. Mostly though, he wanted to kill Peter Darrow and end this nightmare. With an effort, he got his feet under him and stood once more. Mackintosh was afraid of Darrow now; the conjurer couldn't allow this to go on much longer. He needed to kill Ethan quickly.

Ethan had only seconds in which to act. And he still had no idea how to defeat the man.

That is, until Darrow himself gave Ethan an idea. For a second time, the conjurer suddenly stared off into the night. This time his brow furrowed, and when he faced Ethan and Mackintosh once more his jaw was set, his expression resolute. He had seen something through Anna's eyes. Again.

Why couldn't Ethan do something similar?

He closed his eyes and, drawing on the flames once more, summoned another illusion—the first form that came to mind. This one, though, didn't form in the circle of firelight. Instead, he sent it out in the same direction Darrow had gazed a moment before. As before, he drew on the flame. *Videre per mea imagine ex igne evocatum.* Sight, through my illusion, conjured from fire. He felt the power. So did Darrow.

"What are you doing, Kaille?" the conjurer asked, sounding alarmed.

Ethan ignored him. Suddenly he was on a road, or it felt like he was. He could see three people approaching, walking quickly.

"Wha' d' you mean, wha's he doin'?" Mackintosh's voice. "He's not doin' anythin'."

Ethan's illusion approached the men and Ethan saw with elation that he knew them. Mr. Pell, whom Ethan had sent to keep watch on Darrow; Samuel Adams; and James Otis. Ethan had his illusion stop in front of Pell, who regarded the figure with obvious suspicion.

"Who are—?"

"I haven't much time," Ethan made the illusion say.

"Stop it, Kaille!" Darrow warned.

"Ethan Kaille is by that fire, with Ebenezer Mackintosh. They're in danger; they need your help. Ethan said to tell you that if you really want to be a thieftaker, this is the time to start."

Pell had been eyeing the illusion doubtfully, but his eyes widened at this last remark. "She's telling the truth!" he told the others.

"Darrow is a conjurer," the illusion said. "You'll need hel—"

"I said stop it!"

The spell with which Darrow fractured Ethan's knee hurt even more than the one that had shattered his shoulder. He was wrenched off the road and back to the tree and his chains. He collapsed again as far as the shackles would allow, gasping at the agony in his leg and his shoulder. He assumed that his illusion had vanished, and he wondered what Pell, Adams, and Otis would make of what they had seen and heard.

He opened his eyes and found Darrow standing directly in front of him. Rage smoldered in his dark eyes, and Ethan could see that it was all he could do to keep himself from smashing every bone in Ethan's body.

Despite the throbbing pain in his knee and shoulder, despite the gag in his mouth, he flashed a quick smile Darrow's way, which only enraged the man more.

"Tell me wha' he's doin'!" Mackintosh demanded, still panicked and far beyond his depth. "He's a speller, you say. An' he says you are, too. Fine then. Wha's he doin'?"

"An illusion spell, like before," Darrow told the cordwainer. "He's communicating with his friends, trying to bring help."

"Help?" Mackintosh said, his eyes like those of a scared child. "You mean more witches?"

"It doesn't matter," Darrow said. "He'll be dead before they get here."

Uncle Reg had been standing utterly still, watching all of this unfold. Now, though, he turned to Ethan, avid, a plea in his eyes. Ethan had never seen the old ghost so eager for a spell.

But what to cast? Blood still oozed slowly from the finger he had ripped open; the blood on his hand was growing sticky as it dried. He would have only one chance at a blood spell. His best hope lay in surprising Darrow, and he could only do that by attempting something he had never done before.

Imago ex igne evocata. Illusion, conjured from fire.

Power pulsed and Darrow pulled the blade from his belt.

But then he saw the figure Ethan had conjured. The same figure Ethan had sent to speak with Pell, Adams, and Otis.

Anna. Or at least Ethan's best imitation of her.

"Very clever, Kaille," Darrow said.

"I don't want to die," Ethan said through the image of the girl. "And I don't want to be tortured anymore."

"I'm sure you don't. You should have thought of that before you set yourself against me."

"Is it too late for that partnership you spoke of earlier?"

Ethan barely listened to the man's response. He concentrated instead on maintaining the illusion spell while at the same time casting again. *Ambure ex cruore evocatum!* Scald, conjured from blood! It had worked once; Darrow told him as much. Perhaps it would work a second time.

Ethan felt a change in the pulse of his conjuring, and knew that Darrow had, too. He had hoped that by masking the power with his illusion spell, he would catch the man off guard. And since Darrow wouldn't expect him to have access to blood, the spell should have been strong enough to break through whatever warding Darrow used.

For an instant, he thought that it would work. Darrow stiffened suddenly, and he growled through gritted teeth—he was obviously in agony.

And then he wasn't. Ethan felt Darrow's spell, too. It had to have been a warding, cast with nothing more than a thought, fueled by something other than blood. In the span of a single heartbeat, the rictus of pain vanished from Darrow's face, leaving only an angry glare.

"Scalding again? Not very creative, are you?" He dragged the edge of Ethan's knife across his hand. "Fine. Here's an old favorite for you."

It couldn't have been any more painful if Darrow had taken a bayonet, plunged it through Ethan's head, and pinned him thus to the tree. Ethan let out a wail that echoed across the surrounding fields and beat his fists against the tree trunk until he thought the bones in his hands would shatter again.

"Two spells at once," he heard Darrow say. "You're learning. A pity that you won't live long enough to put your new skills to use. Your time is up."

The agony ended. But immediately, Ethan felt a sudden odd tugging at his chest. It didn't exactly hurt. But his heart had begun to labor; he couldn't draw breath. A shadow darkened his sight; the firelight faded. He could barely keep his balance.

And he thought, *This is what it's like to be the source for a killing spell.*

TWENTY-TWO

*L*ife was draining from his body like blood flowing from an open wound. And Ethan could do nothing to stanch it.

"Wha' are you doin' to me?" Mackintosh asked, sounding panicked. Apparently he felt something, too. How ironic. At last, he sensed Darrow's power, and it was too late for Ethan to do anything to save them.

"Darrow!"

Ethan raised his head, the effort taking every ounce of his ebbing strength. Darrow had turned at the sound of his name. So had Mackintosh. Dimly, Ethan saw Samuel Adams and James Otis standing at the edge of the firelight. Both men held pistols.

The conjurer sighed, sounding more annoyed than alarmed. "You shouldn't have come."

"Put down the knife and untie Kaille," Adams said, stepping forward, his firearm aimed at Darrow's chest.

Darrow laughed. "This knife? It's nothing. A trifle." He tossed it to the ground so that it landed beside the fire. "You believe you've tamed me now? You have no idea what you're dealing with. Go home, Samuel, before you get yourself hurt. And take James with you."

Ethan could stand again. He felt stronger, more alive. He glanced at Mackintosh only to find that the cordwainer was already watching him. He still looked scared, but there was anger in his gaze as well. Ethan understood. Darrow had tried to use a conjuring on him; Mackintosh had felt it. At last, he had chosen sides in this fight, and like the good street captain he was, he now looked to Ethan for orders.

"What is it you hope to accomplish here, Peter?" Otis asked, his protuberant eyes alight with the glow of the fire. "And what does Kaille have to do with any of this?"

"He's a witch," Mackintosh said. "They both are. Bu' Darrow—he tried t' work a spell on me."

Darrow held himself still, his eyes fixed on the cordwainer. Ethan could see his thoughts churning, and after tracking the man these past few days, he had finally started to understand the workings of his mind. He didn't like what he saw on the conjurer's face. In the next moment, Darrow shifted his gaze to Ethan and actually smiled.

"New plans," he said, just loud enough for Ethan to hear.

Of course. He couldn't have Mackintosh kill Ethan now, not with Adams and Otis here, knowing what they did. But he could kill all three men, and use power drawn from their murders to compel Ethan to accept the blame. With that much power, he might even convince Ethan of his own guilt.

Darrow glanced off into the night again before facing Adams and Otis. "I don't think you need those anymore," he said.

The ground hummed and a second later, both men dropped their pistols as if they had suddenly grown too hot to hold. Adams rubbed the palm of his hand. Otis stared down at his weapon, his mouth hanging open. Then he looked at Darrow, and there could be no mistaking the terror in his eyes.

"How did you do that?" Otis whispered.

"How do you think?" Darrow answered, a mocking grin on his lips.

Ethan drew on the flame for another illusion spell. Anna appeared before him.

Darrow regarded her sourly. "What now?"

"Mackintosh is right," Ethan made the girl say. "Darrow is a conjurer. He intends to kill you all, and he'll see to it that Kaille takes the blame."

"I'm afraid he's right about that," the conjurer said, looking faintly amused.

Ethan didn't hear what was said next. Once more he used one spell to mask another. Maintaining the image of Anna that stood in the firelight, he sent another image of the girl down the road and peered into the night through her eyes. Doing so, he beheld what Darrow had seen only moments before. Pell was coming; the real sheriff and a few men of the night watch walked with him.

". . . Kaille?"

Ethan forced himself to concentrate once more on what was happening in the firelight. Darrow had said something and now glared at him. The others watched him, too, Otis looking frightened and uncertain, Adams grim but alert. Mackintosh, the street fighter, merely waited.

"I asked you what you're doing," Darrow said.

"I'm keeping this illusion going," Ethan said through Anna. "I'm telling these others that you intend to kill them, and that they should flee while they can."

Darrow shook his head, his eyes narrowing. "No. You're up to something else."

They were out of time. Ethan knew what was coming and knew as well that he needed to be precise in what he did next. The timing of the spells was crucial. He was exhausted; never had he cast so many spells in so little time. Never had he been tortured like this. But he could give in to his weariness, or he could survive the night. He couldn't do both.

He closed his eyes again, drew on the fire, but also on the air, and on the fine mist forming over the nearby fields. And he succeeded in creating an illusion that was more real than any he had conjured before. His image of the sheriff and men of the watch rushed into the firelight, their footsteps scraping on the road, their pistols glinting in the glow of the blaze as they leveled them at Darrow. But he felt his own spell, and so did Darrow. Otis and Adams jumped out of the way of the illusions. Darrow laughed at them.

"They're not real," he said, contempt in his voice. Glancing at Ethan he added, "Really, Kaille, is that the best you can do?"

Ethan's conjurings waved their weapons at the lawyer, making the same motions over and over. They looked pathetic really, as Ethan had known they would.

But he needed them to mask yet another spell.

Discuti ex foliis evocatum! Shatter, conjured from leaves!

Power coursed through the ground. Darrow's eyes snapped to Ethan's. A second conjuring made the earth hum, so that the two spells skirled discordantly, like strings on a poorly tuned violin.

Except that Darrow's spell was a warding against Ethan's assault. And Ethan hadn't aimed his spell at the conjurer. He aimed it at the shackles that bound his arms.

The chain snapped at the last link before the cuff on his left hand, and immediately Ethan grabbed hold of the chain with this right, and swung it hard so that the links whipped toward Darrow. No doubt the conjurer's warding would have worked perfectly against a spell, but it wasn't intended to guard against a physical assault, and he didn't have time to cast again.

The end of the chain lashed Darrow across the side of his face, knocking him to the ground.

Mackintosh dove forward and grabbed the knife that had fallen near the fire. At the same time, Ethan cast a second spell to free his legs, and ripped the gag from his mouth.

Adams and Otis started toward their guns, but they couldn't reach them in time.

Still lying on his back, Darrow roared something in Latin that Ethan didn't understand. There could be no mistaking the effect, though. It seemed that a keg of gunpowder exploded in their midst. The spell threw Adams, Otis, and Mackintosh to the ground, leaving all three men addled. It also hammered Ethan back against the tree. The breath was knocked from his body, and he collapsed, landing hard on his wounded shoulder and knee.

Darrow stood slowly. Blood flowed from his nose and the corner of his mouth, and his cheek had already started to darken. He didn't speak. He didn't have to. Ethan knew what was coming. He saw the blood vanish from his face, felt the ground tingle. Still, how did one prepare for such agony?

He felt as though his skin was being flayed. Molten steel coursed through his veins again. The spike had impaled his head once more. This was torment beyond anything the man had done to him before.

He couldn't escape it, and it went on and on. He thought Darrow would kill him with the pain. Ethan didn't even know if that was possible. He could hear himself howling like a wounded animal, but he couldn't make himself stop.

"Beg me to kill you." Darrow's voice, even and calm, so close that the man could have been whispering in his ear. "Ask me for death, and I can end this. The others are lost anyway. You can't save them. Beg me."

Through a haze of agony, Ethan drew upon the leaves overhead to cast a warding spell. He might as well have tried to block a cannonball with a sheet of parchment. Still, Ethan refused to surrender. He tried to attack Darrow with fire, with scalding, with another shatter spell, and with the blindness casting he had used two nights before. He felt the conjurings tremble in the ground beneath him, and he knew that the spells had worked. But he could do nothing to breach the man's wardings. Darrow was too strong. Even Pell and the sheriff and the men they had brought wouldn't be able to help. All of them would die. Already Ethan felt his life ebbing away. His heart was being seared; he could barely draw breath. He couldn't fight it. He wasn't even sure anymore that he wanted to.

And yet, in the next instant, the pain ceased. Ethan took a deep breath—he could breathe without feeling that his lungs were on fire. A warm breeze touched his face. He wanted to savor the sensation. He wanted to rest.

He forced his eyes open. Darrow loomed over him, but he was staring over his shoulder at Mackintosh. The cordwainer backed away from the man, terror in his eyes, his chest rising and falling rapidly. Darrow turned slowly, and Ethan saw that the knife Mackintosh had retrieved jutted from the conjurer's back, just below his shoulder blade. Blood darkened the man's coat, but only for a few seconds.

Ethan had time to shout a warning to Mackintosh, but it did little good. The blood disappeared, and Mackintosh's coat burst into flames. The cordwainer dropped to the ground and began to roll from side to side. Adams and Otis leaped to his aid, batting at the flames with their hands.

Darrow reached back and pulled out the knife. The blood on the blade caught the firelight, and then it, too, was gone. Ethan braced himself for another assault, but it didn't come. Darrow, he realized, had used the blood to heal the wound on his back.

Ethan drew on the fire for another illusion spell. Two, actually. With the first he sent Anna down the road. With the second, he conjured again the image of Greenleaf and the men of the watch.

The illusions advanced on Darrow with raised weapons.

"Enough of this, Ethan," Darrow said.

He kicked Ethan's shattered knee, and Ethan cried out. But still, Ethan held the image of the men for a moment longer, until at last he heard what he had been waiting for.

Through gritted teeth he said, "You're right. Enough."

Looking toward the road, he let his illusion die away. And there, to take the place of his conjured images, stood the real sheriff and his men with Mr. Pell.

"Now, Pell!" he shouted.

He heard Pell say something, saw Darrow slash at his own arm with the knife. The conjurer's voice rang through the night and then was drowned out by the rapid blasts of four flintlock pistols.

For a second, no one spoke. No one even moved. The report of the guns echoed across the pastureland.

And then Darrow laughed. He opened his fist and held it out for all of them to see. Resting in the palm of his hand were the four lead balls fired at him by Greenleaf and the men of the watch.

"Do you understand now?" he asked of no one in particular. "Do you see at last what you're dealing with?"

Ethan glanced at Adams and saw despair in his eyes. He let his gaze drop to the pistol lying on the ground before the man. Adams nodded.

Conflare ex ligno evocatum. Heat, conjured from wood.

It was a more difficult spell, fueled as it was by the wood of a branch rather than by mere leaves. But it made for a more powerful casting. His conjuring rumbled in the ground like thunder.

Darrow cast as well. Another warding, of course. But again, Ethan's spell wasn't intended for the conjurer, at least not directly.

Darrow cried out, jerking his hand back. The bullets fell to the ground, now a mass of molten lead. And at the same moment, Adams dove to the ground, grabbed his pistol, and fired.

As before, no one moved. Darrow let out another laugh, breathless with surprise. But then he fell to his knees, blood blossoming over his heart.

The stain on his coat vanished as quickly as it appeared. Even now, his face ashen, his hand shaking, the man was attempting to save himself. But a healing spell for such a wound was no trifle, and even the most skilled conjurer couldn't maintain a warding as well.

I need blood, Ethan said silently, staring hard at Uncle Reg. The old ghost nodded and planted himself in front of Pell. At first, the minister took a step back, fear in his pale eyes. But then Reg raised a finger and made a quick slashing motion over his forearm. Pell looked past the ghost to Ethan, who nodded once.

"A knife!" the minister said.

Darrow turned his head slowly to face Ethan. Then he began to climb to his feet.

"Quickly!" Pell shouted.

Otis pulled a blade from his belt and handed it to the minister. Without a moment's hesitation, Pell cut his forearm.

The instant he saw blood, Ethan said, *"Frange! Ex cruore evocatum!"* Break! Conjured from blood!

The earth shook once more. There was a sound of cracking bone—as clear as a church bell. Darrow's head leaned to one side, his neck broken; he swayed and toppled to the ground.

The golden girl—the ghost Anna—looked at Uncle Reg and at Ethan, her eyes wide and bright. For an instant, she was merely a child: scared, alone. And then she was gone.

TWENTY-THREE

or a moment, no one moved. Adams and Otis, Mackintosh and Pell, Greenleaf and the men of the watch— all of them stared at Darrow. Adams was the first to look away. He gazed down at the pistol in his hand, and took a long, shuddering breath. Finally, as one, they turned to Ethan.

Pell hurried forward and knelt beside him.

"Where are you hurt?" the minister asked.

"It would take less time to tell you where I'm *not* hurt."

Pell laughed breathlessly, sounding more relieved than amused. "Can you . . . ?" he hesitated, glancing at the others. "Can you take care of it yourself?"

"I haven't the strength," Ethan said quietly, his thoughts clouded by the throbbing pain in his shoulder and knee. "And I'd rather not put on a display for the sheriff." He looked around. "I don't know where we are. How far are we from my home?"

"Did you just say that you don't know where you are?" Adams said, coming forward.

"That's right."

Adams gestured at the tree to which Ethan had been chained. "This is the Liberty Tree, Mister Kaille. You're on Orange Street, at Essex."

The Liberty Tree. He had heard talk of the place. This was where Andrew Oliver had been hung in effigy, and where the first of the riots on August 14 had begun. More important, they were only a short distance from Janna's tavern.

"There's someone who can help me," Ethan told Pell. "Her name is Tarijanna Windcatcher, and she owns the Fat Spider. It's a tavern down the road toward the town gate."

Pell started to stand. "I'll get her."

"No," Ethan said, stopping him. "Send one of Greenleaf's men. She doesn't like ministers. She doesn't like anyone. But she'll help me. Tell him to use my name."

The minister walked back to Greenleaf and his men and spoke to them in low tones. After a moment, one of the men started off down the road toward Janna's tavern.

"Thank you," Ethan said to Adams. "That was a fine shot. I thought you were palsied."

"I am," Adams said. "My penmanship is atrocious. Shooting is another matter." He looked down at Darrow and shook his head. "Peter was a friend. I didn't want to kill him."

"You didn't," Ethan said, his voice low. "I did." He had taken lives before, and perhaps he would again. But it would never be easy, not even when the man he killed was intent on murdering him. "And you should know that Darrow wasn't your friend. He was a spy for supporters of Parliament and the Crown. He sought to undermine everything that you're working for."

Greenleaf came forward as Ethan spoke, plainly interested in what he was saying. Ethan paid no attention to him.

"He killed Jennifer Berson and three others," he went on. "And he was perfectly willing to kill Mackintosh here, or me. Or both of you," he said to Adams and Otis, "if it served his purposes."

"Why did he kill them?" Pell asked.

"He was casting control spells—using his conjurings to make others do his bidding. He killed Jennifer Berson so that Mackintosh would take his mob and destroy Thomas Hutchinson's home. He killed the girl who was found this morning to make Sheriff Greenleaf release Mackintosh from gaol. Same with the boy who died on Pope's Day. He won Ebenezer's release, and so won his trust."

"That's preposterous!" Greenleaf said, but there was uncertainty in his eyes.

"Is it, Sheriff?" Ethan asked. "Did you have any intention of releasing Ebenezer before this morning?"

"I . . ." He shook his head, his gaze falling to Darrow's corpse. "I don't recall," he said at last.

"I wouldn't expect you to," Ethan said without rancor. Facing Adams again, he said, "The alliance between you and Mackintosh was a threat to him and to those he worked for. Everything he did was intended to drive the two of you apart, to break the bonds between Mackintosh's followers and the Sons of Liberty."

Mackintosh stared down at Darrow's body, murder in his eyes. "You said there were four who died. Who was th' last?"

Ethan considered this briefly. What was it Darrow had told him? *No one died that day who wasn't going to die anyway.* He thought back to his conversation with Holin about the Richardson hanging—about how one of them had kicked violently when the other merely went limp.

"Ann Richardson," he said.

Mackintosh frowned. "But—"

"She was to be executed anyway, I know. But he used her death to keep you and Swift, your North End rival, from declaring a truce. He needed the fighting to go on a while longer so that he could win you over on Pope's Day."

The cordwainer shook his head and glowered down at Darrow. "Bastard. He made me int' a puppet. A toy."

"We didn't know, Ebenezer," Otis said, his voice gentle. "You have my word on that."

Mackintosh nodded, but he wouldn't look at him.

Before Ethan could say more, the man of the watch stepped back into the ring of light, leading Janna, who had a shawl wrapped around her shoulders, despite the warm night air.

"What you done t' yourself, Kaille?"

"Hi, Janna," Ethan said. "I've got a broken shoulder and a broken knee."

"What else?"

"That's all."

She eyed him skeptically. "You look worse than just a broken shoulder an' a broken knee."

"Well, I can handle the rest."

"What happened t' all that mullein I gave you?"

"I used it."

Janna shook her head, scowling at him. But then she sat down on the grass beside him. "Go ahead and cut yourself."

His eyes darted toward the sheriff and then back to hers: a warning. Janna twisted around and looked back at Greenleaf, then dismissed him with a wave of her hand. "He's gonna need more than three men if he wan's t' take me in."

Ethan would have laughed had he not been so weary and in so much pain. He caught Pell's eye and beckoned him over. The minister eyed Janna warily, but handed Ethan Otis's knife. And after Ethan cut his forearm, Janna dabbed blood on his shoulder and began to heal his broken bones.

She didn't speak her spell aloud, or indicate in any way that she had cast. But the ground began to hum, and the pale blue ghost of an old African woman appeared at her shoulder, her face a mirror image of Janna's. Cool healing power flowed over Ethan's tender shoulder like spring rain, and after several moments, the pain began to abate. He took a long breath and exhaled slowly.

"Better?" Janna asked.

"Much."

She had him cut himself again and poured still more healing power into his shoulder before turning her talents to his shattered knee. By the time she had finished with that, Ethan's forearm was raw and sore, but he could walk again.

"Thank you, Janna," he said. "Again, I'm in your debt."

She got to her feet, moving stiffly. "Yeah, you are," she said, and walked off into the night, back toward her tavern.

Pell stood nearby, speaking with the sheriff, as did Adams, Mackintosh, and Otis. The men of the watch spoke in low tones among themselves, eyeing Ethan from a distance. Ethan stood slowly, wincing at the pain in his joints. Janna's healing spells had taken the edge off his pain, but his shoulder and knee still throbbed, as he had known they would.

His bad leg didn't feel much better, and his entire body ached from all that Darrow had done to him this night and earlier in the day. He felt older than his age. Much older.

Seeing that Ethan was up, Pell and the others joined him in the firelight.

"Are you all right?" Pell asked.

"I will be. Thank you." Ethan looked at Adams, Mackintosh, Otis, and even Greenleaf. "All of you. He would have killed me if you hadn't come."

"All the credit goes to your young friend here," Adams said, indicating Pell with an open hand. "He came to us saying that you were in trouble."

Pell flushed. "I only did what Ethan told me to. I lingered by the Green Dragon, looking for the two of you and for Darrow. When I saw him, he was acting strangely, so I followed. Eventually I realized that he had you, Ethan. Once I figured out where he was taking you, I went back for Mister Adams and Mister Otis."

"Well," Ethan said, "I think you'll make a fine thieftaker if you ever decide to give up the ministry. Wouldn't you agree, Sheriff?"

"I suppose," Greenleaf said. He still looked shaken and unsure of himself. Ethan had never been the object of a controlling spell—though he had come close in the past day. He could only imagine how disconcerting it would feel.

"I should have listened t' you, Mister Kaille," Mackintosh said. "You tried t' warn me about him."

"Did you warn him about us, too?" Adams asked.

Mackintosh glared. "Wha's tha' mean?"

"We were ready to let you hang for the Berson murder," Adams told him. "And for what had been done to Hutchinson's house. We feared that your actions would do irreparable harm to our cause." He nodded toward Otis. "As James said, we had no idea that Darrow was making you do these things. He sought to divide us, and so to weaken the cause of liberty. And he nearly succeeded. You have my sincere apology, Ebenezer."

Mackintosh didn't answer. Darrow's fire had burned low, but still

Ethan could see that the cordwainer's jaw had tensed and his gaze had hardened. After a moment, he turned to Ethan.

"Good nigh', Mister Kaille. If you ever have need o' anything at all, you come see me. I'll take care o' you." He glared once more at Adams and Otis, and stalked away.

"Peter may have succeeded after all," Otis said, watching him go.

But Adams shook his head. "He's angry now, as he should be. But he'll come around. He understands the importance of what we fight for."

Ethan wasn't so certain, but he kept his doubts to himself.

Adams extended a hand, which Ethan gripped. "You have our gratitude, Mister Kaille. I wonder if you wouldn't reconsider joining our cause. You know now that what happened the night of the twenty-sixth was not what it appeared. We could use a man of your talents and courage."

"I'm a subject of the British Empire, Mister Adams."

"As am I, sir. But I also recognize that our relationship with Parliament and the Crown cannot continue as it has. Mark my word, matters will only get worse."

"Yes, I'm sure you'll see to that."

Otis bristled. Ethan thought Adams might, too. But the man seemed unaffected by what Ethan had said.

"Our liberties are sacred. They're a gift from God. And if Grenville and King George refuse to recognize this, I can hardly be blamed for holding them accountable." He pocketed his pistol. "In any case, you will always be welcomed as a friend in our struggle, even if you don't yet understand that it is your struggle as well."

"Darrow called you a visionary," Ethan said, before Adams could leave.

The man smiled sadly. "Did he?"

"What did he mean?"

Adams shrugged. "I would guess he meant that I see where all of this will lead." He glanced at Otis, but then faced Ethan again. "Few speak of separation now."

"Separation of the colonies from England, you mean?"

"That's right. People aren't ready to hear of it. But it is coming; we're merely laying the foundation, working out what liberty might mean in a new nation. Peter knew this as well as I. I suppose he didn't approve."

"And he betrayed you because of it. Don't you worry that others will do the same?"

"No," Adams said. "I know for certain that they will. What should I do? Give up?" He shook his head. "Any noble cause will encounter its share of setbacks. The strength of that cause is measured in how the men who fight for it respond. We refuse to give up, which is why we will prevail eventually." Adams smiled once more. "Good night, Mister Kaille," he said, and walked away.

Otis nodded to Ethan and Pell, and followed Adams.

Ethan wanted to leave as well, but Greenleaf still had questions for him; he should have expected as much. He was more weary than he could ever remember, and wanted only to sleep. But he beckoned the man over and told him what he could of all Darrow had done. He skirted around the edges of the truth at times, taking care not to say too much about conjuring. He sensed that his answers served only to frustrate the sheriff more, but in the end there was little Greenleaf could do to him. Pell and the others had already made it clear that Ethan had been tortured; Darrow's death could hardly be seen as anything other than self-defense.

"What do we do with his body?" the sheriff asked at last, as Ethan started to leave.

"What?"

"His body. He was a witch, wasn't he? That's what I gather from all you've said. Do we cut off his head or something?"

Ethan looked back at Darrow one last time. "No, nothing like that. Just bury him." He turned to the minister. "Come on. I'll walk with you back to your church."

"Are you well enough?" Pell asked.

"I think so."

They didn't say much as they walked along the moonlit street. Ethan's legs ached, and he was too weary to make conversation. Pell seemed to understand. But when they reached King's Chapel, the minister slowed, his expression troubled. He pulled up his sleeve and examined the bloodless gash on his forearm.

"Does it hurt?" Ethan asked.

The minister shook his head. "No. It did when I cut myself, but then you cast your spell and . . . It felt odd." He glanced at Ethan. "I'm not sure I liked it."

Ethan nearly said, *You get used to it.* But he stopped himself. He could almost see Henry Caner scowling at him. "Well, let's hope we never have to do that again," he said instead, thinking that the rector would have approved.

Pell nodded, looking at his arm once more. "Do you think Adams is right?" he asked, pulling down his sleeve. "Will matters worsen before they get better?"

"I would think so," Ethan said. "Grenville is determined to have his revenue; Adams and his friends are just as determined not to pay. It's a dangerous game they're playing."

Pell gazed toward the rector's house. "Mister Caner and I are on opposite sides of this."

"You're both men of God. That's what matters."

"Of course," Pell said, though he sounded unsure. "Good night, Ethan. Rest well."

"You, too, Mister Pell. Thank you."

Ethan watched him enter the church. Then he walked on to the Dowser. He knew that he should be watchful as he made his way through the streets. If Sephira and her men chose this night to come after him he would be hard-pressed to protect himself. But he was too tired and too sore to do anything more than walk, shoulders hunched, hands in the pockets of his breeches.

He reached the tavern without incident. Upon entering he breathed in the warmth and the familiar aromas, and knew a moment of relief that almost brought tears to his eyes. The past several days had taken too much out of him. Before learning of Jennifer Berson's death from Abner Berson's servant, he had intended to rest for a few weeks. Now he promised himself that he would actually do it.

In the next instant, though, he spotted Diver sitting alone at a table in the back of the tavern. His weariness forgotten, he stalked across the main room to where his friend sat.

Kelf shouted out a "HiEthan!" but Ethan hardly heard him.

"Ethan!" Diver said, seeing him approach. "You don't look—"

"What were you doing with Derne today?"

The younger man blinked. "What?"

"You heard me. What business did you have with Cyrus Derne?"

Diver stared down at his half-finished ale. "I don't know what you're talking about."

Something inside of Ethan snapped. He grabbed Diver by the collar with both hands, lifted him out of his seat, overturning the chair, the table, and the ale as he did, and slammed his friend against the wall.

"Tell me!" he said, his face just inches from Diver's. "I saw you with them! You and Cyrus Derne and Sephira Pryce and some other merchant! I saw you! Now tell me what you were doing with them, or I swear to God, Diver, I'll thrash you to within an inch of your life!"

He knew people were staring at them. He knew how angry Kannice would be. In that moment, he didn't care.

"All right!" Diver said. "It was the wine and rum! Remember, I told you about them?"

"The wine and rum," Ethan repeated. He didn't know what Diver was talking about, and he actually drew back his fist intending to hit the man. But then it came to him. From France. The shipment Diver had been waiting for several nights earlier.

His anger began to sluice away, though he didn't release Diver. Not yet. "Derne was involved with that?" he said.

"He didn't want to sell them directly, because of the new laws. But he was one of the merchants backing us. So was Greg Kellirand— that's the other man you saw us with."

"And Sephira?"

Diver's gaze slid away. "It wasn't my idea to involve her. Derne wanted her in, and I couldn't just walk away. I wanted to, Ethan. Really. The way she beat you the other day. I didn't want—"

"It's all right, Diver." Ethan released him and took a step back. The shipment—wine and rum. That was what had taken Derne into the streets the night of the riots, the night Jennifer followed him. Ethan probably should have reasoned it out. "I'm sorry," he said after some time. "I shouldn't have . . ."

"It's all right," Diver said in a low voice. He looked past Ethan. "At least it is with me."

Ethan turned. Kannice stood nearby, her hands on her hips, a cloth draped over her shoulder.

"Everything all right here?" she asked, her gaze fixed on Ethan, a hard look in her eyes.

"I'm sorry," Ethan said.

He righted the table and picked up Diver's tankard. Kannice squatted down beside him and began to mop up the spilled ale with her cloth.

"I can do that," he told her.

"I've got it," she said, the words clipped.

"I'm sorry, Kannice. I know how you hate this sort of thing."

She nodded, but said nothing more.

Ethan straightened and watched as she finished cleaning up his mess. Diver held himself still, his lips pursed, steadfastly avoiding Ethan's gaze.

When at last Kannice stood up again, Ethan said, "I owe apologies to both of you."

Diver and Kannice shared a brief look.

"I think we'll both be glad when you're done with this job," Kannice said.

"I am."

They stared at him.

"You know who killed her?" Kannice asked.

"Peter Darrow."

"Darrow?" Diver repeated. "The lawyer? He's a conjurer?"

"Was. He's dead."

Kannice paled. "Did you . . . ?"

"I had help."

Diver picked up his chair, set it down properly, and sat. "I want to hear all about this."

Kannice grinned sheepishly. "Actually, I do, too." She held up three fingers for Kelf. Ales all around. She and Ethan sat, and Ethan began to relate all that had happened to him in the last day and a half.

It was a late night, made even later when, after Diver left, Kannice led Ethan up to her room above the tavern. There she gently removed his torn, battle-stained clothes, undressed herself, and made love to him.

Ethan slept away much of the morning and still woke sore and tired. Kannice had risen early, kissed him, and gone down to the tavern. When at last he dressed and joined her there, she greeted him with a big smile.

"Are you hungry?"

He shook his head. "Actually, no."

Concern chased the smile from her face. "Is everything all right?"

"I have to go see Berson, and then Henry. And I could use a change of clothes."

"All right," she said, suddenly sounding guarded.

He knew why. He would also have to return the clothes he had borrowed from Elli.

"I'll be back later. I promise."

"Of course."

Ethan eyed her a moment longer, then left the tavern.

He went first to the Berson house, and was ushered into the merchant's study. Berson came in several minutes later, frowning at the state of Ethan's clothes and his bruises.

"I'm afraid this inquiry hasn't been kind to you, Mister Kaille," the man said, indicating that Ethan should take a seat.

"No, sir. Which is why I'm glad it's over."

Berson had just turned to close the door, but now he spun back to face Ethan so quickly that he nearly lost his balance. "Over, you say?"

"Yes, sir. I know who killed your daughter. And I know why."

"Tell me. Please."

"Peter Darrow killed her and several others."

Berson's jaw dropped. "Darrow? The man who works with Otis and Adams?"

"Yes, sir. He was a conjurer, and he was using killing spells to control the actions of others. I believe he was working on behalf of the Crown, or someone close to it."

Berson frowned. "I find that hard to believe. Surely this is what that scoundrel Adams told you."

"Actually, sir, it's what Darrow told me. He used the spell that cost your daughter her life to control Ebenezer Mackintosh. Darrow forced him to lead his mob to Hutchinson's house."

"This makes no sense," Berson said, his voice shaking.

"No, sir, I don't suppose it does. But it is the truth."

Ethan thought about telling the merchant why his daughter went into the streets that night, but then thought better of it. Ethan couldn't say for sure that her death was Derne's fault, and even if he had been sure, that was a matter for Berson and Derne to work out between themselves.

"Where is Darrow now?" Berson asked after a time, staring at the floor, his cheeks bright red.

"He's dead, sir."

"Do I have you to thank for that?"

"In part, yes. I killed him, after Adams shot him."

The merchant blinked, then nodded. There were tears in his eyes, but he made no effort to hide them. "Well, I'm grateful to you. Another man might have retrieved the brooch, taken his money, and been done with it. Few men I know would have risked so much on another's behalf. I won't forget this. You have my gratitude and that of my family."

"I'm glad I could help you, sir."

Berson stood. "I believe I owe you the balance of your payment."

"You gave me five pounds the other day, sir, so whatever you pay me should reflect that."

"You're a good man, Mister Kaille. I'm not sure you would do very well down at the wharves, but I admire your honesty." He crossed to a small writing table in a corner of the library and pulled from a drawer a coin pouch. He poured the contents onto the table and made a careful count. From where Ethan stood there looked to be twenty pounds sterling; perhaps more. Berson placed the coins back in the pouch and handed it to Ethan.

"There you go. You've earned every pound."

"That's . . . that's very generous of you, sir."

"Well, perhaps at some time in the future you'll consider working for me again."

"Of course, sir. It would be an honor."

Berson shook Ethan's hand and smiled, though it appeared to take a great effort. His eyes were still red. "I think I would like to tell my wife what's happened. If you'll excuse me, I'll have William show you out."

"Thank you, sir."

The merchant left him there, and his servant came to see Ethan to the door. William didn't say much to him this time, but as Ethan was leaving he asked, "Was I righ' abou' Mister Derne?"

Ethan thought back to their conversation that first day. William had said Derne was careless, a man who could lead Jennifer into peril.

"Yes, you were," he said. "I didn't tell this to Mister Berson, because Derne didn't mean to harm her. But if not for him, she might still be alive."

William nodded gravely. "I feared as much. Good-bye, Mister Kaille. May th' Lord keep you safe."

"And you, William."

Ethan walked back to the lane and turned toward home.

TWENTY-FOUR

s Ethan neared Henry's cooperage, he saw movement out of the corner of his eye and froze. Shelly lay by the side of the lane and had raised her head at his approach. Ethan swallowed, then took a tentative step toward her, remembering his dream from two nights before.

The dog got to her feet and trotted toward him, her tail wagging, her mouth open and her tongue hanging out in what looked like a grin. Ethan knelt down to greet her and she licked his hand before letting him scratch behind her ears.

"Shelly," he whispered. "I'm sorry. If there had been any other way . . ." He shook his head, his throat tight. Was he crazy to be apologizing to a dog?

She padded closer and licked his cheek, and when Ethan stopped scratching her she pawed at his hand to get him to start again.

"I miss him, too," he said, his voice still low.

After another few moments, he stood and let himself into the cooperage. Henry sat on a low stool by his workbench, sipping water from a cup.

"Resting?" Ethan asked, closing the door behind him.

The old man glanced Ethan's way. "Hello, Ethan. Aye, I'm tired today."

Ethan crossed the shop and sat on a finished barrel. "You all right?"

The cooper shrugged, his open mouth revealing the gap in his front teeth. "A bit thad, really. Pitch died."

What could he say? That he knew? That he was a conjurer and had needed the dog dead more than he needed him alive? So he said the only thing he could, meaning it in ways that Henry could never know. "I'm sorry, Henry. I know he meant a lot to you."

"Aye, he did," Henry said, sounding wistful. "Him and Shelly both. The odd thing is, I don't know why it happened. I found him out front this morning. He didn't look hurt; I don't think he'd been sick. There wasn't a mark on him. He just died, like he was old." He shook his head. "But he wasn't. At least I don't think he was."

In that moment, he wanted nothing more than to tell Henry what he had done. But he was afraid. He had faced Sephira and her men, he had fought the conjurer Darrow. But he lacked the courage to tell his friend what he had done to save his own life. "I'm very sorry," he said again, the words feeling woefully inadequate. He leaned forward and gripped Henry's shoulder briefly before standing again and walking back to the door.

"What about you, Ethan? You all right?"

"Tired, but otherwise fine, thank you."

"No more trouble with Sephira Pryce?" He sounded more hopeful than concerned, as if he thought another visit from the Empress of the South End might be just the thing to lift his spirits.

Ethan suppressed a smile. "No, I think I'm done with Sephira, at least for now."

"Oh," Henry said, sounding distinctly disappointed. "Well, that's good, I suppose."

"See you later, Henry," Ethan said, letting himself out.

"Bye, Ethan," the old man called.

He walked around to the back, slowly climbed the stairway to his room, and went inside, taking care to lock the door. He believed what he had told Henry: His inquiry was over. Whatever interest Sephira had in protecting Darrow, there was nothing more she could do now. She might want the money Berson had given him, and she probably would have enjoyed setting her men on him again, but she had no reason to go out of her way to track him down. Still, he felt better with the door locked.

He considered trying to nap, but though still weary from all the conjuring he had done the night before, and still sore from the injuries Darrow had inflicted on him, he knew that he wouldn't sleep. Instead, he changed into clean clothes, realizing as he did that he had ruined a couple of shirts and a coat over the past few days. Before long he would have to dig into the pouch of silver Berson had given him and visit the clothier. Thinking about it, he decided that there was nothing stopping him from going this day, right now. It was an odd feeling, as unfamiliar as it was liberating.

He left his room, fully intending to buy himself a coat and some clothes. But as he stepped onto Cooper's Alley, he saw a carriage waiting in front of the cooperage. Henry was there, speaking with the driver. They both turned at Ethan's approach.

"It's for you, Ethan," Henry said, sounding awed.

"Are you Ethan Kaille?" asked the driver, a young, well-dressed man in a linen suit and powdered wig.

"Yes, I am."

"Lieutenant Governor Hutchinson requests that you join him at his home in Milton. I'm to take you there."

Ethan shared a look with Henry, who merely raised his eyebrows.

"Well," Ethan said, "we shouldn't keep him waiting."

He winked at the cooper and climbed into the carriage. The driver took his place in front and soon they were rattling through the streets of Boston toward the Neck and the town gate. The leather harnesses of the horses creaked, and the horses' shod hooves rang brightly on the cobblestone. Once past the battlements, they crossed the causeway into Roxbury, veered south toward Dorchester, and continued on to Milton and the Hutchinson estate. It had been months since last Ethan ventured out of Boston, and despite the length of the journey—nearly two hours—he enjoyed seeing the countryside and knowing that Sephira Pryce was miles away.

Hutchinson's home stood at the top of a knoll that overlooked the Neponset River and offered a distant view of Boston Harbor. It was a

sprawling estate built of marble, with an impressive portico at the main entrance, and smaller wings flanking the central portion of the house. Large trees shaded the yard, and as Ethan climbed out of the carriage and followed the driver up the path toward the house, he caught a glimpse of colorful gardens along both sides of the home. Birds sang, bees buzzed past, and a freshing breeze rustled the leaves overhead. Ethan could see why Hutchinson had chosen to retreat here after the attack on his home in the city. A servant met Ethan at the door and led him through the house to an open veranda at the back where Hutchinson sat alone, gazing out over his land.

The lieutenant governor appeared rested and in far better spirits than he had the last time they spoke. When his servant announced Ethan he stood and dismissed the man before extending a hand to Ethan and indicating that he should sit.

"Thank you for coming all this way, Mister Kaille."

"Of course, Your Honor. The pleasure is mine."

"Your journey out here wasn't a hardship, I hope."

"Not at all, sir. And if I may, it seems the country agrees with you."

A reflexive smile touched Hutchinson's lips and vanished. "I believe it does." He cleared his throat. "I won't waste your time on niceties. I had word this morning from Sheriff Greenleaf of a shooting on Orange Street that occurred last night. He said that you were there, with Mackintosh, Samuel Adams, Peter Darrow, and James Otis. Now I hear that none of you was arrested, and I will assume there was good reason for this. But I also gather that this incident was related in some way to the Berson killing, and I would like to know what happened."

"Yes, sir. Simply put, Peter Darrow killed Jennifer Berson, and he came close to killing me. He was shot by Mister Adams, who acted to save my life."

Hutchinson gave no sign that any of this came as a surprise. Ethan assumed that he had been told as much by the sheriff.

"Why would Darrow kill the Berson girl?" he asked.

Ethan hesitated, unsure of how much to tell the man about Darrow's conjuring abilities, not to mention his own.

"I'll be honest with you, Mister Kaille. Much of what I've heard about the events of last night strikes me as . . . fantastical, to say the least. I don't know what to believe. Now, you tell me that Darrow killed Jennifer Berson, but obviously you are reluctant to tell me why he would do such a thing. Put yourself in my place, and tell me what I should think of all this."

Ethan gazed toward Boston. It felt wrong to speak of murders and shootings here in this gentle place. But he doubted that Hutchinson would have much patience for evasions.

"Darrow practiced the dark arts," he said, facing Hutchinson again. "He was what some would call a witch, and others a conjurer. He used his powers to bend men to his will, and in order to do this he had to sacrifice the lives of others. Jennifer Berson was one such sacrifice."

Hutchinson stared at him for a long time. "That's quite an explanation."

"Yes, sir."

"I assume that Darrow did these things you describe to further the cause of . . . of liberty." As he had the other time he and Ethan spoke, Hutchinson said the word as if it left a bitter taste in his mouth.

Ethan shook his head. "No, sir. He indicated to me that he was an agent of the Crown, and an enemy of Samuel Adams and the Sons of Liberty."

The lieutenant governor opened his mouth, then closed it again and sat back in his chair. Ethan thought that Hutchinson would object to this as Berson had. But he didn't. Eventually he simply said, in a voice barely more than a whisper, "I see."

They sat in silence for several minutes, until Ethan began to wonder if Hutchinson was done with him and expected him to leave.

But after a time, the lieutenant governor regarded Ethan again, seeming to take his measure with his gaze. "I would think that someone who could draw upon such . . . dark powers would be difficult to overpower. At least he would be for an ordinary man."

"Yes, sir."

Hutchinson watched him, clearly waiting for Ethan to say more. When at last he realized that Ethan had no intention of telling him anything else, that faint smile returned. "Very well, Mister Kaille. It's a long journey back to Boston, and I'm sure you would rather arrive before nightfall. I'm grateful to you for coming all this way to speak with me."

Ethan stood and sketched a small bow. "I'm honored that you asked me, sir." He started back toward the entry hall, where Hutchinson's servant waited for him. He had taken only a few steps, though, when the lieutenant governor spoke his name, stopping him.

"What was Mackintosh's role in all of this?"

"He was a victim," Ethan said, "turned to Darrow's purposes by dark means."

Hutchinson grimaced, as if Ethan's words had wounded him. "Of all that you've told me, I find that most difficult to believe."

"I think I understand, sir. But I give you my word, it is the truth."

"Yes," the man said, a haunted look in his dark eyes. "Yes, all right. Thank you, Mister Kaille. My driver will see you back to Boston, and will drop you anywhere you wish."

Ethan bowed again, and left.

❦

The ride back to Boston passed more quickly than had the journey to Milton. Before long, he could smell the sour mud of the Roxbury tidal flats and see the causeway that led toward the town gate and the Boston Neck.

As the carriage entered Boston and drove up the Neck toward the church spires and brick buildings of the South End and Cornhill, Ethan considered where to have the driver take him. Pell would want to hear about his conversation with Hutchinson, and eventually Ethan would need to pay another visit to Elli's house to see how Holin was doing. That was where Kannice thought he would wind up—he could tell from the way she had looked at him just before he left the Dowser that morning.

The truth was, though, all he wanted to do was go to the tavern, eat a bit of stew, and be with her. So that was where he went.

She made no effort to hide her surprise, or her pleasure, when he walked in.

"I didn't think I'd see you again so soon," she said from behind the bar.

He crossed to the bar and sat on an old stool. "I talked to Berson and visited Thomas Hutchinson's estate in the country. The only place I could go to top that was the Dowser."

Kannice stared at him openmouthed. "You were at Hutchinson's estate? In Milton?"

"Yes," he said, as if it was nothing unusual.

"HiEthan," Kelf said, emerging from the kitchen.

"Hi, Kelf."

"Is it beautiful?" Kannice asked. "I've heard it's beautiful."

Ethan nodded. "It was very nice. I wouldn't mind living there myself."

"Ethan went to visit Thomas Hutchinson in Milton," Kannice told Kelf.

"Nice," Kelf said, sounding unimpressed.

Kannice stared at the barman for a moment before facing Ethan again, her eyes narrowed. "You're not lying to me, are you?"

"I swear I'm not."

She regarded him briefly. "And you didn't go anywhere else?"

"I went home and changed my clothes. But I didn't go to Elli's if that's what you're asking."

"I'm sorry," she said, looking away. "I shouldn't—"

"It's all right," Ethan said, touching her chin so that she would face him again. "I had Hutchinson's driver drop me here, because this is where I want to be."

Before Kannice could reply to that, the tavern door opened and Sephira Pryce walked in, followed by Yellow-hair and Nap.

Ethan stood and took out his knife. Kelf stepped out from behind the bar, and though Ethan put out a hand to keep him back, there was a part of him that would have enjoyed watching him and Nigel have at it. Ethan had seen both men fight and he would have been hard-pressed to choose a likely winner.

"I don't allow their kind in here," Kannice said, eyeing Sephira with open hostility, and pointing to her toughs. "I'm not sure I allow your kind, either."

Sephira smiled and sauntered to the center of the room, ignoring Kannice, her boot heels clicking loudly on the wood floor. She surveyed the tavern, her gaze coming to rest at last on Ethan.

"What a charming place, Ethan. It's like a stable, but for people. I can see why you like it so much."

"What do you want, Sephira?" he asked.

"I just came to congratulate you," she said, flipping her hair. "It's not every day that a man kills someone as well known as Peter Darrow and gets away with it. I'm very impressed. I'd show you how impressed, but I'm afraid your little friend might get jealous."

Kannice stalked out into the main room. "His little friend?" she repeated. "I'll show you just how little I am, you ha'penny whore!"

Ethan grabbed Kannice's arm and pulled her back. Nigel and Nap took a menacing step forward, as did Kelf. For a moment Ethan thought he might actually have to conjure to keep Kannice and Kelf from getting themselves killed.

But though Sephira's mask slipped for an instant, she recovered quickly. "She's fiery, Ethan. I like that."

Ethan stared back at her, toying with his knife. "I think you had better go, Sephira."

She flushed, looking daggers. Ethan couldn't imagine she was accustomed to being dismissed.

"All right," she said, her voice tight. "Remember, though: You might have defeated Darrow, but you're still nothing more than a poor man's thieftaker. You work in this city because I allow it."

"So you've told me."

She eyed him for a few seconds more before flashing one last smile at Kannice and turning on her heel to leave.

"Why did you care about this, Sephira?" Ethan asked her. "What was Darrow to you?"

Her grin was taunting, and he thought she would leave without answering. But then she said, "He was nothing. A means to an end. I like things as they are, as they've been. Change . . ." She shrugged. "Change could be bad for business."

Ethan gaped at her. "You knew he was working for the Crown?"

Sephira sighed and shook her head. "Ethan, the sooner you understand that I know everything that happens in this city, the easier life will be for both of us." She opened the tavern door. "Until next time," she tossed over her shoulder, and was gone.

Nigel and Nap followed her out into the street.

Once they were gone, Ethan took a breath and sheathed his blade.

Kelf watched the door, as if he expected them to storm back in at any moment.

"She's got some nerve coming in here like that," Kannice said. "She may be the Empress of the South End, but if she comes in here again, I'll wipe that grin off her face myself."

"Aren't you the one who's always telling me that I need to be more careful?" Ethan asked her. "Don't you always tell your customers to leave their fights out in the street, away from your tavern?"

Kannice turned her glare on him. "What of it?"

Ethan threw his hands wide. "You just called Sephira Pryce a ha'penny whore!"

"Kind of liked that myself," Kelf said, heading back into the kitchen.

Kannice smiled grudgingly. "She deserved it."

"You'll get no argument from me," Ethan told her. "But now you're going to have to watch yourself, too. You made an enemy today."

She stared into his eyes. "I'm not afraid of her," she said, dropping her voice. "I share my bed with a conjurer."

"And I share mine with the most fearless woman in Boston."

Kannice took his hand. "You want some stew?"

He shook his head. "I need a coat. Come with me?"

"A coat? A nice one this time, or another rag like that last one?"

"Rag?" Ethan repeated. "That was no rag."

"Hmmm." She retrieved her own wrap from behind the bar, took his hand again, and pulled him toward the door. "I'll choose this one," she said. "I know just the place to get it."

He halted, forcing her to stop as well. He pulled her close, and kissed her.

"What was that for?"

Ethan brushed a strand of hair from her forehead. "For being willing to take on Sephira Pryce to defend me."

"That wasn't for you," she said, tugging him toward the door again. "I didn't like her calling my place a stable."

Ethan laughed and followed her out into the city.

Historical Note

Historical fiction is a strange hybrid—a literary Chimera, in a way—in that it blends historical fact with fictional, and in the case of this book, fantastical elements. The central premise of the book, that thieftakers were active in the American colonies, is not true. Thieftakers were starting to appear in England at this time, and made a brief appearance in the fledgling United States in the early nineteenth century. But there were no thieftakers in Boston in 1765. Sephira Pryce and Ethan Kaille have no direct, real-world counterparts.

However, the other historical elements of the novel are largely accurate. The Stamp Act riots of August 26, 1765, occurred much as they are described here, and the relationship between Ebenezer Mackintosh and his followers on the one hand, and the members of the Loyal Nine on the other, was fraught with mistrust and characterized by mutual exploitation.

In writing the novel, and interweaving my fictional characters and storylines with actual events, I have consulted a number of scholarly sources, as well as documents from the pre-Revolutionary period. A partial list of my sources for this book—along with lots of other information—can be found at my website: www.dbjackson-author.com.

Acknowledgments

I've written history, and I've written fiction; this was my first foray into writing them simultaneously. Not surprisingly, I needed a good deal of help along the way and so have many people to thank.

John C. Willis, Ph.D., Professor of United States History at Sewanee, the University of the South, answered literally hundreds of questions, and steered me to some terrific source material. Our morning conversations at the gym, as we pedaled our stationary bikes to nowhere, made this process even more enjoyable than it would otherwise have been.

Christopher M. McDonough, Ph.D., Professor of Classical Languages at Sewanee, translated spells into Latin for me, and during one memorable lunch, taught me more about Latin grammar and syntax than I had learned in the previous forty-odd years. Without his efforts on my behalf, writing about Ethan's conjurings wouldn't have been nearly as much fun.

Dr. Robert D. Hughes, Professor of Systematic Theology at the School of Theology of the University of the South, guided me through the proper honorifics for eighteenth-century ministers, and the steps to ordination for Anglican clergy in the colonies. I'm grateful to him for being so generous with his time and expertise.

I would like to thank as well the Norman B. Leventhal Map Center at the Boston Public Library for allowing us to use the map of Boston that appears at the front of the book. I am especially grateful to Catherine T. Wood, the Center's office manager, for all her help in locating the map and expediting the process. My wonderful friend Faith Hunter read an early draft of the book's opening pages and provided me with welcome feedback. I am deeply grateful to her, and also to Misty Massey, C. E. Murphy, A. J. Hartley, Stuart Jaffe, and Edmund Schubert. I'm grateful as well to Kate Elliott, Stephen Leigh, Lynn Flewelling, Carrie Ryan, Joshua Palmatier, and Patricia Bray, all of whom helped to shape this book through e-mails, online exchanges, and the occasional conversation over a beer.

Lucienne Diver, my agent, believed in Ethan and his story from the start. Without her tireless work, her editorial feedback, and her friendship, we might never have found a home for the series. I would also like to thank Deirdre Knight, Jia Giles, and the other great people at the Knight Agency.

James Frenkel, my editor at Tor, was the first person to suggest that Ethan might be better off living in a historical setting rather than in an imaginary world. With his encouragement, I rewrote *Thieftaker*, and the rest is history. Or at least historical fantasy.

In addition, I'm grateful to Jim's assistants, Leslie Matlin and more recently Kayla Schwalbe, and his intern, Hannah Morrissey; Tom Doherty, Irene Gallo and her staff, Steven Padnick, and all the other wonderful people at Tor Books.

Finally, I want to thank my wife and daughters. Their love and support, their laughter and silliness, make everything I do more rewarding and more meaningful.

About the Author

D. B. JACKSON is the award-winning author of a dozen fantasy novels, a half-dozen short stories, and the occasional media tie-in. His books have been translated into more than ten languages. He has a master's degree and Ph.D. in U.S. history, which have come in handy while writing *Thieftaker,* and *Thieves' Quarry,* the next novel about Ethan Kaille, which will be published in 2013. He and his family live in the mountains of Appalachia.